I0818792

Shadow Play

BY JOHN HARRISON

Published by C. E. R. Ellwood
under the House of Harrison imprint

All rights reserved.

Copyright © 2016, 2019 John Harrison
Map by John Harrison and C. E. R. Ellwood

This novel is a work of fiction. Names, characters, places, and events are either the product of the author's imagination, or used fictitiously.

No part of this book may be reproduced or transmitted in any form or by any electronic or mechanical means, including information storage and retrieval systems, without the express written permission from the author, except for the use of brief quotations in a book review.

ISBN-13: 978-1-947061-11-8

Printed in the USA
Second trade paperback edition, October 2019
First trade paperback edition, 2016

This series is for those that love life… and all of its possibilities.

I also dedicate this book to my three sons: Benjamin, Ethan & Hunter. You three will always inspire and surprise me, and for that, I am forever grateful.

Cennicus
Isle of Senica
Camitia Strait
Storm's Nest
Coluna
Last Pint
Hotis
Jarstil
Reins
Sirelsee
Rock Healm
Galtren
Realm of Elves
Diri Lake
Ithica Bay
Trander's Sea
Three Rivers Crossing
Frelanti Realms
Peat
Bloodles
Keep
Elysium Sea
Delart
Estan Ocean
Haven
Divitian Realm
Darque Woods
Denton Mire
Ba'zed
Forbalt's Clan
Fortyn Sea
Kaurt
Tarkin's Clans
Falsiral
Dolen
Watch Keep
Sea Imbri
Deep Marsh

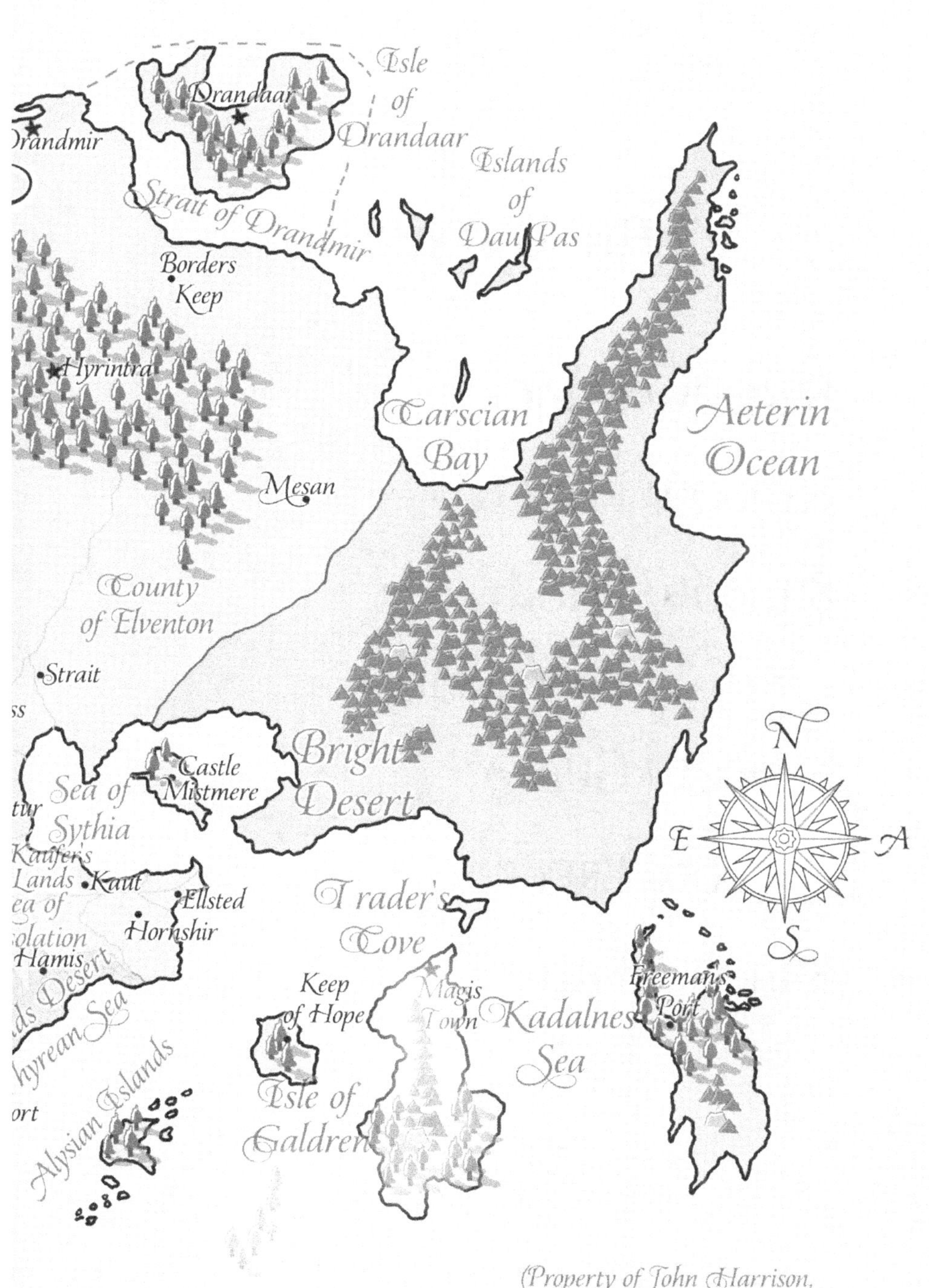
Isle of Drandaar
Drandaar
Strait of Drandmir
Islands of Dau Pas
Borders Keep
Hyrintra
Carscian Bay
Aeterin Ocean
Mesan
County of Elventon
Strait
Castle Mistmere
Sea of Sythia
Bright Desert
N
E
A
S
Kaut
Ellsted
Hornshir
Hamis
Trader's Cove
Keep of Hope
Magis Town
Kadalnes Sea
Freeman's Port
Isle of Galdren
Alysian Islands
(Property of John Harrison,
Drawn by C. E. R. Ellwood, 2019)

Shadow Saga

Shadow Dance

Shadow Play

Shadow Flight

Forthcoming:

Shadow Guard

Shadow Break

Shadow Fall

Prologue

The cold is the worst part of it!

The coldness of change is carried on the winds...
It devours worlds and dreams...
Its victims lay along the path of life,
both the righteous and the condemned.

Stories play along these shadows of change
like images across the ice...distant and distorted.
Yet this shadow theatre plays itself out...
time and again...time out of mind.

Somehow these scenes manage to reflect reality
in their own cold way...a harsh light shed by the
direction of darkness and shades...filtered only
by actions of a small group struggling for salvation.

Will they lead us to this salvation?
Or deeper into the very darkness we seek to escape?

What shall come of them then?

Indeed...

What shall come of us all?

Chapter One: Recollections

"Are you alright?" Nurn's voice boomed across the clearing.

Light cascaded around his brother's massive form and created the effect of an angelic halo. Halin could barely make out his brother's brown hair and piercing black eyes. The rest of the large boy's features were lost in the impenetrable darkness that always accompanies bright lights. The effect unnerved him a little and he shuddered involuntarily because of it.

"I...I think so." Halin stuttered. His reply was a feeble one at best and his head throbbed with each word. He rubbed it gingerly. His steel grey eyes darted around as he fought to find something familiar about his surrounds. Something was off. Although he knew they practiced in a clearing, he should have been able to see some trees in the gloom.

"We've got to get back to the clearing, right?" Halin asked sheepishly.

Halin's vision swam as he watched his brother's shape morph into their father's hulking form, "You should be more careful." Halin could not help but give into the confusion that threatened his sanity as Tipin's booming voice fell from what were his brother's lips less than a minute ago.

Halin shook his aching head as he tried to make sense of

what he was seeing and hearing. His father's words made no sense. Halin knew he had to be more careful. Based on the condition he was in, these words were obviously true. But what did that have to do with whether they had left the clearing?

"Yes sir," he replied hastily. Halin was well aware of the consequences that came from ignoring his father.

A dull ache throbbed through his lifeless legs as he twisted in a feeble attempt to stand. He stared for a moment at his father for help. Halin could feel the pleading look slide off Tipin's muscular body ineffectively. Halin tried to get his arms to move, even a little, with no luck. For some reason neither his arms nor legs wanted to work right.

"I can't seem to get up," Halin whined through his overly taught lips as he struggled. "Please help me up, father." Halin tried to glance around him as he spoke. But the only sensation to greet him was a new blossom of pain every time he moved even the slightest bit.

"Before you can stand up, you have to wake up." His father's light chuckle made no sense to him. "So wake up," Tipin smiled down at Halin as his words boomed over him.

The waning light still lingered in his father's silver mane, but not as much as it had before. It had dimmed almost imperceptibly, but the little sparkles he had seen playing amongst the shadows were lessened. Halin could clearly see the look of concern in his father's grey eyes.

"I am awake," Halin said softly. He wanted to help Tipin cheer up so he added a playful tone to his words.

Somehow, his father seemed younger than he remembered him to be. Although large, his powerful frame was a little smaller and his mane was thicker and less manageable.

"Really, I am awake!" Halin insisted as he saw his father's disbelief. Even Halin's own voice seemed to youthen a little as he struggled to get control over his emotions.

Another shot of pain erupted in his left shoulder as he tried to sit up. His grey eyes darted to his feet and he felt even more flustered. Somehow there was a mottled white and brown blanket over his legs. He thrashed in another futile attempt to toss the blanket off him and his only reward was yet another shot of pain. This one forced him into submission.

"How did I get here?" Halin asked aloud. The lack of response fazed him as much as his own inner silence did.

"Don't dally, my friend," Tipin replied as his body shifted into yet another persona. This time Namir filled the boots once worn by both Halin's father and brother. "We have precious little time before we have to leave. The girls are ready and all of the items are already loaded." There was an odd air of disappointment in Namir's voice Halin hated to hear, especially since he knew he was somehow the source of his friend's pain.

"Namir, where are we going?" Halin fought back another wave of pain as he reached for his friend's retreating shadow. Namir's blond hair was the last thing Halin could make out before another blossom of pain broke through Halin's fevered dream and forced him into consciousness.

Halin squinted against the blinding light that met his eyes. His back ached from the rough rocks that protruded through his cloak and shirt. A light powdering of snow rocks and leaves covered him like a blanket as a low groan forced its way out of his throat. Moving his overly stiff arms caused Halin to wince.

"I have to get out of here." Halin croaked. His overly dry throat ached with each syllable.

A tawny lock of hair fell across Halin's grey eyes as he struggled. Each subtle movement forced a new type of pain to blossom as he struggled to slide the hair out of his field of view. Most of these flowering reminders seemed to center in the middle of his back and shoulders.

Halin fought through his tears as even the small shifts of his weight threatened to stop his progress completely. Halin knew that he had to keep moving or he would freeze to death, but his will regularly balked at the sudden onset of pain.

Reality twisted and shimmied before Halin's eyes as he rolled from his back to his stomach. The moments of pain that followed were so excruciating that he almost passed out. Several short breaths allowed him to focus his thoughts enough to think about his goal. This helped steady the small tremors in his body long enough to move.

An almost endless array of questions flooded through his mind as he crawled along the large pile of stones. Somehow these shattered remains of a decays collapse broke his fall and not him.

"I should be dead," Halin could not deny the truth he found staring him in the face. Every inch of his body screamed in pain as he inched his way out from the circle of light cast by the hole in the rocks above him.

The sounds of the howling wind as it screamed through the jagged opening all but lost in the cavern's ceiling above him only added more desperation into his actions. Halin knew he had to get out of his exposed location and into the beckoning darkness. There was a storm brewing above him and he could already feel the heaviness of the snow-laden air.

"I really need to move!" Halin yelled at himself, although most of the words were said mentally.

He fought back a wave of fear from his mind as he fixated on the thought of being wet and in pain. In his mind's eye, Halin could practically see the rivulets of water pour out of his clothes as he huddled against the icy winds. Cold, wet, hungry and alone; none of those held any comfort in them and Halin shivered at the thoughts.

With each pain wracked tremble, he forced himself another inch closer to the darkness. Halin repeated this grueling cycle until he felt completely entombed by the darkness he struggled to find.

"I need to find something to drink." Halin thoughts swung from shelter to survival swiftly as the urgency of his situation slowly sank in.

He was momentarily blinded by the depth of the darkness

and this urgently as he waited for his eyes to adjust to the gloom that now surrounded him.

"Where am I?" He wondered as he mentally prepared himself for a new bout of pain that he knew would erupt as he pulled himself into a sitting position against the base of the wall.

The large stones were smooth and cool to the touch as he leaned his weary head against them. "Thank you, Tumere, for this blessing," his thoughts whispered from his lips and echoed the message that he felt in every fiber of his being. Halin breathed a sigh of relief as he closed his eyes and forced his overly sore muscles to relax.

"How did I survive that fall?" Halin wondered aloud after he mustered enough courage to open his eyes again. He searched his broken memories while his eyes scoured the scene that spread itself out before him. His grey eyes darted from rock to rock as if he might decipher what it was that caused his fall. His brain, likewise scoured its resources.

Halin easily recalled working with his brother to improve their aim as the two sought to complete the nearly impossible task that the elven general had given them. Unfortunately for Halin, Nurn was far superior to him when it came to weapons.

After all his brother Nurn was three cycles older than him and had quite a few more chances to practice with Namir and their Father, while Halin had spent most of his time learning the practical needs of life from their mother. Halin tried to shake these depressive thoughts from his mind as he recalled the ease with which Nurn had met the goal they had been set.

Even Halin's eventual success with arrows did little to ease the darkness that had descended in his mind. That is when the half-hearted moment that he struck out from the safety of the clearing etched itself into his mind.

"I needed to collect my arrows," Halin's whispered words seemed to fill the entirety of the hushed cavern.

The flecked red and black tuft started shockingly at him from across the room. It was almost as if his words had forced the arrow into existence. Halin squinted against the brightness of the light that flooded the sprawling vista in front of him.

The pile of rocks he landed on was easily as tall as he was and the hole was at least forty feet above that, if not more. His eyes darted from the now invisible hole in the ceiling to the pile of stones and then finally to the fletching of the arrow half-buried at the base of the rocks. "I couldn't have survived," his words held the finality of the tomb.

Another quick prayer to Tumere for his safety spawned a wave of nausea that threatened to purge what little food he had left in his stomach. As he fought against this urge, he felt his senses start to slip away from him.

In the darkness that started to close around the edge of his vision, Halin could hear the low menacing howl of the beat that had attacked him in Hornshir. He struggled against both, but he knew his will was spent. Either fear or nausea that would win and Halin knew it. In the end, it was fear wrapped its arms around him and pulled Halin into its welcoming darkness. The last images that flashed before his mind was a confusing one filled with branches, dirt, and glowing red eyes.

"Let me out!" Faris's gruff and haggard voice was the only sound that dared shatter the deafening silence.

The stone floor was cold to the touch as he lowered himself down to it slowly. His hope fell slightly as the darkness engulfed him once more. Although he had only been in this cell for just over a week, his soul begged for freedom.

The scant amount of light that filtered in lazily through the minute cracks only managed to make the shadows deeper and more pronounced instead of dispelling them. This forced him to fight even harder against the frustration and despair created by his situation. Even the simple task of marking the passage of time proved fruitless due to the softness and infrequency of the light.

"At least tell me where you are keeping my men!" Faris shouted in frustration. He felt his throat ache as his voice scrapped against the inside of it. His vocal chords were raw from his many attempts to be heard through the solid stone walls that surrounded him.

"We are here, sir!" A familiar voice tore at the silence of his cell. Even though it was muffled, Faris could easily tell that his lieutenant was relatively unharmed. "All of the men are present and accounted for sir!"

"At least we have that much," Faris replied snidely to the report. "How could a meager bar owner have bested us?" Faris wondered quietly as he tried to recall the details of the fight.

Most of the images were still too fuzzy. His fingers ran through his oily brown hair as Faris tried to probe his own mind for answers. He recounted giving his men their orders as they sprang into action. From the noises erupting from the inn's main hall, Faris knew that it was only a matter of time before someone was seriously hurt. He easily remembered pushing past a pretty blonde priestess as she dove down the stairs. But everything after he entered the main hall, aside from the pain, was gone. Everything, that is, except a familiar voice that yelled at him to drop his weapons.

"Everyone survived then?" Faris asked as he pulled himself back from his thoughts.

"Yes," his lieutenant replied with military precision.

"Good," Faris responded. "Hopefully our captors will free us soon." He let his anger consume his thoughts as the darkness surrounded him once more.

Faris fumbled with the ring on his right index finger and carefully removed it. He carefully raised it up into the dying rays that managed to still penetrate the inky blackness of his cell. His chestnut eyes focused on the light as is flew across the multitude of cut amber gems that completely encrusted the brilliant silver band. His eyes narrowed worriedly as he carefully examined the luster of each gem.

"I can spare one use if needed," Faris muttered under his breath to himself as he slipped the ring back onto its rightful place on his finger.

The all too familiar tingle that accompanied the heaviness of the ring sparked his memories about the first time he had placed the ring on his finger. He could almost feel the mugginess of the air on his skin as he closed his eyes and let the thoughts take him back to Watch Keep just a few days before the massacre.

"Our mistress would like to give you a token in exchange for your devotion to her," the sultry words rolled off the Darque Traveler's tongue seductively as she spoke.

Her musky voice echoed in Faris's mind as she extended her hand. The way her skintight leather clad body moved leapt in front of Faris's mind's eye as she did so. He recalled how intimidating the silver buckles set against the deepest black leather that he had ever seen looked, especially when her head and most of her body was enshrouded by her charcoal black cloak.

He easily recalled the mixed emotions he approached her with. He hated to admit it, but there was a part of him that lusted for everything she stood for. However, his hesitation was mostly due to the dreadful deeds he had witnessed at her hands. Faris's hand shook like a leaf as he reached out to accept her gift. The weight of the ring surprised him, but not more than its inherent warmth.

"If you can master this gift's secret, you will never have to truly fear death." Her words held a soft and tender quality he had always found odd.

"What do you mean?" He asked innocently as he slipped the ring onto his finger.

That was when it happened, the mind-numbing pain and profound sense of loss. Somehow, he felt something inside of the ring reach into his very being and touch his soul. But it did more than just touch it, the ring and bonded to it.

"I mean what I said. There is a riddle intrinsic to the ring. If you can solve it, you will not know the true hand of death. If you can't, then your soul will meet our glorious mistress sooner than you thought. All gifts have two sides my dear; surely you were already aware of this." The tenderness had left the Darque Traveler's voice and a certain crispness had replaced it instantly.

The muffled sound of metal against stone pulled Faris away from his memories and back into the darkness of his cell. He could only assume the noise belonged to the door of his soldiers' cell as it scraped against flagstones of the floor.

He held his breath so he could better hear the slightest noise that made its way through the thick wall that separated them. To his chagrin, all he could make out was a brief muffled exchange between their captors and his lieutenant. Even this much was far too faint for even his keen ears to make out. Something was said about them leaving. Were they were being escorted away? His thoughts spun as he tried to piece it all together.

"Did they hear our conversation somehow?" Faris's words came out in almost silent whispers as he strained his hearing to the edge of its already overreached ability.

Faris struggled to keep his emotions in check as he heard the voices rise and fade as the receded away from him. He cursed their predicament under his breath as he visually scanned the wall in front of him for some weakness that he could exploit. Finding none, he hunkered down against it and waited for his opportunity.

He wedged himself beside the sturdy door and mentally ran through his plan again. He was positive his captors would decide to come for him at any moment, just as soon as they realized his men would not betray his reasons for staying in Ellsted.

A smile crept to Faris's lips when he heard footsteps approach his door. He laughed inwardly as the familiar sounds of metal scrapping against metal as his jailer slowly inserted the key into in the lock of his cell's door jingled in his ears. 'I wonder how many guards they sent to retrieve me.' Faris thought as he mentally revisited his escape plan.

He braced himself as the door started to creak open. However, Faris felt his confidence fall as the realization hit him that the door opened away from him instead of toward him. He was even more frustrated when a fist-sized cramp seized his hamstring.

Time slowed to an agonizing crawl as he waited for someone to enter his cell. Faris knew he was completely exposed now that the door, the one thing he might hide behind, had been taken from him and Faris hated it.

He did not hesitate, however, when he saw his captor's arm cross the threshold of his cell. In the length of time it took Faris to see the arm, he pounced. He wasted no time and brought all of his rage directly to his jailer in a frantic attempt to free himself from captivity.

Faris deftly knocked the torch out of the jailer's other hand and stepped behind him with the ease of a well-trained dancer. He quickly ran his wrists down along his captor's arms to his elbows in an attempt to restrain him. To Faris's surprise, he could not move them. He twisted his body and brought all of his might to bear against his brawny jailer's arms as a new pain blossomed at the base of Faris's skull.

"Do not struggle." The voice boomed out of the darkness at him.

Faris tried to shrug off the weariness that the blow brought with it, but he was unable to. Shock welled up inside of him as he felt ropes slip over his wrists. "How can this be?" Faris screamed as he tried to free himself in vain. The sensation of his life being compressed filled his senses as he felt a giant hand grab hold of his chest and thrust him into the darkness that waited for him beyond the cell and behind his eyes.

Landolin kept his hood pulled tight in order to conceal his features. He checked yet another time on his men. He hated the long wait that always accompanied an excursion into Hornshir, or any other of the walled cities.

He felt the constant need to make sure his men were scattered randomly throughout the already impossibly long line that amassed in anticipation of Hornshir's gate opening. No one dared to miss their chance to enter because it was obvious the farther back in the line you were, the easier it was to miss out on entering the city. He had heard tales of people that were so unfortunate they missed their opportunity to enter the city three times in a row, and on their fourth attempt, they were severely injured by a group of bandits who tried to force their way in.

Landolin shook his head as he recalled the story he had heard so many times around a campfire. While he hated to force his top soldiers into a mission so soon after one of their dear friends had passed, they knew he had no choice. Aras's death was hard on all of them and the fact that neither his wife and daughter nor the sa'ouvant were able to attend his funeral did not sit well with any of them. Unfortunately, the urgency of their mission did not allow them the luxury to wait.

"Darkness waits for no one." His words, though whispered, puffed out of his mouth in thin little clouds as he recounted the events of the last few days to himself. He allowed the images of his dear friend's funeral to flood back into his mind. The only noise he could remember was the lone cawing of a blackbird and the rustle of the wind as it forced the trees to observe the fallen hero's passing.

Even the sun lingered just below the horizon as if it stood guard into the houses of the gods. Though brief, it was somber. There were no fond recollections or merriment in any of the eyes that watched the body vanish under the stone as Landolin and his personal guard slid it into place.

"It was the perfect seal to the final puzzle for you old friend," Landolin's voice surprised him as he spoke. He had not intended to say anything out loud and glanced around nervously in case he had been heard. He felt a tear threaten to slip from the corner of his eyes, so he dealt with them, in the same manner, he had at the funeral, swiftly and neatly.

As he scanned his surroundings, Landolin took a careful

assessment of where each of Hornshir's guards were heading as they readied themselves for the beginning of their day. Unrest settled into his shoulders as he saw their flippant attitudes and slovenly appearance. He was amazed half of them even bothered to be in uniform, with less than that actually wearing some form of armor.

"Faris would never have let them report for duty this way," he thought ruefully as he adjusted the pack on his shoulders in an attempt to distribute its weight better. It felt good to be in charge of his emotions once more, even if he had to thank the lackluster performance of these guards to thank for it.

As he waited for the acting captain to open the gates, he mentally ticked off items on his list of things that needed to get done. The first was going to be relaxing at the manor, but, based on the actions of these guards, Landolin decided it was a little more urgent to speak with the town council instead. "I fear for this town should anyone decide to attack," he muttered under his breath when he saw a guard get close enough to hear him.

"Keep in one line and only move when directed to!" The nearest guard's orders both snapped Landolin from his thoughts and agitated him further.

He could feel the guards' stare, but he quickly dismissed it. Landolin knew his attire would attract their attention; that was the point. He had purposefully chosen to conceal his features with the white scarf worn mostly by aristocrats and politicians. Finished the look off with a jade green hooded cloak was the perfect way to guarantee their suspicion of his motives. This way the guards would think he was another rich merchant or, worse, a travelling dignitary.

His goal was to distract the guards long enough to allow his men easy passage into the city. With a wave, which he purposely made toward the guard that had berated him, Landolin directed a few of his men to enter Hornshir via the old passageways that had been created during the first war of the ages.

"You there," the guard that replied was not the one that

Landolin was trying to summon, but the elf had noticed the intense stare for quite some time. Landolin acted as if he was lost in his own attempt to flag the nearer guard and ignored him. "Step over here, now!" The guard's tone was one Landolin did not like hearing.

Not only was the elf unaccustomed to hearing it directed at him, but it held an air of ill-fitted authority. Just but the impertinent undertone to the command, he could tell that this guard was used to people following his orders out of fear and not respect.

Landolin nodded his acquiescence and slowly approached the guard. As he made his way over to him, Landolin visually searched him for weapons and paid special attention to the two other guards that turned as if to accompany him.

"State your business in Hornshir," the guard demanded when Landolin was a few paces away.

"I am an emissary from Kaut," Landolin lied easily, "and I am on official business of an urgent nature."

Landolin leveled an icy stare at the guard as he replied. The whole time he prayed that the buffoon would not notice the gem-like color of his garnet eyes or the all too fair complexion of his skin.

"Well, don't you think you're important?" The guard spat back at Landolin as a reply.

"I meant no harm; I am just trying to complete my mission." Landolin did not even try to hide his contempt for the guard as he continued, "But I will let you explain your side to your mayor, that is when I inform him of my unnecessary detention."

Landolin felt a little relieved that he no longer had to lie. He had every intention of reporting this guard's behavior to their mayor and to their whole council.

"If you were an emissary, wouldn't you be travelling with an entourage or in a carriage or something? I would even expect horseback instead of walking." Although the guard's tone started out shakily, Landolin heard the assertiveness that he gained as she spoke.

The elf knew he was going to have to do some creative talking as he listened to the guard's rant. "It is readily apparent that you know nothing of statecraft!" Landolin admonished. "Entourages do nothing but slow the movement of the emissary, as do carriages. You are correct though, I had a horse. Keyword…had!" He leveled another long icy stare at the guard. "Now, are you going to let me pass?"

"What happened to your horse?" The guard asked hesitantly.

"Marauders," Landolin replied evenly. "Another thing I plan on bringing up to your mayor. The treaties state that the trade lanes nearest to each city shall be patrolled and protected by that city. I guess you and your men are just too busy harassing the upright citizens trying to gain lawful entry into your city to do your actual job." Landolin could tell the last few words of his scathing sentence struck a nerve by the guard's reaction.

At first, it looked as if the man was going to draw his sword in anger, then the haunted look of fear took hold of the guard and he hastily waived Landolin through ahead of the rest of the line. "This one has priority. Clear his way." He reported up the line to the rest of the sentries.

"Finally," Landolin muttered loudly as he turned toward the now opened gates. "I can hardly wait to give my report to the mayor." As he walked through the gates, Landolin waived one last time as a signal to his men. He knew each of them had a great cover and their reasons would vary enough so the guards would not think twice about letting them into the city. Everything was going smoothly for once, and that is the way Landolin preferred it.

Pain coursed through his left arm for the second time as his hand started to go numb. Jaconis felt tiny drops of his blood bead along the skin of his upper arm. He could not help but focus his jade green eyes on his assailant's waist and marvel at the richness of the fabric that floated around her hips.

Amazement tore at his mind as he noticed how the light played across, and through, the supple folds of velvet that comprised her tunic. The ease the fabric moved and shimmied across her skin was enthralling and Jaconis could not keep his eyes off her.

Even the small drops of his blood that darkened the red fabric to an almost blackened hue seemed to catch and hold what little light filtered into this chamber. His assailant wore the darkness like a cloak and Jaconis could not make out any of her features, which was for the best. That way he could not seek any retribution in case he took offense to her tactics. The darkness of the fabric mingled with the pain coursing through his body and forced Jaconis's mind back to the last few weeks that lead him here.

The long walks with deacons that ran the abbey Tali was recovering in only strengthened his convictions to join their order and do what he must to help Tali in her mission. He had asked so many questions that he felt confident in his decision to join them.

While most of his questions centered on Tali, and what she meant to their faith, he did recall asking about the progressions from each order and which path he should take. However, Jaconis did remember asking not enough questions about their indoctrinations and the time it would take. Sometimes he cursed himself for his lack of foresight and this was one of those times.

He puffed a stray oily black lock of hair from his face as his assailant corkscrewed around him. He knew she was going to extract more pain from him. That was her job after all. She was supposed to teach him of the freeing power of pain as well as the wide variety of ways that it could be inflicted without becoming lethal. Jaconis could almost sense the anticipation she felt as he felt her gaze dance across his exposed skin. He reflexively tensed his muscles as he heard her steps falter.

Sweat beaded Jaconis's forehead as the tines of her barbed whip pierced his skin and the leather that held him in place cinched ever tighter as he pulled against it. The exquisite pain caused by the tiny barbs burned through his body and forced him to writhe in agony. Try as he might, Jaconis could not hold back the scream that ripped itself free from his throat.

"LOTEVILAR!" The well-rehearsed name rose from him unbidden.

Somehow he sensed the goddess's hand reach into him and peeled back the layers of his soul one at a time. Jaconis felt his sense of perception slide away as the silhouette of his torturer grew larger. He felt a deeper spiritual connection to his newly chosen goddess as the waves of pain washed over him and revealed Her plans for him.

The sounds of his screams enveloped them both and blended with those from the other chambers that made up the devotional wing of the temple. Jaconis was well aware of the fact he was not the only new inductee, just as he knew that not many of them would survive. The difference between him and them was he knew that he would.

"There are things I need to do and they will not be done if I fail," Jaconis reminded himself.

He allowed the climaxing cacophony to pull him into its rhythmic ebb and sway as the deacon of Lotevilar plied her well-honed trade. Jaconis felt completely swept away by an avalanche of sound as he screamed his goddess's name once more.

"LOTEVILAR!" He felt his soul slip farther into Her sway and he enjoyed every agonizing moment.

Chapter Two: Renewals

Faris's brown eyes flew open instantly as the sound of soft leather against stone. He did not recall falling asleep, but he must have. He scanned the room quickly as he tried to ignore the immediate pain of the bright lights as his eyes adjusted to them. "Wher…" Faris started to respond, but his words were forced back into his mouth as his captor jammed a bitter tasting rag down his throat.

"I said do not struggle." The silver-haired giant growled as he pulled his fingers out of Faris's mouth.

Faris attempted to squirm away from the large man and abruptly felt the constricting bonds that held him fast.

"When did he manage to tie me up?" Faris thought to himself.

He cast a quick glance at the heavy hemp ropes that entwined him. He noted to himself they were expertly tied and something in the back of his head found the series of knots and bindings familiar.

Faris felt the uncomfortable sensation of being lifted rapidly, which was closely followed by an abrupt descent onto the large man's shoulder. Unfortunately, the sudden stop was not enough to knock the rag from his mouth.

He dangled from the man's shoulders as his captor quickly carried him through an elaborate tunnel system. Faris attempted to memorize all of the twist and turns, but he knew he missed a few. He knew his only hope of escape hinged on being taken nearer to the entrance than where he had been.

Thankfully, the brute moved slowly enough his eyes were able to adjust to growing orange glow of the torches. Judging from the roughly hewn walls, the musty scent to the air and the overall looming darkness, Faris figured out he was underground in earthen tunnels and not in a catacomb under a keep.

Another turn and they entered a larger room. Faris could see the broad-shouldered back of someone examining metal objects on a wooden slab in front of him. The man had an authoritative air about him and his thick black hair was pulled back into a warrior's braid that hung halfway down his back. Another fast feeling of weightlessness as the hulking man unceremoniously dumped Faris into an awaiting chair.

"He is all yours, Constable. I'm done with this." The hulking man said over his shoulder as he walked back into the darkness that lay just outside of the torch lit room. His silver hair cast an odd dancing effect to the light and caused the shadows around him to fly to and fro with every step.

"A Calanari," Faris thought somewhat confused, "'here? They are all supposed to be dead." Before he had enough time to ponder the implications the fading giant signaled, the black haired man strode up and blocked his view.

Faris's chestnut colored eyes widened in fear as he recognized his old commander from the war. He could never forget the golden wolf-like eyes, even if his once fully black mane now had the tell-tale signs of age along his temples.

"Well…well…well, what have we here?" Carness asked as he slowly paced over to the chair that Faris was slumped over in. "It looks like a lawbreaker and a deserter, but I may be mistaken." Carness's humor was lost on Faris. "Am I wrong or are you the scumbag that abandoned your post in the battle of Watch Keep?" Faris's scathing glare was the only reply that Carness needed. He yanked the gag out of Faris's mouth so fast it chaffed his lips. "Do you have anything to say that might make me spare your life?"

Faris fought down a wave of bile as he glared at his ex-commander. "The war is over, our liege is dead."

"As are at least forty of my men because of your betrayal," Carness spat as he cut Faris off. "Again, why should I let you live?"

"Because my death won't bring them back," Faris replied. He tried to stare Carness down, but failed.

"True, but it will go a long way toward me forgiving you." Carness's threat clung to the air between the two of them for several long moments before either of them broke the enveloping silence.

"It will also destroy the hard-fought agreement that Ellsted has won with Hornshir." Faris waited for Carness to digest his words before he continued slowly. "So I would suggest that you release me." Carness's derisive laugh was not the response Faris had hoped for.

"I would suggest you try harder than that," Carness replied as he brought his face mere inches away from Faris's.

From this distance, Faris could tell that Carness was deadly serious and his only hope was to lose his glib attitude fast. "I am sorry," Faris replied haltingly. It was hard for him to choke out the apology, but he managed to do so after several moments. "I panicked and I ran." He looked into Carness's golden wolf-like eyes imploringly.

"So you would have me believe that you are a coward and not a traitor? Is that the lie that you tell yourself every day?" The incredulous look on Carness's face frightened Faris a little as he recalled the horrors that he witnessed at his old commander's hands.

"Believe whatever you'd like, but it's the truth," Faris allowed a small hint of despair to fill his voice as he spoke.

"Let him go," though quiet, the tenor of the mayor's voice rung throughout the room clearly. "He clearly is ashamed of the part he played at Watch Keep."

"Under whose authority?" Carness spat as he spun to face Armani's glare.

"The council's," Armani met the constable's bloodthirsty stare evenly, although the smoldering hatred in Carness's eyes obviously unnerved him a little.

"I have never seen Carness lose his grip like this," Faris thought to himself in awe.

He could feel the raw hatred that emanated from the constable physically press against his skin. He saw a twinge of terror as it worked its way into the back of Armani's neck and he saw the white hairs on the back of the mayor's neck rise unbidden.

"You heard the man," Faris said to break the fight of wills between the two long enough to give Armani a chance to recover. He let a sigh of relief escape his lips as he saw a look of determination make its way across Armani's face. "Let me go." There was a hint of violence that mingled with derision as Faris spoke and he knew Carness would not respond well to it.

"You want him released?" Carness spat as he spun to face Faris. In less than a moment, he effortlessly hefted Faris from the chair he was in and lifted him above his head. In one fluid motion, Carness flung Faris against the opposite wall as he turned and stepped toward the only door to the chamber.

"Take your traitor and go! You had better explain the laws to him, Armani. I'll not have him, or his men, making any more trouble in this town while they are here!" Carness stormed across the room.

Before he left he shot a glare over his shoulder at Faris and said, "I will be watching you, Faris. If you do anything out of line, I will kill you. No questions asked. Do you understand?" Carness's golden eyes gleamed sinisterly in the torchlight as he vanished into the wintery blackness that waited on the other side of the door.

The cool breeze blew through the clearing as Nurn retraced his steps. His brown hair whipped behind him like fire as several strands pulled free from its queue. "How could Halin have made it this far?" Nurn wondered as he looked back across the valley to the clearing that he had last seen his brother in.

Their brief conversation as Nurn left to go get them some food seemed woefully incomplete and Nurn knew that this was his fault and not Halin's. He was tired and sore from all of the training. On top of it all, he worried for Namir.

The elves had whisked away his best friend when they first entered the encampment and he had not heard from him since. Nurn felt the tension build in his shoulders as he recounted the memories and he took a deep breath to dispel it. No matter how hopeless the search had become, Nurn struggled to stay positive.

"Are there any signs?" Jerine's voice cut cleanly through Nurn's musings as if it were a knife.

"None," Nurn sighed dejectedly. Nurn felt the elf's ice blue eyes trace along the exposed scalp of his temples as he spoke. "Surely Jerine knows that my tattoos serve as a map to my lineage," Nurn thought to himself as he scanned the area again.

"Do not fear, sa'trandon," Jerine said as he walked up and put a reassuring hand on Nurn's muscular shoulder, "we will find your brother."

Jerine's words bolstered Nurn's spirit more than he had thought possible. Somehow, the elf's voice had a reassuring quality to it that made Nurn believe anything was possible and he was grateful for it.

"I know," Nurn agreed. "I know that we'll find him, just like I know that he's still alive. However, I think, it would be better to find him sooner rather than later." Nurn hated he had to let Namir and the others head back to Ellsted without him and this realization bothered him almost as much as his brother's absence did.

"All of our plans have been scattered, like flower blossoms in a late summer breeze," Nurn muttered the snippet of poetry under his breath.

It was one of his father's favorites and, as punishment, Tipin had forced him to memorize it. One of the things that struck Nurn about it was the poem was from the only Calanari book his father owned. Nurn's brow furrowed when he remembered his father saying Aras had given it to him at Watch Keep. His mind churned as he tried to untangle his thoughts enough to make sense of them.

"Why did Aras ask to meet Namir?" Nurn's bass voice rumbled across the short distance between him and Jerine like a threatening storm.

"He had proof of Namir's lineage and he wanted to make sure his promise to Kalta was kept. Why do you ask?" Jerine cocked his head a little, as he answered Nurn's odd question.

"Why did he wait so long? Until he was dying I mean." Nurn asked without looking at Jerine. The unnerving effect Jerine's clothing had was almost too much for Nurn to handle in the whitening forest.

"I guess he waited so that he could be sure about it. I know that Alequa told Landolin that her husband had to finish something urgently before he could hazard meeting with the future heir." Jerine's reply seemed honest, cold but honest.

"I just need to know why we were really brought here. There's a part of me that feels like if I can figure that out, I might be able to find out why Halin was targeted in the first place." Nurn's already deep voice grew deeper with a hidden conviction as he spoke.

"The last part is the easiest to answer. Halin was targeted because Morcant's master misread a communication between your father and Aras." Jerine commented as he paused reassuringly. "Your resolution is a boon and I'm pleased to see that you still have faith."

The elf shifted the conversation expertly. He used the pause to its fullest extent and sealed the transition by saying, "I just hope it proves to be enough to get us through this." Jerine all but whispered these words as he locked Nurn's deep black eyes with his own icy stare.

"I know that we aren't finished here, but we need to head back and see if anyone else has found a sign of him elsewhere."

"Fine," Nurn grunted a little unsure of Jerine's motives. Although his reply was short, each letter dripped with the same disappointment that had etched the recent lines of worry across the youth's face.

Armani cleared his throat for the third time as he cut through the last of Faris's bonds. He hated going against Carness like this, but he had little choice. If anything happened to Faris, or his men, while they were envoys of Hornshir, all of his daughters' negotiations would have been for nothing.

"I am sorry about what happened," Armani knew his apology sounded empty, but he had to say something.

"I understand," Faris's lie was evident by the distasteful expression that creased his face as he slowly rose into a sitting position. "Some veterans cannot let go of the war, even after all these years."

Faris rubbed his wrists as his eyes travelled from the floor to his knees then down to his feet. Armani could tell the soldier was contemplating standing and was debating internally about how steady his muscles were.

"The war was hard on many people," Armani said as he filled the void between them with the almost lyrical tone of his voice. "For those that saw its horrors, it is impossible to forget that the war happened. Many of them are still trapped in its grip, even though it ended close to fifteen cycles ago." Armani said as he offered Faris a hand up. "However, you should consider yourself doubly lucky for surviving as long as you have in our little town," Armani said aloofly as he helped Faris to his feet.

"Why?" Faris asked as he steadied himself using the wall. "I understand, and am thankful, for your help here, but why should I be doubly grateful?"

"Because Carness intervened in just enough time to save you, and your men, from a swift death at the inn," Armani's level tone drove home the urgency of what happened for Faris. "I would strongly recommend that you look twice before you decide to step in and take up arms in this town. Many times in the past, that choice proves to be the last error someone can make."

"You're telling me one drunk bar owner bested, and almost killed, nine highly trained soldiers?" Faris's tone told Armani that he did not believe what he had just heard.

"Aye, that is the brunt of it," Armani agreed with a sardonic nod as he straightened his robes.

"How could one man…" Faris said and then caught himself. "I mean, does this bar owner have a name?"

"That he does. His name is Daffer," Armani paused a little so he could see if Faris would recognize the name. He chuckled quietly to himself when he saw Faris's confused look, "and he bested your men because he was a highly trained soldier as well. I'm rather surprised that the name doesn't remind you of anyone. From what Carness said earlier, you should be familiar with the final battle of Watch Keep? That is the one that happened after you deserted. Daffer is one of the five legendary survivors." Armani stifled a little pride as he spoke. "You see we have three of them here in our little town.

"He is that Daffer?" Faris asked as if lost in thought. Armani struggled to keep his composure as he saw that his final words struck an obvious nerve. Faris's face paled a little as he cautiously asked, "You have three of them…here in Ellsted?" Armani could tell how uncomfortable the soldier had become the longer they spoke. "Who is the third?"

Armani smiled quietly as he heard the slight falter in Faris's voice. "Well, I believe you have met all of them; Carness, Daffer and our smith, Tipin," Armani said as he ticked them off with his fingers.

"The Calanari lives?" Faris's question was more of a

statement and, from his tone, Armani knew that it was born out of fear more than anything else in it.

"Why wouldn't he be alive? He survived one of the bloodiest moments in history." Armani said defensively.

"No reason," Faris attempted to cover his fear up as he spoke. "I just thought all of the Calanari had perished in the war."

Now it was Armani's turn to look at Faris incredulously. "I've never heard that. Where did you hear that news from?"

"I must have heard it from a bard in Hornshir, but obviously those reports were false," Faris offered a little too quickly for Armani's liking.

"Well, let's get you out of here and back to your men," Armani said as he opened the door. "I hope you don't mind, but I've made alternate accommodations for you and your men. We can talk about the laws of Ellsted while I show you to the house that you will be staying in. Then you can feel free to gather your men and relax a bit at our festival."

"Fine, but can we stop somewhere that might get a bite to eat? I feel like I haven't eaten in a week." Faris added his little jab and Armani knew that he meant it as a reminder of the situation.

Armani knew Faris was not going to forget what happened to them no matter what Armani tried to do to ease the insult. "Of course," Armani acquiesced. "I believe that you might enjoy some of the food from the bakery. It's well-known for his selection of pies."

"The boy is still alive, more than that I cannot say for certain." Alequa's voice drifted lightly on the breeze to Landolin's ears. "From where I am, it is hard to sense even that much."

"But it is more than enough to allay some of our fears at least," Landolin replied as he brushed a loose lock of crimson hair out of his face. His garnet hued eyes were shut as he focused once more on the soft whispering threads of sound in his mind. "Can you tell me if his energy is strong or if it is fading?"

"Steady…it is steady for now. Again, I wish that I could say more." Her voice faded momentarily from Landolin's mind as the sounds of the Inn temporarily invaded her thoughts and drowned her out. Alequa refocused her thoughts to strengthen her spell as she continued, "I wish there was more that I could do, but I need to stay here to guarantee the sa'ou-vant's safety."

"I understand," Landolin acknowledged faintly as he marshaled his will once more.

He struggled to maintain the conversation and he could feel his mental resolve falter. His control was slipping faster than he could focus. Landolin knew he could not maintain this communication for much longer.

"Though I long to have you and your abilities at my side once more. My condolences once again for the loss of your husband," Landolin felt a pang of regret as he breathed these words to her. "He will be missed and I am sorry for my part in his end." A tear crept down the elf's face as he sent his message.

"There is nothing more you could have done." Alequa offered sympathetically.

"I could have yielded to your requests sooner." The words hung like a pall over Landolin's head as he scanned the waiting chambers of Hornshir's council once more. He had no idea how much longer the mayor would give him before he was summoned, but Landolin intended to use as much of it as he could to ease some of the burden he felt loom over his soul.

"You could have done nothing." Alequa countered. "Aras had a full life and achieved many great things. His legacy is still writing itself even in his absence," Alequa whispered cryptically. "Please do not try and take that from him with your doubts."

"I just feel ashamed for my deeds, or lack of them." Landolin countered.

"Meishi, the gods have a plan for us, one that we have no idea of or any control over. That is the way of this world. It is our lot, whether we like it or not." Alequa soothed. "I must go."

"Peace be with you, hebasii." Landolin offered as he withdrew from their conversation and smoothed the creases caused by sitting hunched over while he spoke with Alequa from the front of his blood red shirt.

Landolin felt a little of the dread surrounding Aras's death ease as the tendrils of their connection slid away. He purposefully turned his thoughts to the conversation he planned on having with the mayor, should he ever get the chance.

Chapter Three: Impressions

The stifling silence of the room was shattered by an ear-splitting bang as the thick leather-bound book crashed into the oak wall opposite from where he stood. Namir felt little satisfaction as he watched it fly from his outstretched hand and through the stack of papers on its way to the wall.

He dismissed the sense of annoyance that crowded into his mind as the loose pages exploded from the surface of his decrepit wooden table. A pained sigh escaped him as he watched them flutter to the floor of his room. They floated like a premonition of the snow flurries that would soon blanket the surrounding hills in the coming months.

"Feel better?" Haradine asked as she closed the door behind her.

"No," Namir confided as he watched the last few sheets dance along the floor.

They spun in place for a moment, caught in the slight breeze that had managed to slip past the door as it closed. Namir felt Haradine's eyes burn his skin as she stared intently at his features. Based on their previous encounters, he knew that she was trying to decipher his thoughts.

"Why did you throw the book then?" She asked somewhat perplexed.

"I thought it would help." Namir knew that his matter of

fact tone would strike Haradine just as odd as his despondent body language did. He also knew that neither would do much to assuage her curiosity.

"What bothered you so much about it that you felt the need to throw it?" Haradine locked gazes with Namir as if she dared him to lie to her.

"There are too many gaps in Aras's documentation." Namir blinked and broke her gaze as he turned to face the small dust filled window ledge.

He felt somewhat comforted by the growing clamor outside. Soon the town would erupt into activity and the full onslaught of the festival would be upon them. That knowledge brought a sense of peace and order with it.

"It makes no sense. The more I read and study his writings, the more holes seem to appear. It's as if I am missing something vital." Namir said as he pulled himself away from the window and focused his attention on the papers scattered across his floor again.

"I don't understand?" Haradine shot a confused look at Namir as he paced in front of her.

"Neither do I," Namir took a deep breath as he paused midstride and took a moment to look Haradine over.

He carefully took in the worry lines that spread across her face. What really bothered him was the fear that he saw in her eyes. The air of confusion that had settled about her was the final straw. "It's just very hard to follow," Namir said as he let his breath out slowly.

"Maybe I can help," Haradine offered as she watched Namir cross the room and retrieve the book he had thrown.

"Maybe," Namir considered her offer as he recalled the pledge that Aras forced him to make. "Keep this work away from those who might betray it," Aras's voice echoed in Namir's mind as he thought about Haradine's offer. He carefully shrugged each of these thoughts away. "How about we go for a walk instead?"

Namir immediately realized what a poor substitute his suggestion was in comparison, but he had no other options. "Hopefully the air will help me straighten these things out in my head," he said as he laid the book on the table.

"Let's clean your mess up first," Haradine suggested as she knelt down and started to gather up the loose pages that littered the floor.

"Let's," Namir replied. A relaxed grin played across his lips as he swiftly knelt down and joined her.

"Why do you say that?" Hessa felt hurt as she looked across the desk at Aves and her father.

"Because I don't see a need for you to go back to Hornshir with them," Armani's voice was smooth yet commanding as he repeated his decision.

"But why not, father?" Aves asked. Her pain was evident in her voice as she scowled hurtfully at Armani.

"Because your mother would not have approved and neither would hers," Armani admitted. A twinge of defeat filled his voice as he looked at each girl in turn. "You both are so very much like your mothers, so full of anger and defiance. I've noticed it more and more over the years, but never more than right now." There was fear lurking behind Armani's eyes as he spoke, but the air of authority he wore offset the effect.

Armani's response silenced both Aves and Hessa. Neither one of them were used to Armani discussing either of their mothers with them before, no matter how many times that they had asked. It had been years since they had even heard him make any remark about them. Now to find out that he thought about how their mothers would react to their actions astounded them.

Aves broke the silence first. "Father, why don't you ever talk about our mothers?"

Armani looked down at his hands as his daughter's words washed over him and it was obvious by the unexpected creases that appeared on his smooth features that a bolt of pain shot through his heart, "Because it wouldn't help to speak about Shara and Natlia. I loved both of them dearly, in my way, and if I thought either of them would quarrel with a decision that I've made for either of you, I would be more than ashamed. I would rather die than bear that kind of disgrace." His answer was slow in coming and both girls could sense the weight that his words bore within him.

"Even if my mother didn't improve, my Lord, I believe it is necessary for your daughter's safety. Although I loved her, I don't understand how the head of your staff would have any real say about this." Hessa responded. As she did, she realized that she had overstepped her bounds again.

Armani just shook his head from side to side as he continued to look at his hands. "You become more brazen every day," he said, more to himself than to either of them, as he slowly leveled a tortured look at Hessa and then at Aves in turn. "The two of you are so much alike, yet so different. You could have been sisters if things were different."

"I am sorry, my Lord. I didn't mean to overstep…" Hessa interjected after she saw the hurt look play across her employer's face.

"No, I am. Although I do believe you meant to overstep your position, it's forgiven. At least it is, this time." Armani interrupted Hessa's apology with a slight wave of his hand as he rose from his chair. "I know that you can't fully understand my thoughts, and I fear that I don't either."

"Father, are you all right?" Aves asked. The twinge of worry pulled at the edges of her voice. She rose and quickly went to her father's side. Her hand gently landed on Armani's shoulder supportively.

Hessa could tell that Armani was worried and that bothered both Aves and herself. Something other than their conversation weighed heavily upon him and Hessa wished she knew what it was. Last night he had said that he was worried about them. The fact that he was a little leaner than he was before they left was easily attributed to that. Now, however, Hessa was not so sure.

"I am fine my dear. I am simply still recovering from your absence. That is all." Armani responded as he looked up at Aves. "You know, you are the spitting image of Shara. The only difference between how your mom looked when she was your age is that you wear your crimson hair shorter than she ever had. Even your eyes are as expressive as hers were, if not more so." Armani took his daughter's had off of his shoulder delicately and turned to face her.

Hessa stared at the two of them perfectly silhouetted by the fireplace and she was stunned. She always fought back the jealousy that she felt for what they had. After all, not only had her mother died when she was young, but she had never known her father either. She knew that there was nothing that she could do about either thing, but when she saw Aves and Armani together like this she couldn't help but feel her old wounds reopen deep inside of her. She sifted quietly in her chair as father and daughter shared their moment as she thought about his words.

While she was certain that Armani was being confusing on purpose, Hessa could not quite figure out why. She knew that he was lying about why he was so distracted, that much was obvious by looking at him. The lines that gouged his features as he spoke about their mothers worried her. Hessa and Aves exchanged glances at each other. Hessa could tell that Aves and her both knew that Armani was lying to them, she just did not know why.

"Please father," Aves whispered to Armani, "tell me what is really bothering you. I know that you missed us and that you were worried, however, we both have seen the long glances that you take when you look at either of us. You are gaunt and frail looking. Why won't you tell me what's wrong? Was it our trip? Was it not successful enough? Did we not get enough people to agree to come to our Belanui's Feast? I know that there has been a better turnout this year than we have experienced in any of the previous years, but was it enough?"

"There is nothing wrong, my dear." Armani lied again. "You are right. Your excursion to Hornshir was more successful than anyone could have hoped for. We actually have a chance of surviving this winter, especially now that a trade agreement has been made with Hornshir's mayor and their elders."

He dropped his daughter's hands and looked at her lovingly for a moment before he swept a frail-looking hand across his brow. Armani's hazel eyes darted from one girl to the next a few times before he spoke next.

"Whoever the main negotiator was, they did a fantastic job. I just hope that it wasn't Jaconis." A hint of bitterness was immediately apparent in his voice as Armani said Daffer's son's name.

"Although I would love to be able to take the credit for it, Hessa managed most of the negotiations," Aves said as she smiled happily at her maid.

"Good," Armani replied. There was an odd twinge of pride in his voice as he spoke that seemed a little out of place to Hessa.

"I am glad to know that you don't mind that I overstepped my bounds." Hessa smiled as she realized that the pride she heard was directed at her.

Nurn watched the snow flurries with a disapproving scowl. His deep black eyes traced their path as if he memorized their patterns as they fell. A heavy layer of snow had fallen since they called off the last search and he did not like what it meant for his brother. Three more days were lost to the whim of the elements and he hated it. The longer he had to postpone the search, the more chance there was of Halin being injured.

Nurn glared at the black clouds that obstinately hung overhead. There seemed little chance that the storm would lift any time soon and this only darkened his mood. The endless waiting was starting to grate on Nurn's nerves and it was starting to become more and more obvious to everyone around him.

Nurn stretched his cold muscles in rampant frustration. He knew that Landolin would not allow him to continue the search without an escort, just like Nurn knew that there would be arguments against continuing the search at all if the weather did not hold.

"I don't care what they say, I'm going to search alone if I have to." The bass rumble of his voice carried several yards across the fresh snow, even though he had all but whispered them.

"That may not be the wisest choice," Jerine's soft tenor voice filled in the odd awkward silence smoothly.

"I don't care if my choice isn't wise," Nurn growled as he slowly turned his muscular frame to face Jerine head on.

Nurn was silently thankful for their conversation, that way he did not have to bother with the uneasiness that the elf's cloak caused every time he looked at him. His brown hair cascaded across his left shoulder as he locked his dark eyes onto Jerine's ice blue eyes.

"In case you forgot this is my brother that we are searching for. He isn't some missing dignitary or a vagrant. So pardon me if I can't just let him die without trying to find him." Nurn's black eyes narrowed fiercely as his words flew out of his mouth with deadly force.

He struggled to keep control over his senses as the growing sensation of vertigo threatened to consume his senses. All it took was an unguarded glimpse and the unsettling sensation that Jerine's cloak caused unraveled Nurn's hold on reality. Somehow, as they spoke, the elf's ability to blend in with his surroundings pulled at the corners of his mind. It was unnatural and the sense of instability always seemed to follow any encounter with Jerine. This disturbed Nurn more than he cared to admit.

"I know." Jerine paused. Nurn watched the elf's face in an attempt to stop the nauseating sensation from claiming him.

He watched as Jerine's ice blue eyes darted from one part of Nurn's body to another as they spoke. Nurn knew that the elf was sizing him up; he just had no idea about whether he should let him. Nurn felt Jerine's eyes trace the tattoos on the sides of his clean-shaven head.

Then, the elf replied, "But we can't risk losing you in the search for your brother either. You are a sa'trandon now and therefore vital to the skein of things." Jerine assumed a soothing tone as he tried to reason with Nurn. "Although the search has been called off until the weather eases, it has not been, nor will it be, permanent."

"How do you know this?" Nurn interrupted impatiently, his deep voice carried his irritation in waves. "And how do you know that the time we are losing due to the storm is not the very time that Halin needs in order to survive?"

Jerine lowered his head and shook it sadly. He waited a few moments as several strands of his long brown hair fell free from his braid and whipped in the wind. It was evident that he struggled to maintain his emotional control before he answered.

"You may be right," Jerine's voice, usually a light tenor, held a gravelly quality that betrayed his inner turmoil. "I cannot know if the lost time is vital for Halin's survival, just as I cannot know if you would survive if I allow you to go out into this coming storm. What I do know is that your chances of finding him are slim in this weather and your chances of survival are even slimmer." Jerine's words held a sense of pity that Nurn found hard to hear as Jerine locked Nurn's black eyes with his own ice blue stare as he spoke.

"Fine, we will wait until it passes then," Nurn replied hesitantly. "But as soon as the weather breaks, I am going out to find my brother." There was a sense of finality that Nurn purposefully ensured was conveyed by his tone. "I don't care what your general says."

"That's fair enough," Jerine conceded. "Until then, we need to secure our gear and get ready for the storm."

Alequa closed her wearied eyes again. She felt the strain of her search fray the edges of her mind as she tried again. She quickly ignored the knot as it formed in her thigh from sitting cross-legged for too long. "I must find him," Alequa thought to herself. She dismissed the stray thought as quickly as it formed. She drew in another deep breathe and held it as she refocused her thoughts on the missing boy.

The scent of incense filled her nostrils as her body pulsed in perfect rhythm with her own heartbeat. She felt her mind slowly fade from the room she had been meditating in for more than four long hours and back to the peaceful forest that held the elven encampment.

She felt the birds flit through her mind's eye as her consciousness floated toward the clearing the sa'trandon was last seen in. She probed the forest with all of her ethereal senses. She tasted the air and felt the aura of the clearing. Nothing. No feeling of dread or mischievousness anywhere.

She sighed in exasperation as she pulled herself back to her body. Disappointment settled in slowly as she stretched. The annoying tingles shot through each body part as her circulation was renewed and Alequa scolded herself for meditating for too long.

"You should be more careful." The bodiless voice snapped her out of her thoughts.

The deep voice held a commanding tone that cut Alequa to her core. Panic flooded through every corner of her being as she turned to face the intruder. Alequa fought off a wave of nausea as her body tensed. She felt his eyes upon her, a hunter's eyes.

"I could have been a stranger." The unseen intruder's voice took on a haughty tone as he moved in unison with her to stay hidden.

His words did little to ease Alequa's fear. "That is true." She agreed as she lowered her left hand cautiously to her side.

"Let's not play this game," he said as he clasped her hand

with his. “I don’t think either of would be happy with the outcome,” Carness said as he stepped out of the darkness and into her view.

“I should have realized it was you!” Alequa exclaimed as she jerked her hand away from his. “You really should be more careful, my friend.” She chided herself more than her old friend as she felt her tension melt away. “Or have you forgotten my goddess’s wrath when her followers are harmed.”

“Oh no, I could never forget that,” Carness confided. A wolfish grin crossed his lips as he continued, “I had heard that you decided to grace our fair village with your presence and I could not pass up the opportunity to speak with you again. How is Aras?”

Alequa appreciated her old comrade’s sentiment, but it cut her heart in ways that he had not intended and she knew it. She felt the fresh scars rip open again as she fought back her tears. “Dead. He is dead.” Her grip on sanity slipped just long enough to allow her tears to gain the upper hand against her ironclad will and she knew she had lost her inner struggle to remain stoic.

“I am so sorry.” Carness stammered. “I didn’t know.”

His words were not enough, nothing could be, and Alequa knew that he felt like had to say something. Everyone always does. She watched as he walked over to her. His strong arms were compelling and she did not resist him as he pulled her into them Alequa felt her body quake against his hard muscles as she buried herself against him in a futile attempt to help her regain some of her lost composure.

Chapter Four: Schemes

Aves looked at Hessa pleadingly. "Come on, we need to go and enjoy the festivities at least once before we are pulled into the political maneuvers that the council has planned for us." She held two of her finest cloaks tight against her chest as she begged Hessa one more time.

"What would Armani think if he knew you had left?" Hessa replied matter-of-factly.

She eyed her mistress warily as she spoke in an attempt to gauge her reaction. Hessa hated to think that they would be forced back into their previous roles. So much had happened in the last few months and Hessa knew she could no longer be content living a life of servitude.

She even doubted that she could stomach living in Ellsted any longer than she absolutely had to. Hessa felt a new connection to Namir's plight. Neither of them had any real family to tie them to the town and both of them had a taste of what might await them if they could be freed from their current circumstances.

The only real difference was that Namir found his ticket out. He was a king, or at least he had the chance to become one. Hessa knew she had to seize her opportunity to help Namur achieve his destiny if she wanted to ever find her own way out of Ellsted.

"I don't care." Aves's lie was evident. "I just want to spend one final day with us as equals instead of the way it will soon be again."

Hessa looked into Aves's pleading hazel eyes and realized that she longed for the same thing. "Fine, we'll go, but just for a few hours. But if Armani confronts us, I'm not going to shoulder the blame though."

"Agreed," Aves said hurriedly. "Now let's be gone before my father notices."

"So where to…cousin?" Hessa asked with a hint of sarcasm in her voice. She quickly donned the cloak that Aves handed her as the two of them made their way down the back staircase to the kitchen.

"I thought we could start with games of chance and then end at the gypsy wagons," Aves whispered over her shoulder as they hurried through the deserted kitchen.

Both girls knew Armani usually visited the kitchen in search of a late night snack sporadically throughout the night and Hessa felt her pulse quicken as they passed silently through it. This knowledge only seemed to heighten their senses as well as their fear of discovery.

Each subtle creak goaded out the floorboards as they passed through the empty hallways of the house forced them to pause in fear of discovery. Both girls held their breath at even the slightest hint of the mayor's presence. Long moments and longer awkward glances slowed them even further, but both managed to breathe a little easier when they were out in the crisp evening air and well away from the building they had both called home for as long as Hessa could remember.

"Aves," Hessa finally found her voice after they were almost to the main square, "do your rooms feel the same to you now that we are back?"

"What do you mean?" Aves replied. The look on her face let Hessa know that Aves was a little confused by her question.

"Nothing really," Hessa said offhandedly. "It's just that the house feels different. Smaller I guess. And Armani, I mean, the mayor seems different. More distant than I have ever felt before."

Hessa's words flooded from her between from her lips uncontrollably. She had been holding them in for so long and now she was a little surprised by how they sounded coming out of her own mouth.

"I think that I know what you mean," Aves conceded. "I thought I might've been imagining it. But now that you mention it, he has changed." Aves slowed her pace to a crawl as she spoke.

One thing that Hessa loved about crowds is that no one seemed to notice what each other did or said unless it was shouted. She knew Aves liked this as well.

Hessa fought back the numerous memories that filled her mind about their little discussions. Aves had often mentioned the miraculous way crowds had a way of enveloping someone.

Crowds leant their anonymity to those that needed it. Hessa knew that Aves waited for her to catch up and match her new pace before she would continue and she took her own time to do so. Hessa reveled in the little bit of control she could exert over Aves, but she knew not to enjoy it too much.

Aves's impatience was starting to show through the edges of her moral fiber. "My father seems distracted, almost haunted in a way. I've never seen him this way and I'm worried." A tear crept down Aves's cheek as she finally confided her fears to her best friend.

Hessa grabbed Aves's hand and pulled her friend into her. In one fluid motion, Hessa's arms wrapped around Aves and held her close. She knew her friend needed comfort as much as Hessa felt the need to comfort her. Both ladies stood motionless and let their fears free into the night air. After several long moments, Hessa said, "Let's go and lose ourselves in the shops." Hessa offered supportively.

"Agreed," Aves responded hesitantly.

Hessa felt some of the weight lift from her mind and she enjoyed how good it felt to be back on somewhat familiar ground. I forgot how much I missed being here. Hessa thought as she took Aves hand and pulled them into the gathering throngs of carefree revelers.

The bustle of Belanui's feast clamored outside of Namir's window made it all but impossible for him to concentrate on the pages scattered across the roughly hewn table before him. Each time he focused on one piece of information another one would slip away from him.

More times than not, Namir found the cheers of the children that surrounded the Gathering Place more captivating than the spidery writing that filled Aras's journals. Namir closed his eyes as he rubbed his temples in a vain attempt to stay focused.

"Sa'ouvant, it was obvious a few hours ago that you wanted to join the festivities when we took our walk." Haradine's voice was soft, but somehow managed to cut through the noise of the festival outside. "Why don't you just give in and do so?"

"I can't." Namir pushed himself away from the books in front of him. "Not while I know that Halin is missing and Nurn is distressed."

"It's good that you care for your friends, but it isn't your fault that they cannot be here." Her eyes showed how much heart broke a little every time she looked at him.

Namir felt the pity she felt every time he spoke of his friends and their plight. Somehow he knew that she could feel how much his friend's fates weighed on his soul. Namir paced across the floor, to the opposite side of the room in an attempt to gain more distance from the notes that he had been agonizing over.

"It still doesn't mean that I should enjoy myself without them." His voice was flat and distant

"Sa'ouvant," the slight crack in Haradine's voice betrayed

that her defenses slipped a little as she spoke, “you don’t have to punish yourself. Not like this.” Her internal struggle was obvious as she continued her thoughts, “Besides, a sa’ouvant needs to be able to put the needs of his subjects over his own concerns. You need to go and enjoy the festivities. Even if it is to connect to those that you will eventually rule over.”

“But, uh,” Namir stammered as he stared at Haradine in confusion and admiration.

There was more to the elf than he had imagined. Unfortunately, Namir’s surprised look, as well as their conversation, was cut short by a loud pounding on Namir’s door. He turned toward the door as it opened and his uncle’s hulking form loomed in front of him.

“Daffer?” Namir’s surprise was evident as the huge man entered unbidden. “Please make yourself at home, Uncle.” Namir’s sarcasm was as obvious as his lack of admiration for his uncle.

“I will!” Daffer spat in response. “You live here at my discretion and don’t you ever forget that!”

“How could I?” Namir replied vehemently.

“And how can we help you, sir?” Haradine cut in and took control of the situation. Her attempt to disarm the hostility that filled the air around them was obvious as she inserted herself between the two men.

Daffer eyed Haradine as he removed his cloak and threw it onto Namir’s bed. “I have no business for you, harlot.” Daffer hurled the insult at Haradine casually.

“She is not a harlot,” Namir interceded on Haradine’s behalf, “and you are not welcomed in my quarters, so make your visit here short.” Namir finished as he locked stares with the hulking drunk before him.

The inferred threat that Namir’s words held was palpable and obviously took Daffer off guard. “I came to evict you,” Daffer said matter-of-factly. “I don’t know what you did to turn my son against me and I don’t care! I’ll give you a week to collect your things and leave." Daffer never broke Namir's gaze as he said this. "Do I make myself clear?"

"Where would you have me go?" Namir asked. He refused to back down and give his uncle any satisfaction in this decision.

"Quite frankly, I don't care. You can't stay here any longer." Daffer snorted as he turned to face Haradine. "Take your tramp with you when you go. Neither her nor her companion are welcomed here anymore." He spat his final words at Haradine. Namir saw the telltale smirk that Daffer wore when he was pleased with himself when he saw her wipe his spittle off of her face.

"Do you know who you speak to?" Haradine asked coolly before she could think better of her words. Her hands slowly lowered themselves to her belt that the hilts of her awaiting blades.

"Aye, my good-for-nothing nephew that's who." Daffer eyed Haradine's actions as he continued, "But I wouldn't care if he was the heir apparent! Just be gone before the week is out and I lose my temper."

Namir could see there was something familiar to Daffer about Haradine, just as he could tell that Daffer could not figure out what that familiarity was.

"Do you understand me, Namir?" An unsettling awkwardness developed as Daffer swayed menacingly. Everyone present knew he was waiting for Namir to reply and that he was not going to leave until he got it.

"Aye," Namir responded dryly. He motioned for Haradine to be silent as he did so. "I understand your message, uncle, and I will be gone before that if possible. Now, if you don't mind, we will be leaving and I would appreciate it if you did as well." Namir's tone held a commanding quality that obviously took Haradine and Daffer off guard and Namir was grateful it did.

He smiled inwardly when Daffer turned to leave. However, the lumbering barkeep paused momentarily as he filled the door frame with his hulking form and Namir sensed that Haradine feared his uncle was going to stay instead of obeying Namir's orders. A brief sigh of relief escaped her lips as Daffer abruptly staggered out into the blustery wind.

"Typical," Namir commented. He took the look of confusion that crossed Haradine's face as his queue to explain, so he continued, "he left his cloak. Oh well, he can get it after we are no longer occupying this hovel." Namir motioned toward his bed and grinned as he spoke.

Haradine smiled at her liege's words and demeanor. It was obvious by the twinkle in her eyes that she loved the way he managed to take control of the situation and then joke about it. "Aren't you concerned about our accommodations?" She asked a little incredulously.

"No," Namir shrugged. "I have a few ideas. In the worst case, we can stay in the Council Hall." He replied jovially. "Now, let's go before I realize that I just told off my uncle."

Namir could tell that Haradine was still not used to his little quirks. Even this little jest seemed to surprise her. He marveled at how she studied his every sound as if she were trying to decipher his very soul through the urgency of his voice or the little jokes that he told. The eerie thing was that she did seem to understand it and this bothered him. He watched as she nodded her agreement and quickly followed him as Namir walked toward the central road of Ellsted.

Games and mazes lured children of all ages to spend their time and their parents' coins on trivial distractions that they did not need. Everywhere Namir looked, he saw people spending hard earned coin on cheap thrills and he knew that they could not really afford it.

A feeling of nostalgia mingled with loss as he meandered through the throngs of people as they partook of the mindless festivities eagerly. Peddlers' shops of every shape and size met Namir's gaze as he surveyed the Belanui festival grounds that spread out before him.

The once empty pasture that ran from The Gathering place

to the edge of town was filled with throngs of people. Where only grassy fields had been just days before now held all of the trappings of a village in its own right. This year it had almost doubled the size of Ellsted and Namir found it awe inspiring. Roads wound between vendors tents and the semi-permanent buildings hastily constructed by both locals and gypsies alike.

"You seem sad," Haradine's gentle voice cut through the cloud of sentiment that enshrouded Namir's thoughts.

"No…I'm just remembering the days when I gave myself freely to the festivities." A slight smile pulled at the corner of Namir's lips as he spoke.

"Ah, I see," Haradine responded. She still seemed a little confused by Namir's actions and words. As incongruent as they were, Namir knew she would not stop until she understood their meaning. "So what is stopping you from indulging yourself now?"

"Nothing I guess," Namir shrugged. "It just doesn't feel right. I just can't seem to give myself in to the lure of the festival without Nurn and Halin. I guess I've just become too old inside to really enjoy myself."

"Sounds like you just need to let go of your troubles a little." Haradine offered. Her response seemed odd to Namir, it was almost as if she had not thought about how he might take her words. Namir watched as the color drained from her face as the realization of what she had just said to her liege sank in. Haradine quickly turned and met Namir's as a twinge of anxiety spread across her face.

"Maybe," Namir replied absently. He knew that his aloof response would take some of Haradine's anxiety away and strengthen her resolve to not make a slip like that again. "I wonder if Aves is out and about…" Namir wondered more to himself than anyone and did not really expect to hear an answer.

"I think she is," Haradine offered. Namir knew that she saw the quizzical look on his face, so he was not overly surprised when she pointed toward the main square. He assumed that Haradine had last seen Aves in that area when she confirmed it by saying, "She was over there at the herbalist's booth a few moments ago."

Namir nodded as he changed direction and started to weave through the throng of people toward where Haradine had motioned. "Good, maybe there is a chance for some fun tonight after all." His words were a much of a mystery to himself as he assumed they were to his elven guard.

Armani sat in his study alone. He knew that somewhere in the house both of his daughters were trying to make sense of his reaction to their news, just as he knew that they would feel betrayed if they ever discovered the real reason for his reactions.

A deep breath filled his lungs unbidden as Armani cursed the cruel tricks that time had wrought on his life. Of all the lies he was forced to tell, he hated the one he told the girls every day. The only thing that he hated almost as much as was the withering effect that time had on everything that it touched.

"You're late," he said to as he ran all of his fingers through his hair. He had slumped over his desk as he waited for his belated guest.

"I had other errands to attend to," his silent visitor replied half-heartedly. "Why did you summon me?"

"I fear for my family, isn't that reason enough?" Armani replied coolly.

"In a word…no." The response was just as cold as Armani's had been and he was not expecting it to be so distant. "I fear that there is something you're not telling me," his visitor's words fell on his ears with a tender edge to them. The faint rustle of robes as they caught on the footstool a few paces from Armani betrayed his guest's movements. "So tell me, why was I summoned?" It was more of a command than a question and Armani knew it.

"I believe that an assassin has been sent here to dispatch me." Armani started as he carefully picked his words. "Have you any thoughts on the matter?"

"Hmmm, that is a delicate situation." His visitor replied as if in thought. "Am I correct in assuming that you suspect that I am the assassin?"

"Aye," Armani replied calmly as he sat perfectly still.

"Would you believe me if I told you that I wasn't sent to kill you?" There was something in his guest's voice that set off alarms in Armani's mind.

He could not tell if it was how smoothly she answered him or if it was the subtle hint of sarcasm that the well-chosen words hid within their sultry veil. No matter what the reason was, Armani could not quite place what it was.

"No," he shook his head as he lowered his hands to the top of his desk. "I'm afraid that I wouldn't." Armani's matter of fact tone tore at his soul as he fully realized the truth in his words.

"I see." These words were followed by several long tense moments of silence before his guest filled the void with her reply. "What options have I been given then?" There was roughness to the voice and Armani could sense the terse emotion behind them.

"Leave. Never come back. Not even if you hear that I have been killed." Armani turned to face his guest slowly as he spoke his final words. "Then…and only then…can I believe you."

He scanned the room carefully. No one was there with him. Only the subtle movement of the door as it silently closed betrayed the fact that someone had ever been there at all.

A single tear rolled down Armani's cheek as he absently ran his fingers through his thinning hair once more. "I am sorry, but the winds of change have blown upon us and I fear no one is safe any longer." He said quietly to himself as he slowly stood up and made his way to the window.

Armani carefully pulled the curtain aside and gazed out over the bustling city. Although dusk was not far off, the clangor of the festivities drowned out all of the usual noises that he normally enjoyed throughout the year.

The biting cold wind ruffled Morcant's fur as he perched above the elves' camp. He could feel his muscles cramping from the cold and he knew that he had stayed too long overlooking the elves' activities. He could tell that his prey had somehow slipped away in the confusion. Although he saw them bury the old man, there was something wrong.

Aras's scent still lingered in the area. It was as if his old enemy was still alive instead of in the ground. Morcant knew he was grasping at straws, but he had to believe that the elves might reveal where he went. Although it was difficult to find the elves, or their tents, Morcant had finally managed it. He was well aware that his mistress would kill him if he failed to find his target this time.

The wintery winds meandered through the branches that Morcant stood on. His heart fluttered with excitement as the whole tree moaned and swayed with the increased pressure of the coming storm. The refreshing sensation as the coldness worked its way through his black fur like icy fingers that soothed his taut muscles. Morcant closed his pupiless blood red eyes in rapture as he focused on remaining in his precarious perch.

Morcant reflexively licked his lips as he sniffed at the air again in a futile attempt to isolate his prey. Deep down he had hoped to catch the source of his prey's scent hidden in the breeze. He carefully turned his head slowly from side to side as he inhaled deeply through his nose. This most recent attempted to derive one last hint allowed Morcant to figure out why Jerine had brought the boy from Hornshir to the elves, to protect the child from him.

"I wonder what lies Jerine has told the elves this time." Morcant mused to himself as he tried to taste the air for any remnants he may have missed.

Impatience weighed on his nerves as he waited for the

elven sentry to pass below him. He did not dare move from his perch until they had passed. Morcant remembered all too well how keen their ears were from the last time he was in this forest, all of those years ago.

His fingers reflexively traced the intricate pattern on his left gauntlet in anticipation of the now familiar tingle that would alert him of elven magic, but it never came. Once the sentry passed, Morcant deftly moved closer to their encampment and scanned from one barely visible tent to the next.

Even though the encampment bustled with activity, there was something not right about it. None of the elves moved with a sense of urgency or purpose. From what Morcant could remember about this particular group of soldiers. While this was not their normal tendency, he still could not place what exactly it was that bothered him.

"The supplies are ready," one of the tall elves that Morcant had been watching called over to his compatriot. "We can get the camp packed and moved as soon as Landolin sends the word."

Although the elves were out of his field of vision, Morcant could picture the metallic silver eyes of the elf dance across the stowed away supplied stacked in front of him. Unlike his compatriots, this particular elf let his golden spun hair hang unbraided. Long as it was, it barely reached the small of his back.

"Good," The other, raven-haired, elf replied. "Maybe we can get the unused tents broke down and be ready to completely evacuate the camp by midnight.

Morcant had heard enough. Silently, he climbed the tree to ensure that they would not be alerted to his position before he leapt to another one. With each leap, Morcant put a little more distance between him and the elves and closed the distance to his destination.

The small clearing was easily discernable from the top of the tree line. Morcant smiled to himself as he calculated exactly how few jumps he had to make to arrive at Aras's unguarded grave.

"Soon I'll know for sure if the scourge of my people, and the last of his kind, is truly dead," Morcant's words hissed from his hair coated lips in small puffs of steam.

Chapter Five: Tracked

A cold wind whipped his ebon hair around his head as he stared at the rickety gate tied clumsily into the tree line. He silently pondered how many times he had been to this place and never knew the importance that it would hold in the greater scheme of things. He stood in silent observation, like a statue, in the cold night air with only his thick black cloak for warmth. He knew something had moved deep in the thicket below the little knoll that he stood on.

The shadow walker waited as a dark cloud crossed in front of the moon and completely obscured it from sight. As utter darkness enveloped the vale, he saw what he had been waiting for. Several different bushes rustled at the same time as the animalistic creatures eased themselves out of them. He focused his attention and heightened sight at them in an attempt to discern what they were.

Although there was no moonlight, what little light that managed to filter through the clouds and foliage reflected off of the skeleton-like armor of the creatures as they made their way silently toward the cottage that the shadow walker knew was just at the end of the little trail that stretched out in front of him.

"Nassarid," the shadow walker said quietly to himself.

He knew that these were a special class though, not the

normal ones created by Lotevilar's ilk. These were crafted with more skill and power. He also knew that there was nothing for it. They searched for the same thing he was sent to retrieve, which only confirmed his suspicions.

"The dark and the light both seek the same thing, it must be here somewhere." He whispered to himself stoically.

He knew that the only way he could hope to evade them was to do what his kind did best, use the shadows. He mentally braced himself to walk through the shadows again. He just wished that it was easier to move through them.

The scratching snuffling noises of the nassarid as they searched the grounds were the first sensation he experienced as he stepped free from the shadows. He smiled as he saw the mists rise from his cloak and hair.

One thing he enjoyed about travelling through the dark passageways of the shadows was the creeping warmth that claimed him afterward. The soft embrace of life that slowly played across his flesh was spellbinding. These little sensations helped to remind the shadow walker of what it meant to be truly alive and he thoroughly enjoyed it.

The shadow walker crossed the small room quickly. He deftly avoided the side table cluttered with knickknacks and small plates as he moved. Unlike most people, he was able to avoid those things that others could not. He slowed his pace as he neared the door on the far wall. He eased his dagger from its sheath and carefully tested the door's lock.

To his surprise, the door eased open just as his fingers brushed its surface. Carefully he let it swing open just enough to slip through without leaving it noticeably ajar. The shadow walker did not want to make it any easier for the beasts outside to find what they both searched for in case he missed it somehow.

"Empty. The room is empty!" His thoughts matched the speed that his eyes darted around the chamber.

His frustration increased as he came across nothing of any

real value. He was about to leave when he saw it, an almost invisible edge of paper jutting out of the closet's door frame. The shadow walker slowly recrossed the room to examine it closer.

"The paper type is wrong," he muttered quietly to himself, "but it must have been important for Natlia to hide it."

The shadow walker held his breath in anticipation as his hand slowly waivered hesitantly toward the edge of the page. He struggled to move slow enough to remain unheard by the beasts that rooted around just on the other side of the wall.

He painstakingly slid the sheet free from its hiding place at an unbearable snail's pace. "What are you?" He whispered under his breath as he held the page that he clutched a few inches in front of his eyes.

The shadow walker carefully turned it in his hands so the soft light that eased its way through the partially shuttered windows would fall on its face just enough to reveal the contents.

The familiar click and creak of the front door came all too soon and he hardly had any chance to read the spidery writing spilled across its face. The shadow walker had hoped that the inscription would answer all of his questions. Instead, he had to wait.

"There are far too many people searching for it to risk them finding the information on this page," he whispered silently to himself.

"Fan out and find it." A sultry voice commanded from the darkness of the cottage's entry. "Be careful though. It cannot be known that we were here! Break anything and your head will decorate my boudoir." Her last command coaxed a few throaty growls and whimpers from the nassarid that accompanied her.

There was something familiar about her voice, but the shadow walker could not immediately place it. As the creatures meticulously picked their way through the entrance and into the great room, the shadow walker's breath caught in his throat.

Somewhere deep in his psyche, the shadow walker understood that even the slightest noise would have garnered too much unwanted attention. He knew that the nassarid would find him sooner than he would want just as he knew that he had no choice, he had to leave. He gingerly rolled the page he held delicately in his hands and silently slid it into a loop of his belt.

"Hold!" Her abrupt tone made even the shadow walker's heart leap into his throat. "I smell a walker." She said menacingly. He heard her inhale his scent deeply. "He stepped from the shadowy realms here." He heard a tap of metal against stone. "Find him. I want him alive." The words were more snarled than spoken. "He may know where it is."

Her initiative decided his actions for him. He knew that he could not leave the room he was in; it would draw them to the very place he wanted to keep hidden. The last thing that he wanted to do was to lead the dark followers any closer to their goal than they already were. No matter what she was, the shadow walker knew that this particular hunter could not track his scent. Instead, she smelled the scent of the shades and specters that inhabited the shadows he walked through.

He listened to the search patterns of the beasts and knew his timing had to be perfect. The shadow walker waited until the room across the long hall from him was clear. Then he darted into the shadows that waited for him in the room beyond.

"He is down there!" Her screams trailed off into the blackness of the shadows.

The ever-present tug of a million dark hands tugged at his soul as his very breath was pulled from his lungs. In one quick and abrupt gulp, the darkness consumed him.

Landolin looked at each of his officers in turn with a staunch look of disappointment firmly set on his face. "So you are saying that we have nothing to go on."

"Aye," the captain to his left replied as if the question was asked only to him.

"I see," Landolin replied absently. "Then we have little choice. We will have to infiltrate the guard." He cautiously scanned his officer's reactions. When none of them flinched he continued, "I don't know how else to put it. We have to find evidence of his betrayal if there is any. If we can't, then we are fine to leave the manor without fear." Landolin hated the need to verify his friend's motives. "I don't like it any more than you do men, but we must perform our duties without reservation. Whoever is chosen will be truly alone. We will not be able to risk their discovery. No magic and no contact, no matter how brief."

"Who will be sent to infiltrate?" The same captain's voice chimed in as if on cue.

"Feel free to draw lots or someone can volunteer," Landolin replied emotionlessly, "either way I cannot know who was sent."

He slowly crossed the room to the fireplace. He took a deep breath as he stared into the roaring fire. Landolin recalled the first time that he stood in this room. The owner of the manor had stood where he was and he had asked a similar question of him. His answer had been the same. Landolin finally understood why the cryptic order had been given all those years ago. This realization did little to ease his hatred of their situation.

"Have the others checked in yet?"

"No." This time the answer came from the far side of the room. "And I'm afraid they won't be able to." The voice held a silky quality in its subtle tones.

Landolin spun and faced the source of the sinister voice. "And pray tell me how you know this?" His words sprayed like acid as he directed his them at the shadowed figure.

"That much is simple." The words were mild and even.

Landolin could barely make out the person's shape. He

almost had his keen elven eyes adjusted enough to see through the darkness of the person's hooded cloak when the figure stooped and rolled a helmet into the middle of the room.

"I believe this belonged to Harvais…and this," the person continued as a rustling noise all but drowned out her voice.

Landolin's eyes were riveted on the helmet he had given his second lieutenant just a week ago. The sound of metal on stone snapped him back from his memories as he saw a very ornamented dagger clatter across the floor and stop at his feet.

"This belonged to Savril, if my recollection is not amiss." The lady said calmly.

Landolin raised his hand and quickly motioned his officers to sheath their swords. Although he had not heard them draw them, he knew by the tangled mass of heavy air around them they had them poise to attack the intruder. Landolin quickly assessed the situation and turned to Trainor, the captain to his left.

"It seems we have our volunteer," he said calmly.

Trainor looked at Landolin with disgust, "Who, this beggar?" He said as he stabbed the air with his thumb in the direction of their visitor.

"Aye, and that is no beggar…she is my sister. I am very sure she is capable of performing the job, that is, if she doesn't run from this duty like she did her last." Landolin said as he slowly picked up the dagger. He stretched his tensing muscles before he retrieved the helmet from the middle of the room. The silence that had filled the room was almost deafening and Landolin felt his sister's eyes on him the whole time.

"Oh, I shall not run this time, brother." The figure said as she stepped into the light. The charcoal hood slid off of her head as the elf brushed her shouldering crimson locks away from her face.

"Did they make it into the tunnels at least?" Landolin asked as he held the helmet in his hands tenderly.

"These two did, but the other four weren't as lucky." She

said. Her every movement betrayed her caution as she made her way to her brother's side. "It was a trap. Someone else is aware of a few of the old passages." The elf gently placed her slight hand on Landolin's shoulder.

"Gienna, please take your hand off of me." His voice was curt, but held no real malice. "Can you tell me how the trap was sprung?" Landolin's voice was tight with grief even though he tried his best to disguise it.

Landolin watched his sister as she reluctantly removed her hand from his shoulder. He knew she feared that he might lose control of his emotions and he could see the concern in her eyes. He knew that she wanted to be near him in case he failed.

"It was a lilan." Her voice was calm and even.

"What?" Her words startled Landolin enough that he all but dropped the helmet. "Are you sure?"

"No, but I haven't seen any others use wires like they do." She motioned to the side of the helmet to draw her brother's attention to the marks etched into the steel. "I also don't know many races that can move fast enough to kill all of them so quickly." She unfastened her cloak and tossed it into a nearby chair as they spoke.

Landolin felt his men's eyes shift from the two of them to just her. He knew they were looking her over in a much different way than they had been previously and he hated them for it.

He took little solace in the fact that his sister was not the only woman amongst them and that at least one of his officers would not be fantasizing over Gienna's luscious curves as she moved back to Landolin's side. He also knew his sister was aware of the effect she had on most men, just as he knew she had never become completely used to their leering glances. No matter how covered she was, their eyes always lingered overly long.

"From my calculations, the four outside were dead before they knew it and the other two," she paused for a moment as she picked her words carefully, "were caught in its webs and then killed slowly."

Gienna's face contorted as she fought back a wave of nausea. Landolin knew that she was seeing their corpses and he wished that he could spare her from the memory.

"Somethings cannot be unseen," He said quiet enough so only his sister could hear. He knew if it was a lilan, the corpses would have been dried and almost embalmed.

"How did you find them?" Trainor asked with a complete disregard for protocol.

"I use the tunnels every time I enter Hornshir so as not to cause too much disruption." Her tone let Trainor and the other captains know she was not thrilled by the fact she had to answer his question.

"Enough," Landolin said as he lowered the helmet. Though he did not speak loud, his tone mirrored his words perfectly. He was not known as a loud or demeaning leader; instead, he was soft spoken and forced those under his command to really listen to his words. "I'm glad that you survived and happy to have family around." While his words were directed at his sister, Landolin knew his men understood his unspoken chastisement of Trainor's boldness. "I hate to say it, but I need your talents. Will you help us find all of the threats this city offers us?"

"Aye," Gienna nodded. "I know that this manor has long been your haven. Aras swore you to defend it as did the owner before him." She locked gazes with her brother as she spoke. "I've been sworn to the same pact. I know you are doing what you need to in order to fulfill your oath, so I promise that I will help in any way that I can."

As they crossed the room from the roaring fire to the table that sat near one of the many windows that overlooked the manor's central courtyard, Gienna's garnet hued eyes lingered in the faces of the officers that they passed as if she were memorizing their features.

"Good, let's get down to it then," Landolin said. He took a

good look at his sister as they walked.

She was thinner than she had been a few months ago when they had last spoken over tea. Although she was still filled out in all of the places that men look for, she was smaller and this concerned him a little. He found little comfort in the fact that her hair still held its smoldering red color and her garnet colored eyes were just as piercing as always.

At least she isn't malnourished he thought to himself as he noticed her outfit. Her form-fitting tan hunting breaches and dark brown flowing blouse was offset by knee-high green leather boots that matched the hooded cloak she had draped over her arm. If it weren't for the three swords and wide variety of daggers and knives that she had hung from various belts he would have questioned why she needed to use the tunnels.

"I trust you will tell me more about the arsenal?" He said aloofly as he motioned to her plethora of weaponry. "There are a few recent additions to what you normally carry.

"In due time," her response mirrored his manner perfectly. "Let's first talk about something else to tide us over until dinner." She gave Landolin a cheshire grin as she laid her folded bow on the table between them. "I heard that Aras is dead, do we know who the new owner of the manor is?"

"How is he doing?" Tali asked inquisitively.

She found it hard to fully detach herself from her emotions anytime she spoke of Jaconis. She knew this was a problem. Unfortunately, she felt a pull toward the boy that she was not ready to face, at least not yet. She allowed the darkness of the catacombs to hide her feelings from the deacon. He had accompanied her to apprise her of all the new acolytes' progress.

"He does well. He seems eager to learn, but…" the deacon hesitated as if unsure of how to proceed. Their footfalls echoed off of the unused halls that they passed through. No noise other than theirs seemed to exist in these forgotten passages.

"But what?" Tali snapped with an almost lethal edge in her

voice.

His frequent pauses were annoying, especially when concerning Jaconis. Tali hated how her emotions fluctuated when she thought of the boy. She shook her head slightly as she allowed a deep breath to slowly fill her lungs. Another corner seemed to briefly distract the deacon enough to give her some emotional distance.

"I feel he could learn faster if he wanted to. It's as if there is something holding back his pain that he won't let go of." The deacon conceded as they neared the end of the passage. "As you know, in order to pass out of acolyte and into one of the orders, he must allow himself to explore and release his pain. That's the only way that he will be able to help others do the same."

Tali thought about his words as she walked silently to the door of the chamber. She traced her fingers along the almost invisible pattern etched delicately into its face as she let this news soak into her mind. A slight sigh of relief escaped her lips as she felt the door slowly slide open under her fingers' impossibly light touch.

The deacon waited silently beside her in the darkness. There was a sense of fear that seemed to exude from his pores as it filled the primal silence around them. Tali glanced over her left shoulder at the deacon and grinned.

Her response was calculated and emotionless, "Find out what the reason is. I will not allow him to hold onto anything that takes his focus from our dark mistress." Her words fell like freezing rain as they slipped from her lips. Their coldness seemed to even lower the temperature of the hallway as they crossed to where the deacon stood.

"As you wish, my mistress." The soft rustle of the deacon's hood as it brushed the fabric of his robes let Tali know that nodded once in the darkness before he left.

"How I have missed the company of the devout," Tali said to herself once she knew she was alone. She fought back the wave of depression that always seemed to accompany her memories from her younger years in the order. "Their holy view of life is so refreshing and simple."

Her words were comforting as she turned toward the now opened door. "Some things are too much for us, even if we have been immersed in Her will for decades." Tali knew that no one was able to hear her, which is the way she preferred it. She could not afford to let any of the devout know how her own pain pulled at her.

Tali basked in the soft coldness of the air that wafted out of the room that lay beyond the gaping threshold. "I wonder if any of the deacons ever thought about the real reason these halls are kept perfectly dark,"

Tali mused as she stepped through the archway and into the awaiting blackness. The speed with which the small bumps formed along her skin, even under her robes, amazed her. In less time than it took for her to take three breaths the pleasure of the cold turned into excruciating pain. Tali whispered Lotevilar's name as she felt her own breath freeze in her throat. The pain wasn't a new one and she closed her eyes to revel in the refreshing crispness.

She recited the well-rehearsed and practiced instructions as she crossed the room. She trailed her fingers almost imperceptibly along the wall in a well-carved groove until she felt the smooth alter stones meet her extended fingers. Although she had traveled this path numerous times before, she always felt ashamed for desecrating the room with her humanity.

The coldness was just one of the signs of the divine, or so she had learned. The darkness was another. Tali let the short nails on her fingers gingerly trace across the smooth stone surface until the pads of her fingers finally touched the base of the small delicate lantern. Even sitting in the frozen air of the chamber, it somehow managed to feel warm to her touch.

Tali's silent prayer danced along her lips as she carefully removed the top of the lantern. She allowed the wick to breathe for a moment as she recalled the proper incantation to coax the flame from the burning cold. Then, without pause, she uttered it and set the top of the lantern gently into place.

The words of her incantation spilled from her lips heavily. She felt the weight of each word as they dripped from her mouth and fell into the air in front of her. Her voice took on a sing-song quality as she backed away slowly. The notes of her song lifted the heaviness of the words and carried them to their destination. Within moments the area around the altar filled with the buzzing vibrations of their life.

Tali squeezed her eyes closed tightly in reverence as she felt the air congeal around. The final syllables of her incantation all but constricted her throat and she had to violently expel them for fear of them ripping her apart from inside.

Bright flashes and fiery explosions erupted silently through her eyelids. Although Tali expected them, they always took her by surprise. She hated how helpless these words of power made her feel. Especially when she knew that it meant death to see their effects.

"It is about time," the silence around her shattered as she felt the words cut across the exposed skin of her face. She felt their otherworldly sounds for than heard them.

"My liege," Tali replied as she bowed deeply. She turned to face the source of the words as best she could with her eyes closed.

"You may rise and look upon me." His voice was pleasant as always, its tone was soft and light. Tali always had wondered where he was from, today was no different.

"Thank you, my liege," she said quietly as she slowly opened her eyes. The flickering blue light burned as her eyes adjusted to it. She scanned the room quickly and feigned as if she had never been in it before. "This room is wonderful my liege," she said politely as she gazed into the reflective surfaces that completely surrounded them.

Tali watched their reflections shift shapes as the light slid along each surface. The flickering light flew and fell as if it danced through other worlds. She found it hard enough to keep pace with the man's long strides without this distraction. She waited to speak any further until she was asked another question. That is how the divine worked. They expected only her reverence and the answers to any questions that they asked. Their footsteps echoed off of the vaulted ceiling and mirrored surfaces as they walked in silence.

"It is that. It was built as a tribute. Marvelous and safe," he said nonchalantly. "Now, please, tell me what I need to hear." His statement was more of a demand than a request and Tali knew it.

"Your power is great and the leaders of Cennicus still bow unto your might," Tali replied perfectly. The phrases she had learned as a child finally paid off and she was glad of it.

"Enough with the pleasantries," Tali could hear the impatience in his tone and winced. "What have you discovered?" His voice completely surrounded her with its malevolent threat of dismemberment and violence.

"The boy still lives. I fear that he has found at least one artifact." Her verbal vomit flowed unbidden. "A shadow walker helps him, but I don't know why."

She stole a look at her king and smiled. She loved how pale he looked. His golden hair only seemed to draw the color away from his skin and the ice blue eyes that she saw stare past her in the mirrored wall that faced them sent a chill down her back. Although his large black cloak hid the rest of his features from her, she knew how muscular he was and felt the corner of her lips pull into a hungry smile as she thought about his amazing physique.

"Describe this shadow walker." His words carried with them the notes of true curiosity.

Tali felt his eyes dance across her figure and take in her supple curves. She felt their welcomed heaviness along each subtle contour of her gowns. She felt a slight blush flood her cheeks as she realized he was focusing more on the weapons that lay hidden beneath her robes than on her other attributes.

"Like you, he is pale. His hair is long and as black as the heart of the darkest shadows and his eyes…his eyes are pools of darkness." Tali confided as she recalled how easily he had lifted her by her jaw in the alleys of Hornshir. "He is strong and swift. He appears when and where he likes." She recounted the facts from all of her encounters as she ticked them off on her fingers as she spoke. "He seems to be everywhere and he is searching for you."

The last few words rolled off her tongue with an ominous note. She knew that her lord was disturbed that one of his minions was now actively going against him. In her studies, Tali had learned the old gods created the Darque Lords to rule their creations. Each had a handful of shadow walkers created for them. A small part of her thought that this was all myth and legend, that is until she had met her liege for the first time after the great war.

"So Deracai searches for me," he snarled derisively. "Although he is formidable, I am not moved. He is weak like my father was weak."

"Your father?" Tali said before she had a chance to think twice about her words. Her eagerness to learn more about her liege was apparent in both her tone and reaction.

"He was a very wise and lethal man, heavily steeped in tradition." He said as they moved through the dim passageways of the temples under chambers. "That was his greatest weakness…and Deracai's as well."

"I don't' understand," Tali admitted. She hated how her words flowed from her lips in his presence. It was if she had no real control of herself.

He shot a piercing glance at Tali before he continued. "Your ignorance makes no real difference, does it? You can meditate on its meaning after I leave. Now, how close is he to finding us?"

"Us?" Tali asked. It was clear that his question caught her

completely off guard.

"Yes, the church's true chambers and myself…us?" Tali felt his anger rise as he clarified.

"Oh," she struggled to regain her composure. "Not far, but I think it has left the city for a time." She saw him motion for her to continue and blustered. "A couple of my scouts sighted him outside of Ellsted the night before last. I figure that puts him at least two days out by even the swiftest horse."

He laughed at her naïveté. "Deracai travels through the shadow world, which means distance is not an object," He looked around and made a couple motions at a few of the mirrored surfaces that surrounded them.

Tali suddenly felt as eyes were on her from every mirrored surface. She tried to make sure that her mind was not playing tricks on her, but she thought she saw things moving on the other side of the mirrors. With a quick breath, she dismissed the movement as light playing tricks on her eyes.

"I want you to double the patrols on the outer walls and triple the patrols in the inner circles. He could decide to pay us a visit and I want him killed if he does. Do I make myself clear?" He waited for Tali to nod her consent. The contented smirk on his arrogant lips let Tali know that he was pleased that he did not have to wait long for her response. "Good, now go and make it so!"

Tali all but stumbled as she tried to turn toward the door. Her robes twisted together and tangled her feet. With a muttered curse she lost her footing and collapsed onto the smooth reflective surface they had been walking on. With a reverberating and ungraceful thud, she landed with her face against its cold hard surface. Tali thought they were walking on marble and was horrified when he realized it was glass.

Her eyes widened as she peered through the looking glass at the hideous creatures that quickly scurried out of her field of view. She slowly regained her footing and managed to stay on her toes as she rushed out of the room and back into the welcoming warm blackness of the passageway.

"We can proceed!" Jerine yelled across the snow-covered field to Nurn as he ran towards him.

Nurn set down the dagger he was shaving with as he heard Jerine's voice fighting against the wind for his attention. He felt his heart race as his tired brain put together the pieces of Jerine's message. A quick glance drove home the fact that the snow-laden sky had decided not to let loose more snow on them.

Nurn ran his hand across his smooth scalp one more time to ensure that he was finished shaving before he turned and grabbed his belt and axe. His father, Tipin, had taught him that appearance was important for a follower of Tumere. Followers should always be at their best. Whether it was dealing with their looks or their physique, it made no difference. His goddess expected the best of her devotees and Nurn expected no less from himself.

By time Jerine crossed the field to Nurn's tent; he had finished his morning rituals and was in the process of donning his cloak. He could see another look of amazement in the elf's eyes as he approached. Nurn knew the guardian was not only impressed by his size, large even for a fully grown man, but he was also surprised Nurn was so quick and efficient. Nurn's subtle simpleness allowed him an economy of motion and he could tell by the wayward glances that Jerine marveled at it constantly. He knew the elf must not have had the pleasure of knowing many people like himself. Something deep inside of Nurn told him that Jerine would not have the opportunity to know many others no matter how long he lived.

"Is Landolin joining us?" Nurn asked as Jerine approached.

"No," Jerine responded. "And neither are his sentries. It will just be the two of us this time." Nurn could tell that the elf sensed his apprehension when he added, "Please understand, Landolin has more to worry about than just the safety of his troops and this encampment. He has sworn to defend the surrounding areas while he is camped here."

Nurn's anger ebbed a little as he understood the gist of what Jerine did not say. He knew that there was more that the elf was not saying, but he didn't care. Not yet. Eventually, Jerine would tell him the rest when he was ready. Nurn just had to wait and let Tumere guide his fate.

"Very well," Nurn replied still somewhat upset that they would not be receiving any help. "Where are we looking today?"

"There is a valley on the other side of the hill that you two were training in," Jerine explained.

"I know, we already searched there a few days ago." Nurn annoyance at Jerine's comment was evident.

Jerine simply nodded at Nurn's outburst. Nurn knew that his aggravation only helped him vent and hoped that the elf understood it as well. "I believe we might have missed something." Jerine's words floated from his lips softly yet were more than loud enough to be heard in the silence that surrounded them.

"What could we have missed? We searched that valley as thoroughly as we could. Why don't we go farther out instead?" Nurn asked heatedly. Nurn felt his anger build a little more and struggled to keep it in check as best he could. Sometimes these elves seemed to try and infuriate him by their lack of logic on purpose.

"I don't think he went farther than that," Jerine replied calmly. "So far we have been searching under the assumption that Halin was taken, whether by force or not. I'm starting to doubt that's what happened. Maybe he wandered off instead."

"Why would he wander off? What proof is there that he wasn't whisked off by Morcant or a bandit?" Nurn blurted out again.

Desperation clung to Nurn's words and he could see by the look in Jerine's eyes that he was painfully aware of it. Nurn had to cling to the thought that Halin left against his will. If that wasn't true, if Halin had simply left, it would mean that he failed to protect him when Halin had needed him most.

"So far there haven't been any signs of anyone, or anything, other than Halin." Jerine met Nurn's cold stare evenly. "The only way Halin could have been taken without any trace is if he flew or if magic were involved. If it turns out to be one of those, we may never find him." There was a sound of resignation in the guardian's voice that unnerved Nurn.

Nurn grunted as he listened. "So why do you want to go back to the valley that we started the search in?"

"Like I said, to look for something we may have missed," Jerine said soothingly. "So, if you're ready, let's be off."

Chapter Six: Decisions

Skara looked out at the latticework that connected the rooftops of Ellsted and smiled. "I'm not sure who put these together, but it would be a shame not to use them." She thought to herself as she traced her path mentally before she left her safe haven.

The nassarid adapted quickly to the subtle nuances that this mode of travel required and it was not long before her feet deftly flew along the makeshift path with a graceful and well-rehearsed ease. Before long her movements were so fluid that it was as if she had always used these pathways to get around this small city.

Skara's body arced majestically over the large gaps between buildings as she deviated from the path that was laid out before her. Although she had to try harder to maintain her speed, her movements remained just as fluid. She made a point to sporadically change her direction and speed, in case anyone watched her progress. If there were any traps, she was going to be certain that she did not fall prey to them. To her great surprise, there were none. She had traversed the main part of the town and had finally made it to a quieter section near its outer rim.

Only gypsy tents and a few merchant wagons were strung together when she finally set foot on actual soil for the first time in hours. She adjusted her supple robes and easily blended in with the last vestiges of workers as they finalized their plans for the evening's festivities. Quieter than the shadows she darted between, Skara made her way out of Ellsted and to a secluded thicket.

She kept a wary eye as she nestled her back against a weather smoothed boulder. She carefully reached her fingers into a small pouch on her left hip and gently lifted a small metal ball up to her face. She closed her cat-like eyes as she focused her thoughts on the outer surface of the sphere. A low hum, almost imperceptible filled her ears with its tones as the ball itself pulsed with an invisible energy.

"Report!" Tali's voice crackled from the orb as her phantasmal face materialized out of nowhere.

"He suspects that I was sent for either him or his daughter," Skara replied instantly. Although she was still surprised by the efficiency of this device, she had slowly adjusted to its use over the last few months. "But I know how to manipulate him. He won't be a problem." She purred.

"Good. Then let's not dally. He has approved of our plan. Kill her." Tali said evenly. "This time I expect you to succeed. We have tried to kill the little tart three times now and each time we have failed."

"The shadow walker always saves her," Skara offered as if in explanation.

"I know!" Tali shouted. "So we should expect him to try and save her again. Be prepared for once!" Skara could feel her mistress's anger as she continued to berate her. "Plan and set your trap for the vixen. When he shows to save her, kill him. Then kill her. It really is that simple." Skara winced at her mistress's words. She knew they were the truth, but she could not help but fear the veiled threat that they carried with them.

Aves and Hessa ran down another alley in their desperate attempt to stay ahead of Namir and Haradine. Sweat beaded along both girls' brows as they turned another corner. Although they were winded, they could not stop giggling as they shared a knowing glance with each other.

"I think we have gained enough of a lead to let you slip away," Aves said as she made sure that they were not being watched.

Hessa nodded her agreement and placed a reassuring hand on Aves's shoulder. "I won't be long, cousin." She could not hide the wry smile that forced its way to her lips as she spoke.

Aves giggled again as she gave Hessa a quick hug. "Just be safe. I don't know why Namir needs one of us to get a book from his room. It doesn't make sense, especially since he could just have his new shadow do it for him."

"Unless there's something in that book he doesn't want his shadow to know." Hessa offered. It bothered Hessa to refer to Haradine this way, but she played along to spare Aves's feelings.

"I hadn't thought of that," Aves admitted conspiratorially, "all the more reason for us to be careful then."

"Agreed," Hessa said as she swiftly moved to the mouth of a nearby ally. "I will meet you at the gypsy fortuneteller's wagon. Try to delay Namir and Haradine if needed. I don't want to lose another race to him again." Hessa added as she stepped into the awaiting darkness and left Aves to formulate her plans alone.

"I am sorry for breaking down." Alequa apologized softly. She looked across the small table in her room at Carness. He had changed so much since she last saw him. His hair had grown whiter and, although he was still very powerfully built, she could tell that some of his strength had faded through the years. "It…it," Alequa felt her tears start to swell again so she stopped speaking in an attempt to get a better hold on her emotions.

It was obvious by the way that his wolf-like eyes studied her that Carness carefully measured her actions as he spoke.

"Think nothing of it. It was grave news, too great for just one person to bear. By keeping it in solitude, it weighed down your soul greatly." His golden brown eyes reflected here sorrow perfectly.

She noticed that Carness averted his gaze whenever he noticed that she was looking at him. Alequa knew he averted his gaze to hide his emotions. "Thank you, my friend," Alequa said when she was finally able to manage her emotions again.

Carness nodded his response as he waited a few more moments, obviously out of respect. "Hebasii Alequa, although I am glad to see an old friend again, I know that reunions are not why you came to Ellsted." Carness paused again. She felt him watching her for unspoken queues. She knew that he focused on the subtle signals that her posture and involuntary twitches would reveal as he continued speaking, "Was it to tell us of Aras's passing? Is that the reason that I have to thank for this blessing?"

"You're right," Alequa agreed, "like you, I am glad to be back with friends. And although Aras's death has worn on me harder than I imagined it would, I am here for other reasons as well. Two to be exact." She made sure that he knew she held nothing back from him.

Carness was too much of a trusted friend for her to try and hide the real reasons for her visit. She also knew that he would suss out the truth on his own eventually, so there was no reason to turn him against them.

"I have come to keep the next heir safe," she whispered.

"I thought that the elf accompanying Namir was important," Carness replied. Alequa felt Carness's guard slip a little as he pressed his back into the chair a little more.

"I am not talking about Haradine," Alequa said jovially, "although she is important to me as well." Alequa could see his confusion so she continued. "She is my daughter. I forgot how long it has been since we were here last."

"Aras and you sired a daughter?" Carness was a little lost by Alequa's statements, it showed in the subtle dog-like look he gave her. He shook his head as he visibly tried to wrap his brain around what she said. "Then one of the girls is going to be the heir?"

The healer knew that Carness prided himself in his ability to solve puzzles. In fact, for as long as she had known him, the man had done nothing but surprise her with his miraculous insight, so she knew that it was hard for him not to make the leap he needed to figure this one out.

"You accompanied Haradine, Aves, and Hessa back to Ellsted along with the troops from Hornshir and the supplies sent with them. Am I missing something?"

Alequa laughed somewhat amused. "You are." She agreed. "There is one other person that you did not account for," she shared quietly.

"Namir," both of them said the words in perfect unison and Carness's face fell as they did.

"But I know his parents." Carness objected. "I grew up with them on the plains of Jarstil. Neither of them is of royal blood." Alequa loved to watch him rationalize why he could not be mistaken about something that she knew he was. His internal struggle to justify his position was a rare treat for her. "Did they?"

"No," Alequa agreed, "neither of them did, but that does not change the fact that Namir does."

"Cerona would not have cheated on Kalta!" Carness exploded as he defended the memories of his deceased comrades.

"You are right again." Alequa conceded. "But again, this does not change the fact of Namir's lineage."

"Then how does the boy claim that right?" Carness was at a total loss and the healer found great mirth in the knowledge.

"He can claim this right because he was not born to either Kalta or Cerona." She explained, careful not to talk down to him. She saw the vestiges of realization dawn on Carness's face as she said these words. "Now I must swear you to secrecy." She waited patiently for his response; thankfully his silent and decisive nod was not long in coming. "We already have enough problems with at least one traitor in our midst."

"Aye," Carness spat. "But you can count on it that he will be strung up and burned before he leaves Ellsted in one piece."

"You know who he is?" Alequa felt the tension in her breast become heavier as she waited for his response with baited breath.

"Faris," his matter of fact tone threw her into a mental tailspin.

Namir darted down another long row of merchants as they hawked their wares to passersby. He knew that Haradine was close on his heels, but he was focused on beating Aves to the glass blower. He spun passed the lady selling woven baskets and almost lost his footing on a patch of slick paver stones. Scrambling, he dodged around a couple mooning over a decorative sconce set as he sprinted down another of the maze-like arms of the Belanui marketplace. He skidded to a halt a few blocks shy of his goal when he saw them, Faris's men.

Winded, Namir paused to catch his breath and stepped behind some baskets for concealment. He cursed himself mentally when he finally peaked out from his hasty cover. He had lost them. Namir frantically cast his gaze around the nearby shops in a fevered attempt to find the soldiers again. He hated that he had lost sight of them so quickly.

He made a furtive motion to Haradine to stay hidden when he spotted her out of the corner of his eye. A subtle movement caught his eye as he glanced away from Haradine. Faris. Namir breathed a sigh of relief as he recognized the captain of Hornshir's guards in the doorway of a shop almost a block away from where he knelt.

He watched as Faris left Mistress Clara's Clothier with a little parcel tucked carefully under his arm. Namir mentally put together a hasty plan, one that would allow him to accidentally happen across Faris so that he could try and figure out why he and his men were still in Ellsted. When Namir was ready to put his plan into action, he motioned for Haradine to move closer and hoped that she could do so without being seen. He focused his attention on Faris after he motioned for Haradine and was pleasantly surprised to hear her in his hear moments after he motioned to her.

"Aye, sa'ouvant?" Her words were scarcely audible, although her lips were not far from his ear.

"I plan on approaching Faris and see what he is up to," Namir stated quietly.

"I don't follow," Haradine's tone was full of unasked questions and Namir did not really want to explain his reasons.

"Something just doesn't seem right," he offered as an explanation. When he saw the confused look on her face her continued a little more frustrated, "He is still here, in Ellsted."

"So?" Haradine quipped.

He knew that she sensed his frustration, but she obviously did not follow his logic. Namir needed to make sure that she fully understood what he asked her to do. "So, he said they were leaving after his meetings with the council were completed. That was almost two weeks ago." Namir answered as he tracked Faris's movements in an attempt not to lose him. "Why is he still here?"

"What do you need me to do?" Haradine whispered.

"Keep an eye out for his guards. I saw a few of them earlier, but I lost sight of them.

"Ok," Haradine agreed.

Namir purposefully did not tell her what he wanted her to do to the guards if they showed. Namir could hardly wait for Haradine's acceptance. Faris was almost out of his field of vision and Namir needed to act now. He walked up to Faris with a confused look on his face as he spoke. "I thought you said you were going to leave after the Belanui feast ended." He scanned the crowd for Faris's soldiers nonchalantly.

"We are, but I never said how soon after it ended." Faris's reply unnerved Namir for some reason.

"I guess I'm just puzzled that you'd want to stay through the Season of Dread instead of making your way back to Hornshir before snowfall limits travel." Namir broached as he tried to vet Faris's response.

"Let's just say the nature of our business changed once we arrived." Namir was still puzzled and he could tell that Faris could see it in his face when he continued, "Not that it is any of your concern, but after we arrived I noticed how woefully undermanned your town guard is…and with the Season of Dread soon upon us, I decided it would be in Hornshir's best interest to ensure that this town survives the season."

"Have you spoken with Carness about your decision yet?" Namir pried.

"No," Faris said somewhat flustered, "but I have spoken with the mayor. I believe he outranks your constable." Namir noticed that Faris's disposition shifted as if he won a major battle.

"In politics and legislation aye," Namir replied a little more aloofly than he had planned, "but when it comes to the safety of the town and its denizens the constable has final say." He saw Faris wince a little at this and for some reason, it made him happy. "If I were you, I would at least let the constable know of your plans before he finds them out on his own." Namir was a little puzzled that Faris knew Carness was the constable after such a short amount of time in Ellsted.

"I will take your advice for what it's worth, nothing," Faris sneered. "After all, it's nothing more than the advice of a child that does not yet understand his place or the way of things."

Faris's last words bore more contempt than Namir had ever heard anyone utter before. The final response did not sit well with him either. There was something about Faris that bothered Namir and he could not wait to talk to Haradine about it. He hoped that she might be able to shed some light on it.

"The cold is the worst part of it," Halin thought bitterly as he tugged at the overly worn edges of his tunic. He edged closer to the small fire that he had built from bits of twigs and moss as he brushed a stray strand of dirty tawny hair from in front of his eyes.

Somewhere deep inside his mind, he felt a sense of revulsion growing as he thought about his hair being so filthy for so long. He shivered off these thoughts as best he could. Halin then reached his shaking hands toward the flame in a futile attempt to get some sort of feeling into them.

The crackling twigs did little to drive the cold from Halin's bones, although it did dull the brunt of it a little. He knew that the days had been growing steadily colder, which could only mean the Season of Dread must be drawing nigh and that Belanui's feast was long past.

Halin wearily lifted the dead rat from the ground beside him as he studied it carefully in the dim light. As far as he could tell it was free of disease, not that he was an expert. Halin waived these rueful thoughts from his head and added to the list of things he would think about later while he assessed the rat's cold corpse. Once he was satisfied with his assessment, he carefully lifted the rat's body by the shaft of the arrow that he had squewered it with as he slid back from the fire hesitantly.

The fire's warmth, though meager, almost held more sway over him than his insatiable hunger, but not quite. Halin held his stomach tightly as it growled menacingly again. He forced himself to turn his back to the fire as he eased the arrow into the slots he had tediously carved into the rock.

He could still feel the painfully numbing sensations that the cold rock forced through his hands as he had scraped chunks of it apart with the pommel of his dagger. It was slow and tedious work, but it was worth it. Halin still felt the satisfaction his accomplishment gave him just a few days ago, or at least he thought it was a few days ago.

Halin peered intently into the shadows that flew around him as the crackling from his fire echoed eerily through the caverns. "It is so hard to get my bearings in this gloom," the words raced through his head as his frustration increased.

Halin's gray eyes darted back and forth painfully as he attempted to pierce the tenebrous murk that had surrounded him. He tried to make sure he was still alone and not being watched by some unseen attacker. Halin knew that the movements that crept into the corners of his vision were caused by his little fire, but over the last few days, he felt an increasing sense of paranoia. At times he felt as if the shadows were watching his movements, especially when he was preparing his food.

Of all the things that Halin hated the most about being lost in this cavern, the loss of his bearings irked him the most. Even through his increased paranoia, part of him still hoped that Nurn, Namir and the others would find him. Although he believed deep down he would never be found, he just couldn't bring himself to fully accept it.

He gritted his teeth together forcefully to make himself focus on the task of skinning and cleaning the rat as he cleared his mind of the jumbling emotions that threatened to overcome him. It had been quite some time since he had managed to come across food and this was the first rat he had managed to kill, so he was not going to miss this chance to eat something other than dirt.

A thick and pungent odor hit him hard as he accidentally punctured the rat's stomach in his haste. The stench forced him to clench his jaw tighter. He could feel bile rise in his throat as he heard the contents of the carcass's stomach spray against the wall and slide to the floor. Halin cursed his clumsiness as he quickly cut the rest of the stomach and other organs free from his prey's body.

Halin's stomach grumbled again, this time more menacingly as he removed the remainder of the rat off of his arrow and pushed it onto the stick he had carved to spit meat. He licked his lips in anticipation as he lowered the spitted meat over his pathetic little fire. He fussed over the rat's position over the meager flames before he turned his attention to the discarded organs that he had left in a jumbled pile.

His hands shook as he picked through the small pile of discarded organs. He carefully pulled the rat's heart and liver from the pile and set them beside the fire pit. He pursed his lips as he gingerly placed the rest of the organs and into a simple cloth sack and went back into the dark tunnels that he had killed the rat in. "I might get lucky enough to catch another one with these." Halin thought wistfully as he set to the task of placing the bait in a simple trap.

Chapter Seven: Deals

The moon ducked behind some errant clouds as Hessa slowly made her way toward the door to Namir's room. The crisp air puffed little pillows of steam in front of her eyes as she tried to make sure that she had not been followed. She took a deep breath and stepped around the corner of the inn's stables. "Only a few more yards," she muttered to herself absently.

"Then what?" The sneering voice startled her and made her jump. "Jumpy are we?" The voice asked again.

"Who is there?" Hessa said with as much authority as she could muster.

"That's not fair; I asked you a question first." The voice responded, this time from a different place in the darkness that spanned in front of her.

"Then I can get back to my own room." Hessa lied. She had no idea who was waiting for her, but she did not like the attitude that she sensed in their words. "Now quit this game and show yourself."

"Fine. Seeing as how you answered my question like a good girl and all," the voice said as its owner stepped into the feeble light cast by the torches that sputtered behind Hessa. He was not overly tall or attractive. In fact, he was fairly plain looking.

"See I am no threat." He held his arms away from his body as if to show that he wasn't armed. His arms were not quite raised, but they were extended enough to allow the flickering light to disperse most of the shadows from underneath his cloak.

"Then what do you want?" Hessa queried, still a little uneasy by the stranger's presence and demeanor.

"Nothing really. You see, I was taking a little stroll when I saw you creeping around so I thought I would see what a beautiful girl like yourself was doing all alone in the dark." Hessa could smell the stale wine that the Gathering Place served on his breath as he stepped closer to her.

"Well, thank you for your concern." Hessa wanted to get rid of this man as quickly as she could. "But as you can see, I am just trying to get back to my room." She lied again as she took a step backward toward the stable to keep a safe distance between them.

"I see," he said as he slowly closed the widening gap between them. "So where are you coming from? The festivities?" He struggled to sound conversational and Hessa knew it.

"Aye," Hessa replied as she backed into the stable door. "Now if you don't mind, I would like to get past and return to my room."

"Why the hurry?" The stranger said as a smile started to bloom on his face. "I mean, we just started to get to know one another and all." He licked his lips somewhat hungrily as his words dripped out of his mouth. "You don't even know my name." He added hastily as he saw a look of dread cross Hessa's face.

"Please," Hessa whispered, "let me go."

"I'm not stopping you," he added with a smile, "at least not yet. My name is Jasper, in case you were wondering."

"Not yet?" Hessa croaked. She fought back a wave of fear as she watched him creep closer.

“Don’t’ worry Hessa, I will be gentle. I just need you to come with me for a while is all.” Jasper said as he stepped closer. He was almost within reach and her heartbeat quickened.

“No!” Hessa screamed. She frantically clawed at the door behind her in a blind attempt to get away from the man that loomed menacingly in front of her.

“Don’t scream. We don’t want to ruin the moment do we?” Jasper asked as he reached a slightly trembling hand toward Hessa’s squirming figure.

“Get away from me!” Hessa screamed again.

“I said don’t scream!” The back of Jasper’s hand connected with Hessa’s cheek so hard that she rocked backward into the door with a loud bang. She watched Jasper eye a small trickle of blood in disgust as it started to draw its line from the edge of Hessa’s mouth. “Now see what you made me do? Now be quiet or I may have to silence you again.” His voice had lost all of its former mirth. His words now rang with a terrifying deadliness.

Hessa could not believe her ears. “Are you seriously blaming me for your hand hitting my face?” She spat in disbelief. “What do you want?” Hessa screamed as she slid along the wall in a futile attempt to get away from him.

“Shhhh…” Jasper held his hand awkwardly close to her face as he kept pace with her. “I don’t want anything. I just need you to be a dear and come with me is all.” There was an eerie sort of innocence that Hessa noticed in his dull brown eyes, it was almost childlike. “Do you understand?”

“No…I…” Hessa started, but she couldn’t seem to get any more words to pass between her lips.

“Neither do we,” a different voice boomed past Jasper and to Hessa’s relief it seemed to surprise him as well.

“What I do with my dear friend is none of your concern.” Jasper shot over his shoulder at the source of the voice without taking his eyes off Hessa.

"I'm sorry, but we must insist that it is our business." A second voice cut in with more authority than the first. "If you would please move away from the lady and come over here, we would be much obliged."

Jasper spun around to face the people that were trying to stop him. Hessa took the moment to try and see around him. To her surprise, she saw four of Hornshir's guards standing behind him with their weapons drawn.

"I see that you are all in a hurry to hurt someone," Jasper said bluntly. "This is why I usually avoid the bigger cities," he said as if there were someone else beside him. "Hmmm, I guess I should do as you ask then." He shot a quick glance over his shoulder and caught Hessa's eyes with his icy stare. "We are not done, my dear Hessa. I will meet you later, maybe at the gypsy tents or the fortune teller."

Hessa felt a chill run down her spine as his words struck her almost as hard as his hand had. "Don't count on it." She croaked as she moved farther away from him. She focused her gaze on the ground in front of her as she made her way toward the front doors of the Gathering Place.

Namir waited until he was sure that Faris could no longer hear him before he asked Haradine the question that was burning through his mind ever since they had come across Faris in the market. "What do you really know about Faris?"

Haradine was obviously caught off guard by Namir's question because she had been concentrating on keeping track of their winding path. He felt her eyes trained on the back of his head as he bobbed through the crowd.

"What do you mean?" Her question hung palpably between them. So much so that people moved away from them while both of them waited for the other to break the silence. Haradine broke down first. "He is well known for his strategic sensibilities and can be a shrewd negotiator…"

Namir stopped abruptly and turned down an alley while

Haradine gave her response, effectively cutting off the rest of her sentence. He quickly surveyed his surroundings and when he was satisfied that there was no one else around, he stopped and waited for Haradine to turn the corner. He was pleasantly amused when he noticed that she was still talking. He held up a hand and quickly gained her attention as he asked, "do you, personally, know anything about him?"

"I know that he commands his men's complete loyalty." She replied. Her tone betrayed how put off she was by Namir's abruptness. "I also know that either he is really good at training and drilling soldiers or he knows someone who is. His team's reaction times are flawless and they operate in perfect unison when needed."

Namir knew that his pointed inquiries grated on her nerves but the little twitch that pulled at the left corner of her mouth as she spoke, the same tick betrayed how honored she felt at being in her liege's confidence.

"Aside from that, I know just as much as you, sa'ouvant." She gave Namir a slight bow of her head as she spoke the last phrase. Her golden hair spilled across her face to hide her slight smile.

"I see," Namir said as he focused on Haradine's hair as it fell. "Is there any particular reason you let it down?" Namir asked as if to change the subject."

"What?" Haradine's head snapped up and she met his gaze abruptly.

"I was wondering why you would let your hair down while on duty." His tone was firm and he knew that it bothered Haradine. "I expected better from you." Namir intended to have his unspoken intentions hit her hard, as hard as any physical blow. She needed to know that he understood, and expected, her to behave in a way that was not too familiar.

"I am sorry sa'ouvant," Haradine said as she bowed her head again, this time out of respect and duty. "I will not let it happen again."

"I know." Namir's response was as cold as the breeze that

struck up and swirled around them as Namir turned and left the alley.

"I see," Alequa said to Carness as she set her teacup down. She had pulled her hair into a tightly braided queue and they had adjourned to the main hall of the inn. Alequa normally hated to hold private meetings in such a public setting, but with the town locked in the grip of the festival, the place was mostly empty. "So, Faris was a traitor and a coward during the war."

"That is the crux of it," Carness replied without hesitation. Although the two of them sat near the center of the room, he spoke just loud enough for her keen elven ears to hear him.

She picked her ceramic mug up from the table in front of her and leaned back into the padding of the oversized chair. A dark image passed briefly in front of her mind's eye as the delicate fragrance of cooking meat wafted in from the kitchen. "So how prepared would you be if Ellsted were attacked?" Her tone was as serious as her question was abrupt and it caught Carness off guard.

"Attacked?" Carness was at a loss for words. She knew that he was able to handle the occasional raider or a band of thieves, but she meant something more. "In what way?"

"I don't really know," she sighed. "I just know that if the enemies of the crown learn about Namir's heritage, no one that knows him will be safe." She lowered her cup as she said this. As if on cue, Hessa stumbled through the doors of the inn unceremoniously. Carness leapt to his feet and made his way to her side before Alequa's words had fully made it to his ears.

"What happened?" Carness asked bluntly as his eyes traced the thin line of blood on Hessa's face. Her overall rumpled appearance.

"I was on my way to get something for Namir and someone stopped me," Hessa replied automatically to the sound of the constable's voice.

"Who and where is he?" Carness asked as he shot a knowing glance at Alequa. "It looks like your question is about to be answered." He said to his friend as he waited for Hessa's answer.

"He said his name was Jasper and he is outside near the stable," Hessa said, somewhat confused by Carness's comments to Alequa. "The Hornshir guards have detained him, so you needn't hurry."

Carness shook his head at both Hessa's tone and her words. "She is getting used to telling others what to do, my how her trip to Hornshir has changed her," Carness whispered to the elf before he stepped out of the warmth of the inn and into the crisp night air that waited for him.

Aves was pleased with her ability to make it appear as if Hessa was still with her. She had mastered the skill of mimicking Hessa's voice and used the echoes from some of the emptier alleyways to create the illusion that Hessa was not too far behind her.

She was so wrapped up in her charade that she paid little attention to where she was going. One blind corner after another met her as she stumbled over a small stack of loose crates. Aves mentally chided herself for forgetting that nothing was where it should be as she threw her hands out in a blind attempt to break her fall as she braced for the impact that never came. She opened her eyes and stared at the cobblestones that hovered in front of her eyes and blinked in wonder.

"Are you all right?" Tipin's voice floated to her unsuspecting ears.

"Aye," Aves said as she looked up at his hulking from over her shoulder. Realization slowly dawned on her. Tipin stood almost a foot away and had caught a hold of one of her pouches. He had saved her from not only an embarrassing fall, but the minor scrapes and tears that would have come with it. "Thank you," Aves said quickly as she regained her footing.

Tipin slowly released her pouch as he made sure that she

was not going to fall if he did so. "You need to be more careful," he said sagely as Aves straightened out her belongings.

"I know," Aves replied. "Thank you again." She said quietly. "If you don't mind I have to be going."

"What is the hurry?" Tipin asked. There was a somewhat curious tone to his voice and Aves knew it had to do with where she was heading to in such a rush.

"I am in a race with Namir and I think I am going to beat him this time." She shared conspiratorially.

Tipin smiled at the girl's playfulness. "I know that Nurn and Namir were always talking about your races when they thought I was out of earshot. Where are you racing to this time?"

"The glass blower's booth next to the gypsies," Aves said as she started to walk away.

"I would take the next alley and go through the masonry shop, it's quicker." Tipin offered as she left. "It's good that Namir is taking his newfound responsibilities in such good stride." The smith said as she darted down the alley he had pointed to.

"Thank you," Aves called over her shoulder before she shouted her new direction to Hessa, who she tried to make Tipin believe lurked in the shadows somewhere behind him. She smiled as she saw him wave a dismissive had before the returned and went on his way back to whatever tasks he had been off to before he caught her.

The square was alive with activity as Aves bolted into it. People from all around the Three Rivers Shire filled the normally empty space and the electrified buzz that was generated by all of the conversations and movement gave her an immediate contact high.

"I need to be careful and make sure that Namir and Haradine don't slip past me," Aves thought aloud to herself as she narrowly avoided a bum as he dug through a rubbish pile. "I also need to make sure that I avoid them as well." She mentally noted another seedy man and his friends as she walked past a fruit stand. "I don't miss some of the people that the festival attracts every year," Aves said quietly as she cast a hungry eye over the sparse variety of fruit that this stand had left to offer for the day.

"What kinds of people are you babbling about?" The fruit vendor asked somewhat confused.

"All of the homeless that seem to accompany it every year," Aves said as she absently swatted at something that stung the back of her neck.

"Me neither," the vendor said as he warily eyed another group of vagabonds as they neared his booth from behind Aves.

"That and the stinging flies," she looked up at the older gentleman that sat on the other side of a small pile of apples. His hair was a grayish brown and she knew that she had met him before, but could not recall his name for some reason. "I wonder what brings them," Aves said more to herself than the fruit seller.

"Probably the same thing that draws the other lot," the vendor offered as he turned his attention from the mayor's daughter to collecting a wayward orange that had fallen off a nearby table. "Do be careful Aves," he said as he noticed her turn to leave.

"You too," Aves absently brushed a lock of hair out of her face as she strolled off into the square in a slight daze. She suddenly found it hard to focus her thoughts.

"I know that I have something to do," Aves said to herself as she meandered past a throng of dancing children that milled outside of one of the many candy sellers' booths, "but I can't think of what it would be."

Chapter Eight: Rendezvous

Gienna paced through the rafters of the temple as she watched the deacons gather up the evening's offerings. She did not trust the followers of Lotevilar. Gienna could not fully understand what it was that bothered her so much about their faith. All she knew was that there was something wrong with it. Moreover, she knew that they there was something going on somewhere within the temple and she planned on finding out what secrets they were hiding.

Landolin's directive was clear, "I don't care what you do, just don't get caught." His words haunted her each time she delved deeper into the problems in Hornshir she kept finding.

Gienna silently ticked through her report items mentally to herself. Most of the city's guards were on the take. The mayor was being blackmailed by some influential merchants and healers. On top of it all, someone connected with all of it was tied to this church.

From what she had already seen, there were people involved at this church that were funneling weapons and elite killers into Hornshir past the very walls that had been constructed to stop this sort of thing. She thought about the lilan that had taken up residence in the under tunnels.

"It's somehow connected to this church. I'm sure of it, I just don't know how yet," Gienna whispered to herself. She knew that if she did not get a handle on it soon, it would be too late and all that they will be able to do is hide in their manor and wait for the rest of the denizens of Hornshir to be massacred.

Just as she was about to leave, her eyes danced across something moving in the darkness. A shadow moved near a wall, but not across it. "Ah ha," she thought to herself. "I've found it." She revealed momentarily in the sense of accomplishment that she felt. "Now I just have to wait until everyone goes to sleep, then I can see what really lurks behind this church's façade."

Carness barreled out of the Gathering Place and rounded the corner at a dead sprint. His bow was in his hand before he had cleared the steps of the inn and had an arrow skillfully nocked when he saw the four guards and the Hessa's assailant.

Carness loosed three arrows rapidly to separate the combatants before he even bothered to bark his warning. Each arrow made his presence and his intention known as he skidded to a halt a few paces away from the fray.

"That will be enough gentlemen." Carness's words were easily heard over the distant ruckus of the festival. He eyed the three white shafts of his arrows as they protruded from the ground in a perfect line between the guards and the man that he was more than interested in questioning.

The guards' icy stares that they leveled at him brought a wolfish grin to his face. The look of amusement in his eyes mingled with a slight change in stance to stretch to his full height unnerved them just as he planned.

"Are you seriously going to test both my authority and my patience?" His wolf-like eyes darted from person to person in eager anticipation. A small feeling of disappointment pushed its way through the depths of his mind as he saw all of the guards lower their weapons and step away from their prisoner. "Which of you is in charge?" Carness barked impatiently as his hand hovered over the quiver that hung at his hip.

"I am," the prisoner stated nonchalantly as he stepped away from the guards and closer to Carness. "At least if you ask me I am." His cocky lopsided smile irritated Carness as did his overconfidence.

"The question was directed to the guards," Carness said dismissively.

"I know. That's why I'm answering." He smiled his lopsided smile again as he continued, "I see that I have your attention." His eyes scanned Carness's body language as he spoke. "My name is Jasper and I could think of no better way to get you alone. I've been charged by Faris, the captain of our guard, to give you a message, one that you will not forget." As his words slipped from his lips he palmed a dagger and flung it at Carness's face.

With machine-like precision, Carness nocked and loosed an arrow at the dagger as he stepped aside. He calculated Jasper's next move perfectly and had his second arrow flying toward Jasper's second throwing dagger before he even had a chance to get it into the air.

In one fluid motion, Carness leapt across what little courtyard separated them and planted one of his brawny shoulders in Jasper's sternum with enough force to temporarily knock the wind out of him. Carness pivoted easily and while Jasper collapsed in front of him, he nocked another arrow and leveled it at the nearest guard.

"Care to try your luck?" Carness's eyes were alive with the pleasure of the hunt and the threat his words carried was clearly understood. He cast a quick glance at the four guards, in turn, to ensure they all understood him. "You may be the best Hornshir has to offer its citizens for protection, but I think you will find that we are more than adequately protected." Carness licked his lips hungrily as he placed his foot on Jasper's back.

"Now, throw your weapons down, or I will strip them from you in the most painful way that I can imagine. I think it's only fair to mention that I have quite the imagination for these kinds of things." His tone was level and even and brooked no resistance.

"Who are you?" The guard that was the farthest away from Carness managed to ask as he tossed his sword into the pile of weapons that was slowly forming in front of Carness.

With a wolfish grin, Carness turned his gaze briefly to the guard as if to address only him. "I am the constable of Ellsted and the one that just bested your lieutenant."

"That doesn't answer our question," one of the closer guards piped in with a shaky tenor voice.

"You are right, it doesn't," Carness added dismissively.

"I never understood why you can't answer a direct question plainly." A deep voice boomed from behind them and took everyone off guard.

"I have this Daffer, you can return to your drink," Carness replied as he removed the arrow from his bow and settled it back into his quiver.

"I know, I was just told that there was a problem near my stables and I wanted to make sure that none of my property is damaged." Daffer offered as an excuse to remain. "Besides, you need to answer their question. If you don't I will."

"Far be it from me to steal what little pleasure you get to enjoy these days." Carness retorted as he looked over the small arsenal that the guards had discarded.

"What are you two going on about?" One of the younger guards spat impatiently.

Daffer and Carness exchanged a quick glance as Daffer turned to address the four remaining guards. Carness to it as his cue to pull a length of cord from one of his pouches and started to bind Jasper's hands behind his back.

"He is known as Carness the Wolf," Daffer said noncommittally to them and then continued to answer their next, unasked, question, "you may have heard of him when people speak of the last war and the battle of Watch Keep." Daffer grinned as he saw all of their eyes widen. "Yes, the butcher of the marsh is the one that you gave yourselves up to."

Carness scoffed, "Butcher of the marsh, really?"

"Aye," Daffer replied. "It sounds a bit better than the crazy man that hacked up his enemy and ate their hearts. And it's easier to say as well."

"Fine," Carness conceded, "but then I get to call you Daffer, the scourge of the reptiles." Carness did little to disguise the playful gleam in his golden eyes as he quipped with Daffer.

Daffer grumbled and then looked back at the guards. All four of them had dropped to their knees and each one was in the middle of some form of prayer. "Now look what you've done. Scared them half to their graves."

Carness could tell that Daffer felt robbed of the accomplishment. "How is this? When they regain themselves, I'll let you hit them with my club…softly. Agreed?"

"Agreed," Daffer nodded as he watched Carness collect the weapons. "Can I hit him too?" He poked his thumb in Jasper's direction as he said this.

"No, he is all mine." Carness looked forward to finding out exactly what Jasper knew, especially when it came to Faris.

Alequa eased Hessa into the chair that Carness had just left and sat across from her. "Are you alright?" She asked in a conspiratorial tone.

"Aye," Hessa replied. "I am just a little shaken I think."

"From what little you have told me, that is understandable." Alequa eyes quickly surveyed what little injuries that Hessa had sustained before she continued, "So why are you here? Did your mistress send you on an errand?"

"No, Namir just asked me to get something for him from his room." Hessa offered before she thought better of her answer. "I really should go. I mustn't keep Namir waiting." Hessa said somewhat chagrinned as she started to stand.

"Please sit for a moment and collect yourself," Alequa offered." Besides, Namir can wait a few more moments I am sure. Has anyone told you that you look a lot like your mother?" Alequa asked cautiously.

"No," Hessa sat back down and stared at Alequa. "You knew my mother?"

"Aye, you might say that we were friends of a sort." Alequa slowly lifted her tea to her lips and took a sip before she continued. "Natlia helped my husband, Aras, a lot like you are helping Namir now. I can see a good deal of your mother in you."

"Your husband? You were married to Aras?" Hessa asked somewhat confused.

"Aye, is there something wrong with that?" It was Alequa's turn to sound surprised.

"No, it's just that Namir described Aras as old…and … well…you aren't that old," Hessa stumbled over her words as she struggled not to offend Alequa anymore than she may have already.

Alequa laughed, "Thank you, but I am much older than you think. I even have a daughter, Haradine, I think you met her." She added lightly.

Alequa was seemed to be warming up to Hessa in ways that Hessa had not thought possible a few months ago when they had first met.

"Haradine's your daugh…then you are…" Hessa was too shocked to speak and Alequa obviously found great amusement in the effect that her words had.

"Aye," Alequa started, when she finally had her fill of the girl's confusion. "We elves live extremely long and we do not age like most of the other races. We were one of the first brought to life by the Old Gods."

She gaged the impact of her words by watching Hessa's expressions. She wanted to make sure that the girl understood what she was saying before she continued.

"But that is enough about my kind. I think we have dallied enough. What was it that Namir needed you to get for him and where was it?"

"He asked that I bring him a particular book from his room," Hessa had no problem talking Alequa. She was not sure why, but she found it extremely easy to speak her mind to her as if she was a long-lost friend.

"I think I know just the one, let's go," Alequa said as she set her teacup down on the table and helped Hessa rise before they headed for the door.

Alequa said in response to Hessa's obvious trepidation at discussing her mission. "There is nothing my husband kept from me, especially nothing pertaining to Namir's past." Hessa found Alequa's words soothing as the elf walked over to the little lantern on the table and lit it.

Hessa felt a bit better with everything as the warm glow filled the room around her. "I know," Hessa shared, "I'm just confused. If Namir knows that you and Haradine were already in Aras's confidence, why did he need me to get this particular book instead of sending your daughter?"

"Ah, so that is the source of your turmoil?" Alequa said as if enlightened. She turned toward Hessa so that the girl was directly in front of her as she reached out and gently touched her elbow. "I'm afraid that Namir may not know Haradine is our daughter." Her words were warm, yet somehow distant at the same time.

"Oh," Hessa felt some of her tension abate. "I see. I guess that makes sense." She smiled slightly as she realized what this revelation might mean to Namir. "I guess I'll have two things to share with our liege now."

Alequa shook her head mirthfully as she looked at Hessa. She knew that the elf could read her thoughts on her face, but Hessa could care less. She enjoyed the comfort she found in the healer's presence.

"Did he tell you which of my husband's books he wanted?" Alequa asked Hessa to get the girl to focus on their primary task. "I have an idea about which ones he might need, but if he had something in particular in mind I'd hate to be wrong."

"Aye, it is a black bound one. Small, but heavy," Hessa recalled Namir's exact description as she spoke. "He said that there were a few loose pages scattered throughout it." Hessa pulled the note that Aves had handed her out of her pouch and looked over the cryptic message again to make sure that she hadn't forgotten any of the important details as she described it to Alequa.

"He must be thinking of this one," Alequa said as she eased a book from out of the bottom of the closest stack. "But he may also want this one," she said as she shimmied a larger green one from the middle of another stack. "It is going to help him decipher the code that the first book is written in."

"Code?" Hessa asked perplexed.

"Aras and I decided many years ago that the information we sought to gather was not safe if left in plain sight, so we developed a code. No information can be discovered by reading just one book. Aras wrote everything in a way that you needed at least two of his tomes to get the basic understanding of a topic. Each additional book referenced adds more depth to the original information. So, to get a full understanding about any one topic contained in his books, you need access to all of his writings." Alequa explained carefully. "He can only find out so much from the books though. The rest you will need to help him with, otherwise, Namir may never fully understand his heritage."

"I'm not sure what you mean," Hessa said as she tried to absorb everything Alequa just said. "So did Aras write all of these books?"

"No," Alequa's answer confirmed Hessa's thoughts and she let the elf know with a nod. "We also decided that the information was too precious to ever have all of it in one place." She gave the girl a knowing look as she continued, "We hid some volumes in particular places that were important to the topic that it focused on. But there is a master key that can be used to find each of those places. There is a reference to the locations in a few of these books, but there is also a particular journal at the manor in Hornshir and another that your mother hid as well."

"We must not keep Namir waiting then," Hessa said as she took the books from Alequa carefully. She did her best to hide her dismay that her mother had hidden something that she knew was now lost. "Care to join me in town?" She asked Alequa pensively.

"I wish I could, but I have other tasks that await my attention." Alequa declined as she opened the door for the girl. "Don't worry. If Namir has any questions, I will be more than willing to answer them for him. Now go, you have been delayed long enough. He might think he sent the wrong person if you take too much longer." Alequa saw the slight look of dread crossed Hessa's brow before she could rush out into the darkness, she hoped the girl couldn't plum the real reason behind her knowledge.

Jaconis lay on his stiff bunk in a ball of pain and anxiety. His mind struggled to mix his hard-won understanding of Lotevilar's love and graciousness with the teachings that he learned of Ea as a child. The two were in direct conflict, yet neither seemed false and he could not get his mind to console the growing rift in his soul.

He breathed out an exhausted sigh as his eyes lingered on the new scars that now crisscrossed his left forearm. "What have I gotten myself into," the more rational side of Jaconis's mind asked desperately. "Lotevilar give me the strength I need to pass through your trials."

"Sometimes when you are alone and in pain, your mind can play tricks on you. It can make you hear things that are not there, or worse, make you start to believe things that are not true." The reassuring sound of Tali's voice filled Jaconis with strength.

"Thank you," Jaconis answered her as best as he could. "It has been so long since I have heard a familiar voice. I almost thought that I never would." Jaconis could almost hear her smile in the darkness. He quietly turned on his bed so he could face the door of his little cell. To his surprise, it was still closed. "Tell me why I am here again."

"To give love and service to Lotevilar of course, why else?" Tali had responded too fast for Jaconis's liking.

"Leave me be," Jaconis said quietly. "I will wait to speak further until Tali's really here."

"I am Tali," even the inflection in its voice sounded like Tali to Jaconis's fragile psyche.

His heart ached as he forced the words between his clenched lips, "No, you are an abomination! A trial composed by abbots of Lotevilar in an attempt to make me falter and I will not succumb!"

The silence that followed his words was almost as bad as the trial itself. The pitch black moments of solitude stretched on longer and longer as he silently waited for this terrible trial to be over. The soft sound of water as it flowed quietly over the stones outside of his room was the only confirmation that he received. When he heard it he breathed a sigh of relief. As the air rushed out of his mouth, his mind recalled the first time he had heard the soft ripples of water as it coursed smoothly across the face of the stone.

Visions of his childhood flowed into his mind. Stories about Ea's great deeds echoed off of the soft places in his mind as Saril gently spoke the well-rehearsed words of light and love that served as the cornerstone of Ea's teachings. Jaconis carefully banished each of the parables that Saril had taught to him as a young child until; there was nothing but peace left in their place.

"Finally I can get some sleep," he said quietly to himself as he attempted to get comfortable on his bunk.

"TALK!" Carness's fist narrowly missed Jasper's cheek as he made another indention in the beam that he had chained his prisoner to.

"I have nothing more to say," Jasper said carefully. His words stung as they slipped past his swollen and bloodied lips.

"What are Faris's plans? What is he trying to accomplish in Ellsted?" Carness's demands rang off the walls of his interrogation room like the thunder of an amassing storm. His keen eyes lingered on the bloodied daggers and spikes that were strewn across the table to the left of his prisoner.

"I have already told you what I know. Faris keeps his plans to himself and tells us only what he thinks we need to know. I was instructed to go to the Gathering Place and meet…" Jasper spat out another stream of blood as his words were silenced by the constable's club as it hit him in the stomach.

"Daffer I told you that you're not allowed to hit this one!" Carness shot at the lumbering barkeep as he pulled the club out of his hand.

"Sorry, I forgot," Daffer said as a pathetic attempt to apologize. "Besides, I'm getting bored just listening to the two of you squabble back and forth. You're worse than a couple of chickens before they fight."

"I can't get information from him if he is passed out or dead!" Carness spat as he glared at Daffer. He quickly assessed the wounds that the inn keep had inflicted on Jasper and frowned. He shook his head when he realized that he may need to bring Saril in to keep him alive long enough to get something useful out of him.

"Fine, I will be in the next room with his soldiers. Maybe one of them is awake enough to beat again." Daffer's words echoed from the hallway as he left the room.

"They don't know anything!" Jasper shot at the constable wearily.

"I know," Carness admitted in a flat tone, "that's why I'm in here with you." Seeing Jasper's anger rise he added, "You can spare them a lot of pain if you tell me what I need to know. The faster I find out, the faster I can let all of you leave Ellsted.

It really is that simple."

"Fine," Jasper agreed after a few moments. His response seemed to be prompted by the sudden scream of one of his guards, but it could have been from some of his own pain. Carness watched Jasper take a deep breath before he made sure he was the only one that could hear his prisoner as he spoke, "Faris asked me to give the note in my shoe to your brutal friend." Jasper nodded toward the door that Daffer had just walked through. "That's why I was confused when your friend helped beat my men and I."

The defiant look on Jasper's face was quickly knocked off by the back of Carness's hand. "Don't be too smug, everything may not be what you think." Carness offered this advice as he reached down and quickly found the hidden pocket on the outside edge of Jasper's left boot. "It seems that you still use the design I came up with for hiding our orders during the war. That's good to know." Carness said absently as he opened the note and scanned its contents. "I will be back soon." He said to Jasper loud enough for everyone still conscious in the prison to hear.

"What about my men and me?" Jasper asked incredulously. "You promised to set us free if I helped."

"I know and I will, just as soon as I verify the information you've given," Carness said with a wolfish grin. "Sit tight and don't worry. I will be back for the lot of you soon enough. Daffer, let them breathe a bit and don't kill any of them until I'm back!" Carness called over his shoulder as he donned his cloak and left the room swiftly.

Chapter Nine: Relics

Alequa slowly walked toward Tipin's Smithy. She smiled as the sweet scent of honeysuckle wafted from the open windows of the house. Memories flooded her mind as she recalled the pleasant walks that Allair and Tipin would accompany her on when her husband was too busy with things that needed to be done. Alequa's hand fluttered down to the pouch that her husband had given her on his deathbed.

"One last thing that needs to be done my love, then your spirit may finally rest," Alequa said to herself as she walked up to the smithy's gate.

She carefully raised her hand from the pouch and knocked on the gate. Part of her wanted them to answer and another part hoped they would not. After a few tense moments, she knocked again and whispered a prayer to her goddess for the strength she needed to see her task through. Before the sound of her gentle rapping faded from the courtyard behind the wall, Alequa heard the faint rustle of movement.

"Hello, I was hoping to catch the two of you, before you had retired for the evening," Alequa said to the still closed gate.

"Who may I say is calling?" The feminine voice was all but a whisper and Alequa instantly placed it as Allair's.

"An old friend," Alequa gave the well-rehearsed response

that Aras developed with her years before the war. She hated that the needed to put it back into practice so their cohorts would instantly understand the importance of her visit. "One that has travelled far and would like the pleasure of familiar company on this night," she finished and waited for the appropriate response.

"You have been sorely missed," Allair replied. "Let's reminisce in front of the fire. Will you be staying long?"

Her response seemed so innocent and noncommittal, but Alequa knew her friend had to word the response just right. That way she knew it was safe to talk freely once Alequa made it inside. The soft scraping of the steel latch sliding deep inside the wooden door let Alequa know that Allair understood the exchange.

The fact that her friend had yet to open the door prompted her response, "Long enough to warm old hearts, but not long enough for my liking." She knew that Allair's hand would be on her dagger by now. That is assuming that her friend had stayed in practice. Alequa softly placed her trembling hand on the gate softly. "May we adjourn to the fire and speak of glad times?"

"Aye," Allair said as she opened the gate for her old friend.

As the gate opened enough for Alequa to see the face of her old friend she was quickly engulfed in an embrace as Allair threw her arms around the elf abruptly. Alequa felt relieved to know that her friend was as happy to see her as she was to be there. The fact that they had both quickly dismissed all formality brought a slight smile to her face.

"Tipin will be glad to see you, he is inside. Come," Allair beckoned as she led the way through the courtyard and into her house.

"I can hardly wait," Alequa said as she hastened her step in order to keep up. "It has definitely been too long and I feel the need to be around loved ones tonight."

The healer felt the chill of the night accompany them as they moved silently through the house's front door and into the entryway. Although the house was small, the rooms seemed to exude a feeling of space greater than they should, something Alequa had always loved about her visits to the smithy.

"Then come in and let's be comfortable," Tipin's voice seemed to fill the entryway as Allair and Alequa stepped through the doorway to the great room.

He easily gathered both ladies into his vice-like arms and held them for a few moments before he decided to let them go.

Once he was sure Alequa had regained some of her lost composure, he looked at her solemnly, "Please know our thoughts and prayers are with you. Aras was a great man."

"Thank you," Alequa said as she choked back her tears. "He asked me to come and see you two as soon as I was able." She confided.

"Not now," Allair scolded. She shot a stern look at her husband then to her friend as she continued, "We haven't seen you in ages and the two of you want to start right away with business? No, we need to relax a bit first." Her words, though obviously abrasive, were kind.

Alequa hung her head in shame as she spoke. "We have always loved you two, Aras and I. Out of all of our friends in this town, you two were the dearest. I…I," Alequa's voice cracked as she forced the words out, "I need to deliver his last request to both of you before I lose my composure completely." Overly large, hot, tears started to roll down Alequa's cheeks unbidden and it shamed her that she couldn't stop them.

"Sh…," Allair said as she placed a reassuring hand on her old friend's shoulder. "It will be alright. I'm sorry for my ignorance. Of course, all of this has taken its toll on you. Please continue." She gently rubbed the elf's shoulders as they waited for Alequa to regain herself again.

Tipin, obviously taking the slight lull in the conversation as his cue, guided the two ladies to chairs. Alequa felt his eyes linger on the tracks that she knew her tears were leaving on her cheeks. She knew they were waiting for her emotions to cool.

She watched Tipin stoke the fire helplessly as her emotions continued to tear at her soul.

The elf watched the giant of a man discretely look through the nearby windows. She knew that he was checking to see if anyone had followed her. For some reason, his vigilance calmed her enough to regain some of her lost composure.

"Thank you for your kindness," Alequa finally said. "As I was saying, Aras gave me these and directed me to give them to you two as soon as I possible." She carefully pulled two envelopes from her pouch and handed them to the couple. "He insisted that you read your letter aloud," she said to Allair quietly.

Although her strained voice was barely more than a whisper, Alequa knew that both of them heard her fine. She just hoped there would be no more objections so that she could put this task behind her quickly.

"Very well," Allair agreed.

She carefully removed the wax seal and opened the envelope. Alequa could tell by the slight smile that pulled at her lips that her friend was thinking about all of the odd requests that Aras had made of her throughout the years.

"It is with a heavy heart that I put these words onto the page for you to find them." Allair started. "It is unfortunate that your son is lost and I am dead. I had hoped to be with you when you heard of Halin's disappearance." The tug in her voice easily indicated that it now was Allair's turn to struggle against her emotions. "Allair, I am sorry for the pain that our cause has given you to bear. Know that in my final days, I thought about you and Tipin and wished that it could have been different. I know this next part is hard to read, but please know …" Allair's voice broke and her tears flooded down her cheeks. She was a mess and could barely hold the page aloft.

Tipin reached over and gently eased the page from his wife's hand. His face was streaked with tears as well, but he seemed in more control of himself than either lady was at this point.

"I know that this next part is hard to read," Tipin's deep voice had a calming quality to it as he read from where Allair had left off, "but please knows that Halin loves you both more than you can imagine. He asked me, in a dream before I died, to tell you that in the event you never see him again, within your lifetime, know that he will always hold your teachings dear to him, especially the songs."

Tipin cleared his throat once before he continued, "I know this sounds odd, but I need you to swear that you three will share this information with no one. The Gods work in mysterious ways and it is best that the pathways of light be guarded and protected at all costs." Tipin's hand trembled as he continued, "Tipin, I know that you are reading the letter by now. Thank you for all that you have done, especially for your wife. You have proven to be just the man our cause has needed to survive. Over the years I have come to love the two of you like the parents I never knew. Thank you for that. I know that I have asked too much from you and the next thing that I ask is going to be no different. Tipin, please keep our pact. Although I have passed, it is important that we both protect the secret we shared as long as possible if we hope for our plans to succeed." Tipin leaned back in his chair heavily and took a deep breath. Tears streamed down his face as he visibly stabbed his thumb into his eyes in a vain attempt to stop them.

Alequa knew that he was doing his best to banish the painful memories they shared from his mind with his crude gesture. "My final gift to you both is this one piece of hope. Halin has been chosen to do great things, know that he does those with all the grace and all the love you have given him over the years. Although he is frightened, he is alive and is far braver than you could possibly imagine. Yours in service, Aras." Tipin lowered the page and pulled Allair into him tightly. He buried his face in her chestnut brown hair and the two of them shook in the obvious grip of their rampant pain.

Alequa was the first to recover from the impact of the letter. She carefully stood up and moved closer to her friends.

"In my loss, I had almost forgotten that you both have lost a son. I am so sorry."

She said a quick prayer to Tayant and placed her soothing hands upon them. Almost immediately the room filled with a soft blue glow and the healer physically felt the almost electric sensation of energy build up all around them. The throbbing heat gently pulsed against the deep sense of loss she knew they felt.

"If it helps, I know my husband's words are true. Halin is still alive." She whispered to the two of them before she let her Goddess's energy consume her to do its bidding.

Hessa managed to catch a glimpse of Aves's auburn hair as she hurried toward Ellsted's central square. Hessa sprinted around the corner and barely slid to a stop before she careened into the new makeshift wall of the potter's shop.

"We are almost there!" Hessa shouted to where she had last seen Aves as she smoothed her skirts and took a quick assessment of her possessions to make sure that she still carried both books. "We should be able to get there well before Namir!" Hessa offered aloofly.

She absently tugged a stray lock of hair back into place as she slowly looked down the street to get her bearings. The sight that greeted her was anything but cheerful and quickly knocked her mood back into the depths where it had started.

The area before her was in pure pandemonium. Several people milled about aimlessly while others were trying to regain their footing. Hessa stared in shock as she watched people shout instructions back and forth in a chaotic attempt to control several small fires that broke out all across the square. Several of them were directly between where she stood and the glass blower's stall where Aves and her had agreed to meet.

A throng of people still separated her from the gypsy seeress's wagon. She quickly wrote off worrying about what happened amongst the gypsies. They could take care of their own and she knew better than to venture too far amongst them alone. After all, most gypsies were thieves or worse. Hessa banished the filthy sensation that always accompanied thoughts about gypsy from her mind and focused her attention on smothering the many little fires threatening to consume the makeshift marketplace.

Something bothered Hessa about the way several of the gypsies just stood by and let the fires burn. "What is so interesting at their seeress's wagon?" She wondered to herself completely aggravated by their lack of assistance.

It took far longer than she anticipated, but Hessa finally managed to get the final blaze in check. The subtle warmth of confidence spread through her and she instantly knew that none of the other flames that still burned posed any real threat. Somehow she knew that they were isolated enough that they couldn't spread anywhere.

Hessa hurriedly waved to the others that had helped her with buckets of water and sand as she turned toward the glass blower's stall. Another quick survey of her surroundings allowed her to breathe a little easier. A sigh of relief snuck past her lips as she realized that she hadn't seen any sign of either Namir or Haradine.

Her feet slowly started to move toward her goal as she scanned the withering crowd for Aves. Hessa's elation quickly fled as she peered through the almost impenetrable throng of gypsies that were still gathered around the seeress's wagon. There was a brief small gap in the crowd that let her see what had held their attention for so long and her blood froze as her hazel eyes carried realization of what it was to her brain.

It was just a fleeting glimpse of Aves frozen in place, but it was enough. There had been little specks of blood laced Aves's dress and exposed skin, while the gypsy seeress lay at her feet sprawled amongst her wares. The cards that the old lady used to look into the future lazily careened to the ground all around them.

Hessa slowly moved toward the ring of gypsies that cordoned off the scene. It felt as if she moved through molasses.

She struggled against the sensation as she forcibly placed one foot in front of the other. Somehow she managed to squeeze through the outer circle of bystanders at a frustratingly snail-like pace.

The thing that struck her the most about all of this was the strange immobility of everything and everyone around her. She forced herself to move faster through the throng of onlookers and felt her muscles strain with the added exertion. The dull and elongated sound of metal on stone as she saw a small ring roll slowly passed her pulled at her mind. The unnerving effect of a delayed sound tore at her psyche. It was all Hessa could do to force herself to slip past the third and final ring of gypsies.

Bile rose in Hessa's throat as the full extent of the scene assaulted her senses. Aves stood a few steps away from Hessa and another few paces away lay the gypsy seeress. Her old and lifeless body was pierced by several different glass and metal items that Hessa assumed once adorned her shop. Necks of bottles and wooden rods protruded from the gaping holes and a thick brackish blood seeped lazily out of the oozing wounds.

While the odd slowness of everything was hard to deal with, the tipping point for Hessa was the stench. The odor of oils and incense mingled with burnt flesh and pooled blood made her stomach churn and she could do nothing about it. She turned away from the scene involuntarily and doubled over. In the back of her mind, Hessa knew Aves needed her, but she could not fight her body's urge to expel everything she had consumed this evening. Unfortunately for Hessa, even her retching was a drawn out and delayed chore.

Armani paced the room restlessly. It was bad enough that Faris had asked him to meet tonight, but to meet him in a storage shed behind the inn was worse. "He better get here soon," Armani muttered darkly to himself. In an attempt to better his mood, Armani sat down on an old oil cask and thought about his daughters. He did his best to focus on how things were when they were growing up. The pride he felt when he recalled seeing Hessa for the first time.

She was fair, even back then, and so full of life. He hated having to force her into a life of servitude, but he really had no choice. He had a reputation that he had to maintain after all. He had just been elected as the mayor and he couldn't let anything jeopardize his new found status.

Armani shook his head in frustration, "What is taking him so long?" He wondered aloud.

He let his mind drift to thoughts about Aves. She also was a precious little girl. She was only born a month after his precious Hessa had been and unlike her, Aves was frailer. They shared his hazel eyes and the red tinge to his chestnut hair. Or what his hair had been before the stress of the many years as mayor had a chance to take their toll on him.

The sounds of Aves's phantom childish giggles faded into the soft steps of padded boots against stone as one of Faris's soldiers approached him amongst the throng of revelers outside of the market less than an hour ago.

Armani recalled that the soldier was lithe and moved more fluidly than almost anyone he had ever met. Although her face was covered by the customary chainmail sash that Hornshir guards wore when they patrolled, Armani could tell that she was comely. The way her boiled leather armor formed to her body did little to dissuade this impression.

Her silence was unnerving. She seemed to know his routine, which bothered him a little more than he thought it would. Not only did she not say anything when she hand-delivered the sealed parchment, she said nothing when she approached him. Her piercing green eyes betrayed nothing as she held out the paper expectantly.

Once he touched it, she let go of her end and melted into the crowd effortlessly. Something about her reminded him of his other visitor from a few nights before. Both moved too well and seemed to know too much about him and his habits.

His mind shifted its focus from the past and into the

present. Armani's eyes flew across the piece of paper he held in his slightly trembling hands. The rough feel of the paper was almost painful to him. His fingers traced the remnants of the broken wax seal that Faris had closed it with.

With a slight flick of his finger, Armani flipped open the page and read its contents under his breath, "I know what you have done and I expect you to meet me where the pact was started." It was signed by Faris and it was sloppy. Which meant Faris had to have penned it.

Armani had no idea how Faris had found out about the pact, but he was going to make sure he could tell no one else. His hand dropped to where his dagger hung at his belt as he steeled his nerves for the encounter that he knew was to come.

The squeal of the heavy door as it swung slowly opened on its rusty hinge split the heavy air around him. The sudden change in humidity and sound made Armani flinch unwantedly. "It's about time you arrived. Now we can..." Armani said as he turned to face Faris, however, his words caught in his mouth when Carness's wolf-like gaze stared back at his instead if Faris's brown ones. "What are you doing here?" Armani's alarm as he faced the constable was palpable and he felt the cold tingle of sweat that started to bead along his scalp.

"I could ask you the same thing," Carness replied somewhat amused, "but I won't."

"He knows something," Armani muttered to himself silently. "Good," he said in an attempt to hide his nervousness.

"So my question, for you, is," Carness started as he paced a circle around Armani, "why is it that every time I go looking for Faris I find you?" He stopped a few paces away from Armani and locked gazes with the mayor.

"That is a good question Constable," Armani did his best to sound unfazed by the Carness's actions. He knew he was shaken and he hated the feeling that formed in the pit of his stomach. The way the constable moved made him feel like he was a hen before it's devoured by a wolf. "I suggest you forget about it and focus on the safety of Ellsted instead of your petty revenge." He leveled his most intimidating stare at Carness and hoped it worked. "Now if you would please move," Armani motioned his intention to leave as he said this.

Carness stepped out of Armani's way as he replied, "Of course mister Mayor, anything you say." He bowed deeply and motioned toward the door as he showed his acceptance of Armani's wishes.

The mayor walked around the front of the Gathering Place as he wove through the collected masses that eagerly waited for the commencement of evening's activities.

He deftly avoided each and everyone one of them as he looped around the other side of the inn and back toward the storeroom. Armani knew Daffer had a secret entrance into his stores. It was a throwback to his service in the war.

"No good soldier builds a room with only one exit," Armani recounted the words the innkeep had said to him those many years ago. He breathed a little easier when he found the small switch that he watched Daffer pull to open it the last time he had invited the mayor over to discuss the future of their alliance in the wake of Namir's trip to Hornshir.

Armani watched as Carness studiously scanned the visible recesses of the room. A small twinge of respect for Daffer's ability to hide the existence of the small space he hid in from the main chamber. He peered past the casks that blocked him from view and watched as the constable pulled a roughened piece of parchment from the small pocket inside of his cloak.

With a quick flick of his wrist, Carness unfolded and whispered its contents to himself, "Murderers meet tonight in the Inn's storage. Old allegiances are revealed and new pacts of silence made."

"I assume there is a reason for you to be in my storeroom, Constable." Daffer's voice boomed from behind Carness.

"No...not anymore at least," Carness replied quickly as he refolded the note and turned to face Daffer. "I thought you were going to keep an eye on our prisoners," Carness replied smoothly.

"I did. At least until they all passed out." Daffer shrugged as if his choice to leave was a natural one. "I tied them up good then left." There was an air of normalcy about the way Daffer spoke about his actions that bothered Armani on a deep level.

Carness shook his head in frustration as he listened to the innkeep's statement. "Very well, I'll see to them. I'm finished here anyway," the constable said over his shoulder as he stalked out of the storeroom.

Several long moments passed as Armani sat in his hiding place. His eyes were riveted to Daffer's hulking form. The way he stood silently peering out into the night was a little unnerving, especially considering the conversation that he had just heard.

"You can come out now Armani," Daffer's booming voice filled the entirety of the little structure. "He won't be coming back anytime soon and I think there are things that we need to discuss."

Armani pulled the lever in front of him and shoved against the back of the shelves. After several strenuous moments, he felt it start to move. Daffer turned to face him as the weight of the shelves had shifted enough for them to open on their own.

"There are things we need to talk about," Armani confirmed as he stepped into the main part of the storeroom. "But first I need to ask. How well do you know both Carness and Faris."

Namir slowed to a stop as heard the commotion from the square. He quickly motioned for Haradine to stop and waited for her to approach him before he signaled her to duck into a nearby alley.

"Why are we stopping again?" Haradine asked as soon as she was close enough to whisper. He knew that she was confused by his erratic actions by the quaver in her voice just like he knew she did not want to fail him again by the hardness that had taken over her azure colored eyes.

"There is something going on in the square and I want to know what it is before we just barrel into it." His tone was even and he could see that this surprised his bodyguard.

"So what is the plan?" She asked as she scanned their surroundings.

"We find a different view," Namir said with a knowing smile as he pointed up. He felt the odd sense of déjà vu as the words fell from his lips. A sudden pang of remorse hit him as he recalled Halin's reaction to learning about the secret path that he and Nurn had built above the city. Haradine's face took on the same look that Halin's had perfectly as her eyes traced the direction his finger indicated.

"I don't understand?" Haradine commented. She looked up at the night sky and marveled at the stars that peaked around the rooftops above them. "How do you intend to get up there?"

"Carefully," Namir responded as he walked over to the nearest wall and motioned for her to follow him.

The look of confusion that Haradine wore on her face was priceless and Namir enjoyed it completely. Once he was certain that she had followed him to the wall, he slowly pulled a silk rope from its hiding place in the crevice where the wall that separated the alley met the walls of the next building. Namir waited until the initial wave of shock finally released its hold on Haradine's face before he motioned for her to climb the rope first.

"Very interesting," Haradine said as she took a hold of the rope. "Is this a well-known route, or do you reserve it for those you wish to be alone with?" Haradine asked suggestively. She quickly tested the rope to ensure it would hold her and then started to climb.

Before she could get far, Namir reached out his hand and placed it on her shoulder to stop her from climbing. A sideways smile creased his lips as he spoke, "No I don't usually take anyone up there, only those I know I can trust. But I do have a question for you that I need answered before I let you climb to the top and discover the rest of my secrets." He failed to keep a stoic look on his face and he knew it, but he refused to let his gaze soften until he was sure of her answer.

"There's more?" Haradine answered playfully. He saw her joviality fade as she realized his seriousness. The redness in her cheeks betrayed the embarrassment and shame she felt for not using more restraint. "I am sorry sa'ouvant for my candor. Please ask anything."

She bowed her head and waited. Namir knew Haradine found it hard to contain her excitement about discovering more about her liege's life. Especially the life he had lived before he knew about his destiny and heritage. He just wished that she wouldn't let it show so much.

Namir waited until he was certain he had her undivided attention before he asked, "Why do you believe that I am your king?"

His question was so simple it caught Haradine completely off guard, "Because you are." He knew that she was trying to get a better look at his face in an attempt to figure out whether his question was a serious one.

"Don't you doubt it?" He could tell that the elf was unsure of how to answer him, but he could care less. "Why are you so certain that Aras was right? I don't understand how all of you can be so positive that he didn't make some kind of mistake about me. Namir knew by the taught look on her face that Haradine could hear the frantic twinge in his voice as it grew stronger, just as he knew that same knowledge is what prompted her to reach out and put her hand on his shoulder in a somewhat awkward attempt to reassure him.

She leveled a rational stare at him as he lips parted just far enough for her words to slip past them. "It is simple, sa'ouvant. We know that you are the one chosen by the Gods to restore order to Cennicus. We can feel it just as we can feel the slightest breeze that dances on our skin."

The certainty in her voice snapped Namir out of his emotional downward spiral. He took a couple deep breaths to regulate his pounding heart and managed to steal just enough time from the certainty of his encroaching fate for him to regain a bit more of himself.

"But what if you are wrong?" His gaze danced from one of her azure blue eyes to the next as he pressed his line of questioning, "What if this is truly a bizarre case of mistaken identity. What if…" Namir's words caught in his through as he struggled to control his inner turmoil.

"What if what, sa'ouvant?" Haradine's tone betrayed her true feelings. The exasperated manner in which the normally strong notes fell from her mouth pulled at Namir's heart. "I know that you have read too much from those accursed journals. I know Aras was studious and careful. I also know that some of the things he listed was meant to lead those that read it astray. What part of these books has you so lost, sa'ouvant?"

"What if I am the other?" Namir finished. His words sounded hollow and haunting, yet menacing at the same time.

"I don't understand." For once Haradine's words held no hint of joy. Namir visibly saw Haradine's heart fell as she watched his own face contort against his internal struggle for control. "Please help me understand," her words were little more than hints of sound on the wind and Namir could feel the hopelessness his questions put into them as she spoke.

"Two dragons born of this world will fight. One of dark and one of light. Twins in both, birth and might. Should the one prevail, then the world shall unite. If it is the other, then the Gods shall smite." The words seemed to fall from Namir's lips unbidden. A vacant look stole across his features as he recited the simple rhyme he had read a few hours before.

"Where did you hear that?" Haradine asked plainly. All of the color had fled her features as she gently shook his shoulder. "Sa'ouvant? Namir? Are you all right?"

Without warning, a bright flash erupted from underneath Namir's tunic. Haradine staggered back from her, obviously blinded. Namir watched as he felt the almost familiar tingle of mystic energy course along his skin. It was a sensation that he had felt on each of the prior moments Zelios flexed her power.

The ripple of pure power pulled at Namir's mind and lifted him from his fears better than anything else could. Amazed by the experience, he stared as he bodyguard and when he noticed that her sight was returning, he made sure to flash a playful smile at her in an attempt to ease some of the fear he knew that he had caused her.

"You had me worried. Where did you hear that rhyme?" Haradine asked in a conspiratorial tone.

"It's a prophecy," Namir responded off-handedly, "not a rhyme." He continued. "And I read it in one of Aras's journals." Namir wiped an errant bead seat from his brow as he spoke. "I am sorry that I delayed us for so long. Sometimes my questions get the best of me. If we have any chance of beating the girls we should go, so go ahead and climb." He let the rope slip from his grip and winced at the small jolt of pain it caused him.

He knew Haradine understood that his brusqueness was a defense of his, but he did not want her to panic before he had a chance to pick her brain about either the prophecy or what she was thinking that caused Zelios to react to her actions so drastically.

"As you command," she grasped the rope and quickly ascended to the rooftop at the end of it before he could think of anything else to say.

Chapter Ten: Tributes

Allair gathered her things as the two women started to leave the room. "Tipin, Are you sure you won't come with?"

The pleading tone in her voice was more apparent than he would have liked to hear. He knew that she hated to leave him alone, especially now. Tipin felt a tear start to build in the corner of his eye as he thought about how much both of them had lost.

Many of their friends were now either dead or missing and on top of that, both of their sons were lost as well. He knew that the pain he felt was almost more than he could bear and Allair had always felt things deeper than he could even understand. That last thing he wanted was for her to be alone, but he knew he had no choice.

"I would, my love, but I have one last task to do for Aras." Tipin soothed as he motioned to the letter that sat on the table a few paces away.

"Fine," her words were sharp and she did nothing to hide her disappointment as she turned to Alequa. "Please tell me that you will at least walk with me into town like we used to."

"Aye," Alequa agreed. "That is one thing that I think I miss most of all. Do you have anywhere in particular that you would like to go?"

Allair nodded, "I need to have some bottles made, so I was

thinking we could wander the main square and see the glass blower. That is after we've had our fill of the other booths and festivities."

"That sounds fun," Alequa said as she looped her arm in Allair's after she donned her cloak. "Ready?"

"Ready," Allair replied as the two ladies stepped out into the omnipresent darkness.

Tipin watch the ladies leave with a heavy heart. Although his eyes followed them, his mind raced along the edges of the page that he now clasped delicately in his fingers. He was grateful that his wife had left as the solitary tear finally left the safety of his eyelids and made its way down his cheek.

A sigh of relief stole from his lips as they faded from his view and his ears could scarcely hear their light banter. When even the subtle soft scuff of their feet was lost amongst the rest of the noises that accompanied the festivities of the town, he knew that he as truly alone.

Tipin's eyes scanned the ancient Calanari script that lay just under the sealed fold of the page. He whispered a quick prayer to Tumere as he slowly tugged on the outer edge and coaxed the folded piece of paper to bulge against its seal. With just the right amount of force, he perfectly cracked the wax seal in half and smiled as he recalled the simple technique he had perfected during the Great War. Tipin scanned the shadows around the room before he opened the letter before he lost himself in the words that he found waiting for him.

Faris crouched just behind the gypsy juggler's stage. From his vantage point, he saw everything play out in front of him just as they had planned it. The mayor's daughter was a sight to behold indeed.

Watching as she darted through the throng of people, twisting and arching in just the right ways not only enticed him, it forced him to watch her even more intently. She was a rapture in motion and the fact she was completely oblivious to their trap only added more excitement for him.

The captain spared a quick glance from Aves, just as she all but flipped backward over the handles of a stationary cart to avoid hitting a passerby, to find Skara's hunkered form lurking in the shadows directly across from him. From their positions, they had a clear swath of coverage. Anyone that either one of them decided to target could be assassinated in a very short time.

A quick nod let the feline know he was ready when she was. Faris had always believed that a manual trigger was always more reliable that one sown into the environment, which is why he insisted that Skara set the spell and then activate it when they were certain of the moment.

In less than a second, a slight pop erupted all around him. Everything in his line of sight was enhanced, while everything else was blurred into an incomprehensible mass. An odd pricking sensation slowly worked its way across the inside of his scalp and it was unnerving. Faris absently ran his fingers through his hair as the feeling of spiders moving underneath his forehead settled itself into a tolerable rhythm.

His eyes darted from one painfully pristine to another. Each thing was too perfect, even Aves. Faris sucked in a quick breath as he eyes fell on the girl's perfect stillness. She could have been mistaken for a statue. She was beautiful, yet motionless. Not even her long hair moved in the muted breeze.

The tableau was almost too tempting for the old guard to resist. Aves had been caught in mid-turn. From her body's position, it was obvious that she was moving toward the gypsy seeress's wagon, but her head faced the glass blowers tent. Her hair, with its subtle scarlet and amber hues, arched over her shoulder in such a way that it screamed motion, even though she, herself, was not moving in the slightest.

Faris struggled against its animalistic lust to lead this highly attractive, and well-formed, girl away from the prying eyes of the townsfolk and have his way with her. It was a hard pitched fight, but he squelched these carnal urges before he had a chance to act on them. He was well aware that their ultimate goal was too important to sacrifice their impending success for a brief moment of ecstasy, no matter how fulfilling they might make him feel at the time. Although he was in control of his desires again, Faris let his eyes drink in every luscious curve that Aves's statuesque form presented him for a few more moments before he gave Skara another nod.

He watched as she slid easily from her hiding place and started a few small fires. He too slipped away from his cubby hole and purposefully bumped into some of the immobile onlookers. By the time they were both done, the once tranquil scene had been transformed into a sea of chaos and turmoil. All that remained was the command from the nassarid witch to set their work into motion. Faris barely saw Skara's nod that signaled she was ready to put the next part of their plan into action.

Faris deftly darted back to his cubby and waited. His eyes were closed, his heart pounded and a dull ache formed in his chest from their exertion. These sensations were all that he was able to focus his mind on. Skara's warning about being caught in the spell if he were to fixate on anything other than himself thundered through his mind louder than even the sound of his own heart as it sought to escape his chest.

After a seeming eternity, the sensation of time started to flow again. Not like it had prior to the spell, but it was there. He felt it as an odd pressure just beneath and behind his left ear. Uncomfortable and bothersome, it persisted as he scanned the area for his real target. Skara had to have seen her approaching, that's why she triggered the spell. His thoughts were like a whirlwind in his mind when he saw her careen around the corner.

The fact that his target failed to immediately notice her friend's plight made him a little happier than he had anticipated. A smile threatened to break across his lips once he saw the realization of her situation sink into her features.

Her step slowed almost to a stop as she visibly absorbed the pandemonium around her. Faris watched her scan across the sea of faces in a vain attempt to peer through the commotion. Her brow furrowed in frustration as she struggled to move faster than the spell would allow her to. Even witnessing this confirmation that the spell worked as Skara had promised it would, did little to elevate his mood any higher than it already was.

He found more pleasure watching the girl fight against its effects as she started to extinguish the little fires they had set a few minutes ago than he could possibly find in the knowledge that everything progressed as they had planned it.

Faris tugged his dagger free from its scabbard silently as she approached him. He could tell that she was completely unaware of his presence. When she was less than a few paces away, he carefully allowed his weight to shift from foot to foot. He could see the hem of her skirt caught in the molasses-like pull of the spell. It was captivating in its own odd way. Once the captain was certain that his blood flowed freely through both legs, he pivoted his stance to maximize his reach. She was less than an arm span away when he saw Hessa step up to the stage and grab the pail of water from where it sat just above Faris's head.

His hand trembled in eager expectation as he heard the folds of her dress rustle cautiously across the very boards that he leaned against. His mind leapt to what he was about to do and momentarily pulled his focus away from his task. Faris's base urges flooded his mind as he struggled to regain his purpose. She was moving farther from him and he knew, deep down, that his window of opportunity was slipping away with every heartbeat. Desperation tugged at the edges of his mind as he shook the deprived thoughts from his brain.

With newfound resolve, Faris leapt. The release of tension in his legs released an all too familiar of endorphins and adrenaline, one that the captain had come to rely on in his job. He drove the point of his dagger toward Hessa's exposed shoulder blades. He knew she had strayed from the spot he had planned on hitting, but he should still be able to sink his dagger in far enough to bring her down. His mind stayed a step ahead of the strike. He was instantly planning his next move.

His offhand reflexively reached for the railing as his thrust took him over it. Sprawled out across the top of the rail, Faris realized a little late that she had somehow move a bit farther away than he had thought she could. In one deft motion, he pulled himself back into the obscuring embrace of the shadows. In the back of his mind, Faris felt the uncomfortable twinge of regret that he had mistimed his shot. "Hopefully Skara will be more accurate than that," he brooded quietly.

The sounds of metal against stone pulled his thoughts back from the path of embarrassed shame that his failed attempt had led him toward. Faris stared in disbelief as he saw one of Skara's daggers skittered across the cobbles of the market toward him. "Skara missed?" The thought was as alien to him as his own mishap had been. "Her aim is legendary," he muttered to himself. An odd sensation of disbelief mingled with hope as he realized he had another shot at finishing this for them. Deep down Faris knew that his aim was nowhere near as accurate as Skara's, but he didn't care. He knew that he had to succeed.

Faris quickly picked up the discarded throwing dagger from the cobles near him and tried to clear his mind. As he raised Skara's throwing dagger and leveled it at Hessa's back, his thoughts raced. He knew that if they had been in Hornshir he never would have attempted this. The fact that he had never sworn to protect the people of Ellsted only made his actions easier to justify to himself. Faris forced all extraneous thoughts out of his head, leveled the dagger at Hessa's stooping form one last time to judge his distance. A few deep breaths as he waited for the timing to be right. As soon as he felt his breath catch on its own, he let the dagger fly.

Alequa sprinted toward the person she saw plummeting from the rooftops. The small elf's golden braid slipped from her shoulder as she dodged around an unexpected shopper.

Here azure blue eyes darted from the villager that she had almost collided with to the ground and then to the next obstacle, a gypsy juggler that had started his routine when she saw the falling person. The healer knew that she had no time to waste. She just hoped that her friend, Allair, had seen what she had and could predict her actions.

Deep down Alequa knew she would have precious little time to help the person. That is if she was not already too late. The dull thud as the body hit the flagstones head first echoed through the streets eerily as she barreled toward it. All thoughts of impropriety left her mind as she literally dove in order to cross the final few paces faster. Although still a few paces away, the motionless body filled her senses. The subtle shifts as the golden hair danced in the breeze as she scanned what small bits of flesh she could see for signs of life. The soft patter of Allair's steps behind her gave her the needed strength to continue.

Without thinking, Alequa fell to her knees as she ran. Her lips danced in a rhythm of their own as the all too familiar prayer to Tayant for healing and protection slid from between them. The stones, though smooth, cut into her knees as she deftly skidded to a stop less than an arm's length from the body reminded her that she too would need some healing once her work for this poor soul was finished. The elf deftly ignored the small blossoms of pain that accompanied flecks of her blood as they rose to the surface of her skin and made their way to the ground.

"Blood will always find its way back to the earth," she reminded herself as her mind danced along the gift of healing that her goddess started to channel through her. She knew that it was for healing. A small sigh of relief escaped her lips as the familiar blue energy swelled within her. The crackling sensation that came along with it always made the healer want to move. She focused her thoughts on the words of her prayer so that the temporary restlessness she felt could be quelled.

The spark danced underneath her skin from her crown,

along the back of her eyes and finally through her chest and into her hands. The soft blue glow pulsed brighter with each breath and she knew that he skin had taken on an otherworldly hue. The blue light threatened to pierce through her tightly closed eyelids when she finally felt the release. A crack of power, like the sound just before an avalanche, pulsed through her from somewhere deep inside her chest. This new surge of energy flowed rapidly from its source, through her outstretched hands, and into the body in front of her.

For a brief moment, Alequa was lost in the flow. A new feeling of oneness with everything filled her soul. This gift from Tayant was the addictive part of being a healer. The unparalleled sensation of being connected to the very source of the universe was overwhelming. Although she knew to be guard herself against it, Alequa knew she could not fight it. The anguish of separation and aloneness that flagged the end of the surge was the worst and she knew that tonight would be no different.

She slowly pulled her hands away from the body as the power ebbed in her hands. An odd tingling sensation started in the tips of her hair as she did so. "What is happening?" She wondered aloud as she watched the energy arc from her fingertips into the deathly still body in front of her. Before she could brace herself, another pulse of energy swelled through her body and discharged as abruptly as it built. Sweat beaded her forehead and her body pulsed with an ecstasy she had never felt while healing before.

A palpable and sickly sweet fragrance filled the air around her as she slowly reached out and gently tugged on the person's shoulder. The elf hoped to get a better look at her patient. Her heart almost stopped then, when the firelight flew across the person's features. Alequa stifled her scream abruptly enough that she felt its pressure as it squeezed against the inside of her throat. Although she commanded the healing powers of her goddess, the elf felt her heart stop as she looked upon her daughter's face

"Your friend is in danger." Zelios's words erupted in Namir's mind as a soft flash of blue light shimmied through the seams and edges of his shirt.

"I know," his response was whispered, but he was certain the spirit within his necklace could hear him.

"I have already done what I can," her voice seemed a little distant to Namir and it bothered him. "The rest is up to you."

"I know." It took all the will he could muster to whisper his response.

The stinging tears pulled at the edge of his vision as the disturbing scene unfolded below him. All his childhood memories seemed to center on the fountain at the heart of Ellsted. Seeing this place caught in a series of small flames and destroyed tents was almost more than the boy could endure. He forced the memories of his childhood out of his thoughts and attempted to fill their void with thoughts about his new found past.

"Where are you?" Namir asked silently. Somehow he knew what the spirit inside the amulet was as the question started to form in his mind.

"I am here, protecting you. Now see to your friend, or she will die." Zelios's matter of fact tone did little to spark any urgency in Namir. Another blue flash erupted from the amulet as she spoke and Namir knew the sharp truth her words conveyed.

He closed his eyes in an attempt to stop his emotional pain from consuming him. I did not work. "It's in the gods' hands now. I just hope I can pick up the pieces fast enough." He glanced around for Haradine and let out a frustrated grunt when he could not see her. Namir knew he could not afford the time to wait until he could. He just hoped she had seen him exit his hiding place. Then she might be able to follow him from a safe distance and provide help as needed.

Namir calmed his mind as he deftly sprinted toward the farthest edge of the roof and jumped. His heart fluttered for a fraction of a second as the momentary doubt that always seemed to accompany this jump came sent its tingling tendrils jolting through his nerves. It ended as abruptly as it has risen when he felt the rough rope brush against his palm. He closed his hands on the rope as quickly as he could and immediately kicked his legs for more momentum.

Namir's brawny frame arced out over the square. At the height of his swing, he let go of the go and felt the cold night air overwhelm him. His aim was perfect. Within moments he felt the soft embrace of the hay bin that sat outside the potter's shop.

Namir scrambled out almost as soon as he had entered it. He needed to be out of the way in case Haradine was had followed his lead. It was the subtle whisper of steel as it cleaved through the brittle air around him that forced Namir's mind to focus his senses on the chaos all around him. The stark clangor of sound assailed him as his eyes darted from person to person. He knew he had to find Hessa soon; he just had no idea about how he was going to do it.

Chapter Eleven: Misgivings

Skara stared in disbelief at the turn of events. She shook her head angrily as she recalled her first throw and how her prey had somehow managed to twist free from her spell. "Her freedom was only temporary," the feline reminded herself.

She watched in anticipation as Faris leveled one of Skara's daggers at Hessa. "He throws like a human," Skara thought to herself ruefully. She knew the old soldier could not help his race, but his throw was clumsy and off target. "I will have to teach him to have more grace with daggers if he's ever going to be of any real use." Her mind raced faster than the spin in Faris's throw as she moved into a better position.

Skara easily plucked the dagger out of the air as she changed positions. She wanted to make sure her next throw ended her prey's life. Skara had grown bored of their little game and was eager to be on her way to warmer places. She carefully lined up her target and waited. Skara visualized the outcome she desired and allowed everything else about the scene in front of her fade into a black nothingness.

Every possible motion her target could make played through Skara's head in less time than it took her to blink. Anticipation of her prey was a skill she had honed over a great many years and the slightest inkling of the kill sent a shiver down her spine.

She silently chanted a quick spell into the steel. A brief flare of heat, akin to that of an open flame, passed stealthily from her lips and into her dagger. A sigil of flame cast in heat waves hovered momentarily in front of her as it searched for its tether. She gently caressed the carving she made earlier on the pommel as she guided the real power of her spell to its home.

A brief blue flash erupted above her as she drew her last dagger to her lips. "I hope that wasn't lightning," Skara brooded as she cast a worried look to the clouded sky above her. She quickly noted where it came from as she forced herself not to get distracted by the abrupt display.

Skara, however, did not let the momentary lapse of concentration break her desire for revenge. Instead, she steadied her dagger one last time. She quickly visualized its path and mentally willed it to strike her target. Then she let it fly. "I hope the shadow walker likes this present," Skara thought as her eyes traced its path toward her intended victim.

The imaginary line between reality and willed visions blurred as she strained her keen eyesight to its limits. Skara's head inadvertently twisted to the side and she listened for the soft thump that always followed a perfect throw.

The sound of metal striking metal snapped her from her anxious thoughts and back to the present. She felt her heart fall when she realized that she missed. Somehow her prey still lived. Puzzled, Skara frantically scanned the square for her dagger. She had to find it before anyone else did. If the spell was released, Skara knew that she did not have enough strength to cast it again. She also knew that she had to make sure that her efforts were not wasted.

Another, more deadly, sound stopped her frantic search. The unmistakable thwack of a bowstring as it slapped the arms of the bow. Instinctively leapt behind a basket of apples as an arrow skittered off of the cobbles where she stood a moment before. She shouldn't be alive and she knew it.

"My spell must have slowed the arrow," She thought to herself as she scanned what she could of the square.

Skara silently cursed her luck as the weight of another arrow impacted the woven basket of fruit in front of her. She waited until she heard the thwack from the bowstring again before she dared to move and when she did, she was a blur. Up and over the stall behind her and in three fluid strides she leapt. The nassarid's fingers closed the dangling rope as if she planned her escape. With a quick kick, she free from the confines of the square.

The weightlessness of her swing lasted only a short time. Although her flight was only momentary, Skara reveled in the freedom it had provided her. In less time that it took her to think about the archer somewhere below her, Skara silently landed on the roof. Her heightened senses instantly registered the almost imperceptible impact as the balls of her feet touched the board. She tucked her lithe body into a ball and rolled onto the main part of the roof easily. As she skidded to a soft, she glanced around to see if she could hide anywhere. The soft flutter of canvas as it flew in the wind let her know of the perfect spot.

Even in the dim light of the smoldering flames below her, Skara easily made out the shape of the laundry pile. It was only a midsized pile made up from dirty canvas sheets from the makeshift shops of the market, but it would do nicely for what she needed. She easily molded the pile of canvas sheets into a non-conspicuous hiding place. Her new vantage point gave Skara a wide view of the square with very little movement needed, which she planned to take full advantage of.

With efficient arcs, she searched for her attacker. Skara quickly ruled out each of the villagers and the gypsy that she saw one at a time. Her eyes darted from face to face to face where they stood close together. When she had to cover a gap, her eyes traced the lines between the large cobbles of the street for any sign of her missing dagger. Her heartbeat was erratic and loud in her ear. With each calming breath Skara took, she half expected another arrow to pierce the flimsy cloth that surrounded her.

“Mother of Pain guide my sight,” She breathed her words quietly and instantly regretted it. All it would take for her would-be-assassin to find her was one word uttered too loud or an out of place noise. The muscles in her neck and shoulders ached with tension as she deftly scanned the crowd for her attacker and the cobbled streets for her missing dagger another time. The nassarid felt her frustration grow deeper inside her with every person she was able to dismiss. “I don’t even know what my assailant looks like,” She mused quietly. Her eyes skimmed through another throng of people. Every dull thud of her heart drove home the futility of her search, then she saw them; the piercing brown eyes of a hunter.

To Skara’s surprise, her would be assassin was a small lady with an almost mousy look to her. Long Chestnut colored hair whipped in the growing breeze as the lady started through her. Skara watched as her attacker carefully hung the bow she had used back onto the awaiting hook of the stall she stood beside. With a slight nod of approval to the overly distracted shopkeep, she pulled her green hood back into place and stepped back into the shadows that she had obviously emerged from.

Although she was impressed by the lady’s skill, Skara was disappointed and a little frightened as well. This lady looked no different than anyone else in the crowd. Part of her mind fixated on that and she found it hard to beat down the finger of paranoia that threatened to take root in her mind.

“She could be anyone,” Skara’s thoughts voiced themselves as she searched the streets below her for the missing dagger. “And she used regular arrows against my spell. How did she do that?” Her voice was ragged as she spoke. The slight frantic tinge that crept into her tone made her realize exactly how scared she really was.

A deep sigh of relief helped her to ease some of the tension in her neck and shoulders as Skara realized the lady had lost track of her. “She doesn’t know where I fled to,” Skara breathed quietly to herself. She knew what a boon this was and planned on using it to her fullest advantage. She quickly recalled the lady's features. She knew that she needed to find out who this lady was. As she made plans on how she was going to determine this, Skara mentally added her to the growing revenge list she had started just a few years ago.

Her eyes continuously skimmed the cobbles below her as her mind raced. She was completely unaware of the differences between her thoughts and actions until she saw it. Her dagger rested less than a foot from her prey. It gleamed menacingly as the light around it was drawn to its wickedly sharp edge. Horror washed over Skara's catlike features face when she saw Faris's bare hand reach for the blade.

Her heart hammered in her chest as she tried to find a way to warn him of the danger. Skara knew Faris was dead before she even saw him touch the blade. Her mind raced as time seemed to stretch infinitely slow. Unsure if it was panic driven or the effect of the spell she had cast, Skara reached for a pebble at her feet. This was the only way she could think of. "Lotevilar, please guide my hand," she whispered as she felt the stone fling free from her fingers. Silence flowed over her as she watched the small stone zing toward her comrade.

A brief yelp of pain the only answer she heard in response to her actions. A lump formed in her chest as she watched Faris quickly snatch her dagger from its resting place. Less than a second later she saw it slip from his fingers and clatter silently back onto the hard stones at his feet.

Skara knew the pain he felt. She had felt it before once when her mistress had been angry with her. Flames danced inside of him. They danced through his veins and along the underside of his skin. His panic, visible to anyone that watched, rose steadily as he frantically searched for water. Skara knew it wouldn't help, but she prayed that he might find something to ease his mental anguish. After all, mental anguish was the only thing he could find release from. She knew full well that even if he had found some water, there was no way for it to get inside of him to where the flames lived. It was under his skin and in his blood. Worse yet, it was going nowhere.

Skara said another silent prayer to Lotevilar as she saw Faris dash from the square toward the council hall. There was a morbid part of her that wondered how far he would get before the flames consumed him, but the rational part knew that she had to find his body. Not just to make sure that he was dead, but to ensure that there was no way the constable and the council could tie his death to her.

"Tali is not going to like this," she said softly to herself as her feet darted along the rooftops. Her eyes followed the path she had seen the captain of Hornshir's guard stagger as he writhed in pain. With each step she took, hope built inside of her that no one else would find his ashen remains before she could.

Aves hazel eyes looked down at all the gypsy tarot cards that littered the street. The world seemed muted and distant as her unfocused gaze scanned over the patterns created by them. The seeress's tools were strewn all across the street in front of her. The little piles of cards were the least of them. Shattered glass fragments law amidst broken wooden boxes. Tattered remains of cloth, once serving as decoration for the inside of the old lady's wagon, added small accents of red and gold to the debris as it fluttered in the breeze trapped in the square.

Everything around her was in shambles, even time seemed damaged somehow. Aves turned her head as she watched a scarlet scarf rip away from the board that had it pinned against the ground. The silken material fluttered birdlike past her face slowly. Her eyes drifted from it to the few strands of her own hair that had managed to escape her braid. Her mind marveled at the slow patterns that it moved in, almost as if they were also caught in a thick invisible liquid.

Her sleeve caught on something and Aves pulled against it. She started to turn to see what it was, but a part of her resisted. After all, why should she care if something pulled at her? She was like the scarf. Caught in the invisible eddies of the world, finally free of her bonds.

Another sharp tug, this time it pulled her arm. It felt forceful and urgent. Aves tried to resist it, but knew she wasn't going to be able to. There were sharp voices saying something, what exactly she could not say. But whoever was speaking to her sounded like they were in charge.

Her hazel eyes darted toward the voices. There were two, or was it three, ladies nearby. "Were they the ones I heard talking?" Aves wondered as she tried to make out their faces.

A single card flittered along the street in the growing breeze. It danced and swayed along the cobbles near her feet and then, abruptly, decided to fly. Little leaps at first, as if the card tested its skills. Then, after it had clearly decided that it was capable, the card launched itself into the air. The card, obviously used for divining the future, soared in little circles. Its loops steadily became larger with each pass and its altitude increased as well. The invisible cyclone that the card was obviously trapped in directed it in flawless circles for the amusement of those who cared to watch.

Aves understood that neither the card nor the breeze that moved it was alive, but the cards were so lifelike that her mind toyed with the idea that it might be. Even so, it was all Aves could do to focus her attention on only the card and not the chaos that surrounded her. Every time she let her eyes shift to look at what someone was doing, or even to inspect a different piece of debris, a sharp pain ignited just behind her eyes. The only thing that seemed to banish the pain was this card and its lifelike movements.

The almost imperceptible flapping noises as its yellowed edges sliced this way and that through the air in front of her eyes drew her attention back to its location. For a few moments, it hovered just before her eyes before it flitted off into another circle. The first time, its checkered back flashed for a long enough time that Aves could see the artistry that its creator had used to make it. The second time it hovered it was at more of an angle. As it started to spin in place, Aves reached for it.

Her motion was reflexive and uncontrollable. Like her strange urge to watch the card, she felt powerless to resist this simple motion. Aves felt another small tug against her outstretched arm as her fingers stretched toward the floating card and she thought it was odd. The pressure was from the top of her arm and Aves could clearly see that there was nothing restraining her. Then, as her fingers brushed the edge of the card, the timelessness of the moment ended.

All of the noises of the festival assaulted Aves's ears at once and completely robbed her of her senses. The sudden cacophony was deafening and painful. Each sound and each flash of light hit Aves so hard that the very fabric of her soul reeled in pain as if struck. Here senses were bombarded and completely overloaded by the sights, sounds, and scents of everything all around her as they invaded her mind. The only sanctity she found was in the too smooth surface of the card she had barely managed to snag with her outstretched fingers as the onslaught from the world of the living continued to incapacitate her.

"I'm telling you, there is more to this church than you would think." Gienna's words seemed harsh to Landolin. He never knew her to particularly care for religion of any kind, but she seemed so adamant there was a bigger conspiracy surrounding this particular faith than he was unaware of.

"What makes you so sure?" His skepticism was as apparent as the doubtful look on his face. "All that you have given me is a list of Hornshir's council members that frequent the monastery. I understand the mayor is one of the names on the list, but I don't see what their religious beliefs have to do with anything."

"They are not visiting the monastery to go to a sermon!" Landolin could hear the hatred in her voice and winced from it. He hated talking to his sister about some things. The religion of the seven races was one of them. Her lack of tack and acceptance of other's beliefs grated on his nerves. "Never mind that the church is based on Lotevilar's strange teachings," Gienna spat as she spoke. "Let's also put aside the screams that can be heard well after the night has grown old."

She sat directly across from him at the long table in the meeting hall. Their garnet colored hair bobbed in the same subtle breeze from the courtyard below them and their violet eyes were locked in a competition of will and Landolin knew she meant to win. He did his best to speak with her as an equal instead of the child she acted like, but the weary elf knew he was failing by the scowl he felt pull at the corners of his lips.

"There are passages that lead to secret parts of the monetary. Older parts that are so well hidden that even magic cannot feel them out. The passages that lead from this house down to the harbor are not as forgotten and ancient as those the Disciples of the White Rod use."

The twinkle in her eyes betrayed her conviction and Landolin knew she sensed the onset of realization start to form in the back of his head. "The monastery is the only place a lilan could have hidden and crept out of undetected." He watched as she confirmed his words with a soft nod of her head. "Which means that the Disciples of the White Rod are somehow tied to the menace that killed my men?" Landolin's question completed his sister's thought seamlessly.

"Aye and that's where everything gets blurry," Gienna added. "From what I can tell, all five of the council members on the list were introduced to the monetary by Faris."

"What?" The incredulous tone in Landolin's voice betrayed his disbelief. "Are you certain?"

"Unfortunately I am." She waited for her words to sink in before she continued. "I found several letters from Faris to each of the council members. All of the letters directed the councilors to contact a specific person. These meetings were spelled out and detailed what needed to happen during each meeting. Each elder was instructed to bring money and all of them were promised that their wildest dreams were going to be granted by Lotevilar."

"I wonder how far his treachery extends," Landolin hated to think about all the years he conducted business with this traitor. Even if his negotiations were made under different pretenses, he still could not help but feel betrayed by him. His sister's words mixed with the proof she had shown him only cemented Faris's guilt in the general's eyes. "I sent Haradine to him with gold to escort an envoy back to Ellsted. I hope he proves trustworthy for that task at least.

"There is only one way to find out," Gienna admitted. "I need to go into the passages and trace them to their source myself." Landolin eyed his sister warily. "I need to do it alone," she added as he continued to ponder her request.

"Absolutely not! I won't have my sister go into a place as dangerous as you say it is without me and that is final!" The determination in his voice took on an ominous note as his words struck Gienna. "I will accompany you and we will see what we can find together."

"Do you honestly believe that I have never been in dangerous places, brother?" Gienna chastised. "Thank you for your concern, but I can take care of myself." Her sarcastic tone lashed at her brother's ears.

"I know that you have been. And so far you've been lucky. I refuse to let you risk your life foolishly." Landolin took a deep breath before he continued, "Is it too much for me to want to ensure my only sibling's safety?" He violet eyes locked with hers as he pleaded. "We are twins. Cast at birth to share our fates." Gienna's look of disdain was only accented by the blatant eye roll that his words provoked. "I know that you don't like hearing about it, but it is true. Anything that befalls you, affects me as well. It's fated."

"You know how I feel about fate," Gienna warned.

"I do, which is why I need to remind you. You may have left to avoid your responsibilities, but I have never forgotten how our souls are entwined into the greater scheme." He waited while the weight of his words worked on his sister's mind before he continued. “This is why I must insist on accompanying you into the tunnels beneath the church.” He knew that she could hear the sincerity of his words and was relieved once he spoke them.

“Fine, I can agree to that, since it means so much to you. When can we go?” Her words hung between them momentarily as Landolin thought about his decision.

“At first light,” Landolin was relieved when he saw her acceptance. He was only prepared to give her that much of an answer. After all, he needed to select the proper escort for them.

Hessa allowed the slowness of time to close in and restrict her movements. She felt comforted by the sensation and sought its painless release. Once she was fully recovered she focused on Aves. Hessa was amazed at how easily she managed to slip through the slowing effect once she focused her mind on where she needed to go instead of on what she wanted to do.

The girl focused her attention on her longtime friend’s side and then she gingerly stepped past the debris that littered the space between them. Hessa gently tugged Aves’s sleeve and guided her friend closer to herself carefully. She was worried. Aves stood so still that Hessa feared that she had been turned to stone somehow. Only the color of her skin and her breathing betrayed the effect.

Hessa stared at Aves and carefully brushed a single amber strand of hair out of her face. As an afterthought, she quickly waved her hand in front of Aves’s face with no response. Hessa snapped her fingers and nothing happened. She still wondered why she was immune to the effect that held everyone else so tightly in its grasp.

Delicately Hessa tugged on Aves’s sleeve again to lead her farther away from the danger. She reflexively brushed a tarot card from in front of Aves’s face. It seemed to be caught in the wind and spiraled in front of them. As soon as her fingers touched the card, the odd slowing effect ended. The first sound that Hessa could remember hearing was the slight flutter of cards and then the square erupted into motion and noise once again.

"It is no longer safe here." The words were simple, yet hard for Hessa to understand. She quickly scanned her surroundings for who might have said them, but nothing around her seemed to make any sense.

"What do you mean?" Her question was a pathetic attempt at deciphering the chaos around her and she knew it.

"There is no time." A more musical voice chirped. It was familiar, but Hessa could not quite place it. "We must leave now. You already have the other girl, just grab this one so we can go." These final words were more direct, yet non-threatening at the same time.

"The other girl?" Hessa asked as she felt strong, yet thin fingers, latch onto her arms and heave her into a standing position. "I thought I was standing," Hessa muttered absently.

She scanned her surroundings for the source of the second voice. The only people close enough to her to have spoken was Aves and the demur cloaked figure that now guided her through the square. Hessa's mind was still reeling from the sudden change from silent slowness to overwhelmingly loud speed. Her guide was not helping much by jostling her along as they retreated from the chaos of the square and deeper into Ellsted's heart.

Chapter Twelve: Little Comforts

Allair lead both girls back to where she had left Alequa. The elf still knelt beside Haradine's unmoving form. The healer's hands moved silently and drew arcane symbols over the girl's body. The cobalt blue glow, that always accompanied Alequa's healing, emanated from her fingers and left the symbols etched in the air between the elf and her patient.

There were still a few yards separating Allair from the elf, so she deliberately slowed her pace. She knew that she had been moving swiftly, but she had made sure not to go so fast that she left neither of the two girls behind. Her eyes darted across the scene again as they approached. The chancellor did not want to be surprised. She scanned the shadows a third time for any unwanted movement. When she was certain they were alone, Allair refocused her attention to the girls.

Both of them were out of sorts and seemed confused, although Aves seemed to be in less control of herself than Hessa was. Relief slowly took its hold on Allair's shoulders when she noticed that neither of them had any serious wounds.

"Any idea about what happened?" Alequa asked as she repositioned her daughter's unconscious body into a more comfortable one.

Allair knew that although the elf had healed Haradine's wounds, it would take a little while for the mind to recover.

Until then Haradine would be helpless and needed someone to watch over her. Allair wondered what the bond was like between her friend and her daughter. Would Haradine squirm knowing she was in her mother's care once more or would she be glad that she was in such capable hands? The pained smile that pulled at Alequa's lips answered the question for her better than any words could.

"None," Allair answered.

Although she was somewhat distracted by looking over the girls, she knew that her friend needed some time to gather herself as well. She led both girls into the light so she could better assess their wellbeing. Allair's soft brown eyes scanned Hessa again thoroughly. She paid extra attention to the burn holes in her chemise and an odd bit of sliced fabric near the girl's shoulder.

"You know as much as I do," she added somewhat snappishly. Allair spared a glance at Alequa and saw the growing look of anger etch itself into her brow so she continued a little softer, "We both saw the commotion. You reacted before I could and went to help that girl, your daughter. I ran into the square to see if there was anything I could do to help," her voice took on a conspiratorial tone as she spoke.

"And was there?" Alequa pried. Her tone quickly lowered as she all but whispered the question.

"There was," Allair agreed. Her soft whisper stretched and filled the small area they were in ominously. To Allair it seemed as if something had stretched her words to make them understandable to everyone close by. Although she hated the odd sensation, she continued her story. "I saw two shadows wreaking havoc in the square. They took turns throwing daggers at random people. I managed to put an end to it with an arrow borrowed from a street vendor, but I'm not certain if this is truly the end of it."

"Me neither," Alequa added. "Carness and I discussed our thoughts on the odd turn of events earlier this evening. This just seals it. Someone, other than Namir, is being targeted."

Then elf blinked as if she tried to clear her almost too blue eyes of smoke. When she continued, she spoke softly and looked past her friend the whole time. "Who are they?" She motioned to the two girls huddled behind Allair.

"The mayor's daughter and her maid," Allair replied easily. "I found them wandering around the scene aimlessly and somewhat confused, so I thought they might need to be looked after." Allair looked at her friend inquisitively. She quickly dismissed the questions that she wanted to ask. After all, Alequa had a lot on her mind. She may have forgotten the girls, even if she did spend a few long days on the road with them.

"I'm glad you did. I think that they might be the assassin's other targets." Alequa's reply was not easy for Allair to follow.

"Why do you think that?" She glanced at the girls as her question fell from her lips tentatively. Aside from their overly nice clothes, Allair saw nothing that separated these two girls from any of the others girls their age. There had been quite a few in the square that she easily recalled. She glanced at her friend with an imploring look as if she could coax the answers she needed from the healer with a desperate look.

"That's simple, they returned from Hornshir with Namir and my daughter. You know that I hold no faith in happenstance. These two were involved in this somehow. Otherwise, they wouldn't have been in the square. Especially since my daughter fell from the rooftops, you know that she is too sure-footed to fall. That is unless she was in a hurry." Alequa moved just enough to allow the sputtering torchlight illuminate Haradine's face.

Seeing the young, and capable, soldier lying on the cobbles drove home the seriousness of the healer's her words to Allair's mind. Allair gasped at the implications. "We need to find Namir and make sure he is ok." A new sense of urgency filled her heart and she knew her friend felt her resolution as she spoke.

"Go get him and bring him back here. I will heal these two. When I am done, I keep them all safe. At least safe enough for you to get the boy and bring him back." Alequa instructed unnecessarily. "After that, I can make no promises," the elf's tone became as ominous as her words. Allair felt the healer's fear rise a little. Somehow their very words were like cannons. Each of them struck a nerve or an emotion and forced both of them to act.

"When we come back, I will take us to my secret chambers in the council hall." Allair agreed quickly before she sped off back to the square in search of their king.

Skara looked down at the bloody mess at her feet. "Pathetic," she thought to herself as she eased past it. With a quick flick of her wrist, she easily dropped a loop pf silken rope around one of the corpse's boots. Once she was certain that the rope was secured, she quickly pulled the body into the alley behind the great hall. "Faris, you shall be missed," her catlike speech was more pronounced as she whispered her grief. Although Skara was fairly certain she was alone, she dragged the dead guard's body into the darkest shadows in case she was wrong.

With the alacrity of a gypsy thief, the nassarid deftly freed anything of personal value from her comrade's pouches. She carefully inspected the half-charred remains to make sure that there was nothing left on it to lead anyone to think that it used to be Faris. If she hadn't seen him ignite from the inside, she would never have believed that this corpse was really the Captain of Hornshir's guard.

"I will have to let Tali know of your demise as soon as I can," Skara whispered to her fallen comrade. She licked her lips absentmindedly as her thoughts turned her remaining tasks over in her mind again. "I just have a couple more errands to take care of, then I will send her the news," she promised.

Deep down Skara hoped that these last few things would give her a little consolation. Enough hope, at least, to ease her flagging spirits and put her in a better mood. That way she might be able to bear Tali's wrath a little easier.

"I hope my mistress is still awake when I'm done," she said quietly to the shadows around her as she bolted down the alley. At the end, she leapt instinctively and all but flew up the wall at the end of it.

Carness quickly surveyed the scene at a complete loss. It looked as if a major battle took place. There were small charred areas surrounding some of the shops. In the very center square was the most damage. Debris from destroyed shops and broken glass littered the area. All of this right here in the heart of his town and he did not like it one bit.

"So, let me see if I understand," the constable said as he turned to the nearest gypsy.

The man's long dark hair was well oiled and matted against his scalp by a combination of sweat and blood. Carness's wolf-like eyes easily gauged the man as a thug just from his build and the transient nature of his people.

"A girl ran around this corner," his baritone voice held the subtle edge of authority as he spoke. He gestured toward the street leading from the in as he continued, "She stumbled over something and then fell into the glassblower's booth. There she destroyed everything in the booth as she tried to get back up. In her haste to leave, she then threw the seeress onto her own display?"

"That is correct," an old gypsy said from behind the man Carness was questioning. The brute in front of him still seemed somewhat distracted by the muted chaos that surrounded them. The extra trill of the r's that the older gypsies used always made it harder for Carness to understand. The guttural tones that every gypsy spoke with did not make it any easier.

"What happened next?" Carness asked as he turned to face the old man. This gypsy had a smaller build. His long greyish-white hair was pulled back into a light queue and, as was customary for their kind, not confined by a braid. His clothes, though dirty, seemed to hint at a more noble birth than the rest of the gypsies around them.

"She died," the gypsy said with a shrug as if nothing more was needed.

Carness knew that the old man may have been a little confused and he expected no less. "The seeress died, not the girl." Carness clarified.

"Aye, the seeress died. That is what I meant." The old man scratched his head absently as if he could pull his thoughts together somehow. "Then, then I do not remember. I know there were fires, because I can see things are burnt. I know that someone must have put them out, but I cannot say who." The gypsy motioned around at the debris as he spoke.

Even through the thick accent, Carness knew he believed what he said and that was as close to the truth as this man could give. The problem Carness had with it was it matched all of the other gypsy accounts perfectly, almost verbatim.

"Thank you for your time," Carness said casually as he turned away from the witness and scrutinized the scene again.

"Looks familiar doesn't it." The deep voice resonated over Carness's left shoulder and startled him.

Carness swiftly turned to get a better look at the man that had managed to sneak up on him. Without thought, his right hand fell to the hilt of his sword and his left squeezed the haft of his club in his left hand. As soon as he saw Tipin's massive form he relaxed. How that large of a man moved so quietly was always beyond Carness, although he knew that it had come in handy on several occasions in the past.

"It does," Carness admitted to the smith. "That's what bothers me."

"Just like Watch Keep," Tipin completed the constable's unspoken words ominously. "I'm afraid we might face the same enemy."

"You may be right." Carness agreed halfheartedly. "Things have a way of coming back when deeds are left unfinished."

"That they do," the calamari nodded.

"What brings you out, a sense of morbid curiosity?" Carness probed unobtrusively. Although Tipin was a dear friend and ally, the constable needed to unravel the mystery he was given earlier. He desperately hoped that the smith was not wrapped up in the conspiracy, but he had to be certain. After all, at least one of his ex-soldiers had already been implicated.

"I have a few tasks to do before the sun comes up," Tipin replied conspiratorially. He looked around them and then continued in a much softer tone, "I believe the future of Ellsted rests on the shoulders of one of our young more literally than we thought. I aim to make sure this child is fully supported and safe." As he spoke he placed his large hand on his friend's shoulder reassuringly. "Hopefully I haven't just betrayed my cause." His steely grey eyes locked with the constable's amber stare as a subtle tension started to slip between them.

Carness shook his head slightly and smiled a wolfish grin at his friend's question. The slight tension that had weaseled its way between them started to melt as he nonchalantly turned away from the large man.

"By all means, go and do what is needed. But be fast about it, I'm not sure when things are going to get worse. I just do, as do you I fear," he hated the fact that he had doubted Tipin, but he had to be sure. After all, Alequa would not have let Tipin know the crux of their discussion if he couldn't be trusted. From what he could tell, she had filled the smith in on important details. "Let me know how I can help." He said as he stepped away from his friend.

"I will," Tipin said bluntly as he watched the constable head toward the remains of the gypsy seeress's tent. He turned and left Carness to his work and made his way back to his smithy.

Carness could not help but notice the increasing effect Tipin's hair had on his surroundings. Even without looking at the man, he knew he was leaving because of the growing darkness that seeped back into everything. The way Tipin's silvering hair distorted the light was a little unnerving, but refreshing as well. This time, however, he welcomed the effect.

Somehow the dancing light highlighted just the right areas that the torches had failed to. At the base of the fountain, Carness's amber eyes fixated on a discarded throwing dagger. "I just might have a clue about what really happened here," he muttered to himself hurriedly as he walked over and retrieved it.

Haradine looked across the table at her mother's door in silence. She waited patiently as Alequa finished her prayers. The moments stretched on as her mother's trance only deepened. Haradine started to worry.

The healer had been in her trance for two hours and showed no outward signs of ending it anytime soon. Although the older elf was renowned for the depths of her devotion, she never allowed herself to get lost like this in her meditation before.

Haradine wished she knew what was happening with Namir and the others. She was on edge ever since the attack in the square. There was something not quite right about it, but she could not fathom what it was. It was as if there had been a spell in place. Either that or a trance of some sort had been cast on her.

She recalled the roof falling away from under her feet as she ran after her liege. It was still so unsettling that she had to steady herself. Haradine placed a reassuring hand against the wall as she refocused her mind back to her current mission, collecting her mother and their things from the inn.

She shook off her concern for her liege and his friends with a quick shake of her head. After a few more silent moments, Haradine decided to see if there was anything she could do to hurry her mother's prayers along.

Her heart filled with guilt as she lifted her hand to knock on the door that separated them. A quick rap closely followed by another one. There was still no movement from the other side of the door.

Haradine knew her mother had been disappointed when she walked away from the temple. Tumere was a stern goddess that required so much from her followers. Every first daughter of her family had been called to worship at the great temple and she was the first to decline. In a way Haradine knew she had betrayed more than her mother's trust, she had turned her back on her elven lineage. That was the real reason that Alequa had never forgiven her for her choices and she knew it.

"Mother, are you ready?" Her words fell from her mouth, mouse-like and timid. Scarcely words at all. Instead, they puffed out from between lips in a staccato of brief whispers and sounds.

Silence was the only answer from the far side of the door. Another lump filled her throat when she realized she would have to know louder. She hated to do it because she knew her mother would see it as another failure. "Lack of patience is a sin," she heard her mother's voice chiding her in her mind. "Why did I have to take on so many of Aras's traits?" She asked herself tersely.

Deep down she used to revel in the fact that she was her father's daughter. Another pain erupted as she recalled her father's still form lying in Landolin's tent. She stifled her tears and said a quick prayer for him to Tumere.

"I wish I was more elven instead of whatever my father was," She said under her breath. "Maybe then I might be able to persuade my mother that the life of a soldier is one that I am better suited for."

Her mind slipped to the many swordsmanship lessons Aras had given her. Long summer days in the training yard melded into even longer evenings practicing archery or knife throwing. She readily recalled the stories he would tell her about his training when he had been younger.

"Even the best elven warriors weren't half as good as my

father was," Haradine thought wistfully. "I miss you, dad," a solitary tear crept down her cheek as her words caught in her throat.

"Mother, we should really be going. We need to leave before the innkeep, Daffer, realizes you haven't left." She did her best to sound stoic. Haradine knew her mother always seemed to respond better to those that had a firm tone. She just hoped it would work for her as well. She strained her elven hearing for any sort of response, but the only answer Alequa gave her was more silence.

Chapter Thirteen: Unearthing

Armani blew out what little flame the candle on his desk provided as he stretched. He hated himself for the betrayal he committed all those long years ago. Carefully the mayor closed his hazel eyes and carefully locked the memories of his youth away.

"These are thoughts best left to the ages," he said softly to himself. His words were like a mantra, slow and deliberate. As he spoke, Armani delicately pulled a note from his pouch. Without looking, he tossed it into the open flames of the fire-place in his room and breathed a deep sigh of relief.

"So, did the meeting not go well I take it?" The sultry voice purred from the darkness near the only window to his room.

"I didn't expect to see you again," Armani said quietly. The sound of fear in his voice was all too apparent for his taste and he hoped that his guest might take the hint and change the topic. The course sound of her tongue as it played across the unseen guest's lips let the mayor know she was not going to let the topic go.

"That should make it this feel just like last time then," Armani could almost hear her catty smile as her lips formed the words carefully. "Besides," the seductive voice from the shadows continued to purr as Skara sauntered out of the shadows toward him slowly, "I'm not here for your daughter this time."

He knew she was watching and when he felt her words hit him, her smile broadened. He knew she was in complete control of their situation. The problem was that he knew she knew it as well. He watched helplessly as she licked her lips sensuality. He felt himself shudder uncontrollably as she sashayed toward him. No matter how hard Armani fought against it, she felt the sharp burn of desire smolder behind his ribcage and in his pants.

"Either of them?" The hope in Armani's voice was almost too much for Skara.

She knew that his charade was eating him up inside, she could smell it in his pheromones. Her biggest issue was that she enjoyed watching him suffer. Humans were so adept at torturing themselves that she understood, at a young age, why they flocked to Lotevilar in droves. She did her best to hold in her laughter as she replied to him playfully.

"Two daughters? I thought you only had the one," her left eyebrow arched of its own volition and almost gave away her charade. "My dear, you have been busy since I was last here," she purred as she finally was able to touch his chest with her hands. Skara licked her lips briefly in anticipation as she raised her fingers to his face and cupped it in them tenderly. Their eyes locked momentarily as she lowered her face toward his and tasted the saltiness of lips with hers. "Mm... I've missed that." She said when they finally pulled away from each other.

"So have I," Armani admitted reluctantly. His breaths were a little more rugged than she thought they would be as he pulled her closer. The mayor's hands buried themselves in Skara's hair and she reveled in the feeling of strength he exerted over her with each tug. "Please tell me you have some time to spend with me tonight."

"I can't stay the whole night," Skara admitted, "but I do have a few hours to pass however I'd like." ." She purred in pleasure and pressed herself against him as she spoke. To accent her desire better, she arched her body with catlike grace against his harder as she leaned over his taut frame and smothered him with another impassioned kiss.

"And just how do you plan on spending it?" A glint of passion and playfulness filled his eyes as they broke away for air.

"I guess my intentions for the next few hours were not made clear enough," the felinoid kissed him again deeply. This time, as they pulled away, she shot a playful glance across the room toward his bed.

"What happened exactly?" Namir was the first to break the silence. He scanned the small room in an attempt to give someone a chance to explain it to him.

"There isn't much to explain," Aves said meekly. "I held the ruse for as long as I could. I made sure to make it seem like Hessa was with me so she could get the book you wanted her to get."

"I know that much." Namir's tone was terse. There was too much going and he knew so little about the finer details that it pulled at his conscience. "Let's fast forward to the square." He let his gaze slip from Aves to Hessa a few times before he let out an expectant sigh.

"I…I don't know," Aves said after several, too long, moments passed. She fought back tears as she spoke. "I'm sorry Namir, but I can't even remember entering the square."

"All I know," Hessa chimed in in an attempt to relieve some of her mistress's unease, "is what I already told you. The place was a mess. People staggered around as if they were lost. There were little fires burning everywhere I looked. Even the animals were either frozen in place or roaming around dazed." Hessa shook her head as if she could get more information to come out of it that way. "There was also a weird sickening feeling. It was as if," her words caught in her throat as she tried to describe it. "I felt like I was drowning, but I could breath."

Namir could tell by the pleading look in her hazel eyes that Hessa was not going to be able to give him anything better than that. "No matter then," Namir added. He hoped to change the topic to something that might be of more use, but before he did he needed to make sure that they were alone.

"Thank you for your help Allair," Namir said as he turned his attention to his best friend's mother. Her long brown hair flowed freely ass he finished stacking a series of loose pages on the desk in the far corner. He marveled briefly at how well she aged and was slightly embarrassed as his steel blue eyes met with her soft brown ones. He looked away hurriedly as he spoke, "If you and Alequa would not have happened by when you did…" Namir stammered a little as he searched for the right words. "I guess what I'm trying to say is that without you two, there would be at least one less person to help me in what I need to do."

"It was our pleasure," Allair's soft voice filled the small room easily. "Now if you don't mind, I need to take my leave. I believe that someone is waiting for me at home, so the sooner I am finished the sooner I can help him get some rest. You will all be safe here, it's my little secret and I rarely share it with others." Her last few words made Namir blush.

"You honor me with your help, as always." Namir agreed. "Like you said, no one knows of this place. This means that I can use it as long as I need to without raising any suspicions." He looked over the small group and felt a twinge of pain as his mind noted the two missing elves. "Thank you again. Please return with news of what happened as soon as you can." Namir said humbly as he bowed to the chancellor as she left. Once he was certain Allair was out of earshot, he turned to Hessa. "Did you get the book?"

"Aye," Hessa said quickly as she pulled the two tomes from her skirts. She noticed Namir's surprise and smiled. "There was a little incident, but Alequa was there to help me understand a few things."

"Please continue," Namir said in eager anticipation.

"It has been a long time Alequa," Saril's voice slide from the shadows and startled her as she made her way back toward the Gathering Place to collect her belongings. "I never thought to meet you again."

"Nor I you," Alequa's musical voice answered Saril's tenor tones easily. She felt some of her concern slip away once she realized who had addressed her. "I see you still cling to the beliefs of the God of Sweet Waters."

"Ea? Of course, He oversees us all." Saril nodded sagely as his white hair danced in the light breeze. "And you still embrace the teachings of the Ancient Ones I assume?"

"Of course," Alequa acquiesced. "Haven't you ever wondered how it happened that so many of you from Jarstil came to rest in Ellsted? Not just rest, but prosper?"

"Ea's bidding my dear," Saril answered coolly.

"You think?" She lowered her head and her voice as she continued. "It seems odd to me that the last of the yearlings to pass Jarstil's final rite of passage fled so far from home. Let alone them bringing their beliefs and doctrines with them in a way that the river folk of the Three Rivers have almost all converted." Her energetic blue eyes pierced his clouded ones. "You know the Ancients prophesied this, yet you fail to see… why do you, of all people, choose not to see?"

A part of her yearned to make him understand the truth that lay behind her belief. She knew that she could if she just took the time to lay the groundwork for him. It wouldn't be too hard, humans tended to be moldable. All she would have to do is bring him in front of her goddess once. That was all. Saril would be able to feel Her presence and understand the peace she felt every time she communed with Tayant. The only problem with her plan was the fact it was forbidden, and as such, impossible to do so.

"Because I am, and always will be a cleric of Ea." He closed his clouded eyes as sorrow clouded his face. "As you know, Ea also prophesied this…and the passing of the

Ancients. Please know I harbor no ill toward you and yours." He waited for his words to sink in before he continued. "I just miss our old talks. The debate about which belief was right as well as what limits mankind has been given." He took a deep breath as he continued, "So much has happened that now cannot be undone."

Alequa placed a comforting hand on Saril's shoulder and nodded her agreement. She looked at the aging cleric one more time before she squeezed his shoulder gently and started to walk away.

As she took her leave she whispered one last message into Saril's mind, "We both mourn the losses of the past my friend. One day I hope to have such debates with you again. Please know that Tayant has forgiven you for your part against the crown and my kind. We understand that your faith made you do things that you will forever regret. I just hope your faith sustains you in the coming war. As you know, more of the Young Ones arrive every day. They will take believers from your flock. Watch Lotevilar and Her following closely my friend. They sow their seeds in the fertile bed of Ellsted as well and they bring ruin with them."

Her soft footfalls echoed eerily in her mind as she made her way toward the inn. She knew that her daughter would worry if she entered her room and found it empty. "Some things are best left unspoken," her last words, though sent to Saril, were more for herself than their conversation. The dying lights and sounds of the festival only added to the sense of dread that pushed against her heart as her last words drifted on the breeze and into his mind.

Namir sat in silence as Hessa finished her explanation. He would not have believed the intricacy of the code she laid out if she had not insisted on demonstrating it to him. "Wow," it was the best response he could manage. He wrapped his mind in tangles around the seemingly scattered information. "So I will have to literally travel the whole world in order to find all of the books just to have a full understanding of my fate."

"It seems that way," Hessa answered comfortingly. "At least we will be there to help, so it shouldn't be too hard."

Namir appreciated Hessa's attempt to console him. He forced a soft smile to hide the panic he felt. He did not want to let them how distraught he really was. The unbearable weight of the task started to push down on his heart as they spoke and he hated how it felt.

"Besides," Aves added, "it isn't as if you wanted to stay in Ellsted for the rest of your life."

Namir's forced grin shifted into a genuine one at Aves's perfect timing. "You're right, both of you. I'm just a little overwhelmed with everything. When Haradine gets back, we should call it a night. It's late and the two of you should go home before Armani starts to worry about where you have gotten off to. Besides, I need to get a few more of these passages deciphered."

He knew they would argue with him and he braced himself for it. Just as Aves started to speak, he waved his hand and completely cut her off. "Please, for my sake, go and get some rest. We can talk more about this in the morning."

Namir allowed the awkward silence to build between them build as he poured over the two texts Hessa had provided. It didn't take long for the girls left and when they did, Namir breathed a small sigh of relief. It was the soft sound as the door latched behind them that betrayed their departure.

He hated to dismiss them, but he knew they needed to keep up appearances, especially if he was going to address the council tomorrow. After all, Aves's father was the mayor and he was a tricky man to decipher.

Even though the mayor had supported Namir's trip to Hornshir, he had a sinking feeling Armani was not going to be so willing to believe him. The idea that Namir was the heir apparent was hard enough for him to believe himself, how could he expect to convince the council it was true?

Namir's carefully pulled Zelios from under his shirt. The warmth of the metal contrasted wonderfully with the cool feel of the blue stone set within it. He closed his hand around it as he felt some of the tension ease away. Namir briefly closed his mind as he centered his thoughts and cleared away some of the painful memories that tried to flood into his mind. The soft pale blue light that emanated from the stone in response to his touch only soothed Namir even more.

"I can't believe Aras forgot to tell me about this code," Namir muttered to himself once he felt in control of himself again. "At least now I might have a way to decipher some more of the information and fill in some of the gaps."

It was not so much the sound of feet swiftly pattering down the hall toward her as it was the overwhelming sense of foreboding that forced Skara to drop down into an awkward and uncomfortable crouch. Exhilaration and fatigue battle against each other as she hovered protectively over Armani's unconscious body. The scent of his sweat overpowered her delicate sense of smell. Its primal musk caught in her nostrils and tried its best to distract her from her vigilance.

Grudgingly Skara crept silently toward Armani's window. She hated to leave him, but she needed to make sure that she had a way out. A momentary glance was all it took for her to ensure he was still safe. The content grin on his face reminded Skara of a cat that had just finished a bowl of cream, content and satisfied.

"Morcant is right. I do have too much affection for these humans." She chided herself as she pulled back the curtain enough to see through the leaded glass. Every shadow was under her scrutiny. Something had caused her unease and she wanted to know what it was. Although the window was closed, Skara focused her heightened senses in a vain attempt to determine the source of the panic she felt welling up inside her chest. "There has to be something must be happening," her thoughts only served to reaffirm her suspicions and it worried her.

"There," she thought as a subtle shift in the slight whine, caused by the trickle of air, which made its way through the closed window.

The soft noise, though not much louder than the rustle of fabric, repeated itself and confirmed its existence. Somewhere far below her, someone moved in the darkness. Although she wasn't sure who it was, Skara was positive they meant harm to either the mayor or herself. The hairs on the back of her supple neck stood at attention as she narrowed in on the slightest hint of sound.

"They are talking," Skara noted to herself in disdain. Although she strained to hear more, she was not able to make out any of their conversation. "At least I know there is more than one," the acknowledgment felt hollow to her.

Skara grabbed her armor and shimmied into it silently. Her mind filled with images of other times where she had to hurry into her protective clothing. Skara smiled and whispered a thankful prayer to Lotevilar for her past experiences as she quietly opened the window the rest of the way. She cast a furtive glance at Armani's as he slept. She worried about disturbing his rest.

After all, he had such a big day ahead of him. Soon he would even have to plan a funeral for one of his daughters. Another sidelong glance brought both peace of mind and determination. He was still sound asleep and seeing his chest rise and fall in its unhampered way eased her fears.

"Sleep well, my plaything," she whispered gently.

Skara would rather curl up next to him and feel the rhythmic motion of his body as he breathed than sneak out to kill one of the few people capable of ruining her mistress's plans, but she had no choice. Although she longed for peace and the chance to live the rest of her days with a man of her choosing, Skara knew her mistress would never allow it. Skara chastised herself for longing to crawl back into the bed with Armani and allow him to lavish more of his attention on her.

“Tali would never forgive me if she knew I forsook my responsibility to her for this dream,” Skara chided herself mentally as she pulled her green eyes away from Armani and turned to face the window.

“I will be back, I promise.” She muttered more to herself than to the mayor.

She paused as she struggled with her emotions. Skara tried to squelch the inner turmoil and turn her attention to the task at hand, but she failed. With a brisk turn, she walked away from the window and over to Armani’s desk. There was an unusual urgency to her step that mingled well with the catlike silence of her movements. She quickly pulled a piece of paper free from the stack it had been sandwiched in. With a few quick pen strokes, Skara hurriedly scratched a note to her lover and sealed it with a little kiss. She laid the note on his side table and crossed back to the window.

“I wish that I could stay longer,” she said under her breath as she slipped her leg over the window sill. Skara paused just long enough to blow the mayor one last kiss before she dropped silently into the awaiting darkness.

Haradine gently rapped on her mother’s door again and waited. Her nerves would not settle themselves as she waited. She was not sure which annoyed her worse, her unsettled nerves or the fact her mother was keeping her waiting. “I know she hasn’t slipped past me,” she reassured herself as her patience wore thinner than it already was. Another group of long moments sauntered by before the elf decided she had waited long enough.

Her fingers instinctively pulled at the underside of her belt nervously. Without much direction, she cautiously retrieved her picks from their hidden pockets inside the lining of her belt. Another quick glance around ensured her privacy.

With the ease of a burglar, Haradine deftly picked the lock on the door. Then, before anyone had a chance to get a good look at her, she quietly pushed open the door. “Thank you again for all of your lessons, dad," she whispered affectionately as she slipped her picks back into their hiding place. Her appreciation of the variety of skills her father decided to teach had become a habit, especially when she found uses for things she never thought she would need when she learned it.

Memories of her childhood flooded into Haradine's mind as she thought about her father. All of the 'secret hours', the term Aras used to refer to the time they spent together without either her mother's knowledge or approval, were filled with unusual lessons and activities. These moments were the ones she longed for as a child and when her father felt more like a dad and less like the diplomat that he was.

Haradine smiled as she thought about all of the fun skills, like how to pick locks and divert the attention of others from her actions, and activities, like fishing and hiking, that they did. "I miss you, dad," she whispered as she opened the door wider. A small tear crept down her cheek unbidden.

"Mother, are you here?" Haradine called softly as her keen half-elven eyes rapidly adjusted to the darkness of her surroundings.

She felt her trepidation increase when the soft breeze and rustling fabric of the curtain were her only response. She looked around the room frantically. The room seemed normal. Everything was where it should be, but something seemed off.

She took her time as she looked around, careful not to disturb anything. It was all here. Her mother's notes and books were neatly stacked on the table with her robes neatly draped over the back of the chair. The ceremonial candles and incenses were still nestled in the satchel on the floor beside them. Even the brush and fragrant oils the priestess used daily were in their place next to the wash basin near the window.

"Alequa...mom are you here?" Her voice held the early tremors of fear. Haradine struggled against the rising tide of dread that threatened to consume her as she strained her ears for any response. Nothing. No answer. Her heart sank as she scoured the room one more time in hope of seeing her mother meditating in an unusual place.

Haradine walked slowly over to the open window in a panic. She mouthed a silent prayer to Tayant for her mother's safety as she stretched her hand gingerly toward the curtain. The half-elf's mind filled with dark images as her fingers brushed the course fabric this inn had decided to use as a shade. Her eyes dropped to the sill as she absently moved the curtain aside. Without expecting to find anything, she scanned the glass of the pane and then let her eyes fall back and trace the wooden frame.

A slight glint of light briefly caught her eye as it reflected oddly off an odd section of wood. Haradine's head cocked to the side involuntarily as she stooped closer to the shiny spot on the wood. The sight of the small metallic hook forced her breath to catch in her throat. The black metal allowed the light to play across its dark surface and only gleamed if it was seen from just the right angle.

Haradine knew she had been lucky to even spot the thing to begin with. Her eyes lingered on the small, normal looking, hook as she moved again to inspect what it was latched onto. It took her less than a second to determine that it was hooked to the soft wood that had been added to the window sill for ornamentation. That fact it was secured in an unobtrusive way signaled Haradine that whoever placed it didn't want it to be found.

Her eyes narrowed as she did her best to figure out who it was that placed the hook in the first place. "There are a few odd markings scratched into the outside edge of its haft," Haradine said softly to herself. Knowing that she was alone did little to stop her from her verbal musings. She leaned closer to the sill as she studied it further. "It's not really scratches though. It's more like a pattern of some kind." Her hollow words floated between her and the window. She ignored them just long enough to force them into nonexistence.

"Did you find what you were looking for?" Alequa's musical voiced chimed quietly from over Haradine's shoulder and startled her.

The stern edge in her mother's voice was instantly recognizable. She squared her shoulders and slowly rose to her feet. "I have now, mother," Haradine said as she recovered her composure. The half-elf did her best to squash the defensive tone she heard in her own voice Alequa's voice took as she spoke, but she knew Alequa had heard it.

She could practically hear her mother's reprimand form in the building tension between them. She had always hated her mother's ability to catch her at a vulnerable point. The worst part was her knack for pouncing on it to keep her off guard in their conversations.

"We must go before we are found here." Haradine let the icy urgency in her voice relay the rest of her message for her.

Chapter Fourteen: Impacts

The gentle rapping on her window threatened to drive Hessa mad. Although she had opened the window several times, the soft rhythmic thud of a branch as it scrapped across the cold leaded pane proved itself to be enough to irritate her to no end.

Hessa carefully lowered her feet back into her slippers once again. She gingerly crossed the expanse of her room and was careful not to make any noise. The last thing she wanted to do was disturb either Aves or Armani with a stray noise. Her tired mind made the room seem much larger than it was.

The vertigo that gripped the edges of her consciousness did little to make the jaunt any easier. It had started to take hold the last time she tried solving the tapping problem and refused to let go. "I just need to get to the table and lite the lamp," she thought aloud to herself.

"Don't." The voice, although quiet, startled Hessa and forced her to stop mid-stride.

"Why not?" Fear strangled her voice and what she managed to say could scarcely even be considered a whisper.

"Because you won't need one," the reply echoed across the room toward her.

There was something about how direct this person was and

the otherworldly tones in his voice that Hessa recognized and she knew he wasn't about to enter into a discussion about the light. The maid ran her fingers through her tangled locks in an attempt to straighten them out as they spoke. "I wish I knew his name," she mused as she determined that she must look awful to him.

"Where do you want me to go?" Hessa asked the darkness. Her fidgety hands moved from her messy hard to her shift and pressed against it in an attempt to smooth out the wrinkles. She was certain he stood in the shadows between her and the door, so, once she was certain she looked a little more presentable, she turned to face him. Hessa hoped to at least catch a glimpse of her visitor before he dodged away.

"I will meet you in the courtyard." This time his voice came from the corner of the room near her bed.

She shot a wary glance over her left shoulder. "How does he move so fast?" Hessa thought to herself. She squinted into the darkness in the hope that by doing so she could see through it better. To her chagrin, it did not seem to work. The best she could make out, even with straining her eyes, was his ebony hair as he faded back into the shadows. That brief glimpse was enough for her though. Hessa felt her heart skip a beat with this confirmation. "He was in my room," her mind flew with the implications. "He was in my room at night and he wants to meet me!" She fought against the urge to scream in excitement as she quickly slipped on her favorite pair of slippers.

Her heart pounded harder in her chest as she realized that he had just seen her in her nightgown. Him of all people, the man she could not stop thinking about ever since he saved her life that first time in the alley. Hessa smirked at the thought of their brief conversation. "Was he embarrassed to see me in my shift?" She wondered aloud. A playful smile made its way to her lips as she absently twirled an unruly lock of hair in her fingers.

It took a few moments for the shadow walker's last words to interrupt her wistful musings, but when they did she froze.

"He wants to meet me in the courtyard. I'm such a fool!" Hessa cursed at herself under her breath.

Before she could think about what to do, her feet drew her toward the door of her room. As soon as her door was closed, she was running with catlike skill silently toward the stairs. Her feet rarely touched a step, but when they did Hessa made sure to only touch the very edge to minimize the sound her footfalls made on the stone. Only the soft rustle of her night-gown betrayed her path as she moved shade-like toward the back door.

With trembling fingers, she fumbled with the latch. Normally it was a little stiff to open, but tonight it was proving impossible and she muttered quiet obscenities to herself at its reluctance. With each creak from the house around her, she froze. The last thing she wanted was for her meeting with him to be interrupted by either Armani or Avis.

Hessa closed her eyes and focused once more on being quiet. No matter how hard she tried to be silent, everything seemed to make too much noise, especially this latch. She willed her fingers to stop shaking long enough to grip the knob on the latch tightly. With a final twist, it opened and the loud click echoed around her as it did.

Hessa took a deep breath as she waited to see if it had disturbed anyone else in the house. Once she was certain she was still the only one awake, she slowly opened the back door. The crisp night breeze brought out goose bumps along her exposed calves and arms. A slight tightness in her chest reminded her that she should have grabbed a cloak. "I'm such a fool," she thought as she hesitated a brief moment before she ventured into the awaiting darkness.

"Don't be afraid." The wind whispered his message. His words had an odd calming feeling to them and she felt her heart beat a little slower as she heard his deep baritone notes. "Come," the voice caressed her ears as the wind gently tugged at her pale gown.

Hessa's careful steps led her gradually away from the

house and toward the center of town. Her feet found the little trail that wound through the long grass of their yard and led to the little courtyard before her eyes ever did. She paid extra attention to her surroundings. After all, she couldn't afford to knock over an unexpected bucket or step on an errant yard tool.

"Not much farther," his voice sounded her as she moved and it startled her. She did her best not to jump, but the little twitch mixed with a sharp grip of wind proved enough for some of her hair to pull free of the leather thong that held it in place.

Hessa scrambled to catch it, but failed. The familiar tug of disappointment took root in her heart as she watched the leather string fly toward the street. "Dang," she said under her breath as the string melted into the darkness.

"What is wrong?" His voice startled Hessa again as it poured over her shoulder.

"Nothing," she lied as she took a half step away from where she thought he was. "It's just that I am running low on those." Hessa smiled as she turned to face him. She struggled to hide her disappointment as she glared into the eyes of the statue that stood at the outer edge of the Gazebo in the mayor's courtyard.

"Here, take mine." This time she visibly flinched as he reached around her from behind her.

His voice resonated through her body in waves. It was hard for her to resist closing her eyes and losing herself in it. Her saving grace was the black leather string he dangled in front of her face. The soft immobility it lent her was the anchor she needed to stay grounded in their moment. "I couldn't," Hessa's heart beat faster as her eyes moved from his fingers and along the muscular bicep that seemed to materialize beside her.

"Think of it as a gift." His tone sent chills down her spine. It was so deep she felt it more than heard it, but it was also soft and inviting.

Hessa slowly turned to face him. Somehow the black

leather string held by his outstretched alabaster hand moved with her, even as she backed away slightly. Her hazel eyes lingered on the string floating in front of her the whole time. It was entrancing the way it hung there in the darkness, yet separated from it. Several long moments passed before she shifted her gaze to the dark depths of his eyes.

"Why would you give me a gift?" Her words came out haltingly and her voice was scarcely louder than a whisper as she spoke.

She saw a hint of a smile crest his alabaster lips as he leaned toward her. The string remained in place as his other hand gently brushed up her shoulder and traced, almost imperceptibly, along her neck. With an uncanny ease, his fingers moved through her unruly hair and gathered it into a loose queue. That's when the string moved. It danced and twisted in the air as if to an unheard tune. Then, in one fluid motion, it was tied gently in place.

The shadow walkers face hovered inches away from hers and she felt an odd heat building between them. The involuntary flush of her cheeks forced her to close her eyes. Even with them closed, she could feel his heavy gaze on her and she enjoyed it. She wanted him to see her. A new thrilling sensation ran down her spine as she felt his warm breath play along the nape of her neck. It was an inviting difference to the cold air and she quivered slightly at its touch.

"He is so close," Hessa's lips darted along her unusually dry lips as the words rambled through her mind. Breathing in ragged puffs, she leaned closer to him. She ached for the soft feel of his touch as her lips parted expectantly.

"THINK OF IT AS A TOKEN THEN." A slight smile played across his face as his whispered words brushed her eager lips.

"A token?" Hessa's voice broke as she tried to hold her composure together. She could feel his closeness and leaned closer.

"A TOKEN." Again his breath teased her skin.

The pressure of his heavy gaze as it moved from her closed eyes to her lips and back was almost too much for her to bear. The anticipation of his kiss was almost too much. Her heart raced and she felt an odd feeling form in the pit of her stomach. "A token of what?" Hessa asked as she felt him breathe in her scent. Her lips puckered her lips slightly as she tried to close what little gap separated them.

"OF MY ESTEEM," although his words felt right, Hessa was a little confused. She felt him slowly step away and that did little to quell the yearning she had for him. "YOU ARE PROBABLY WONDERING WHY I NEEDED TO SEE YOU," he said as if there had been nothing between them. Although his voice was soft, it was burdened by a great deal of emotion.

It took Hessa a few moments to dispel the cloud of confusion that wracked her being before she managed to open her eyes. "Why didn't he kiss me?" She wondered. Her eyes darted across his features. The turmoil she saw stopped her heart for a brief moment. "Well," she stalled, "I must admit the question did occur to me. But it really wasn't the first one that came to my mind," Hessa replied as she brought her raging emotions under control. She tried to sound nonchalant, but she doubted her own success at it.

"I NEEDED TO SEE YOU. I HAD TO GIVE YOU THIS," His words were forced and the odd pause between his sentences confirmed her suspicions that there was more about him than she imagined. Something troubled him deeply and she wished she knew what it was.

Her eyes lingered on his face for a few seconds after he spoke as she searched for more clues to his erratic behavior. The smooth sway of the parchment in his hand drew her gaze from his face and down to his hands. "What, a piece of paper? You came to me, in the night, to give me a piece of paper?" She scoffed. The rawness she felt inside hurt her more than anything she had experienced so far. "Couldn't that have waited until the morning?" She struggled against the swell of feelings that threatened to rip free from her control.

"Maybe so, but if you knew what was written on it, you wouldn't want me to wait," his words hung between them palpably and lent his voice an ominous tone.

"Wh…what is it?" Hessa blinked rapidly. "I mean what does it say?"

"It's not what it says, as much as what it represents," his raspy voice added extra weight to his words as he continued. "It represents your freedom and promises to give you many of the answers you have been searching for." She knew that he paused to wait for the puzzled look on her face to fade before he continued. When it didn't he added, "This piece of paper is your mother's will." The shadow walker held the parchment in front of her expectantly. As her fingers closed around the ivory page, the shadows gathered around him and swallowed him into their darkness.

Haradine threw her mother's pack down on the dusty bed in the overly cramped room. Angry little clouds of dust and dirt immediately leapt into the air around them in response. She was unsure how her mother knew about this abandoned house and, currently, she didn't care.

"Don't worry, I will be safe enough." The healer said as she saw the lines of fear etched themselves across her daughter's delicate features. "Go on back to our sa'ouvant and help him understand your father's texts," Alequa almost begged her daughter to leave. "Besides, I have friends on their way. They know where I am and should be arriving soon," she added hopefully.

"No," Haradine's resolution was complete and her tone conveyed it perfectly.

She crossed the room with a few small strides and took her mother's hands in hers. "I have already lost one parent; I refuse to lose another. Not through negligence at least, especially not while I have the chance to keep you safe." She leveled an icy blue stare at her mother. Haradine knew deep down her mother understood the veiled threat it contained, she just hoped her mom wouldn't force her to carry it out.

"But," Alequa started, but was cut off by another stern look.

"If our liege cannot understand the importance of my duty to you, then I don't care to protect him." Haradine saw the scared look in her settle in mother's eyes, so she quickly continued her thought. Her steady hands gently pressed against her mother's shoulders as she spoke, "I know Namir won't be cross. He is a compassionate ruler. I've seen the leniency he has already given to both myself and others when he didn't need to. Although it his compassion may prove to be his undoing, I'm certain he will shine through the loyalty he earns through his actions. Now, please rest and let me make sure you stay safe."

"How long are you planning on babysitting an old lady?" Alequa's words were barbed and Haradine understood why. After all, she had just shown her mother she was more than capable of taking care of herself and others.

"At least until the first of your guests arrive," her words were soft, yet held enough harshness that she knew her mother would not question her resolve. "After that, I'm not sure. It really depends on how much time passes between then and now."

Alequa nodded at her daughter's wise words. "Very well, at least let me make you a cup of tea. The wait may prove a bit longer than you'd like," the soft singsong nature of the healer's voice calmed Haradine down enough to relax her guard a fraction.

Skara spied on the two of them from the roof of the mayor's gazebo. She eyed the parchment her prey held close to her bosom and followed the shadow walker's movements with her other senses.

"He is a hard one to keep track of," Skara thought to herself darkly. "Very clever to give her something to track her with," she was amazed by the level of strategy that the devanargari possessed. She believed shadow walkers were the mindless slaves of their masters, the incarnations of the old Gods.

To the nassarid's knowledge, they were only able to carry out simple tasks and great bloodshed. However, this one shook her whole image of them. "Something seems different about him," she mused as she watched him offer the girl a leather ribbon.

Skara studied the two of them for a few moments longer. Something deep inside her warned her to be ready. He could attack her at any moment and she knew it, so she wanted to make sure she would be ready. One of the few things she could never forget about this shadow walker was his speed. The few times she fought him, that one recurring attribute of his made it impossible to beat him. The felinoid knew she needed to skew their next encounter in her favor before it even started and Skara had the answer, magic.

Skara silently slid three throwing knives from her belt and intoned the spell to imbue them with the same ethereal flames she had placed on the dagger Faris had unwittingly succumbed to. Her thoughts melded into the spell and for a few moments, everything around her blended into one fine thread of reality. All of her senses were filled with the scent of steel and the heat of the flame. Her eyes flew open as the spell's final words fell from her lips. Black, lightless, flames danced momentarily along the edges of her vision and mirrored their movements along the sharp edges of her knives.

All of the colors drained from the world leaving everything coated in an odd blue and black hue. Images swam in and out of focus as her overloaded senses tried to make sense of her surroundings. She understood the blue hue of magic, but the blackness was new and she had to force herself not to concentrate on it. Three deep breaths were all it took for Skara to regain enough control over her senses to see her target standing alone in the courtyard below her.

Her connection to everything shifted subtly as she raised her first dagger. One quick glance let her gauge the distance and her instincts took over. Without hesitation, her arm coiled across her chest. She crouch shifted to allow her to use her whole body for the throw. Skara knew what the outcome was going to be. She could feel the black flames erupting in her target's body and smell the acrid irony sulfur smell of the body as it gets consumed by the infernal flames of her Goddess.

"That will not do," the shadow walker's voice cocooned her in its commanding reverberations. "Skara, do not make me kill you," his words froze her blood and her muscles.

A little finger of panic spread through the recesses of her mind as Skara realized she was paralyzed. She could not move. Even if she had wanted to, which she did, none of her extremities would respond. The only part of her she could control was her voice and even that was muffled by her half closed, motionless, mouth.

"How do you know my name?" It took all of her strength to form those six words and for a moment they seemed to be the only words that mattered.

"Your name is but a fraction of my knowledge about you, but none of that is your concern right now," he said dismissively. "I need you to know, not just understand, that that girl, Hessa, is under my protection. Any further attempts to kill, or injure her, will be met with death. Your mistress knows this and still she disobeys my simple command." His words hung between them as Skara felt a sense of hopelessness start to settle into the back of her mind. "I have given her a few chances now, but she still sends her minions in to test me. Should I be lenient?" Skara knew he no longer spoke to her, but it didn't make any of his words less impactful.

A brief moment of fear clouded her thoughts and she thought he might have forgotten about her in his musings. She had never heard any shadow walker rant like he was and the otherworldly sound to his voice was entrancing and oddly irritating at the same time. She forced her eyes to move. Skara knew she needed to find an escape path, that is, if she could ever get her muscles to respond. Her glowing green eyes stopped as she locked gazes with his depthless black stare.

"No, I think she needs a reminder," his eyes narrowed into thin black slits that contrasted severely against his alabaster skin. In the darkness that surrounded them, his skin shone eerily. "The pathetic spell you placed on those daggers of yours will be as effective against me as the pebbles you are standing on," as if to add emphasis to his words he reached toward the darkened blade of the dagger she held in her relaxed hand. Her anxiety increased with each moment as his hand loomed closer and closer to hers. "These knives are useless to you. Your spell disintegrates them and only you can safely use them without dying. Well you, and anyone immune to such trivial magics."

Dust slowly fell away from the center of the blade she held poised in front of her. It grew thinner with each second. To her surprise, as the breeze shifted, Skara could actually see the metal dissolving before her. The disintegrating blade brought with it a crude sense of disbelief. "How is he doing this," her brain fired off the question even though she dared not voice it. Helplessly, her slitted eyes absorbed the scene in front of her. No matter how hard Skara tired, she couldn't force her eyes to move from the single dagger.

In just a few seconds, only the handle of the knife remained and even that felt a little smaller and lighter to the nassarid. She knew he watched her and even though she could only see him out of the corner of her eyes, she knew he had a sly grin plastered on his smug face. His words replayed themselves over and over again in her head when she could finally turn it. "How is he controlling me?' Skara wondered to herself. She purposefully leveled a defiant stare at him, but made sure not to meet his gaze directly.

His sly grin twisted itself before her eyes to a cruel one as his fingers touched her chest. A tendril of pain broke out instantly. An impossible coldness spread from where his fingers lightly pressed against her armor. Ice crystals formed between her fur and the tight leather armor she wore to protect herself. They chafed against her skin bitterly as he leaned his face closer to hers. Skara saw a slight ice blue sheen play over his depthless ebony eyes as the foggy tendrils of his breath escaped his mouth.

"Do you understand my message for your mistress?" His words left icy tracks along the soft thin fur that coated her cheeks.

She knew he sensed her understanding, Skara just hoped he would stop before her heart stopped from the frozen feeling that now coursed through her veins. Skara nodded her understanding as quickly as she could. She also focused her will to open her hands in the universal signal of surrender. As her fingers slowly opened the hilts of all three knives slipped from them and landed by her feet. The clatter of metal on stone punctuated their interaction perfectly.

"Good, then I will let you live. For now," his message sent a chill down her spine.

The realization she that was still frozen, helplessly locked in a throwing position only added to the depthless fear she felt. All of her weapons were shattered, or out of reach, and she knew that she was completely unable to defend herself against him if he decided to do anything to her.

Skara's eyes widened as she saw him literally meld into the shadows and vanish right in front of her. A few moments later she regained control over her body again. By then, both the shadow walker and the maid were gone. She rubbed her sore muscles and stared at the gazebo where her target had been as the sun started to crest the horizon.

Chapter Fifteen: Relic

Armani woke up in a pool of his own sweat. Disorientation set it instantly and he fought desperately to keep the vertigo that threatened to consume his consciousness at bay. He hated this feeling and lately it had been happening every time he saw that feline witch. His biggest problem was that always looked forward to their encounters.

"You are a sick man, mister mayor," he muttered to himself under his breath. His throat was dry and sore.

It took a few more deep breaths and silent curses before Armani was certain that he was in full control of his body. The floor was oddly hard and real feeling to his bare toes and somehow, that was comforting. He slowly stood, stretched and then made his way to the wash basin in the far corner of his room.

He poured some fresh cold water into the basin and splashed a few handfuls onto his face vigorously. The soothing sensation as the icy water wicked the heat from his skin was just what he needed to force him into complete command of his senses.

Armani slowly walked over to his dressing area and pulled down the curtain from the full-length mirror that he covered it with. Some of the old habits he learned as a child still haunted him. He shook his head at the stupidity of his mother's customs. "I wish I had known my father," Armani's words were only a brief whisper.

The welts and scratches from his last nocturnal encounter brought him back from the thoughts of his past. His hazel eyes traced the puffy red lines that arced across his chest and upper arms. "Fortunately I have to wear my robes of office today," Armani mused as he traced a particularly long gouge across his chest with his fingers.

A slight rapping at his door pulled him quickly back to the present. "State your business it's early," Armani called. He quickly pulled on a dressing gown to hide the souvenirs Skara gave him to remember their time together.

"Father, it's me." Armani could hear the break in her voice and it pained him. "Hessa's gone."

He paused momentarily and took stock of the state his room. He heard his daughter open the door as he assessed where everything was. The only thing that seemed out of place was a letter sitting on his desk. "Come in my dear," he called over his shoulder as he stepped back behind the divider of his dressing area. He hurriedly crossed his room and pocketed it as Aves's footsteps betrayed her arrival.

He turned to face his daughter, careful not to let his dressing gown open enough to reveal Skara's claw marks. "What do you mean that she is gone?" Armani did his best to hide the real reason for his concern from her. "Skara had better not have had anything to do with this," he thought to himself. Dread gripped his heart as he hung on his daughter's next words.

"Her bed doesn't look to have been slept in…and there was a note," Aves said timidly with heavy tears threatening to pull loose from her hazel eyes. Armani could tell by the tremor in her voice she had been crying. "I woke up. I went to her room. She wasn't there. Her bed was perfectly made." Aves paused again to get her emotions back under control, "And then…then I found the note on her dresser. I know she left it there for me, but it doesn't make any sense."

"Now…now, my darling," Armani tried to soothe her fears the best he could. "Go back to your room and I will be there once I make myself presentable," he instructed. Armani could barely contain his eagerness to read Skara's note in light of this. "I promise I won't be long." The crispness of the paper felt good under the weight of his fingers.

"Ok," Aves said obediently. "Please be fast, I am worried for her."

Gienna eyed the entrance to the kitchen again. "There isn't another delivery scheduled for a few more hours." She muttered more to herself than to her brother.

"I know," Landolin replied caustically. "We have gathered what we can from the other places last night. All that is left is the secret passage that you mentioned before."

He hated that his sister was right about this and not just because she was his sister. It meant that he was lied to by the very people that he had risked both his life and the lives of his men defending. Landolin motioned for both of his men that had accompanied them to circle back around to the front of the monastery. They knew that they needed to report if a large group was approaching so that they had a chance to smuggle themselves in unnoticed. Otherwise, they would have to wait for the delivery and enter in through the kitchens.

"All we can do now, brother, is wait." Gienna's words punctuated Landolin's thoughts perfectly.

"Let's just make sure that we are ready when the time comes then." He replied grudgingly. "Somehow this faith is behind the murder of my men and I promise on their very souls that I will not rest until I find out why," Landolin vowed to himself silently as he watched the sun rise a little higher over the towering spires of Hornshir.

Namir paced around his new room in a vain attempt to stay warm. He muttered to himself as his mind swam with the new found knowledge he had managed to glean from Aras's journals and notes. He crossed the hard packed floor of the old holding cell in the basement of the Council Hall for the hundredth time since he awoke a few hours earlier. His breath caught hung in the air in front of him. He paused momentarily to fight the growing desire to shirk this new, unwanted, responsibility and leave his new found destiny behind. "I never wanted this," he reminded himself as if his thoughts could erase the all of the truths he learned in these last few months.

Namir sighed deeply as a thin beam of sunlight darted through the heavy curtains that covered the dingy windows behind him. Another chill ran through him as a few loose snowflakes drifted onto his face from a few of the more neglected rooftops.

The weathered pages seemed to move by themselves and he found himself looking over them for what seemed like hundredth time. Namir felt his initial shock wash over him again as he read the line from Aras's personal journal. "…and although none can say who the queen's tryst had been with, many believe her lover was a renowned fighter from the southern deserts…" Namir read it aloud again in disbelief.

Namir mentally mulled over the many stories he had heard told by the various travelers in the Gathering Place when he was younger. All of the war stories that he had heard about from the Great War and before that spoke of the greatest fighter ever were about the Calanari warrior Halin was named after. "Could that have been my father?" He asked no one in particular.

"Who?" Haradine asked from the doorway behind him.

Namir could tell she knew he had missed her company by the playful smile that tugged at the corner of her lips. It was her entrances that he missed the most. Just when he thought he was alone, she would make a poignant comment. He already felt some of his tension seep free from his shoulders as he turned to face her.

Namir allowed a look of disdain to briefly cloud his features. After all, he can't let her know exactly how much he had missed her. His thoughts quickly turned back to the revelation he just made and he decided to mull it over a few more times before he answered her question. "Who do you think of, when I say a fighter of renown from the southern deserts?" Namir asked. He knew she hated it when he answered a question with a question, but it was a game that he enjoyed.

"I'm not sure," Haradine replied somewhat perplexed.

The confusion that played across her face conveyed to Namir that her stymied response was caused form more than just his question. Her soft and delicate features contorted themselves as she thought his question over. The mix between his question and his scrutiny forced her to writhe uncomfortably and he absorbed every little fidgety move with his steel blue eyes.

Although Namir usually found it fairly easy to read a person from their expressions, she was a challenge, especially now. Somehow Haradine became harder to read the farther she went from her comfort zone.

"I mean…I know that I heard my father talk about the southern deserts. There was this one time when he thought I couldn't hear him, he mentioned a few fights and some names." Her words held a depth of feeling Namir had not heard from her. It was as if this fleeting memory of her father was the most real thing that she had ever experienced. His heart sank a little as she continued, "But that was ages ago. I'm sorry sa'ouvant, I cannot remember who that would have been." Her brows furrowed as she met Namir's expectant gaze with her clear blue eyes.

Namir sighed deeply, "It's alright. I didn't mean to interrogate you. I was probably just jumping to conclusions." He turned away from Haradine as he his words escaped his lips. The last thing he wanted to let her see was how frustrated he was at all of this. He had been making such excellent headway, and now this. "Maybe I'm wrong," he muttered quietly to himself.

"What happened to you last night?" He asked. The obvious attempt to change the topic of their conversation was apparent to both of them and Namir knew it, he just didn't care. It would take more effort than he cared to expend get them away from his thoughts any other way.

"I was delayed longer than I expected by my mother." Fatigue dogged her words and she shot sidelong looks at the bed in the corner of the room. "My mother has far too many things for one woman to really need," she admitted to her liege. "But we had little choice. She had to leave the Gathering Place before your uncle sobered up enough to know she was still there. Thankfully my mother knew of a little abandoned house deep in the forest." She rubbed her temples wearily as she leveled a determined stare at Namir.

"I know there are a few people living in this that had served in the wars," Haradine shifted the topic back to her liege's question. Before Namir could object she offered, in a more comforting tone, "One of the veterans might be able to answer your question more objectively than I can."

A subtle hint of dread haunted her eyes as she spoke and Namir could tell it was because of him. He knew she hated seeing him beat himself up over deciphering her father's tomes, but he had to internalize as much of the information as he could. A nagging suspicion had taken residence in his mind. One that insisted he would soon have to leave most of them behind.

"That is a great idea," Namir eventually responded somewhat lackadaisically. He ran his fingers through his golden as he assessed the room around him. Once he was certain they were alone, he slowly walked over to Haradine and said, "The better part is that I know just who to ask." The heavy sound of his cloak dragging across the back of the chair beside them accented his words dramatically. "Are you ready to go back out?" He said as he let the warm fabric settle onto his shoulders evenly.

"Who are we going to see?" Haradine replied. He could hear the aggravating confidence build up behind her words.

Her tell when she thought she knew what was going to say.

"Carness," Namir replied as he ushered her out and carefully closed the door behind them as the left.

"The constable?" Haradine asked a little confused.

"Aye, the constable. Why is that surprising?" Namir replied a little abrupt. Her confusion about his choice of veterans bothered him. He unconsciously lengthened his stride as if to get to his destination before she had a chance to change his mind about who he should be talking with.

"I just figured that you would consult either Saril or your uncle." She added quickly as she struggled to keep pace with her liege.

Now it was his turn to be surprised. "Why would I ask either of them over the commander of Watch Keep?" He slowed his pace and paused long enough to allow her to catch up to explain her reasoning. The shadows flew across her haggard face brought a contemplative smile to his lips. "I wonder what she was really doing last night to make her so worn out today," he mused to himself. Her breath was a little more ragged than he could recall ever seeing it, but there was a lingering smile on her face.

"Because, according to my father, Daffer was stationed in the same division as the fighters from the southern deserts and Saril was not only your mentor, but he was a healer during the wars. My mother says he has a real good memory about the goings on he witnessed back then." She shrugged as her words bubbled out and then flashed a coy smile at Namir as she continued, "So I figured if anyone had a chance of knowing who you were curious about, it would be one of them." Haradine's smugness was apparent and completely inappropriate and Namir knew that she could do little to contain it.

The problem was that her suggestion made sense, a lot more than his choice had and she made a good case for it. "Hmmm…good reasons," Namir said as he led Haradine down the street toward Carness's house. "But Carness is the best fighter I have ever met and he served in the war with both of our fathers. So we will go see him first. Namir's matter of fact tone surprised even himself. "What am I saying?" Namir wondered briefly, "I'm not even sure who my father is." Astonishment about how his words seemed normal settled in as he continued, "If he doesn't know, we can visit Saril. I want to avoid my uncle if I can."

Aves stared at the note. It still made no sense to her. "Why would Hessa leave like this?" She wondered aloud as she reread the note for the fourth time. There was something odd about it. Aside from the fact Hessa actually left it and was gone, there was a style to it that Aves had never witnessed from her maid. Hessa was warm and loving. Her hazel eyes flew along the page again as she tugged at a strand of her auburn hair absently. This note was cold, both to the touch and to her heart. The words were dispassionate and distant, almost as if Hessa left it to drive a wedge between them.

"So, she is gone then?" Armani's crisp voice startled his daughter and she almost let the piece of paper fall from the fingers as she turned and faced him.

"Yes," Aves replied as she did her best to hold back her tears. "I just can't understand it."

"She is her mother's daughter." Armani offered as if it was explanation enough for Hessa's departure and the fact that she had only left a note as an explanation

"What do you mean by that?" Aves asked after a few moments had passed. She knew that her father could tell that his answer bothered her and, for once, she could not care less.

"Her mother was the same way," Armani whispered as if he was afraid that their conversation would be overheard. "She was always going off to who knows where for days on end in pursuit of one errand or another."

"Do you have any idea where she went?" Aves asked. She had to find Hessa and her father's behavior about her friend's departure only added to her curiosity.

"I never asked." Armani lied. The matter of fact tone in

his voice betrayed none of the emotions that played across his face as he spoke.

"You never asked?" Aves replied incredulously.

"No," Armani said quietly, "it never occurred to me." He replied as he walked over to Aves and gave her a reassuring hug. "You have to understand. Although I loved her, I loved your mother's memory more. I gave her the space she needed because I needed the distance too." A pained look crossed his face as his words cascaded from his lips.

Aves clung to her father's sleeve as she listened. The soft baritone of his voice washed over her and soothed her raw emotions as they spoke. Somehow his vague answers and reluctant comments gave her the strength she needed to come to terms with what was going on. Aves slowly pulled herself away from the safety she always felt in his arms and sat up.

Tears still rimmed her eyelids and she felt their warm grittiness against her eyes as she asked, "Did Hessa's mother ever tell you about the places she went?"

"Natlia, her name was Natlia." His words were soft and the look in his hazel eyes exuded compassion.

Aves felt his hands, as Armani placed them gently on her shoulders, and enjoyed the loving squeeze he gave her. Deep down she knew he was trying to spare her from the pain he felt every time they spoke of either her mother or Hessa's. Just as she knew that every time she spoke about the secretive little errands she did for Namir, he worried. Aves just hoped that she could help ease her father's mind more.

"You know, even to this day, I can still feel the shadow of resentment for the man who asked Natlia to do the little tasks that stripped her of her life." His white hair cascaded over his face as he kissed the top of his daughter's head. "Even when she shared the horrific stories about the many places she went to and the adventures she had, all I could feel was shame and unease. She loved him, you know. The man that sent her ominous notes in the middle of the night," his voice cracked a little and Aves could sense the pain he felt seep out of his very being.

"I think that was the hardest part. The woman I turned to, the one that I loved, was in love another. It's so much more than a hunch, you see. Her eyes would light up anytime she mentioned him, or that manor house in Hornshir they used as a meeting place before they left for some unthinkable journey." Armani's tone deepened and his emotions ripped the edges of his words making them gravelly and hard.

"From what I could determine this other man, this friend of hers, owned it. Or at least that's how she made it seem." A distant, more haunted look, seeped into his hazel eyes and Aves could tell that he struggled with his thoughts and emotions.

She saw a small tear trek along the edge of his cheek and race for his jaw. The distance that she heard in his voice only mirrored his struggled and it hurt her to know how much her father suffered even after all these years. Abruptly, Armani dropped his hand to hers and raised it to his lips. His actions were stilted and she knew he could tell she was worried about him. His lips pressed softly against her hand for a few moments before he let it go.

"A manor?" Aves asked as she stepped a little bit away from her father. "In Hornshir? Are you sure?" She was stunned and she knew her feelings clung to her expression.

"Yes. And from what she described, it was glorious," Armani replied. There was a hint of surprised that laced his words as he continued, "She described it as having a large stone wall that completely surrounded it with a huge gate manned by an elven sentry…"

"The manor itself was made from the same grey stone as the wall that surrounded it," Aves completed her father's sentence perfectly.

"Exactly," Armani failed to keep his surprise in check as he added, "did you get a chance to see it then?"

"You might say that," Aves shot her father a quick smile as she added, "we stayed there."

"You stayed there?" Armani's voice became heavy with dread and concern as his words spilled out haltingly, "Was its owner there while you were?"

"I don't think so," Aves replied as she walked over to her favorite chair. She mulled over her father's question as she replayed her stay at the manor in her mind's eye. A soft breeze blew through the window behind her and tugged at a stray lock of hair that had pulled itself free from her braids. "I don't remember anyone saying that the manor was theirs. Do you know the owner's name?"

"Aras," Armani answered succinctly as he took the chair across from her.

Aves felt her blood drain from her face as she heard her father's answer. "Did you say Aras?" Her voice quivered as she forced the words out of her mouth.

"Yes," Armani replied. "I take it that he was there?"

"No. I never met him, but Namir did." She struggled to regain some of her lost composure. "I think I should let Namir know that Aras owned the manor."

"Doesn't he already know?" Armani asked somewhat confused. "Isn't that where the two of them met?"

"No, they met at an elven camp a few leagues south of Hornshir," Aves said as she rose to her feet and started to look around the room for her jacket.

"They met where?" Armani's demeanor conveyed his growing confusion better than his words did.

"An elven camp just south of Hornshir," Aves said once more as she donned her jacket and left the room.

Chapter Sixteen: Crisis

Faris crawled out from under the bush he slept in and brushed the soot and dirt off of his tattered trousers. "I hate having to do that," he muttered under his breath as he removed the ring from his index finger and held it up to the light. He turned it until the tiny amber crystals caught the light and started to glow. About half of them had lost their luster and seemed to be fading in color. "I only have a few more uses before it's completely used up," he continued as he let his irritation at his situation consume him.

He took a few minutes to get his bearings and then he set off toward Ellsted. "Hopefully my men will have been released by now and I can meet up with them on the way back into town," he thought bitterly as he purposefully lengthened his stride. "Then I can see about settling my score with Carness," the last thought brought a cruel smile to Faris's face and seemed to lighten his step.

Carness looked at Namir and marveled at the boy's directness. The boy he knew would never have been this brazen and he liked the change. "I really don't know where most of my men were from," he answered after a few moments of deliberation. "Even if I did, I probably would have forgotten by now." Namir's confusion was obvious by the way his eyebrows furrowed and created dark shadows over his normally bright eyes in spite of the early morning light. "My job was to defend the keep. I had to know what each soldier under my command was good at. How they best fit into my overall plans. Where they came from played a trivial part of things in the grand scheme of things. In order to perform our duty, we were forced to put our rivalries aside. Those that couldn't, were sent back to other commands. The luxury of speaking with my men for prolonged periods was something that I avoided. If I hoped to send my men off to die, I had to maintain a certain level of distance." His explanation sounded hollow, even to himself and Carness hated.

"Isn't there a need to know everything about each soldier in order to know how best to use them?" Namir asked incredulously.

"No. In fact, most commanders will tell you the same thing. You want to know as little as possible about the personal lives of your troops. All that a general needs to know for strategy is each soldier's strengths, their unit's strengths, and their division's strengths. You can predict a man's weaknesses based on his strengths." The obstinate look Namir had set on his face let Carness know that most of his words were not making it through to him.

The constable stretched to loosen the kinks that had formed in his back during his investigation. With a wolfish gleam in his amber eyes, Carness decided to change tactics. "If you spend too much time getting to know everything about each soldier, you lose your objectivity. Deaths of strangers placed in harm's way by my command already weigh heavily upon my conscious. If I knew each of them, I'd be tempted to send the ones I cared for to safer places, even if their skills were needed more in the dangerous ones. More people would die because of it." Carness locked gazes with Namir as if he could force the child to understand what he tried to say.

"It just doesn't seem right," Namir said again, mostly under his breath. Carness knew the youth hadn't really meant to direct it to either Haradine or himself. "I know you must be right, I just hoped you would know more about this one particular person." The frantic tinge to Namir's voice let Carness know how much the boy wanted the answer. He just wished he could give it to him.

"I wish that I knew more," Carness shared heavy heartedly. "Let me see if any of the other survivors knew of him. It is going to take a little time, though." The constable offered. He quickly ran through his growing list of things as he tried to decide how best to squeeze Namir's request into it.

"That's fine, I'm going to ask them myself," Namir shared. "It is too important to let it rest and I'm not sure how much time I can really spare." There was a resolution in Namir's voice that surprised Carness.

Carness nodded his understanding and he marveled at how far this youth had come in the last few months. The idea of Namir as king sat better with Carness and his reply flowed quicker than he had expected it to, "I will still see what I can find out for you. Some of my men will respond better to me than they will you. Even if you were to tell them that you are their rightful king, they won't feel right talking about one of their own to an outsider."

"Thank you," Carness felt Namir's appreciation in his tone as he spoke. "How is the investigation into the fires going?" Namir added as he deftly shifted the topic away from his original request.

"Nowhere," Carness confided. "It seems like magic was involved. Some spell was cast on the square. No one can seem to remember what they were doing before everything exploded. I can't even get two people to agree on who they think was the target."

"Could it have been either Aves or Hessa," Haradine asked. Carness could tell that she carefully picked her words. She seemed extra careful so Namir would not get too upset by the answer.

"Possibly," Carness nodded, "I'm not sure that the motive

would be, but I'm not willing to rule anyone out just yet. I wish I could find Faris and question him." He looked over the two children in front of him as he continued, "You mentioned that you saw Faris hiding near the fountain, right?" Haradine nodded her agreement after he saw Namir shoot her an approving glance. "I need to get him in for questioning. Although Armani thinks he can protect him, I know how to get that traitor to talk." Caress muttered darkly.

"I'll keep my eyes open for him and let you know if I find him," Namir offered. "Now, you said the council is meeting later for an emergency session. Is it because of the attack last night?"

Carness watched the little movements Namir made as he spoke. The boy was smooth and Carness was even more impressed. He nodded his agreement and waited to see what response he received before he decided on the best way to advise the would be king.

Namir nodded in unison with the constable for a few moments. The look of deep thought seemed at home on the youthful face and his grey eyes scanned their surroundings. Hesitantly, as if he spent his words like gold, Namir added, "I see. Then I'll need to approach them before they decide what to do about it. They will need to know what changes need to be made in order to ensure Ellsted's survival." The boy's words were stark and laden with dangerous underpinnings.

"I won't put a wall around Ellsted," Carness felt his pupils harden as he locked his wolf-like stare onto Namir. "We are not Hornshir. We don't have the guards or the money to hire them. There has to be a better way. Walls breed corruption and worse." His brain twisted around Namir's unspoken threat as he held the boy in his deadly gaze. He knew his amber eyes could convey the seriousness he felt better than his iron tone ever could.

"Neither do I, my friend," Namir said solemnly as he placed his hand reassuringly on Carness's shoulder, "but I really can't see any other way. If you can think of one, please let me know, otherwise, we will have to discuss it in front of the council. Maybe more minds working on it can come up with a better plan."

Carness was not happy with this solution and he knew Namir was well aware of it. The problem is that the boy was right. "I have to admit that your reasoning is sound. I just wish it wasn't. Then we might have other options to explore." The pained sound of defeat did not sit well in Carness's deep voice, but he could not stop it no matter how hard he tried.

"Who do you recommend that I ask about the southern warrior?" Namir asked as he stood and gathered his cloak. "From the references Aras left in his journals, he is my real father and I want to learn as much as I can about him."

"Based on the description you gave me, I would ask Tipin," Carness advised as he helped Haradine into her cloak. "He knew almost all the folk from the southern desert."

Alequa looked at the glowing orb in her lap and visions of the future slipped in through the edges of her mind. The blue mists clouding the secrets of events yet to come slowly parted and the image focused slowly in front of her third eye. "What an odd term," Alequa heard her thoughts tumble around in her mind as the image struggled to appear. "I know why they use it, but they should come up with a better one," she mused briefly before she banished the thoughts entirely.

The odd sensation of seeing the image with her mind as clearly as she saw with her eyes pulled at the center of her forehead. An odd tingling played across the soft skin and she willed the haze to lift. Abruptly the image of two men locked in deadly combat leapt out at her. Although her window into the vision was small, she could tell that neither would yield. The pool of light that they fought in swam and moved away from their faces.

However, she could clearly see one of the men was clad in all black cloth and held a sword shaped like something from a nightmare. The wicked looking blade was as black as the shadows that surrounded them and moved like water. Nothing solid could hope to slide through the air in such an effortless way. The fighter's steel blue eyes reflected the passion he fought with.

The other man was bathed in a halo of light. It took Alequa a few moments to realize that the pool of light she saw them fighting in was created by this warrior. His white clothes and blond hair reminded Alequa of the angels she had seen in Tayant's temples.

From what she could tell, he was as pure as he looked. However, his sword, though longer, was as deadly looking as the dark one his opponent wielded. Its jagged blade looked sinister and it somehow reflected light cast by its wielder into the darkness like a dagger. With each shift more of the blackness shredding into messy pools of light and dark.

The cold trickle of sweat as it beaded along her brow helped her to bring the rest of the image into a crisper focus. Her mind studied and dissected the image until the liquid blue mist finally fell away. Alequa had hoped that the image would get larger as it sharpened, unfortunately, it did not. Instead, she had a better view of the area they fought each other in.

After another barrage of attacks, the two men circled one another in ever-shifting loops. As they stepped farther away from one another, the walls defined themselves for her.

The priestess's eyes widened as she saw the stone walls of the temple. They fought in a circular ring defined by a circle of marble set into the stone floor, half black and half white. Stands of spectators completely encircled them. The seats were completely filled with guests of all races and each one held the engraved image of a dragon in their hands. One white, the other black.

The crowd sat motionless and watched in complete silence. The only sound that dared to disturb the solemn silence was the sound of combat. Steel against steel, flesh against stone.

"The Arena of Fate," she muttered to herself as the mists flooded back in and washed away the image. The paradox of time and prophecy was not lost on her. If viewed too much, the thread of the future could unravel. Likewise, Alequa understood the problem with self-fulfilment. If she wants something viewed to happen enough, she would always search for a way to see it through.

She was spent. The rigors of scrying so far ahead frayed the edges of her thoughts and undermined her desire to live. She tried to shrug off the indifference as she recomposed herself. The priestess remembered she had guests and fought to maintain a level of control. The elf wiped her brow as she placed the crystal sphere back on the table. Slowly she stood and stretched before she motioned to her guests that she was ready to speak with them again.

"Did you find the information you were hoping to?" The question hung in the air and mingled with the dim light of the little room.

This lady sat across from Alequa and patiently watched her. What little skin was visible from beneath her gowns and veils was dark, almost pure black. Her darkness was beautifully offset by her almost glowing crystalline blue eyes. Although she had an otherworldly quality and smooth skin, Alequa could tell that she was older than most of the elves she had ever known.

The emasculate gowns she wore only added to her sense of ancientness. The priestess marveled at how the light red sheen of her visitor's gown caught what little light there was in the room and trapped it within its gossamer folds.

"Maybe," Alequa responded quietly. She felt drained and wished she was alone instead of being forced to deal with her guests. Although she loved both ladies dearly, she desperately needed time to recover and mourn. Too much had happened in such a short time.

"What did you see?" Another other girl asked as she set her glass of tea gently on the table next to the sphere. Her voice held an air of authority and her tone implied that she was used to getting whatever she asked for immediately.

This lady was the only other person in the room with Alequa and her dark-skinned friend. The priestess somehow sensed that this lady had planned it so that just the three of them would be privy to the scrying. Like her compatriot, this lady's eyes were crystalline as well. However, they seemed to glow with a violet hue instead of the blue Alequa had grown accustomed to.

Long dark locks cascaded around her and framed her pale features. The contrast made her look younger than she was and far too inquisitive. The illusion of agelessness was completed by her overly smooth skin. Although this lady was pale, her skin had a subtle honey tone to it that made her appear more exotic and desirable.

"I saw a battle and a world divided." Alequa saw the confused looks play across her visitors' faces, so she continued, "There were two generals and they were locked in single combat. One fought from the shadows and the other was bathed in pure light. It was the prophecy fulfilled." Her words came haltingly as she mentally scrambled to gather the fleeting scraps of memory that held the images on them. Alequa felt her frustration rise as some of her vision faded from her mind.

"Prophecy, which prophecy?" The older lady asked. Her blue eyes locked with Alequa's as her words fell icily from her lips.

"They were dragons, one of light and one of dark." Alequa heard both of the ladies gasp as they heard her words. Alequa let the suspense build a little more before she continued thoughtfully. "As you know, the prophecy is about the time of judgment. It speaks about the time when the Old Gods deliver their verdict upon the world. When they take those they hold dear and depart leaving this realm, or what is left of it in the hands of the new regime." She felt the tension crescendo as she spoke and stared at each lady in turn. "Have either of you heard the prophecy before?"

"I…I've heard of it," the younger one said as she cast her violet eyes at the other lady.

The older one shook her head as she responded, "No. I have heard the elders speak of it and the sermons from upon high, but the words themselves have been guarded."

Alequa nodded in agreement as the ladies words pooled between them. In a conspiratorial tone she added, "The Old Gods made sure the masses were protected from the words of prophecy. They are powerful and can cause strange and unexpected things to happen in the world if proper caution isn't taken first." She leaned back in her chair as she planned her next words carefully. "I believe it is time that you heard them. But I fear I cannot show them to you like they normally would be shared, I don't have the strength for it."

Her apology felt weak in her mind, but she needed to instill upon her guests the true weight of the words she was about to share. Alequa waited until each of them nodded their understanding. Then she slowly stood up. Without a word, she crossed the room and latched the door. Before she turned to walk back to her chair, she marked Tayant's sigil on it with a piece of chalk she pulled from one of the hidden folds in her dress. Once she was finished, she made her way back to the others.

"What I'm about to say you do not share. Never speak of it outside these walls. Not even an utterance. Even the smallest bit, spoken aloud, can crack the foundations of the world and unravel the skein of time." Her words hung heavily in the air as she motioned for the two ladies to stand and take her hand. Once she was satisfied that they were in the correct places she lowered her head and spoke the prophecy.

"Two dragons born of this world will fight.
One of dark and one of light.
Twins in both, birth and might.
Should the one prevail, then the world shall unite.
If it is the other, then the Gods shall smite."

Everything around them shifted and warped as the words fell from her mouth. Time seemed to crawl to a stop. The crystal Alequa had used to see the future developed a blood red glow. The overall effect was eerie and otherworldly. Within moments the effect ended and all three of the ladies stared at each other in wonder and confusion.

Since she had braced herself for the effect, Alequa was the first to recover. Her mind fixated on the effect, the slowness of time. It was the same feeling that both Aves and Hessa had admitted to feeling in the square. Something was amiss and Alequa hated the sinking feeling that took residence in her stomach.

Her blue eyes flicked between her guests as she pooled her strength. "The disorientation will pass," Her musical voice carried her words reassuringly. "Until then, please stay seated so that you don't fall." She left them and walked into the kitchen. She had planned for something to happen, not this, but something. The priestess quickly filled three cups with tea and set them onto a silver platter. Deftly she grabbed a small handful of the dense biscuits she baked before they arrived.

"There was something strange about my vision though. They fought in the Arena of Fate instead of somewhere in Cennicus...and they battled each other alone." Her words echoed along the adjoining hallway. "It doesn't make sense. The Arena of Fate is used by the Gods to determine the fate of the lands of the living. Armies amass to fight, not individuals. The Gods use these armies as pawns in the ever-shifting game.

"Did you see anything else?" The younger one asked completely enthralled by Alequa's recounting.

"Not really," Alequa admitted somewhat ashamed. "It took everything I had to even get this much."

"Not really?" The older lady asked as she arched her eyebrow inquisitively. "Normally you would say no, not really implies more. What else did you see?"

"Nothing. I saw nothing else. It was more of a feeling than anything." Alequa shared. "Things seemed obscured. No matter how clear they seemed, something was wrong. Almost as if things were not exactly as I saw it." She tried to explain, but knew her words were so inadequate that her companions were left with more questions than answers.

"Please say more," the younger one said.

It was obvious to Alequa that the girl was still enraptured by the prophecy. A deep sigh did little to clear her mind of the anxiety she felt brewing in its depths. The elf's voice, though authoritative, held a little tremor in it as she continued, "I'm sure one of the combatants is our sa'ouvant, Namir. But to be honest, I couldn't tell if he was the one wrapped in darkness or bathed in light."

The older lady was the first to take the slight pause as an invitation to speak. "You know, in symbols, darkness and shadows portray the vileness of life. Everything that lurks in the embrace of night waits for one thing, the chance to kill you." The power hidden in her words was only enhanced by the somber feeling that had settled in the room. "Light, especially pure light, represents goodness and the true Gods. We can only hope that Namir was the one on the light. Otherwise, we are on a fool's quest indeed."

D'barei was a symbolist. Alequa quickly recalled her first meeting with her in Tayant's Temple in the trees. D'barei was called to help unravel a vision that she had as an acolyte. Back then this old lady was never known to be wrong. This time, though, her words seemed off. Like there was something amiss about the whole situation. Nothing seemed to fit and that was what worried Alequa more than her vision had.

"The one bathed in light scared me," Alequa said after she had a chance to sip at her tea. "He was cruel, not kind. There was a feeling he exuded. It's hard to describe. It was as though he was indifferent to the needs of the world. As if he wanted to kill everything and everyone. The other one was more passionate. The man cloaked in darkness fought with a zeal for the living and I could feel his spark. It was exhilarating and real. His movement belayed a need. I could tell that for him there was something to fight for, something to gain. The white dragon, because they really were, you know, dragons, fought to win. Not because there was a reason other than being the victor." She did her best to keep her feelings in check as her words only added to the strained heaviness of reality that surrounded them.

"Be that as it may," D'barei said. A knowing smile pulled at her upper lips and turned it into a cruel looking sneer. "Ours is not to outguess the Gods. Your feelings of what you saw, though important, do not outweigh the interpretation of the symbols. We, my brethren and I, agreed to support this child because you assured us that he was the white dragon. If he isn't, then we can no longer help." The way her crystalline blue eyes studied Alequa unnerved the elf a little as the weight of her words landed on her chest. "So, the real question is what is next?"

Alequa knew that the older lady studied her every twitch and movement as they both waited for a response. "Next we need to travel. I'm not sure how far and who will be going, I just know that Ellsted is no longer safe," Alequa confided. Her eyes danced between them as she made her plans aloud, "Namir will have to believe it was his decision to go and that might be more challenging than I anticipated."

The priestess refocused her eyes on her visitors again as she lifted one of the dense biscuits to her lips. The satisfying crunch as it crumbled against her teeth helped her gather her thoughts. It also helped conceal the pause she needed to choose her next words carefully before she continued.

"Sori," Alequa locked gazes with the younger of her guests, "I need you to ready your ship. How soon do you think it will take before you can set sail?"

"That depends," she asked. Alequa ignored the inquisitive stare. She knew that Sori wanted to get more information by the way the young lady's violet eyes probed hers. "How long of a voyage will it be?"

"I am not sure." Alequa admitted, "But I promise to let you

know as soon as I do."

"Is it mostly along the shore, or will we need to be out to sea for a bit?" Sori's posture betrayed nothing and this irritated Alequa. She was used to reading people and this woman was practically impossible. "I see," she replied thoughtfully. "If we are to be along the shore I can be ready in two days, I would just need time to ready and replenish my crew. If we are going out to sea, I would need a week. The longest my ship can last away from a port, or land is a month. Anything longer and I'll need to get a larger ship."

"Very well, let's plan to meet you in a week then. It will take me at least that long to reach Hornshir with those that will need to travel." Alequa turned to D'barei as she continued, "And you, D'barei? How long will it take you to be prepared for the same type of voyage?"

D'barei was taken a little off guard by Alequa's question. "Are you going to need both ships?" She asked incredulously.

"We may. I am unclear about how many will be travelling, but I know we will need to sail to Freeport at least." Alequa clarified. "Your ship may not be as large as Sori's, but I hope it is still capable of an ocean voyage."

A thoughtful frown creased D'barei's lips as she replied, "I can be ready in a few days, but a week would be better. So if you need a week, I can promise to have the necessary arrangements made by then."

"Good," Alequa said somewhat relieved. She felt the invisible beads of sweat start to form as she held their communication together. "I will see both of you in a week then. May peace and safety travel with you until we meet again," Alequa prayed as she watched the two ship captains fade into the gathering gloom that had overtaken the room she sat in. A few moments later, Alequa found herself alone in her little house and she was glad for it.

Chapter Seventeen: Plights

Tipin opened the gate to his smithy as he saw the two of them walk up. Although they were almost two blocks away, Tipin was certain they headed toward him. The way Namir walked let him know that the boy was intent on something. What he wanted, Tipin was uncertain of, but he knew the boy was going to demand some answers about things.

The rag felt soft in his hand as he lifted the frying pan he finished a few hours before. He kept an eye on Haradine and Namir as he carefully polished the bottom of the pan. When his guests were a few paces away he said, "Allair is at the council hall readying the schedule for the day. My apprentices are gathering coal for the forge. And this is the last piece of cookware for the old gypsy's order. So I can spare a few moments for you two, if needed." The bass of his voice reverberated around them. Carefully he placed the polished pan in a small stack of other cookware he had made. There was no need to make his new apprentices struggle to fulfill the order. In a few more moments the smith jotted down made a quick list of things for his apprentices to do after he had left the smithy. A smile tugged at the old calanari's lips as he realized he was well ahead of schedule for the day. The rest of the tasks he could easily leave for his new journeyman and his three apprentices.

"How can I be of service," Tipin said to Namir as the youth and his guard stepped into the smithy.

The smirk that played across Namir's face as he approached Tipin eased a little of the smith's tension. Somehow Namir could always make Tipin feel a little better about things. Although the boy had a pleasant demeanor, Tipin could tell that he waited until they were closer before he responded. Without comment, Tipin took a few steps back and half turned toward the passage to his courtyard. He understood Namir's desire to reduce the prying eyes and ears constantly surrounding them.

"I have a few questions that only you might know the answer to, that is if you have a few moments." Namir all but whispered.

"I can always make time for you, my friend," Tipin replied smoothly. He knew Namir had not been taught all of their secret phrases, but Tipin hoped he might have stumbled upon a few. Unfortunately, that hope seemed fruitless. "There is much to teach the young sa'ouvant still." Tipin thought to himself as he motioned for his guests to follow him deeper into the smithy.

"Well for starters, how is the smithy's business faring with your sons away in Hornshir?" Haradine chimed in. Her soft voice carried through the smithy's main room better than she had anticipated.

Tipin smiled at the seemingly innocent question. "This one knows a little about the subtle art of distraction," Tipin thought as he crossed over toward the door to his inner courtyard. "Better than I had hoped," the jovial tone betrayed none of the worries for the coming winter and his missing sons. "We are about a week ahead of schedule, which is rare for this time of year." The hushed tones that the smith used to loudly whisper the last part of his message added to the lighthearted feel of their meeting.

"That's good," Namir commented as they passed through the smithy slowly. "I told you he was an industrious man."

Namir said to Haradine in a brash attempt to stay included in the conversation.

Once they were inside Tipin's courtyard, Namir let out a long sigh. "I need to know more about my father," Namir stated carefully. Before he could continue, Tipin cut him off with a quick hand gesture and a glare. "So I was hoping that you might be willing to tell me one of your old stories, like you did when I was younger." Namir finished awkwardly.

"Of course I can, young master," Tipin said easily. He was relieved by Namir's quick thinking. "Let's retreat to my study so we can get a little more comfortable and find some inspiration among my souvenirs. You know, my wife, Allair, makes the best tea in all of the Three Rivers Shire. Would you two care for a glass while we reminisce?" Tipin directed the last bit at Haradine, like any good host should.

"Sounds great," Haradine said gleefully. Tipin could not help but smile as he saw her face light up. "I really love tea. I can hardly wait to taste it."

The smith's smile widened at the girl's enthusiasm. His grin lasted the whole way through the various twists and turns through his unusually cluttered courtyard. The slightly heady aroma of the flowers Allair cultivated met their noises instantly. Although it wasn't pungent, it was strong. Tipin recalled the conversations his wife and him had about them. She won few arguments, of course, but he felt the need to bring it up now and again.

The giant lead them easily through the adjoining great room and up a set of stairs. The stairs were narrowly built and did not seem wide enough to accommodate his girth, but somehow they did. Light struck his silvery hair from a variety of small stained glass windows. The colors they cast mingled with the reflected silvery light from his mane and bathed the walls around them in wavering colors as the three of them ascended the stairs in solitude.

The higher they ascended, the deeper the silence became. By the time they made it to the large room at the end of the stairs, it was obvious Namir could not handle it any longer. He fidgeted incessantly with his amulet. His tone was uneven as he said, "Are we able to speak about my father yet?"

"Aye, sa'ouvant, we can," Tipin remarked quietly as he walked over to the chair at the desk against the window.

He paused for a moment and opened a small drawer that blended into the molding so well it was almost invisible. Carefully, he reached into it and lifted out a small amethyst sphere. With a gentle motion, he slowly lifted the crystal into the light. An amber fire danced inside the orb as the light played along the gem's violet surface. He knew that neither of the youths had ever seen anything like it before by the way their blue eyes were transfixed by it.

"What is that?" Haradine asked. Her eyes tracked the motion as Tipin lowered it into a small wooden stand on his desk.

"Protection," Tipin said as he closed the drawer he removed the gem from. Once he was certain that the orb was secured, he settled into his desk chair and motioned for them to do the same in the remaining two chairs in the room.

"It was a gift from your father," Tipin said to Haradine. "He left it for me when he went to search for more items of power. You know, like the one Namir can't keep his hands off of." He motioned toward the chain Namir worked through his hands worriedly. "Your father, Aras, told me to use it to prevent scrying and unwanted visitors when we need to discuss the real business of the realm."

"I didn't know you knew my father," Haradine said. Tipin found it amusing that his good friend's daughter had no idea that they knew each other. "Did he come here often, my father I mean?" Her question held an odd edge to it.

Although the smith was not as sensitive as the elves were, he could tell how much of a shock her father's visits to Ellsted were by the look on her face. He had no idea why Alequa and Aras would have kept their visits to this small town a secret from their own daughter. No matter their reason, Tipin felt she deserved to know as much of the truth that he could safely share.

"He did," Tipin said thoughtfully. "He was a great man, but I am sure you know that much already." The tears that tugged at the corners of her eyes let Tipin know he needed to continue. There was little sense in forcing the girl to endure any more pain than she already had. "Some wounds are best left to heal on their own," he whispered to himself sagely.

Without any explanation, the hulking man turned his gaze to their young ruler. "Now that I am certain we're safe from prying eyes and ears, how can I be of service my liege?" Tipin bowed his head as he spoke and cast his eyes down to the floor in front of him.

"Please rise," Namir said. Just by the tone of his voice, Tipin knew he was uncomfortable with the shift in power.

"You have to get used to displays like mine," Tipin offered as he raised his eyes back to look at Namir's face.

"I know," Namir replied. The slightly haunted look in the boy's steel blue eyes let Tipin know how uneasy he still was. In an obvious attempt to change the topic, Namir cleared his throat and added, "The reason I came to talk to you has nothing to do with my claim to the throne. I have found some references in Aras's notes about my father and I hoped you might be able to help," Namir offered as a way of explanation. "The only real description Aras offered in his encoded scribbles is that my father was a well know warrior of some sort from the southern deserts."

Tipin let Namir's words hang between the three of them for a few moments. He knew Namir waited for a reaction from him, he just had no idea which one to give. If he let Namir know the truth, all of their lives would be in peril. Yet he hated to keep any secrets from his king. Before he realized what he was doing, Tipin bowed his head again and whispered a prayer to Tumere for guidance.

"Before we discuss that, or anything else, I need to say something." Tipin leveled his famous stare at Namir and chuckled to himself as the youth squirmed a little under the pressure of his gaze. "The two of you will be staying here, in this room, until you decide to leave Ellsted." He waived off their attempts to interrupt him as he continued, "It's far too dangerous for you to stay at the council hall, or anywhere else. I've made sure that my house is the safest place in the entire village." Tipin waited until both Namir and Haradine both nodded their understanding and acceptance. Once they did, Tipin smiled and added, "With that settled, I want to let you know that I think I know who your father really is Namir."

"You what?" Namir asked. The incredulous ring to his words proved impossible to disguise. "How long have you known?"

Tipin felt Namir's steely blue gaze harden as the two of them stared at each other. The smith knew this look well and understood that Namir wouldn't settle for anything less than the truth. "I just managed to piece it together," Tipin lied. "Based on what you told me, and the conversations Aras and I have had in the past, I believe your father is Halin."

"As in the missing child?" Haradine asked a little confused by the giant's statement.

"No," Tipin chuckled a little nervously, "My son was named after the great Calanari hero, Halin. Although he was a half-breed, he was an unrivaled fighter. By some accounts, he was the greatest warrior that ever walked the face of Cennicus," Tipin continued with a mirthful look. It was the only way he could think of to hide the real meaning of his words.

"Your son is the missing sa'trandon?" Haradine asked. The concern in her voice was evident.

"Aye," Tipin replied, "Don't worry about him though. My goddess has assured me that he will be with us again soon enough. The worried look that Namir and Haradine shared was not lost on Tipin. He knew what sort of reaction they expected and laughter was definitely not it.

"It is good to know we are so close to finding your son,"

Namir interjected to help break the uncomfortable silence that threatened to settle in. "As for my father, is there any way we can prove your theory?" Namir held his breath as he waited for Tipin's response.

"Aye, there is." I believe Aras found one of Halin's, the great hero and not my son's, journals." Tipin stroked his short beard as he spoke. "From what I recall, your father hid it somewhere safe. I think he may have even hidden it in his manor in Hornshir, but I am not positive." Tipin took a breath and gazed out the window as if he were lost in thought. He wanted to make sure to word his next statement correctly. There were certain things that he needed to have proved and he hoped Haradine's answer would help him find what he needed. "I guess the deed to that manor was willed to Alequa and you, now that Aras has passed," Tipin watched Haradine closely so that he could see her reaction.

Namir nodded at Haradine and then looked directly at the smith. "He actually left the manor to me," Namir stated without batting an eye. "It was one thing Alequa insisted upon. I tried to give her the deed, but she refused. She said something about a king needing a safe place to hide and strategize if needed." There was a hint of puzzlement in Namir's voice that confirmed Tipin's suspicions and his smiled deepened when he heard it.

"That place would serve adequately in that capacity," Tipin nodded his approval of the idea. He waited for Namir to address the unasked question that had loomed over them for most of their conversation.

"So, that means that I must go back to Hornshir, again, to find out more about my father," Namir said more to himself than to anyone. The disappointment in his voice was evident as was the slight irony about his situation.

"Before you do that," Tipin interceded, since it was becoming apparent Namir was not going to bring up the topic, "you must the council. You have to let them know about who you really are. Whether you want it or not, you have an obligation to ensure the safety of this village and part of that obligation is to inform the council about what you have in mind for Ellsted. This should be your first responsibility. Finding out more about your father will come with time, but regaining the throne and doing right by its denizens must always come first."

Namir thought over Tipin's words carefully as he visibly digested their meaning. "I know there is logic in that. When do you think I would be able to get an audience?" His question came as he stood and stretched.

"You should be able to get one later today, that way we don't waste too much time. The sooner you can address the issues, the better received it will be." Tipin said sagely.

"I see," Namir responded. He motioned Haradine over and discussed something under his breath. Although Tipin was used to listening in on conversations, he found that they spoke a little too quietly for even his keen hearing to make out their words.

Once their brief discussion was over, Namir nodded at Tipin and said, "Then let's make it happen. The sooner my duties in Ellsted are done, the sooner I can return to Hornshir and decide what my next steps need to be in order to regain my throne." The level of conviction in Namir's voice sent an exciting chill down Tipin's spine and the smith knew things were about to change.

What little heat the winter son could muster soaked into the fabric of her cloak as Hessa stood in front of a little trail that wound its way up to mother's house. From what she could see through the thick overgrowth, the house was fairly small. Although it was quite a bit bigger than what she had imagined, she was still startled by the variety of vegetation and the overall feelings it generated. She slowly made her way down the path and took special care to note each type of plant. With every step, her mental listing of the plants grew. The girl was careful as she made her way along the overgrown path. She wanted to make sure she did as little damage as possible as she made her way toward the door.

She somehow felt as if she intruded on something sacred. Deep down a part of her believed that her mere presence tarnished the sanctity of this place and her mother's memory. No matter how hard she tried, Hessa was unable to reconcile her feelings with the knowledge she was now the owner of everything she saw.

The crisp air felt good as it entered her lungs. Although it was cold, it was refreshing. The scents of the woods mingled nicely with those of the surrounding flowers and created a heady, yet relaxing, aroma. Another deep breath gave Hessa the motivation she needed.

A large, overgrown, hedge had grown across the path and made it unpassable. Although she was unwilling to leave the narrow path, she needed to get by it or stay on the trail indefinitely. The girl's thoughts ticked through her options as she wondered exactly how her mother managed to tend to this garden before she died. After all, it wasn't like her mother lived in the house while she worked for Armani. Travelling between the two houses would take up all of her time.

Hessa's eyes lingered on the hedge as she forced her mind back to the task at hand. From her vantage point, she could tell the hedge was filled with blue and purple berries that she had never seen before. Painfully she tore her eyes from the bush and carefully made her way around it. Little delicate steps ensured she didn't do much damage to the variety of plants that grew all around the hedge's base. "I need to trim this one back," she mused aloud to herself as she looked at its massive shape. "Or, I could make another path around it. That might be easier." She noted as her eyes scanned across the ground from the bush's base to the larger surrounding vegetation.

She let her eyes absently move up along the lush foliage to the leaves of one of the larger bushes that lined the trail and her jaw dropped. The canopy of branches and leaves intertwined with thick brambles and fronds from the hedges and trees around her made Hessa feel small.

The vegetation created a massive natural tunnel that lined the path and kept it dry. Her eyes flew along the gorgeous pathway and marveled at the fact there was not a single break in the plants all the way to the cottage's door. An amazing variety of flowering plants and bushes met her gaze and filled the air with a plethora of scents. Her eyes traced the walls of this natural tunnel from its base up to its top. The massive branches all but blotted out the sun and lent a mystical quality to the trail.

"Impressive isn't it." His tone was even and deep.

Hessa spun around instantly as her look shifted from amazement to shock as she realized who had snuck up on her. "Yes it is," she agreed as she let herself relax a little.

"I thought I would find you here." Although his intention remained hidden, Hessa felt reassured by his tone.

"And why are you looking for me?" She replied coyly.

"Because, I need help with something and you are the only one that can assist me with it," A slight smile played across his alabaster lips as if he found her attempts at innocence humorous. "We must find the gift your mother left you. It is somewhere in the house and we have little time before the nassarids that have been watching the house realize that you've come. The last time they searched for it, they were held in check by Skara. Unfortunately, the witch is busy in Ellsted and there is nothing to stop them from destroying your house in their haste to find their prize."

"What do you mean? Nassarids…like Morcant? They were here?" Hessa asked. She was genuinely intrigued, and mortified, by the shadow walker's response.

"Your mother left an artifact here. It was given to her by an avatar of the Gods. She hid it in this house, for safe keeping. She also hid instructions on how to find it. This gift is powerful enough to help stem the tide of darkness set to take over Cennicus. Without it, our chances of surviving are slim." His deep voice echoed ominously off of their surroundings and Hessa felt a chill run up her spine.

Confusion threatened to take over her mind and Hessa knew the shadow walker could see it plainly on her face. "An artifact of the Gods? An avatar gave my mother an artifact made by the Gods?" Hessa's mind reeled as questions flooded into her head. After she managed to collect herself a little, she asked, "Why should I help and let you have it. If it was given to my mother, shouldn't I keep it for myself?" Her mind latched onto the only set of questions that seemed to make any sense to her.

"Those are good questions," he nodded in appreciation as he responded, "and the answers to both are simple. Your mother and I helped Aras find artifacts left behind by the Old Gods when they last visited Cennicus. We kept them safe with the intention that they never fell into the wrong hands. The one I am looking for here, at her house, is the one she was entrusted with safeguarding." He paused for a moment, as if he chose his next words carefully, before he continued, "Your mother was given a journal, one of two made by the hand of Reus himself."

"Wait, Reus made the journal? Isn't he an Ancient, one of the creators of the Old Gods?" Hessa's mind spun when she saw the shadow walker nod. "Who gave her the journal then? The Ancients and the Old Gods have long been absent from Cennicus. How can these things even exist?" Her brain hurt from all of the questions that threatened to consume her. She tried to keep track of his answers, but she knew that she had already started to forget some of it.

Deracai took a shallow breath and turned to face her squarely. "I can only tell you the man was the avatar of Faesin and he trusted your mother very much. Indeed, he had to in order for her to receive the second journal of the set. You see, there were two journals crafted a single blank page removed from the Tome of Destiny itself." He watched her wince as the weight of each word as it hit her.

"But why am I the only one that can help you find it?" Hessa interrupted him quickly. She was afraid that if she waited to ask, she would forget to altogether.

"Only the one given the artifact, and their direct descendants, are able to see the book and understand its purpose. Likewise, if anyone else opens the journal, they will only see blank pages. The very blood that flows through your veins allows you to see and use this gift of the Gods," he said calmly.

Somehow Hessa knew he was telling her the truth, but he expected her to accept all of this too quickly. "And what should I call you? If I'm going to trust my mother's gift to you, I need to know your name at least." As she spoke, Hessa realized precisely how little she knew about her protector.

"My name is Deracai. Now, our time here is limited. Please understand I want to tell you more, and I will. That is, when we are not as rushed as we are right now. Once we find this gift and we have retreated to some place that is safe I will tell you everything I can about your mother." His words flowed as if he knew what she was going to ask even before she did and Hessa hated it.

"Do you promise?" She asked as innocently as she could manage. "Do you promise to answer all of my questions?"

He cocked his head as if he wondered about why she would ask this simple question. It was obvious that Deracai had not anticipated it and that made Hessa smile. She hoped to bind him into an agreement. She just hoped he wouldn't realize it because of their current circumstances.

A quick smile flashed across his handsome features as he replied, "I promise." He extended his hand and waited for her to clasp it and seal their impromptu pact.

Hessa wasted no time. She eagerly took his hand in hers and quickly shook it. Before she could react, Deracai deftly lifted her hand to his lips as he bowed. Blood flooded into her cheeks as she felt his warm lips press gently against her knuckles. Images of her mother curtsying as men greeted her this way flooded into her mind and Hessa followed suit without thinking. Flustered, her hazel eyes darted from his hands to his dark eyes and said, "I appreciate all you have done for me. I hope you know that."

"I do," Deracai's soft and warm response only made Hessa's blush deepen.

"Can I ask one more thing of you then?" Hessa asked. She was well aware that he still held her hand although he no longer bowed. "Will you stay with me as protection until I can find the journal for you?"

His smile broadened as she spoke. "I will stay with you as long as I can, but I do have other tasks I need to perform as well. If need my help, I will know and I will come," he nodded his approval of her terms. Once she nodded her agreement as well, he continued, "Good, now I must go. One of those other tasks begs for my attention," he said as he faded into the dwindling shadows of the garden.

Hessa watched as the center of the shadow visibly darkened before her eyes. She stared in amazement as his body seemed to melt into the shadows and vanish. The last thing that faded was his hand. Even after he was gone, Hessa could feel the soft touch of his hand on hers.

"It seems like you may need my help after all." Faris's voice cut through Skara's thoughts like a finely honed knife.

"You're still alive?" Skara said. She turned around slowly, not sure of what she would see when she did. She was pleased to see that Faris was not only alive but looked just like he had before he picked up her enchanted dagger. "I could have sworn I saw you die, burnt from the inside."

"I am a bit harder to kill than that. It takes a little more than a blood-fire spell to end me." Faris said slyly. "From what my men have reported, not only was the girl allowed to live, so was the boy. I am sure that Tali is none too happy about this turn of events." Skara felt Faris's scrutinizing gaze follow her gestures and knew that he was trying to read her body language as he continued, "What did she say when you told her that our ambush failed?"

"Nothing," Skara said as she looked away from him. She attempted to make it look like she simply scanned their surroundings instead of avoiding his gaze. She now understood the emotions Morcant had struggled with not that long ago outside of the inn in Hornshir.

"You haven't told her, have you?" Faris grinned at her audacity. "Do you really think Tali isn't going find out the girl is still alive?" He asked incredulously.

"I know she will. I'm not a complete idiot," Skara retorted. She struggled to keep her emotions in check as she replied, "I just want to offset the bad report with a good one, which means we have one more chance to redeem ourselves before we face her wrath." Skara pressed. She knew that she hated to feel her mistress's wrath and Skara was certainly not going to face it alone.

"What do you mean we?" Faris asked somewhat confused. "The last time I checked you were the one in charge, not me. Tali won't hold me at fault for your failed attempts." He sneered.

Skara laughed hysterically at Faris's reply. "Either you are naive or you really don't understand how Tali rewards her people for failure." Skara calmly paced a circle around Faris ominously as she spoke, "It's a good thing you're hard to kill. You will have the opportunity to embrace every agonizing moment of her displeasure. You see, Tali is not known for either her leniency or her mercy. What she is known for is her success when others have failed and disciplining those in her command that fail her." Skara smiled inwardly as she heard

Faris swallow hard. “Besides, do you seriously believe I would take the blame when I have an obvious scapegoat?”

“You wouldn’t dare!” Faris shot back in response to her veiled threat.

“Wouldn’t I?” Faris visibly cringed at the tone that took over Skara’s voice and seeing it made her smile wickedly.

“Then what choice do I really have?” Faris spat acidicly. “What do you intend to do and how can I help?”

The cold wind pierced the thick wool of his heavy cloak as Nurn plowed through the almost hip deep snow. He forced himself to keep up with Jerine’s almost impossible gate, but the deep drifts he plowed through pulled at him harder than he thought it would. It forced him to move a lot slower than he cared for and this just added to his frustration. Every time Nurn glanced at Jerine he was amazed by the ease the elf pranced across the cold white surface without disturbing even the tiniest of flakes. Much to Nurn’s appreciation, Jerine chose to continue the search even though the near blizzard-like conditions threatened to obscure the world from view and had done so for the last hour at least.

“Over there,” Jerine motioned to their right as he spoke.

Nurn followed Jerine’s signal and turned toward a clearing on the other side of a copse of trees. Nurn nodded his response and fought his way through the snow. Nurn had been tunneling through knee deep, and sometimes hip deep, snow all morning and his cold muscles burned as he exerted himself further. He noticed that there was very little snow under the trees and breathed a small sigh of relief. He needed to get his feet out of the cold or he might lose his toes.

“I think there is something of interest over here if we can just continue a bit further,” Jerine said when Nurn was in earshot.

Nurn felt the elf watch him intently as he shambled into the cover of the trees. Nurn approved of the elf’s actions as he brushed off the majority of the snow from his cloak before he entered the center of the shelter.

"I think we need to wait a little while for your clothes and boots to dry. Help me get a fire started," Jerine did not wait for a response, instead, he quickly started to gather bits of needles and tinder from around them. As he did, the elf made sure Nurn understood that he expected him to do the same.

Chapter Eighteen: Escapes

Hessa listened intently to the soft creaks of the house as the wind blew outside. She rummaged through a trunk in, what she believed to be, her mother's bedroom. She laid out each piece of fabric and every article of clothing carefully on the floor around her in little piles. Although she searched for the journal Deracai had asked her to find, she also needed to catalogue the artifacts from her mother's past. Might as well take care of both tasks at once she had reasoned.

There was an uneasy feeling that had settled in the back of her head. The subtle feeling of being watched by someone she could not see. Her ears already strained to hear anything that might be out of place, the problem was she had no idea what to listen for.

With each creak of the eaves or the floorboards, her mind imagined a nassarid walking around in a room below her, or worse yet, in one of the rooms beside her. No matter how hard she tried, Hessa could not shake the unsettling feeling.

She paused as she lightly placed another bundle of white linen into a pile she had created to her left. Her ears probed the recesses of the room one more time before she dared to take another breath. Nothing…no unusual sounds or telling noises…no hint of the imagined clicks of claws against wood to betray their presence…not even the subtle drop in temperature that would hint of Deracai's presence.

She scanned the immediate shadows around her. Hessa's hazel eyes darted furtively from shadow to shadow and then into every corner. She did her best to tamp down the first pangs of fear as she searched. "I am the owner of this house," she said as forcefully as she could. "I forbid anything within its walls to bring me harm." She felt a little foolish at her outburst, but she felt better for doing it. "At least I'm me," she thought as she mulled over the fact that she simply had no idea of what else to do.

A slight breeze blew through the open window behind her and played with the piles of fabric surrounding her. Hessa ran the back of her hand across her forehead and took stock of her progress. Of the five large trunks lining the wall furthest from the door, four of them stood empty. Their contents splayed our along the floor in front of them in neat little stacks. The soothing calmness that relief brings swept of her and her breathing became a little easier. "At least I found the real cause of the noises," she thought aloud to herself as she eyed the slightly drifting piles of cloth the wind had displaced.

The small laugh was irresistible as she continued to rummage through the contents of the fifth large trunk. "Wind," the word fell from her lips completely coated in the mirth and sarcasm. "At least I'll be able to focus on finding the journal now," she giggled to herself as she continued looking through the small precious pieces of the past.

"I might even be able to take a good inventory before the end of the day," she marveled as her eyes drifted over the assorted stacks. "Ea knows my mother lacked any form of organization for all of this stuff." The fact that her mother had so much of such a wide variety of things baffled her. "How did she collect it all and where did she get the money for it? Not even Aves has this many clothes," Hessa said in astonishment. Four heaping piles of dresses, shifts, tunics, and jackets littered the floor already and she was about to great a fifth just from the stash of trousers she discovered in this final trunk.

The cascading light pulled her mind away from the clothes and the rest of the contents of the trunks. From the odd shadows that meandered in the room, Hessa knew a storm was gathering outside. Although there was still plenty of light cascading through the half-opened shutters, there should have been more. After all, it was still early, well before noon, and she looked forward to making more progress before she was forced to decide about what she should eat.

"I hate how murky the clouds make things," she muttered to herself. "They always trick me into thinking it's later than it really is." Her hand settled on her stomach as if to stifle its emptiness with just a touch. "There's nothing for it, but to do it." The few words she remembered he mother saying came naturally to her.

With a decisive nod, Hessa refocused gaze from the assorted piles on the floor to the, as yet unopened, cabinets. "Quick decisions are often the toughest to bear," another of Natlia's sayings fell from her mouth unexpectedly and left her a little bewildered about it. "Why are my mother's old sayings coming to me?" Hessa wondered as she stared intently at one of the piles of underdresses.

"Before I delve too far into those, I should at least assess the larger items," he words were firm, but held the air that most people took when they spoke to a child. "Something is definitely odd here," the girl muttered to herself as she tucked an errant lock of hair behind her ear.

One intent glance around the room made was all it took for Hessa to make a mental inventory of the furniture. A small end table was tucked into both sides of the bed, almost as if they were a part of the headboard. The little dark wood coffee table was guarded by three comfortable looking chairs. They were leather-clad and empty. One of the final pieces was a smallish writing desk. A functional chair was pushed up to it, but the difference in sheen between the white wood of the chair and the golden polished surface of the desk let her know that the two were not originally intended as a set.

Near the third cabinet stood the final piece of furniture, from what Hessa could tell, it was a tall free standing mirror. A very heavy looking blanket was draped over it and added to the ominous pit in her stomach that formed when she looked too long at it.

Her plan of attack formed as soon as she could fully pull her eyes away from the shroud that covered the mirror. Without any other thought, she pivoted and moved toward the third cabinet. Hessa carefully tugged at one of the two large doors. Her efforts were rewarded with a deep, and eerie, creak as the much heavier than it looked door slowly opened. Hessa's eyes widened as the door swung upon and revealed even more clothes than she had found in just one of the trunks.

She was speechless as she reached in and touched the shoulder of the nearest gown. Her amazement only increased as her fingertips slipped across its smooth silken surface. Hessa was in awe she pulled the elegant gown free from its hanger delicately. The clothes were packed into the cabinet so tight she was afraid the cloth might tear just by taking it out.

Hessa backed away from the doors carefully and held the gown up against her. The dress looked amazing. Light danced along the dark folds of the midnight black fabric as if its edge was the horizon and the light was the awakening sun. She could not help but stare at the contrasting white pearl beads and the glittering gems that were woven into the very fabric of the dress. Like a girl with a new toy, Hessa clasped the dress to her and spun as if at a ball. One of her favorite memories was Aves letting her wear some of her elegant gowns and now she had her own.

"I wish there was a mirror close by so I can see how well this would fit," she wondered aloud. She knew she had seen something recently, but, for some odd reason, she could not remember what it was.

Her eyes searched the room for anything, even a little hand mirror she could prop up to get a better look. The bed and end tables met her gaze and then her eyes skipped to the opened trunks. The feeling of déjà vu crept into her mind as she realized that she was the one that had emptied the trunks.

"Why can't I remember what's in this room?" Hessa said aloud. The tinge of panic mingled with worry as she spun in place.

A tickle on the nape of her neck, as if someone touched it lightly, caused her to turn. The mirror, cloaked in a heavy white blanket caused her fear to melt away almost instantly. "That will do," she giggled to herself as she nonchalantly tugged the blanket off with a quick swipe of her hand.

As she pulled, the girl used her other hand to hold the dress against her waist. Her eyes were riveted to the way the dark fabric moved with her. It was simply elegant. Thoughtlessly, she let go of the blanket and quickly smoothed the material against her body as best as she could before she glanced up to see how it looked and her eyes froze.

Her throat constricted as Hessa tried to scream. All of her muscles were paralyzed by the horrible sight that floated in front of her. Her reflection was flawless, by different. The dress was gorgeous. It was the rest of her reflection that made Hessa want to flee.

Maggots pooled under her lidless left eye and her complexion bore the bluish tinge of the dead. Her long auburn hair was matted and wispy. Reflexively, she traced her skinless fingers across her cheek. Hessa breathed a sigh of relief as she felt her own soft smooth skin instead of the putrid decaying mess before her eyes. Her stomach roiled and dizziness pulled at her consciousness as she tried to make sense of the image.

Without thinking, she stretched her hand toward the mirror. Her horrific reflection reached toward her in exchange, but there was something different about it. The subtle gleam in the bluish-hazel eyes of her reflection forced Hessa to pause. She desperately needed to feel the reassuringly smooth surface of the glass. Knowing that there was something between her and this thing was the only way she knew of to reassure her that it wasn't real.

"Do not touch it!" His words erupted from every shadow in the room and startled Hessa.

Somehow his voice pierced the soft noises of the room and froze Hessa where she stood. Deracai reached out of the shadows next to her and grasped her wrist. His cold alabaster skin pressed against hers with just enough force to prevent her from moving any farther.

Reassuring as it was, Hessa cast a pleading look into the shadows his arm extended from. "I need to feel the glass," her tone was more assertive than she felt. As absurd as they were, her words somehow fit and made perfect sense to her.

"No, you don't. It is very real and wants you to touch it. It needs you to," Deracai's voice was soft, yet still commanding.

A furtive movement out of the corner of her eye caught her attention and pulled her gaze back to the mirror. Her reflection stood just like she was. It clasped the same beautiful dress against its chest. The same alabaster arm seemed to hold it in its place as well. But that is similarities ended. The thing in the mirror struggled against Deracai's grip. It writhed in constant attempts to pull away from him as if his very touch caused it pain.

"It is trying to find a way into our world. It has been trying ever since the mirror was given to your mother," he whispered in Hessa's ear.

"The avatar gave this to my mother?" The words came haltingly and brought more confusion than anything.

"No," Deracai explained almost silently. "It was a gift from her betrothed. She was sworn to your father when they were young. The dekki way is to arrange marriages. The husband is supposed to give his bride to be a gift that represents the future he sees for their union. This is the gift Armani gave Natlia. The gift of their future." Hessa's surprised look forced the shadow walker to pause.

"Armani is my father?" she whispered as she shook her head. Her confusion only deepened the more Deracai spoke.

"I see," he nodded as he continued, "then you probably don't know that Armani is one of the Iohai Dek Kir, a gypsy lord." He explained carefully.

"No, I didn't," Hessa admitted. "But if he was her betrothed, why would he give her something like this? Did he know what was trapped in it?"

"Oh, he knew. He just didn't care," Deracai's voice grew noticeably colder as he spoke. "He gave it as a gift because he wanted her dead. Although he loved her, she had outlived her usefulness to him. He sought power and realized he could only get it if he left his family and the dekki, gypsy, way of life." Deracai paused briefly, as if to gauge her understanding, before he added, "In short, your mother couldn't help him like Shara could, so he sent Natlia this gift in an attempt to remove her from his life permanently."

"My father tried to kill my mom?" Hessa's voice broke as the words fell from her lips. She felt, more than saw, the shadow walker nod as she all but mouthed the words. "Why would she leave me with him then?"

"Love and respect," he said softly. "Natlia loved Armani, she always had. She spoke with Aras about it often. You see, your mother started to help Aras with his cause because she was trying to forget your father. Although they had been sworn to each other, their marriage was never performed. This didn't matter to Natlia. She grew up believing they were meant to be together, so she respected Armani. She looked up to him and could never accept that the man she loved could betray her, and his blood, the way he had. "

His deep resonate voice comforted Hessa in an odd way. The otherworldly tones that carried his words in them only added to the almost hypnotizing effect.

"I believe a part of her hoped that when he found out she had given birth to his child, he would take her back and everything would work itself out. This is why Natlia waited until she knew Shara was ill. Why she made certain to find out his bride would not survive the birth of their second child before she decided to let Armani know that she was still alive. Your mother lived here, with you, in this house. She wanted to live close enough to Ellsted so that if she had a chance, she could let Armani know she not only survived his present, but that she had born him his first daughter. "

He let go of Hessa's wrist and the creature in the mirror shrank away from them as soon as he did.

"But we have wasted too much time on this. I promise I will tell you more when we have time to talk, but that time is not now. Please continue your search."

"Thank you," Hessa said quietly as she pulled the blanket back over the mirror. She was careful not to touch any part of the ornately carved frame as she did.

"It doesn't look like they are coming back anytime soon," Skara growled to Faris. "Have one of your men watch this place just to be sure."

"And if they do, can my soldiers kill them?" Faris asked hesitantly.

"Only if they make it look like an accident. Fires work well with stables and inns," Skara said as she ran her claws along the pathetic mantle in the converted storage room. "Make sure whoever you use is someone we can trust. I want nothing unexpected to happen." Skara gave Faris a withering stare as she spoke, "This matter is far too important to leave anything to chance."

Faris nodded his understanding as he turned to face his

remaining men. "We need to find the boy that lived. I really don't care how you find him, just that you are discrete. I think his name is Namir and he has three girls that usually follow him around. One of them you are familiar with, Haradine. Be careful around her. In case you forgot, she was the one that tested your skills in Hornshir. She's older than she looks, as are all elves, so be on your guard. I can't stress the importance of your task." He paused as he purposefully locked eyes with each of them. "We all know Carness not only resents that we came, but he has personally tortured and threatened each of you with the promise of death if he sees you in Ellsted for any reason. Find me where the boy is and get back to me as fast as you can."

Faris scanned the faces of his men for weakness, any subtle hint that the soldier had lost either his nerve or his faith. His chorded neck muscles loosed a little when he determined there were none of the telltale signs of either in his men. With a quick nod, Faris dismissed them.

As his troops left, he reached out and tapped his lieutenant's shoulder. "Jasper, I need you to stay here and oversee all of the efforts. There is something I have to do and I want to be sure someone is here to handle the situation should any of them find Namir before I can get back here. I expect I can count on you to do this for me," Faris smiled inwardly as his lieutenant nod in agreement.

Aves walked into the gypsy camp timidly. The note Hessa had left for her was clasped in her left hand and she was very conscious of it. In her other hand she gripped the tarot card. Some little voice told her to bring it. Her eyes danced around the encampment as she tried to blend in. Every placed she checked proved useless. Hessa was nowhere.

The town, although full of travelers, was empty. Almost all of the shops in the main square were closed and everyone was skeptical of each other's motives. Even the Gathering Place proved fruitless and Aves couldn't think of anywhere else to look.

She walked carefully into the center of the camp. Each successive step forced her to swallow an ever-increasing amount of fear. Aves looked around warily, she had never done anything like this and she was sure it showed. Whether the eyes she felt were real or imagined made little difference to her. The overall effect was unnerving and it only intensified the farther in she went.

"Are you lost?" The smooth sounding baritone voice cut through the silence neatly, "Because if you are, I may be of some assistance."

Aves felt too afraid to turn her head far enough to look at the man. Instead, she dropped her eyes and focused on the ground. All of her instincts screamed at her to run, but she knew that if she really wanted to find Hessa, she would have to stay and find someone who could help.

"What am I doing?" Aves screamed at herself in her head. She could not stop the stories she had heard as a child from running through her mind. Sordid tales of gypsies stealing young girls from their homes and marrying them off to one visiting nobleman or another in exchange for some coin pressed themselves against ones that told of the violence that always accompanied these cursed folk.

Her left arm rose all on its own shakily. The card she had guarded for so long revealed itself perfectly in her now outstretched hand. The whispered words that forced themselves past her dry lips were more from the countless stories she had heard and less from her own planning, "I come bearing a gift from an old woman, a card, and request your aid in exchange for its return."

"I see," the man replied. There was a cautious tone to his voice and it set Aves's nerves on fire. "Thank you for your willingness to return the card to us," she could tell that he found her gesture funny, even if he held in his laughter. Aves could hear it in the staccato rise and shortfall of his voice. By the time he continued, she could feel the redness of her growing anger threaten to unleash itself across her skin, "I'm afraid that it doesn't work that way. But I would be willing to help regardless of who gave you that card."

"What do you mean? That is how it works in all of the stories." Aves pouted. The only other reaction she could think of was rage. The girl hated how this man treated her. She had rehearsed the moment mentally all morning and his reaction and arrogance ruined it. It was almost as if all of her trepidation was a giant waste of time.

With a slight cough, the man obviously choked back his mirth and responded, "Do you always believe everything you hear in stories, or is this time your one exception?" Sarcasm dripped from each of the irreverent words that he spoke.

Aves found it harder to decide if the man was being rude on purpose or if he struggled against her ignorance of their culture.

Either way, she had enough of it. In the most authoritative tone she could manage, she replied, "If I know the person telling the story is usually truthful, or if the same story is shared by many different people on many different occasions, then aye, I do believe them. How else am I supposed to get your help then?"

She hurried through her spiel to avoid being cut off. Although Aves still found it impossible to tear her eyes off of her tan shoes, she felt more empowered.

His lack of response worried her. A cold breeze picked up and pulled at her cloak. She felt her breath pull from her mouth by the air's icy fingers. Aves knew he was being silent on purpose. She just wished she knew why. This little mystery bothered her more than both his rudeness and his newly discovered joy of silence combined.

It took all of her mental resolve, but she forced herself to move her eyes from her own shadow and over to his. From there, she let her hazel eyes make mall leaps across the grass that separated them. Her mind took refuge in each random blade of grass and used it to build up her resolve to finally let them rest on the man's dirty black leather boots.

Although they were well polished, and large enough to belong to a man of Carness's stature, the little splatters of dirt caked around his heels and toes let Aves know he did more than walk in them.

Her eyes wandered from his well-kept, but soiled, boots on up to his legs. His reddish brown leather breeches were tight and fit him well. She could tell that they were made to accentuate his well-developed muscles and, although Aves saw they were well worn, there were not visible holes in them.

Her mind wandered from her task as she visually traced each of the little creases and folds up the leather up from his thigh. Some of the seams had ornate patterns on them, while others were simply laced with thick black leather chords.

A crimson blush flooded over her face as she realized the seams she was looking at so intently were situated between his thighs and belt. Ave quickly averted her eyes and let them jump up his broad chest and the soft silky looking violet shirt that was draped over it.

Even though his shirt was loose fitting and floated away from his firm muscles easily in what little breeze there was, Aves could still see every little ripple that played across his chest in the cold.

The warm flush spread down her cheeks and spilled onto the top of her neck and what little control over her eyes started to slip away. She felt like the little helpless girl she had been the first time she saw Nurn without his shirt. The soft folds of this gypsy's tunic pulled at her mind as she struggled against the odd burning feeling she felt welling up deep inside her.

Before she could bring herself to look up at the man's face, his baritone voice shattered the tepid silence that surrounded them. "I've already offered to help." The sound of confusion littered his voice as he spoke. "Were you thinking about that, or was there something else preoccupying you mind?" His right hand slipped over hers as he spoke.

He stepped closer and, for whatever reason, she felt her

lungs start to burn. "No," Aves replied. The light red hue that had settled on her cheeks deepened into a darker shade of scarlet as she continued breathily, "and I do accept your help."

In one brilliant act of courage, Aves tore her gaze from his chest to meet the soulful stare of his hazel eyes. Her breath caught in her chest as long dark locks tumbled around his face and swayed lightly in the breeze.

She wanted him to think of her as an adult instead of the scared girl she felt like on the inside. He was gorgeous and he held her hand. Blackness threatened to consume her mind as she forcefully swallowed her fears in a valiant attempt to act aloof,

"And what should I call you?" She asked carefully.

Her eyes wandered from his eyes to the bridge of his perfect nose and moved along to his cheeks. From the distinct lack of wrinkles, she could tell he wasn't old. Unfortunately, she found nothing else to use to gage is age. His smooth bronzed skin contrasted with his dark hair. While it was almost black, she could see that it wasn't. Instead, there were signs he had been in the sun for quite a few hours by the subtle lightening she saw around the outer edges of his hair.

"My name is Onas," he replied coolly. "I'm assuming that was what you wanted to know, right?"

"Aye," Aves responded. She was a little surprised by how calm her own voice sounded. "So how can you help? What do we do first?"

"Tell me a little bit about your friend. When and where did you last see her?" His voice sounded like smooth honey as each word passed through his lips.

"She is my best friend and maid," Aves said more to herself than to Onas. "This morning I found the note on her bed," she said meekly as she handed him the note Hessa left for her.

The gypsy took the note and scanned it quickly. "You didn't tell me you're Armani's daughter." He added as he finished reading the note. "You also failed to mention your friend is really your sister." Onas's voice took on a somber tone as he spoke.

"What difference would it have made if I had?" Confusion threatened to cloud her mind as he spoke. The fact his mood shifted so drastically only added to the uneasy feeling that formed in the pit of Aves's stomach.

"It makes more of a difference than you can imagine," Onas's tone dropped to a whisper as he spoke. "I shouldn't even be speaking with you."

"But you are," she replied. It was a struggle for her to find the right words to say. The ones he needed to hear to make him help her still. "I promise not to tell my father that you helped me. He can't make things hard for you if he doesn't know you did anything," Aves offered quickly.

She knew most of the townsfolk seemed to fear Armani for some strange reason. He always told her it was respect, but she knew the look of fear when she saw it.

"I'm not afraid of your father," he answered as if he read her thoughts. An annoying aloof tone settled slowly into his voice as he continued to speak, "But you're right. I did agree to speak with you, so I guess your ploy worked. Very little will change if I help you find your sister at this point," His stance shifted a little as she felt his eyes linger on her face. "Come with me, I have an idea where we can start looking."

"Where?" Aves asked a little incredulously.

"The same place you would expect to find anyone, especially a girl, her mother's house." He said somewhat enigmatically as he turned and started walking toward the picket line and the horses. "Do you know how to ride?" He called over his shoulder to Aves as she realized she was being left behind.

"I didn't know her mother had a house," Aves said as she caught up Onas hurriedly.

Haradine dodged through the congested courtyard on her way to the council hall. Mentally she berated herself for not using the route Namir instructed her to use. After her last encounter with Ellsted's roofs, she had reservations about leaping between the rooftops of the town. "It's just something else I'll have to face," she mumbled to herself as she quickened her pace. Heights had bothered the half-elf before, but now the thought of them sent small quivers down her spine. "I will get there faster if I stay on the ground," she reminded herself again. "Besides, I have more option if I run into someone." Haradine's encouraging self-talk paled in the face of the fact she had already taken almost an hour and she was still trying to dart through the throngs of people inhabiting what was left of the festival.

She knew the festival was nearing its end and everyone she avoided was either packing up their wares or doing last minute shopping. Most of what she saw amazed her. People were haggling on trinkets in an attempt to get the best deals on overpriced odds and ends. The things people were buying simply amazed her. A whole gold crown for a carved lantern or 6 silver drams for a set of wooden dishes, it was ridiculous. However, Haradine couldn't decide which was worse the fact people bought these things at such a high price or their determination to get them.

Haradine silently scoffed at the logic humans used to justify almost everything. She narrowly avoided a person carrying far too many glass containers as she careened into another with armfuls of bread and fruit. "I'm almost to the council hall," she thought to herself thankfully as she helped the person pick up the last stray apple she had knocked from their bag.

The wide street that led up to the Council Hall was a blessing and she felt her heart beat a little easier. Haradine managed to lengthen her stride as she made her way to the less used middle part of the street. She easily maneuvered past the remaining people around her as they wound their way through the temporary shops and stalls.

"There are too many people," her mind raced as she scanned the small opening in the bushes that lead to the secret room in the Council Hall. Without thinking, her feet turned toward the nearest alley. "I'll have a better chance at the other end of the path," images of the little trail buzzed through the half-elf's head. Mentally she spun the images and connected them together like a mosaic. It wasn't until she smelled the stench of cheap oil and smoke that she realized her mistake.

Various games of chance littered the alley in front of her. Gypsies and other transients greedily lured some of the more adventurous townsfolk and travelers into their lurid traps. Although there were less people, the alley felt more crowded than the street did. Constantly dodging around the random drunken fights and disagreements between the games' contestants, Haradine was surprised to find that she had somehow managed to gain some headway.

"I just hope Allair is still there," she muttered under her breath. Yet another large man loomed ahead of her and forced her to weave around him. The stench of far too much ale mingled with heavy incense clung to him as she passed too close.

The subtle scent of flowers wafted to her as she spun free of her newest obstacle. Its heady scent was a pleasant change to the almost stale fragrances of the alley. Barren cobles bereft of aimless meanderers called to her and Haradine felt herself break into a sprint. Her feet danced across the intricate pattern of alternating smooth and rough stones.

"Step, step, spin," she thought. The rhythmic staccato of her stride drummed in her mind. With each step, her breath became more rugged and her pace more determined. A few more steps carried her onto the garden path that wound around the base of the Council Hall. Another few led her to the hidden door.

"It's a wonder no one really notices this place," Haradine panted to herself. The door in front of her was completely overgrown by ivy. Although a wrought iron handle obviously emerged from the large leaves, it somehow managed to blend into its surroundings.

Haradine took a moment to catch her breath as she grasped the wrought iron handle of the door. With very little effort, the smallish door swung open silently. Another oddity that made her believe the entrance was always meant to be hidden.

While it was finely crafted, the door was made of oak like the other, oversized, doors the rest of the Hall was decorated with. Unlike the rest of the building, however, this entrance was humble and starkly contrasted to the pompous construction of the main entrance. It was grand and designed to make people feel as if the building, and by extension, the people who worked there, were far more important than they were.

"Allair?" Haradine called as she stepped through the crack in the door. The door closed behind her under its own weight as she stepped softly into the stone passage beyond it. A thick rug cushioned her step and absorbed some of her words. "Are you still here? Tipin said that you might be," she called out a little louder as she walked into what appeared to be the central chamber.

"It seems you found me just in time," Allair replied from somewhere to the half-elf's right. The chancellor's voice held a note of weariness to it and the long lines surrounding her mouth added to the effect. With a raised eyebrow, Allair asked, "How can I help?"

"Is there any more time available for tonight's session?" Haradine blurted out abruptly. She realized too late that she had disregarded all protocol with her request and held her breath in anticipation of a reprimand.

"It depends," Allair replied, obviously taken aback by the girl's brashness, "Who asks and why do they need to speak to the council?"

"The sa'ouvant has requested to address the council," Haradine said with a slight tone of superiority in her voice.

"The sa'ouvant? What is that, an elven camp leader?" Allair replied dismissively. Her left hand rubbed her forehead as she started to turn away from her friend's daughter.

"I'm sorry," Haradine said with a bow. "I forgot myself, I

am among humans now. Please accept my apology. When I say sa'ouvant, I mean the ruler of Cennicus." A twinkle appeared in Haradine's eyes when she noticed Allair stop in mid-stride. "So I ask again, is there any more available time for our liege to address the council?"

Allair shook her head in response. "Unfortunately there isn't. Please let Namir and my husband know that I will work him into tomorrow's session, at the end probably. That way he can take as much time as he needs."

"I thought tonight's session was the last one of the season," Haradine rebutted. It was obvious to her that her mother's friend did not understand the gravity of the request.

"Normally it would be, but there was more to do this year than there was last year, so the council agreed to hold two more council sessions to wrap everything up, one tonight and the final one tomorrow night. Armani will announce the additional session tonight. So please let them know I will get them into the schedule, just not tonight. There are far too many things that need to be addressed for the need of the town. Now go and leave me to my work."

Her words were more of a command than a suggestion and Haradine knew it. A quick nod was the only response the half-elf gave before she turned and left.

Chapter Nineteen: Ascension

The tip of her dagger silently pierced the outer edge of the bag. The sound as the cloth pulled and split open across the blade's edge seemed deafening in the silence of the room. A few more slices and Gienna managed to make the hole large enough to squeeze through. The elf took a deep breath and enjoyed the feeling. It had been hours since she had climbed into the bag of wheat. Although it had been her plan, she now wished she could have thought of another way to sneak past the temple's guards unnoticed.

A few quick flicks of her wrist, she carefully brushed off the chaff off of her exposed skin. With skillful precision she made it look like a large rat or some other animal had made the hole in the bag. She hated having to travel this way, especially because she had to strip down to almost nothing so the bag would not seem unusual if inspected.

"It's going to take months to make myself feel completely clean after this," Gienna thought to herself. Even the thought of retrieving her gear from the bottom of the bag made the elf's skin crawl. The cold stones of the church's floor made her choice easy. She had to get warm.

Shivering, she dug back into the large sack of wheat and retrieved the leather bag containing her weapons and clothes. A cold brisk breeze caused the little bumps along her skin when it touched. The combination of the bone-chilling cold radiating up from the floor and the strength stealing cold the wind promised made the task of unpacking her gear almost impossible.

"I can hardly wait to be done with this," her thoughts raced as she pulled her chemise free from the bag.

She shimmied into it as quickly as she could and pulled it tight for added warmth. Another involuntary shiver forced its way through her body. "This is the last time I let my brother talk me into something like this," Gienna thought bitterly as she freed her breeches from the sack and slipped into them.

A small smile played across her lips as her fingers touched hardened leather of her boots. Careful not to make the rest of the gear clatter inside the bag, she slipped her boots out and placed them quietly down on the stones beside her.

Gienna stepped into them gratefully. She felt a little warmer now that she had some sort of barrier between her and the warmth leeching stones. Her violet cat-slitted eyes scanned the room as she quickly slid her belt, with the rest of her belongings neatly arranged on it, into place. It didn't take her long to spot the containers that her brother and his men had hidden themselves in. and then set about freeing the others from their hiding place.

"At least a bag of wheat was a better hiding place than the cask of pickles Trainor suggested," She whispered aloud. The tip of her dagger bit into the outer edge of the wooden lid. With the skill of a cooper, she deftly twisted her wrist and freed the lid with almost no sound.

A quick glance was all Gienna needed to make sure no one heard the subtle noise as she pried the lid the rest of the way off. Soft and easy arguments voiced from the keg were the backdrop of sound she worked with. Several pieces of dried meat obstructed her view of what was really in the cask.

Without hesitation, she plunged her hand deep into the barrel of meat and smiled as her fingers closed around the leather straps of the bags she had hidden. "At least I chose the right one," she smirked.

Removing the three large leather bags was the easy part. Shaking off the small flecks of salt and meat that clung to them was a little harder. "The hardest part of this is always the setup," Gienna's thoughts flew through her head as she set to work disguising the scene. The elf reached into the cask and took a small amount of the meat and carefully placed it on top of a couple of the closer bags before she put the lid mostly in place. She then cautiously scattered the debris cast off of the bags to make it look like an animal somehow managed to get into the meat before it hurried off.

Her attention flitted to the three casks nearest the door. "I thought so," she said silently in her mind. "They need to quit moving or they will be spotted for sure."

Her violet eyes played across wooden lids as she deftly made her way over to them. The tiny knife cuts along the outer edge of each lid let her know which one each of her companions was in.

"I'm glad I made each of these a little differently," she thought as she moved over to the barrel with her brother in it.

This one, she opened differently than the last. Instead of driving her knife into the edge, she placed her hands against the boards that crossed along the outside if the lid and twisted. A sense of relief spread through her cold muscles when she felt the lid slowly start to move. Then, after she had moved it half a rotation, it started to move on its own.

"Calm yourself," Gienna whispered to her brother. "If you make too much noise trying to get out you'll alert the guards."

"Fine," Landolin's replied dourly. Although he whispered his response, she could tell how upset he was about having to travel this way.

Another few turns and the top of the barrel slid off. Smirking, she peered around it. The sight of her brother floating naked in the church's red wine was almost too much for her. His glare was the only thing that stopped her from laughing outright.

"It's a good look for you," she whispered in his mind as she reached down and took his arm. It took a few tries to pull him free from the liquid's embrace, but she eventually managed it.

"Laugh while you can," he thought back.

She could see he appreciated what little warmth the towel she handed him offered as he dried himself quickly. The lines that sporadically creased his face let her know how much his muscles ached by the combination of the bitter cold and the stiffness from the awkward position he had been in for so long.

"Next time you get to travel by cask and I'll take the grain," Landolin threatened.

Gienna knew threat was a hollow one because of their size. Although Landolin was lithe, she was still smaller. Which is why she had been selected to smuggle herself into the bag of grain.

Landolin finished dressing and pulled his long crimson hair into a tight queue. As he did, little rivulets of the wine made their way down his arms and into his sleeves.

"I'm going to smell like fermented grapes for weeks," he muttered in elvish.

With an impish look, Gienna motioned toward the two casks closest to the door. With a quick flick of the wrist, she silently assigned which one he needed to open. "This might prove useful," Gienna said in his mind again as she handed him one of his daggers.

"Thank you," his thoughts raced as he pressed the dagger's tip into the lid. "I hate to think of my soldiers suffering as much as I did." It was obvious her brother cared for those in his command. "We need to hurry," he added with an odd tone in his voice, "or they might get too cramped to be of much use."

"Or too intoxicated," she shot back mentally. Gienna knew her brother was trying to hide his true emotions behind a façade of bravado. "That is if the stories I've heard of Trainor's drinking are based on some semblance of the truth." She smiled as she pressed her dagger into the lid of the cask in front of her in unison with her brother.

"Why don't these tops just screw off like mine did?" Landolin asked as he followed his sister's lead.

"Yours was a larger barrel. I chose it so you would be easier to get to." Her tone had the same ring to it that a teacher had during a lesson. "Depending on the storage, these smaller barrels," she motioned toward the two they worked on, "might have been put into a larger stack. If I had to unstack all of the barrels to get someone out to help, we would never be able to finish what we came in here for."

"I see," Landolin replied. The way the corners of his mouth pulled downward as he spoke let Gienna know exactly how much he hated her lectures.

She shot her brother a playful smile as she focused on freeing the lid from the cask. She had purposefully directed Landolin to work on the barrel Trainor was in, while she focused on Farvais's hiding place. Although she was sure her brother was the consummate professional, she didn't think it would be fair for one of his female captains to be ogled by him as she tried to climb out of the cold wine.

Without planning it, the two elves slipped into a routine. Their furtive glances to ensure their privacy alternated with their struggle to free their compatriots. The sound of Trainor's muffled belch as Landolin finally managed to ease the lid up enough to slide his fingers under it almost forced both of the siblings to laugh.

"I see you were a little thirsty," Landolin commented jovially under his breath. "I thought this cask was full after you climbed in. Now it seems to be at least a few pounds lighter. Between the humorous looks and the tone of his voice, Landolin was obviously amused by his captain's efforts to stand inside of the cask.

"Aye, and it kept getting in my face," Trainor explained as he carefully stepped free. "It was self-defense mostly really," he jested as he dried himself off. "I may have drowned otherwise."

"I thought you'd say something like that," Farvais commented as she too stood up in her cask. Although she was much shorter than the other three elves, her nudity was barely contained by barrel's outer edge. She quickly swept her sopping black hair away from her face and turned to face away from the men. Wine ran down the pale skin of her back in a myriad of rivers as she twisted her hair into a tight braid.

Without any hesitation, the diminutive elf readily took Gienna's outstretched hand and carefully hopped out of the cask. She shivered as Gienna helped her get dry and into her clothing. "I hope the rest of the trip is warmer than this part was," she joked as they all belted their weapons into their respective places.

The floorboards creaked angrily as Hessa walked carefully across the room. The attic was small, cramped and dark, not to mention dusty. None of which she enjoyed overly much. The annoying tickle-like sensation of a sneeze refusing to release only added to her irritation.

"I wish there was a window to open at least," Hessa muttered as she raised the candle a little higher above her head.

Although the candle was new, its light barely penetrated the gloom of the attic. Crates and chests seemed to line the walls and, from what little she could see, several large sacks were piled in the middle of the floor ahead of her. Hessa decided to start with the sacks.

After all, there seemed to be fewer of them and if she could get them cleared out, she would have more room to move around. She slowly stepped from the top of the steep stairs and into the room. As she did, her skirts accidentally brushed through a mountain of dust from a nearby chest and launched it into the air around her. That was all it took for that annoying sneeze to finally release.

"My mother said it was here," she sniffled to herself in

disgust. Her hazel eyes darted across the chaotic mess strewn about the cramped attic. "It must be in one of the crates," she thought frantically as she forced herself to remain calm. "At least that's what her note said."

Hessa recalled the little box she found hidden in a hutch her mother obviously used as an armoire. The box was small and looked as if it had been carved out of bone. Hessa could still feel its cold smooth surface as if she still held it in her hands. She closed her eyes in an attempt to remember every detail about the strange and exotic thing. As she did, the moment of discovery played itself perfect before her mind's eye.

Hessa recalled her anticipation as she gingerly opened the box. A slight disturbance moved the air around her. Somehow the little shifts added an odd energy to her surroundings. Something inside her seemed to roil uncomfortably and felt as if the contents of the box tugged at her soul. The more the box opened, the harder it was to breathe. Even her vision pulled at the sides as if whatever was inside the box pulled at everything outside of it.

Hessa recalled marveling at the little eddies of dust that swirled around the little table in front of her as she fought to regain control of her breathing. The most amazing part of it was how quickly these strange effects ended. The odd tugging abated so fast her stomach filled with a phantom pain.

The distraction forced her to tear her eyes away from the box for less than a second, but that was all it took. When she looked back a little piece of paper attempted to escape the little box. Hessa recalled reaching down and catching it as it managed to free itself from its prison.

Her hands trembled in remembrance of how much they shook the first time she opened the note. The paper bounced around so much, Hessa had to read it a few times before she realized what it was. It was so much more than a note her mom left for her to find, it was a map to her hidden journal.

Jerine looked up at Nurn's hulking form. Both of them

panted after their most recent search of the clearing. The elf visibly braced himself for the youth's disappointment before he spoke. "I can't find any sign of Halin. I had hoped I was wrong before, but there isn't any sign of him here."

Nurn glared past the elf and into the small crevice Jerine stood in front of and growled, "Now what?" His deep voice and even tone held an air of malice and despair.

"There is one other place, but…" Jerine started to say, but was cut off by Nurn's next question.

"Where?" It was more of a demand than a question. "Where is this next place and is there even a chance my brother is there?" He knew his words would hurt the guardian's pride and he didn't care.

"About four leagues from here is an old dwarven keep. I didn't mention it before because of the distance, but Halin is a clever boy. He may have found a way to get there." Jerine said in a reassuring tone. "I know it's a long shot, but your brother may have run the wrong way if he had been caught in the storm or thought he was being chased. Has your brother been taught what to do if lost in the forest?"

The elf's expectant tone forced Nurn back from his thoughts. "No, I don't think so," Nurn replied somewhat downheartedly.

"So there is a chance that he may be wandering around, looking for us, while we are searching for him." Jerine summed up.

"Aye, I guess it's possible," Nurn agreed reluctantly. "You really think dwarves would just let him in?" Although it was a blatant attempt to change the topic, Nurn felt the need to ask. The idea of dwarves just opening their doors for Halin seemed so absurd, especially since the dwarves closed themselves off from the world before the last Great War. Nurn couldn't believe Jerine would even entertain such an insane thought.

"No, I don't believe they would," Jerine replied thoughtfully as he shook his head. "Good thing the place has been abandoned for almost a century then, isn't it?" A slight twinkled crept into Jerine's eyes when he said this last part and Nurn noticed it.

"Why are we just standing here then?" Nurn asked as he spun around. Some of the hope he had felt draining from him seemed to rekindle as he started to leave the clearing.

"Nurn, there is just one more thing," Jerine said as he reached out to the youth before he walked too far away.

"What is it?" Nurn replied. Sometimes he wished that Jerine could move at his pace. For whatever reason, Jerine always seemed to move at a slower speed. It felt as if the elf had no understanding of urgency and this bothered him.

"It's this way," Jerine replied casually as he set off toward the keep. The humor in Jerine's voice was lost on Nurn, until he realized Jerine left in the opposite direction than he had.

Landolin motioned for his men to be silent as they all crouched in the rafters above the secret door. After the next deacon passed, they would drop down from their hiding place and slip through the secret passage. "Finally we will know what these clergymen are up to," the elven general thought to himself silently. Several more long minutes passed as they waited in utter silence. All four elves were relieved when the deacon finally walked made his rounds.

As quietly as the wind, the elves dropped from the rafters and landed within yards of the hidden door. In less than a second, all four of them crouched against it, each hidden from view in case the deacon came back looking for something.

Gienna's fingers flew over intricate carved sigils and faces that adorned the altar's wall. Before Landolin could take a breath, his sister had it pivoting open. With a flurry of movement, she vanished into its awaking shadows. Her hand flicked back less than a second after she stepped through as a signal it was safe.

"Stay sharp," Landolin directed as he followed his sister into the darkness. Although he knew that his men were always alert, he felt they needed to exhibit special care given their location.

The stairs that waited for them stretched into the darkness forever. Even with his keen elven vision, they seemed endless. The slope was low and each step took him two or three just to get to the next one. The smooth steps seemed to have been carved from the very foundation of the city.

Landolin focused his eyes straight ahead as he motioned for his sister to move in behind him. Another signal to Trainor and Farvais to pair up and keep watch from behind was all he needed to do before he stepped off the third step.

His ears focused the noises as they moved. He easily discerned the sounds of his sister, who followed a few paces behind him, from those of his captains. "Nothing, not even the sounds of moisture on the walls," he marveled to himself mentally.

He knew Gienna would be just as focused as he was. The half shadowed bluish hue of his elven sight cast the world in a surreal shade as his eyes scanned the extremely old stones of the steps under their feet and the walls that bordered them.

"Come up here," Landolin whispered to his sister and noticed that even the sound of his voice was almost muted by their surroundings. "We can easily fit two across. Let's tighten up our rank a little"

"You and your military terms," Gienna replied quietly as she moved beside him. "Not all of us are under your command, brother," She taunted.

"You are while you're here with me," he shot back in a hushed growl. "Any of you notice anything odd?"

"Aside from the lack of sound?" Farvais asked as her and Trainor moved in closer to Landolin and Gienna.

"Can't even hear the water on the walls," Trainor added as he pointed at the small rivulets of water as it etched little finger-like lines through the well-worn granite walls that surrounded them.

"Ok, we need to stay close," Landolin said urgently.

"Something is muffling the sound, so we cannot trust what we hear. This means we need to stay alert, more so than ever." He knew his captains would understand his meaning, Landolin just hoped Gienna would as well.

Without any other words, Landolin turned and spun his fingers over his head before he made a sharp, knife-like, motion ahead of him. He quickly moved forwards down the stairs in a crouched and ready stance. He felt a small wave of relief spread through him as Gienna kept pace in a similar manner.

The other two elves, but faced in the opposite direction. Trainor walked with his back toward Landolin's and focused on the walls and ceiling as they inched along, while Farvais ensured nothing surprised them from behind.

Landolin felt an odd sense of comfort in the fact that Farvais, though young, had volunteered to come with them. She had the keenest eyesight out of all of his soldiers and her speed with a sword was unrivaled.

As they finally neared the bottom of the stairs, Gienna motioned for the group to stop. "I can feel a draft coming from two different sides," her words formed in all of their minds at once.

Landolin allowed his eyes focus on the splitting path before them as his sister delicately placed his next few words into their thoughts. "It would appear that we are in some sort of cistern. I believe we should follow the least worn path," Landolin motioned toward the path on their left with a subtle flick of his wrist. Beads of sweat formed along his sister's brow as she concentrated on their unique form of communication. He hated how much mind speak taxed her, but there was no other choice.

"That sounds about right," Trainor agreed as he warily glanced up the stairs they had just descended. Landolin's approving nod was his cue to continue his thought, "I suggest we each pick a tunnel to explore. Hopefully, we can ferret out what these priests are up so can be on our way home before someone has a chance to notice us."

"While splitting up is a good idea, I refuse to let us spread ourselves so thin," Landolin's words resonated within all of them as if their bodies were instruments that he played with masterful strokes. "Even if we were able to somehow stay in contact, we would all be alone if something happened. No, we should pair up," he added in response their unasked question.

"Good idea," Gienna added. "What do you think the pairings should be?" She asked.

Landolin knew his sister suspected how he was going to divide them. She just had to ask as a formality. He just hated that even with them mentally linked, he still had to say what he wanted to express. "Why can't they just know," he thought privately to himself.

"How about Trainor and I go as one team and the two of you be the other one," Farvais said. A lock of her ebony hair fell over her gleaming violet eyes as she gestured toward the siblings. She skillfully brushed it out of the way as she added, "The two of us have trained together for years and I am sure you have become quite adept at fighting side by side as well." The elf reached out and fondly touched Trainor's shoulder as if to drive a point across to everyone present.

Landolin nodded his approval as he added, "My sister and I will take the left two passages. That leaves the right ones for you two. Make sure to be extra vigilant and let me know the moment you come across anything out of place." He handed each of them two charms. One of them was a pure silver charm and the other was made of wrought iron. "These parishioners are not what they seem to be; hopefully these will help turn the tide to your favor if something goes wrong." He said as he pulled each of them into a quick embrace. "Be safe and good luck," Landolin said as he motioned for his sister to follow him this time.

Morcant watched the large man and the guardian leave elves' the main encampment. Something tugged at Morcant's mind as he saw the direction they headed in. An oddly familiar feeling pulled through the pictures in his mind. "Where are they going?" Morcant wondered to himself silently. His warm breath created small clouds around him and his mind spun like the center of a turbulent storm. "And why does it feel so familiar?" It was all the lupinoid could do to not growl in frustration at the sensation.

Morcant moved deftly from tree to shrub. Long pauses followed by a sharp, soundless, flurry of motion. He had developed this method of traveling to minimize any chance of being spotted. Although he paused often, Morcant only stopped long enough to make sure he was still downwind of the pair. There was no sense in giving them a chance of detecting him, even if their noses were not nearly as sensitive as his was.

Without sparing any thought to why, he changed his path in mid-stride. Only the soft shush of snow as he inadvertently displaced it from its beds noticed his change of course.

Instead of concentrating on his prey, Morcant thought about the odd urge that had moved from his gut to his spine. The tug became more apparent the farther East they moved.

The subtle sounds of leaves being moved as the elf searched for a sign of their missing comrade. "That's right, guardian, keep looking for him. The harder you search, the less I will have to." He snickered to himself wolfishly.

A modicum of enjoyment bubbled as he watched them search. He knew they searched for the same thing he needed to find, the sword bearer, so he languished and allowed them to do his work for him. Morcant just hoped would at least turn up some trace of the boy before he had to kill them.

"It would be a pity to end them too soon," he thought to himself, "I might have to actually get dirty then." He stifled a little laugh that threatened to escape and betray his position.

One thing Morcant hated about his situation was how close he had to stay in order to share in their discovery. That is if they if they actually found anything.

He strained his ears as he saw the large boy signal to the elf. "The way he motions and communicates, he could be mistaken for an elf. That is if he wasn't so large." Morcant thought. An odd prickling of admiration developed as he watched them.

His warm breaths came in small puffs as he crouched under the tree. He had managed to scramble under it low hanging branches before his prey had a chance to spot him, but just barely. He did his best to keep them within earshot, but he also needed to see what the two of them were up to.

Morcant wanted to make certain he knew everything they found. That way he could predict their moves and maybe get to his real target before these two could stop him.

He struggled to keep still. Although he was large, he knew how to hide. Just so long as he didn't move or tremble. He forced his lungs to take smaller breaths and made a point to only breathe through his nose. It limited the sound and forced his steamy breath to be less noticeable.

The less than subtle shift to the branches around him almost made him cringe. He could feel them moving around him, circling, and unnerved him a little.

"How did they know I was here?" Morcant thought vigorously about the route he took from his previous perch to here. "Leave it to the elves to misplace the one person I needed them to keep track of," he thought vehemently to himself.

"We're not far," the guardian's tenor tone made Morcant flinch as it cut through the stillness of the clearing and rang off the nearby cliff face.

"You've been saying that ever since we left the practice clearing." The deep-voiced boy replied. His words boomed throughout the clearing in a way that made it impossible to pinpoint exactly where it came from.

Morcant fought the urge to lash out at the two of them as his thoughts reeled. "I've got to get out of here." He forced himself to breathe deeper and slower so he could minimize his anxiety while he listened intently to the voices that circled him.

The beast hunkered smaller as he tried to accurately discern their whereabouts. Even this little motion disturbed the latticed branches he hid behind. The immediate silence was haunting as both sets of steps stopped. Even the sound of each snowflake as it landed on leaves around him sounded like thunder in Morcant's ears. He knew they were listening for him. Waiting to see if he was going to make another mistake.

Silently he cursed himself for his carelessness. His breath burned in his lungs as he played all of his options through his head. "I need to be more careful," he thought disgustedly.

Morcant slowly released the air from his lungs the second he heard one of his prey shift his weight. "They've given up," a wolfish grin pulled at his fur covered lips as he realized they hadn't noticed him. He stifled his breathing just short of a sigh as he let the tension drain from his shoulders. He could hardly wait for them to get back to their task of finding his target for him. Even under all of his fur and armor, the cold stiffened his muscles to the point of pain.

Morcant shifted his weight slightly from one foot to the other as the guardian and his companion continued their thorough search of the clearing. With each burning tingle that flooded into each leg his anticipation, and smile, deepened. Just as the feeling returned he froze. He heard the leaves of his enclosure rustle again.

"What was that?" The large man's voice rumbled all around Morcant.

Several tense moments passed before he heard the guardian exclaim, "It must have been a bird."

Time twisted and stretched endlessly as Morcant waited to hear them resume their search. The second they did, Morcant allowed the tension to melt from his aching shoulders. "I need to get out of here." Morcant thought desperately. "One more slip and I'll have to kill them before they can lead me to the boy."

His plans for killing these two played through his mind as he instinctively studied his surroundings. A pang of fear crept into his mind as he realized how slim his chances of escaping without being seen really were. Each option weighed itself in front of him and his gaze darted from leaf to twig to stone and back to the leaf.

He calculated every scenario subconsciously as the veritable labyrinth of noisemakers spanning the entire thicket in front of him spread itself out. That's when he noticed it.

The soft glint of aged metal flashed in the underbrush just a few feet away from his steel-shod toes. Morcant allowed his body to sway just a fraction of an inch to get a better look. There was something familiar about it, but the idea of what it was kept slipping away. Another long sway and the golden brilliance shifted into more of a brassy one.

"Could it be?" he thought rapidly.

Morcant slowly lowered himself closer to the ground. He burrowed his hand deep into the snow to help hide his movements. Painfully slowly, his clawed hand snaked through the snow and out from the cover of his hiding place. He crept ever closer to the edge of the delicate branches as he stretched his arm farther from his body and closer to the subdued metallic thing hidden just a few feet away.

The bite of cold and weathered brass instantly soaked into the exposed pad of his hand as Morcant grasped the object's reflective surface. In less time that it took to touch it, Morcant brought it back to him through the small snow tunnel he created.

Delicately he listened for any noise from the two searchers as he silently leaned against the trunk of the slender tree. Morcant eased his weight slowly into it so as not to allow it to shift abruptly.

His wolf-like tongue nervously licked his lips as he gingerly brushed the dirt away from its surface. The blackened bronze symbol burnt like a dark diamond in his hand and made Morcant's thin lips pull hungrily tight across his leering teeth.

"It is," Morcant thought as his eyes traced the embossed dagger on the surface of his lost medallion. "I have finally found what was taken from me," the thoughts played through his mind as he greedily closed his hand.

His canine lips pulled even tighter over his teeth and his face contorted into an eerily haunting smile as recognition flickered behind his red eyes. He easily recalled his brush with the shadow walker as he barely escaped from the elves a few months back.

"I know where my prey has gotten off to," Morcant though wolfishly. His thoughts turned to the crevasse he had faced the shadow walker at. "It's not too far from here," he realized. "And, unless the shadow walker told them of it, the elves have no idea of its existence. Which means the guardian and his boy won't find us until it's too late," the dark thoughts rushed through his twisted mind as fast as he darted from the security of the brush and into the waiting darkness of the evening shadows. Morcant had abandoned all thoughts of stealth as he left the thicket far behind him.

Chapter Twenty: Manifestations

Farvais motioned quickly to Trainor. The path was clear and she wanted him to waste little time getting over to her. She waited impatiently for him to cover the short distance and wondered why he always seemed to take so long doing things when they were trying to be stealthy.

She made a mental note to make him pay for keeping her waiting when they were finished here and alone. Her eyes traced the seam that ran between the huge double doors in front of her. It was unusual to look at and went from the floor all of the way to the ceiling. The lack of a frame around it made it massive. The fact they had been carved out of basalt only made their daunting size that much more intimidating.

The light shuffle of Trainor's footsteps reminded her to check if the sentry was still unconscious. He was and this made her smile broaden a little. As Trainor finally managed to make it to her side she asked silently, in ways only elves can, "Should I kill him?"

"No," he shot back as he visibly smoothed his clothing. "Although Landolin said we could if needed, he did emphasize the 'if needed' bit."

"That's too bad. If he were dead it would be so much easier for us to check out what's on the other side of these doors." She motioned to the looming edifices as she spoke.

"It is odd," Trainor's voice echoed around her in such a way that it disturbed the almost peaceful silence around her perfectly, "so far I have only seen this one guard. There are no light sources to mention either." His confusion was apparent in the tone of his voice as he continued his thought aloud. "I know many of our citadels are built like this, but I have yet to see this style of construction in a place built by any other races. Our eyes are accustomed to the darkness, but few others can, especially not humans. Why would they build a place like this?"

"That is an interesting question," Farvais responded as she finished tying the guard up and ensuring that he had no weapons. "Almost as odd as the fact that this guard was not only unarmed, but untrained as well. It's almost as if whoever built this place wanted it to be infiltrated."

They both looked over the unconscious body one last time before they turned their attention to the door in front of them. "I wonder how they open it?" Farvais thought as she watched Trainor inspect it closely.

"Maybe they don't," he suggested. He turned to face her as if he gave up on trying to find a way through the door.

The ease at which he gave up turned Farvais's stomach as she watched him walk slowly back to her and the guard. Her eyes narrowed as he inspected how well she had tied the guard's wrists and ankles. "Does he think I'm a novice?" she thought to herself in disgust.

"That is what I thought," there was a mocking tone to her voice that she hadn't intended. She did her best to cover it up and reassure him with her tone as she continued, "but then I saw these fresh marks on the floor." She motioned to the base of the door as she spoke. "I'm pretty sure they use a magical charm of some sort to pass, I'm just not sure how they activate it."

"You may be onto something," he agreed easily as he crossed back over tot eh face of the door to inspect it again. "We don't have a lot of time, so hopefully we can figure it out before his superiors miss him and come to check on their missing sentry."

Farvais nodded as she brushed a little dirt away from the door's surface in front of her. "Does that door have a pattern of any sort carved into it?" It was all she could do to hold her frustration in check as she scoured every inch of the stone.

Trainor squinted his eyes and slowly ran his fingers along the almost frozen rock face. From the way he moved them, Farvais could tell that he had all but lost feeling in them. His posture slipped as his fingers pulled away from the stone's surface briefly as it passed over the subtle edge of the hand carved design.

"Well?" Farvais's patience with Trainor wore thin and she knew it showed. "Does it have a pattern etched in it or not?"

"These marks could have been caused by anything. Water, the breath from the mountains, even chisels," he muttered quietly. "Wait. What's this?" Trainor leaned closer to the wall as if doing so would make the stones reveal their secrets to him. "This edge is too long and perfect to be weathering or accidental fracture," he exclaimed softly after studying it for several long moments. "It's odd, because there isn't a discernable pattern from it, but it was made nonetheless."

"What do you mean?" Her voice echoed around them like subtle whispers in a crowd. "Either it does or it doesn't. It can't be both."

"It does," his whisper invaded in her mind as he traced the contours of the carving with his index finger. "Watch," Trainor's voice seemed to grow distant as a slight rumbling noise emanated from the stone. Then, as abruptly as it started, it ended. Nothing seemed different or out of place. "I guess that wasn't quite the right charm," Trainor said disappointedly.

"I guess you're right," Farvais thought to him as she reached out and touched the door. To both of their surprise, the door swung open silently. "Then again, you may have used the right one after all." She looked up at Trainor playfully before she stepped through the open doorway.

Trainor caught her arm as she stepped past him and said quietly, "Be careful, I will stay here and keep an eye on the guard. Let me know if there is more than one room or if we need to search it.

"Agreed," Farvais said coyly. She longed to take him with her into the darkness. Before she could resist, she quickly leaned forward and kissed him. The taste of his lips and the look of surprise were tantalizing gifts that she cherished as she darted through the open doorway and into the darkness.

She felt her lover's eyes on her and thrilled at the feeling of the combined heat she felt from him and the cooling sensation as the darkness engulfed her. She could still feel his emotions whirl around inside his head through their shared bond.

It was one of the few binding spells she had ever allowed someone to cast on her and she was more than glad for it now. The elven warrior did her best to tame her rampant desire for her captain as she explored the cavernous room.

Although her eyes usually adjusted to the almost pitch blackness that surrounded her, this time they didn't. An unsettling feeling settled into her heart as she stepped farther into the darkness.

"Where are the walls?" She thought to herself.

Her left hand was stretched ahead of her as she attempted to find something to use as a point of reference. The whole time, her right hand darted off to the side in a similar manner. She was so intent on her task that the slight click from under her foot took her by complete surprise.

Before Farvais had a chance to react, the sound of stone scraping against stone filled the room. What little light she was using to see with slowly dwindled as the cacophony increased. Frantically she spun around in just enough time to see the brilliant edge of light extinguish itself as the door settled itself back in place.

"TRAINOR!" She screamed. Her voice choked on the force of the word as she dove at the door.

A dull thud resonated through the stone as if in answer to her. She knew her lover was trying to free her. She felt it in every fiber. With each successive thud, she felt another tingle of dread reach through her mind and fasten its vice-like grip around what little hope of escape she clung to.

The door didn't move under Trainor's assault. Not even the full weight of either the elven captain or his armor seemed to have any real impact on the door.

"FARVAIS!" His words were faint and distant. If she wasn't bound to him she would have doubted she even heard his thunderous voice.

"I'm ok, just a little trapped," she hoped he could hear her. Although she wanted to scream, she restrained herself. It would use too much energy and she knew better than exhausting herself so quickly. Instead, she focused on the tenuous bond that gently pulled at the corner of her mind.

"I will find a way to get you out," Trainor bellowed again.

"Shhh. Calm down. I know you are doing everything you can," she reassured her love. "Have you tried the charm again?" She knew he would have to focus in order to work his magic. Farvais just hoped that her words could ease his mind enough to allow for it.

"I have, but it didn't work," Trainor confided a little quieter. She could feel the tears burn the corners of his eyes as she slowed his pounding.

"Let's try it again. But you have to be calm my love," she soothed again. She reached her mind through their mental tether and she felt him physically relax.

"This bond will allow us to do amazing things," his voice played through her memories as she lowered herself into a sitting position.

"Let's see how true that is," she thought to herself calmly. She took deliberate breaths. With each inhalation, Farvais felt her mind slip further into his. She closed her eyes and allowed herself to completely slide away from her body and into his.

It was odd. The tingling sensation slowly faded and left her feeling weightless. She could see out of his eyes, but what she saw was wreathed in golden flames. Everything felt raw, even the air as she breathed through his lungs.

"What is this odd pounding?" She wondered to herself.

"It's my heart," Trainor replied through what felt like her lips. "I can't lose you." His words were less than a whisper, but they resonated through her soul harmonically.

She felt a pit form in her stomach as she thought about how real of a possibility it was becoming. "I won't. We will find a way out of this. I promise. I will not die here." She could feel her words lend an inner strength to him as she spoke them.

"Lose something?" An odd voice called out of the darkness behind him. "Pity, she was so attractive too. I do hope you can find a way to free her from the cistern before it finds her." There was a finality to the words and neither of the elves liked how they sounded.

"Who are you?" Trainor said reflexively.

"The guard must have woke up," Farvais thought in an immediate response to his question as if she was in the room with him.

Trainor as he swiveled to face the source of the voice. A fiery sting erupted along his biceps and brought Trainor to a quick halt. The sensation seemed to scald its way through his armor and into the all too exposed flesh underneath.

The golden haze of her vision shot down to look at his arms. She felt the overwhelming need to see what it was that hit them.

Two impossibly black whips wrapped tightly around his arms. The angle they were being pulled in prevented Trainor from turning to face his assailant.

"Aww, you needn't worry though, I promise to take good care of her if something … unexpected … happens to you." The subtle notes of these words only added a malicious and sinister air to the situation. "After all, it would be such a shame if a big strong elf, like you, found himself in more trouble than he could handle."

"Get out of my head," Trainor pleaded. The fear in his voice broke Farvais's heart. Which is why it took a few moments for her to realize he was speaking to her.

"Why?" Her confusion was too infectious to him and she felt it start to unravel some of his resolve.

"I can't do what I must if I know you are going to be hurt." There was a finality to his words that she hadn't heard since she first met him in the training halls.

He was her instructor then and his word was law. She hung on his every utterance back then for an entirely different reason than she did now. "Alright," she replied meekly. She did her best to stifle the terror she felt building deep with her.

"Why so quiet?" The somewhat effeminate voice asked from the shadows behind them. "You seemed so full of life before. Please tell me that was just a show."

Farvais carefully unhooked her mind from Trainor's and slowly detangled herself from his body. With each connection she severed, she felt an odd distance build. By the time she managed to retreat back into her own body, a small part of her felt empty. It felt almost as if something inside of her died.

"I see," the voice cut through the gathering silence perfectly. "There was another in there as well. Intriguing." The inflection of the words did little to betray the speaker's intention. "I hope this will still be fun." Trainor's assailant's pout was audible.

A chill ran down Farvais's spine as she heard these final words. She was fully back in her own skin and the oddity of it all was slowly settling in. "Please be safe my love," she whispered to Trainor as she felt their bond fade away.

Confusion fought with desperation and despair as she struggled to stay still. Although Farvais wasn't certain about what was happening, she didn't want anything she did to distract her captain.

"What is happening?" She wondered quietly to herself. Her knees pulled themselves involuntarily to her chest and she slowly rocked back and forth.

What little comfort she was able to get vanished as Trainor's screams burrowed through the stone that separated them.

Hessa turned the tome over and over in her hands again. Its black leather surface felt cool to her eager hands. Another quick glance around the room let her know she was still alone.

Her fingers traced the compass rose masterfully engraved in its cover. Although it was not large, the book seemed to weigh heavily in her lap. Thoughts about who could have managed to create such a perfect design danced through her head. The maid found it almost impossible to keep her thoughts focused on one thing.

"My mom kept a journal." She tried the words out on her tongue. They felt foreign and strange. Even the idea was unbelievable when she heard her own voice out loud. "Why didn't she tell me about it?" She wondered aloud.

"That isn't as hard of a question as you might think," his voice floated to her ears softly. "As I said before, the things written in her journal needed to be kept away from those who would destroy it and all of us." A distinct edge slipped its way into his voice and sent a chill down Hessa's spine in a very unnerving way.

"I know you've said it before," Hessa started, "I just can't understand how my mother, of all the people in Cennicus, was selected for this."

"So, I take it you found it?" He asked as he stepped free from the shadows to her right. "You found her journal?"

His attempt to change topics was abrupt. More abrupt than he had been in the past and it concerned her. "I did. Its right here, can't you see it?" Hessa said somewhat bewildered.

As she spoke, their previous conversation about the journal flooded into her mind and she smiled involuntarily. "So the enchantment you mentioned before, it affects all races doesn't it." She watched for the subtle signs of confusion. As they melded through his smooth skin, Hessa couldn't help but grin.

Her smile broadened as she saw him at a loss for words. For once Derecai was speechless and she reveled the moment, although it didn't last long enough.

"Now what?" She asked tentatively. A pit formed in her stomach. She didn't want to give up either the journal or the house.

She finally had a tenuous bond with her mother and she hated to lose it. Not to mention all of the little secrets her mother seemed to have hoarded. There was so much she needed to find out about and Hessa knew the answers less than a breath away. She wasn't strong enough to ignore either this temptation or her own obligations. Everything was so overwhelming, she found it hard to breathe, let alone think.

"I don't want to give any of this up." She managed to say after an overly pregnant pause.

"You won't have to. At least not permanently. Go back to Ellsted. Find your sister. If they ask, you only found an abandoned house full of debris left over from a life half lived," Deracai replied evenly. "Then, when Namir leaves for the manor, find a way to go with him. You can let him know you really found once Ellsted is far behind you. Then you can explain to him how he can find the lost relics. Let him know you want to help. Give grace to the Gods for allowing you to change the course of history and, after it's all done, you will be able to come back here. It really is that simple."

Hessa stared at the shadow walker. She couldn't help it. He made very little sense. From both his words and his demeanor, it seemed as if Derecai actually believed what he was asking her to do was that simple.

"What if I can't find a way to do it? To go to Hornshir with him, I mean." Hessa inquired nervously. Thoughts of

Armani's words floated into her mind. She knew he wouldn't let her go again. Not this time.

"You will find a way, I am certain of it," his tone bore an odd finality to it. Hessa knew he was ending the conversation and she hated it. "I must go, you have visitors. Friends of sorts. Don't worry, they aren't here to hurt you. They may even be able to help you get back to Ellsted." His words faded with him as he melded into the shadows the darkening shadows.

"Hessa, are you in there?" Aves's voice careened through the open window a few paces away from her.

Hessa wondered how Aves had figured out where she was. Her mind raced as she slowly stood up and walked the few steps to the window before she answered, "I'm upstairs. I'll be right down."

Before she walked to the stairs, Hessa snatched up her mother's journal and one of the many leather bags that her mother had kept in a trunk. Without pausing, she deftly slipped the journal into the bag and scooped up the bone case, the note that had been in it, and a few scarves to conceal everything under.

Stairs slipped one after the other under her feet as she satisfied herself with the placement of everything within the bag. She quickly slid the strap over her shoulder as her fingers touched the cold brass knob. There was an odd sense of familiarity settled in and somehow it felt right. A content smile tugged at her lips as she pulled open the door.

Landolin and Gienna traded glances as the passage gracefully split into three more. They had only made it a few paces into the first hall when it had split off into two passages. Now with this new split, neither of them felt good about their first choice.

"Normally I have an exceptional sense of directions, but I fear this catacomb might best me," Gienna shared with her brother.

"Me too," he responded easily. He quickly took a stick of chalk from a small pouch on his belt and lightly drew a quick sketch of a moon shining through two trees. "This should help." He said after he had finished.

"Nicely drawn, brother," Gienna replied as she looked over his work with a slight sense of amusement.

"Why the cattish grin then?" He asked as he caught the slight hint of a smile at the corner of her lips.

"It has been a while since I saw our family sigil. You would have made father proud." She bowed her head and then continued past it. "If we want to have any chance of finishing this search sometime tonight, we should get going."

The first blood curling scream stopped them in their tracks. They exchanged a worried glance at each other as they both strained to hear where the sound had come from. They stood silent and still as if they were statues. It was the second scream that drove home the source of the sounds, Trainor.

Landolin turned to leave as Gienna placed her hand on his bicep lightly. "It is too late for him. We can pray that Farvais survives, but he will be dead before we reach him."

The weight of her words and the truth they carried forced Landolin to his knees. "I have lost too many," his thoughts whirled faster than he could contain them. The stones bit into the palms of his hand as he leaned forward. The bitter taste of bile crept into the back of his throat. His thoughts slowly formed in both of their minds as he pushed himself up from his knees. "I can't bear to lose any more of them."

"Then we must go. If we linger here, Trainor's death with be for nothing. Honor him by continuing. We will avenge him by forcing light into this darkness."

Her words bolstered her brother's strength and he saw a determined smile force its way to her lips. Her increased resolve only added more credence to his own.

"Let's see what we find and learn how we can bring this

church down," Landolin replied with a steely edge to his voice.

Halin followed the music deeper into the caverns. Each time he turned a corner he wondered how much farther it would lead him. The odd pulsing melody of the otherworldly song tugged at his soul and pulled him forward. Halin knew that he wasn't able to stop. Even if he had wanted to.

This is the point where he always woke up. Sometimes he was able to go farther than others, but it always ended the same. He woke up with a huge knot in his stomach and a growing pain erupting from behind his ears and he hated it.

Halin hoped to find the source of these strange dreams. He figured that if he followed them, they might reveal themselves. His mother's stories flooded into his head as he struggled in the dark.

Her dreams were vivid and always a source of great wonder to him. He remembered how some of her dreams came true from time to time. The God's had touched her when she was young, his father would say.

Before Nurn and him had left for Hornshir, Halin distinctly remembered Allair taking the time to tell him about her dreams one last time. This last time there was something else, something different. There was a longing in her voice, and a sadness. Instead of laughing his mother told him that as she got older the dreams became more vivid and frequent.

A tear crept into Halin's eye as he thought about the last words he heard his mother tell him, "Trust your dreams, Serah. You never know when their guidance will save your life." The pet name his mother used for him always brought a smile to his face, no matter how miserable he felt inside. This time was no different.

"I promise to," his words mirrored his memory. Tears from the past mingled with those that had already started to burn their path down his cheeks. His warm tears streamed down his face as he wiped at them with the back of his hand ineffectively. "I will mom," Halin sobbed as he collapsed to his knees.

He fought against the growing tide of fear that threatened to consume him. Inside it felt like the tiny thread of sanity he had cultivated over the last few days was slipping from him and he hated the feeling. Halin felt his hold slip as his mind railed against the thought he might never see his mother again.

Darkness thickened in his mind and images loss accompanied them. His thoughts spun from person to person, face to face. Namir, Aves, Hessa, Tipin, Allair, Armani, Jaconis, Jerine, Carness, the list seemed endless. Even the little elven girl he saw playing in the encampment on the way to the clearing. In the back of his mind, a terrible certainty that he was never going to see any of them again took hold.

Tears flooded through his closed lids. His voice erupted from somewhere deep, somewhere raw. Even the sounds of his screams did little to ease the darkness, so he screamed again. His agony flooded from him into the void around him. He felt the pain as his hot tears etched their way down his cheeks and he savored the sensation.

Chapter Twenty-One: Torments

Farvais shook with fear as she peered through the inky blackness. No matter how hard she tried, it seemed impossible to even make out the largest shape. It had been hard enough to see in the room before the door closed, but now it was utterly impossible.

The captain struggled to recall anything. Some little detail about the room. How far away was the wall? Were there any ornaments or torches attached to it? What else was in the room? The only thing she could clearly recall was the mirror-like floor and nothing else.

Even in the darkness images seemed to shift under its surface. Farvais knew it was just what little light that managed to make it into the room playing with the shadows, but it was eerie. "If there was only enough light to see by," she exhaled to herself.

She slowly backed her way back to the door and breathed a small sigh of relief when she felt the cold stone beneath her outstretched hand. Carefully she turned around and caressed every contour of the door. She recalled Trainor tracing the carvings in a certain way before the door opened the first time. Her only real hope of escape was mimicking it from the inside.

Farvias strained to hear the slightest noise as her gloved hand moved skillfully along the light carvings. Muffled sounds of Trainor's efforts were the only real noises she could discern.

"Open it already," she yelled at the door. She knew he was on the other side, but she had no real recollection of how thick the door had been.

"I'm trying," although it was extremely muffled, she could still hear the frustration in his voice.

"How about the charm. The one that you were showing me the last time," Farvais tried not to sound too hopeful as she spoke.

"I've already tried it a few time. For whatever reason, it isn't working." A slight thud accompanied his words, but he continued speaking before she could ask about it. "I have traced the sigil on this side of the door at least a hundred times," although he exaggerated, she knew what he meant. It felt like she had traced them at least that amount as well, even though she knew she hadn't.

"What else are we going to do?" She asked as she lowered herself to her knees. His voice seemed to be lower now.

In her mind Farvais pictured Trainor sitting with his back against the door. A few strands of his hair pulled from his queue and dangling in front of his face. The look of defeat she imagined set into his countenance broke her heart.

"We can't give up." Her voice was hardly more than a whisper and she knew he wouldn't be able to hear her. "What about the guard?" She asked a little louder. "Do you think he might have something on him? A key or a handle or something?" Her voice sounded frantic to her, so she took another deep breath as she waited for his response.

"That's an idea," he replied.

From the scuffling and scraping noises that made their way through the stone door, she knew he had been sitting. Deep down she hoped she had been wrong about the defeat she imagined he felt.

Silence replace the faint sounds of her lover as he retreated from his perch outside the door. Farvais strained her ears to try and capture any part of the interrogation that she imagined taking place.

"He is going to murder the guard if he doesn't tell him how to get me out of here," the elf said to herself smugly.

The conflict played out in her mind as she settled into a sitting position with her back to the wall. From what she calculated, she was far enough from the door to be clear of it in case Trainor found a way to open it. She pressed her ear against the wall in a desperate attempt to hear anything.

The first sounds of a scuffle only bolstered her hopes. She could make out the slight sound of fists as they smacked against armor and it brought a smile to her face.

"Doesn't the guard know he can't hit Trainor hard enough to hurt him through his armor?" She puzzled aloud.

Slaps turned to solid hits which in turn shifted to the sounds of full-fledged combat. Metallic sounds of steel against stone forced her to press herself harder against the wall. She had to know who was winning. The cacophony of the fight ebbed and flowed. Time blurred for her in the darkness as she drank it all in until there was nothing left.

Silence reigned supreme again in the darkness. Not even the ragged sound of her breathing did much to displace its dominion.

That's when she heard it, the ever so slight gurgle. A death rattle. Her blood froze as she recognized the pleading voice. Trainor was wounded, possibly dying and she couldn't do anything about it. Helpless clawed at her mind as she fought to merge with the wall.

Then Trainor's scream hit her ears and her world shattered. Even though they were extremely muffled, she could tell he was in pain. Worse, he was dying and he was afraid.

"What have I done?" She whispered to herself in the darkness.

"Nothing my dear," a familiar voice called to her calmly through the darkness.

"Who are you?" Farvais demanded in the most commanding tone she could manage. Given the situation, she knew she was in trouble. But there was something familiar about the soothing tones, something that slipped from her just as fast \as she noticed it.

"I am no one to be concerned about," The voice replied in the same soothing way. An effeminate way. One it had just used a few moments before.

"I doubt that," Farvais responded snidely. The cold metal of her dagger felt good in her gloved hand as she pulled it part way from its scabbard. "Why should I believe you?" She added as an afterthought.

"Why, it's simple," the voice replied. Farvais was able to tell it belonged to a woman, but she was unsure of the race and the build. "I know the way out of here. You would like to know it, wouldn't you?"

Farvais strained to see who spoke to her, but failed at every attempt to plumb the darkness with her senses and it frustrated her. "I would, but please I am having a problem seeing you. Can you please step closer?" She said coyly. Farvais hoped she might trick the other woman into coming close enough to grab her. It would be easier to get answers from her once she was contained.

"But I'm right here," the lady replied in Farvais's same coy tone.

The sound of the voice even shifted as Farvais listened to it. The way the vowels were sounded out and the staccato rhythms of the consonants moved to mirror the elf's in every way. By the time the last word was spoken, Farvais felt the odd sensation of hearing herself answer the questions she posed.

A warm puff of air played along the back of Farvais's ear and an odd sensation of fear and intimacy struggled for dominance. She felt the tips of the other lady's fingers press against the back of her armor as the lady spoke again in her own voice, "And you do look scrumptious. In fact, I might just want to keep you here with me forever."

A shiver ran down Farvais's spine as the words oozed down her cheek. Although she could not see her visitor, she could smell her. Her scent was a putrid combination of sweat and grime. The noxious combination made the elf's stomach roll in disgust.

"I think I will pass!" Farvais shouted abruptly.

In one fluid motion, she pivoted on the ball of her foot and swung her balled up fist at where the other lady's face should have been. Nothing slowed her swing as she followed through with her opposite elbow. She must have moved a little farther away and Farvais wanted to make sure she connected this time. The unexpected elbow managed to brush against something hard and left the elf puzzled at her opponent's speed.

"This will certainly not do!" The lady shouted back. Her words mimicked Farvais's perfectly now, as did her actions.

It became hard to breathe as the lady hit Farvais in the stomach with something hard. Tears welled up in Farvais's eyes as she struggled for air. Even though she was wearing leather armor, it felt as if she wasn't. Whatever her opponent had used, hit with enough force to completely knock all of her air out.

The crippling pain in her gut stopped her from pulling in a deep enough breath to recover. Even the small gulps of air she managed to drag in only brought her more pain.

Small lights started to dance at the edge of Farvais's vision as his mind started to spin. The odd weightlessness that always accompanied dizziness settled in as she squeezed her eyes shut.

"I need to breathe," Farvais screamed at herself mentally.

She fought uselessly against the growing vertigo. She felt her legs turn rubbery and knew it was over. Even the sharp jolt ass he hit the floor did little to help her situation.

The lady's fingers slid along the side of Farvais's face and gently turned it upwards. Her limp body rolled with the motion. She was completely helpless against this thing.

"All this spunk and a pretty face too. I think I will have

some fun with you." The delicate words were the last thing that Farvais heard as she gave into the dizzying darkness that had overtaken her.

Namir poured over the tomes again. He needed to find more information. He desperately needed to understand if the great Calanari hero, Halin, was really his father.

"It is good to see you so studious," Alequa's voice was more melodic than he had recalled it to be.

"I feel like I am close to figuring out who my father was," Namir shared as he looked up from the four open books in front of him.

Alequa looked at him somewhat confused. "I'm not sure I understand your devotion. Why does it matter who your father was when it's your mother who secures your title? It is through her side that your birthright has been decided, not your father's."

"I understand that, but I need to know if he was a good person. I need to know if I will be a good ruler if I choose this path." Namir's pleading eyes conveyed more to Alequa than either his tone or his words possibly could.

She walked over and wrapped her arms around him while she gently pulled him close. "For better or worse, you are our best hope. Please understand that who your parents are, or were, makes little difference on the kind of ruler you will be." Her words wore soft and Namir closed his eyes and settled into her velvety embrace. "Whether your father was a great man or a vile one makes no difference. Even if your mother had been a horrible person, her blood in you is what gives you the chance to make a difference."

Namir leaned his head back against her should as he found his voice. "But I don't know who I am." The odd edge of fear was overly apparent in his simple sentence and he hated how it sounded.

"You are Namir Merides. Rightful ruler of all of Cennicus. You are the one great hope for your people and for mine.

Nothing else matters anymore." Her words were full of inspiration, but Namir couldn't help but feel worried.

"What if I fail? What if I am really just a boy that lost his parents and all of this is a misunderstanding?" His words were flowing like a stream. Babbling uncontrollably over the bumps of his teeth.

"Shhh," Alequa soothed. She ran the fingers of her left hand through Namir's tussled hair as she spoke in a calming tone. "I know you are frightened. You should be. So much depends on you now. But don't let the unknown drag you down."

"It would just help to reassure me if I knew more about my parents, both of them," Namir said hopefully.

"I know. I just wish I could help more." Alequa responded softly. "I can tell you everything you want to know about your mother, but your father is a mystery to me. All I say about him is that he knew it was best for you, and the country, that he not reveal himself. He understood that by him remaining hidden in your life he wouldn't be a distraction from what was important."

"And what is that?" Namir cut in. "What did he think would be more important than being there for me?"

"He knew that when you came of age you would focus on your birthright. Without him, you are a king without a mold. You will have only yourself to dictate what you do and how you accomplish it. If he had stayed, you would always be judged by his actions and accomplishments. No matter how great or how limited those may have been."

"And what is that?" Namir asked. He knew she was going to talk about the legacy his mother had left him, but he wanted to hear her say it.

Alequa smiled subconsciously as she held onto the future king. "Your birthright of course," she said plainly. "And we need to discuss your plans on how you are going to reclaim it from those that would keep it for themselves."

"Do you know who we are talking about and how many?" Namir blurted out before he could stop himself. He hated that he had just ruined the moment and would have given anything to have kept it alive for just a little longer. Alequa's arms felt heavenly around him and he could not recall a moment in the last few months that he felt so serene.

"No, but I think there are a few things I need to tell you so you fully understand the importance of your role," Alequa said calmly as she stepped back from Namir toward a little chair close to the desk he had been working at. "You see I occasionally have prophetic dreams and recently they have all centered on you. That is how I knew to find you here. I also know you need help, a task that I'm more than willing to assist with." Alequa confided.

"What do you mean?" Namir questioned her, his interested obviously peaked.

"Recently I have seen you fight someone. It's as if you two were in an arena. In the dream, the arena is a figurative one and symbolizes Cennicus. Who the other person is, remains a mystery, for now." Alequa lied smoothly as she held his steely blue eyes with her shining azure stare.

"THERE IS SOMETHING SHE IS NOT SAYING," Zelios advised Namir in his mind.

"Do you mean she is lying to me?" He thought at his amulet. Namir felt a little stupid trying to communicate with an inanimate object. He wished he understood more about how it worked and what its limitations were. "Evidentially it can read intentions and thoughts." He said in his head guardedly.

"AYE, I CAN READ THOUGHTS," Zelios replied in his head again, "EVEN THE THOUGHTS OF AN ELVEN PRIESTESS. SOME OF WHICH ARE TRUE, BUT THE MORE RECENT ONES SEEM FALSE."

Namir's eyes narrowed as he contemplated what to do or say next. "It feels like there is something you're not telling me," Namir said several short heartbeats later.

Alequa studied the boy for a few tense moments before she

finally decided to answer. "It seems little gets past you sa'ouvant," she commented aloofly. "So I guess I must answer your questions, even if they were unspoken." She nodded as she watched his body language for clues so she could better read him in the future. "I have contracted at least two ships to set sail after we reach Hornshir. I believe you would like to gather the Items of Power that my husband and Natlia worked so hard to hide away."

"Why didn't you talk to me before you did this?" Every time Alequa answered a question, Namir always had another three take its place and he hated it.

"Was I wrong to believe ships would be needed?" Alequa asked feigning a perceived insult. She waited until he shook his head no in the brooding manner he had recently adopted. "Where I'm from we anticipate what our leaders need us to do. We rarely wait to be told. Waiting sometimes causes more problems than acting immediately. And, after all, for this cause time is of the essence." Alequa offered her explanation apologetically.

"I see," Namir replied as he dissected her answer. "Next time, tell me first. And, whatever you do, don't make me pry it out of you." He knew Alequa now believed that he was upset about her little charade. What she did not know is it was mostly an act. He needed her to think of him as having less insight than he had so he could make the needed changes with little or no resistance from those around him.

"Very well sa'ouvant," Alequa bowed her head in deference, "as you wish."

Gienna and Landolin raced down the pitch black hallways side by side. Whatever chased them did not anticipate elves would infiltrate these catacombs. It obviously had not planned on any intruder having their elfish ability to see in the dark, which was something the two of them used to their fullest advantage.

"Turn down the next passage on the left," Landolin whispered into his sister's mind as he pulled an arrow free from the quiver on his back. His mental words held the same reverberating tones that he used when he spoke to his soldiers and she hated it.

"Ok," her thoughts raced back as she freed an arrow as well.

The two of them nocked their arrows in unison. Each pivoted and sighted their respective targets as they ran. The slight hum of their bowstrings joined the whisper of their feet as they brushed the stones of the floor as they leapt around the corner.

Their arrows released in perfect unison as they flew toward their marks. Landolin's arrow arced down the corridor they just fled and Gienna's darted down the hall they just turned down, but the other half of it.

Ahead of them, in the inky blackness, both siblings noticed an unusual outcropping. It was obvious, even to their untrained eyes, the architect struggled to make it blend in with the natural cave-like structure. Overall the effect was good, but not great. Instead of blending the outcropping seamlessly into the ceiling, their keen night vision made it stand out. The two of them slowed their pace in perfect unison as they neared it.

They visually probed the darkness and found another useful feature. A large metal door, barely visible in the darkness, was nestled into the cavern wall at the upper end of a short flight of stairs. Although there were not many stairs, the number of landings was remarkable.

Each landing looked large enough to hold at least five well-armed men. The numerous locations were only separated by two or three stairs before another one took over.

As if the construction of these platforms were not odd enough, two types of markings vied for dominance across the floor's surface. The first set were deep and well-defined grooves easily visible along the edge of each platform. The other marks were shallower and crisscrossed the exposed faces of every surface.

"Don't try to go through the door," Gienna shot to Landolin.

She recognized the simple, yet effective trap and she hoped her brother would as well. With a quick flick of her wrist and a nod, she motioned toward the roof of the cavern above the stairs.

The elf watched her brother's smile crease his lips and she knew Landolin understood it. His garnet eyes played along the deeply gouged gutters in the roof pensively.

From what her brother mentioned in passing, he had first witnessed this kind of trap during the War of the Races. One of the fortresses in some remote mountainous area was full of them. And, while it had been a long time since he would have seen a guillotine trap, she knew a part of him loved their sadistic simplicity.

She watched as he silently counted and calculated the number of blades needed to make this particular trap effective. "Well? How many?"

"From the cuts along the floor and the tracks in the ceiling, between ten and twenty. Without triggering them, we won't be able to really know for sure." There was a gleeful longing that she detecting in his words. As if he wanted to see the trap activated in all of its horrific glory.

"I see," she responded coolly. "I take it these are the spinning blade traps you spoke of?" Gienna felt bile rise in the back of her throat as she thought about what would happen to the unlucky idiot that attempted to open the door.

"It is," Landolin agreed quietly.

"So anyone that tries to open the door dies," she hated how simple it sounded.

"Aye, them and any of their friends foolish enough to stand on these platforms." He motioned toward the stairs and their adjoining landings.

"All of them?" Gienna felt a look of horror etch itself into her features as the words slipped out of her lips harshly.

"All of them," the solemnity that filled her brother's voice as he responded was slowly replaced by awe as he continued, "These blades are housed in the ceiling and poised to launch silently toward their unsuspecting prey. The best part of this particular trap is its layout. You see, it was designed to separate, then kill, a large group of people. Those that don't die immediately are separated from each other. If they try to move from the stairs to another landing, they will be cut down by the blade on one of its many returns. Each of these wall-like plates partitioned off the areas and allow the blades controlled and unfettered access to the platforms. Even if someone were to avoid the first pass of the deadly blades, they would be worn down by the necessity to move constantly in order to avoid the blade on its return. And that is assuming there is only one blade per platform. More than likely there are two or three each."

"This is monstrous," she knew her brother could see how appalled she was and she didn't care. "No matter how horrible a person is, they deserve a better death than this. How do you open the door without triggering the trap?"

"You can't. That's part of this device's beauty. Once the door opens, the trap is sprung. I'd bet that it doesn't lead anywhere, just to a wall." His smugness did little to make Gienna enjoy the device's design.

"Why would someone need to build something as devilish as this?" She spat as she slowly stepped off from the first step.

"To kill intruders. It would be especially effective against people running form a monster locked away in the caverns." She knew he hinted at their situation so she responded with a sneer. "But it does give me an idea."

Landolin's thoughts outpaced his ability to structure them into a coherent message, so instead, she saw his thoughts flood into her mind. She knew he allowed them to transmit directly into her head instead and there was nothing she could do about it.

In most situations, this sort of laziness could be lethal to the receiver since most people think in completely different ways, so the invading images cause an overload in the receiver's mind.

However, Landolin's thoughts were similar enough to her own since they were twins. She hoped that if he was trying to communicate to anyone else, Landolin would show more restraint.

"Interesting thought, it just might work," she replied mentally as she carefully removed her quiver and set her bow delicately on the floor to her side. "I will wait by the door to spring the trap; you hide up by the top of the plate release closest to the artificial outcropping to secure our exit."

She purposefully flooded his mind with her thoughts and efficiently mapped out her whole plan. She knew their success hinged on his ability to control the blades without being seen. Within seconds she calculated the possible outcomes and restructured her plan until it satisfied most of them without Landolin needing to ask anything.

She could feel her brother's amazement at both the speed she formulated her plan and its thoroughness. She knew he had served under quite a few commanders that could learn a few things from her and his thoughts flattered her in a way he never had before. She beamed with pride as she watched her brother quickly set off to ensure escape route from this mess.

Chapter Twenty-Two: Impressions

Skara carefully padded down the silent hallway cautiously as she crept closer to Namir's room under the council chamber. Her eyes scoured every crevice as she passed in an attempt to take in every detail that would give her an edge in the confrontation that was about to happen. She had no idea about who the boy had managed to get to protect him and, based on their previous encounters, he had a certain propensity for having very proficient guardians on his side.

"I hate not knowing if he is even here," she thought to herself bitterly. She occasionally glanced back at Faris to make sure that she had not lost him. "Another waste of my talents," her thoughts grew darker as she realized she could tell where her compatriot was based solely on the sounds he made. The combination of his heavy ragged breathing and the way his boots scrapped the floor etched themselves into her mind in a very unforgettable way.

"Try to move a little quieter!" Skara admonished in a harsh whisper. "The last thing we need to do is let him hear us before we lose the element of surprise!"

She narrowed her glowing green eyes at Faris as she glowered at him. The feline knew the effect this had on humans and enjoyed every minute as she watched him squirm under her gaze. Her stare burrowed little holes through his soul until he finally nodded his understanding and changed how he moved.

"I hate having to work with some humans," she thought to herself as her mind drifted back to the activities she had pursued with Armani for the last few nights. Her left hand slid down the belly of her armor unconsciously and her tongue flicked across her lips lightly at the memories.

"The door is just head, what's the plan?" Faris's whisper forced Skara to refocus her attention back to their task.

"What is happening to me?" Skara wondered as she studied the door at the end of the hallway. It was completely shrouded in darkness. Not even one glimmer of light seemed to penetrate its surrounding gloom. "I think it best if you open the door quickly and dash in," she instructed evenly. "I will stay here, in the shadows, and strike when needed. I think this is the best way to ensure both your safety and the successful completion of the mission."

Her voice was quite enough that it forced Faris to lean in closely or miss the specifics of the plan. She heard him struggle to choke back a snicker as he muttered under his breath, "Just make sure that's the order you do it in." She could tell that his mood was dark and his patience was thin.

"I might not," Skara hissed her response to his sarcastic comment. "Our mistress wants the mission completed at almost any cost. Do your best to remember that so you stay out of the way of my daggers this time." She knew her words stung, she just hoped they had the desired impact on him.

Faris grunted something else under his breath that even her keen ears couldn't make out as he maneuvered in front of her and carefully placed his hand on the door's handle. She watched him pause as he waited for her signal. Before he could rethink his utterances, she tapped her signal on his shoulder.

Without thought, Faris depressed the latch and threw his full weight against the door. He purposefully rolled himself into a ball and threw himself across the room as far as he could. His sword and dirk were drawn in mid-spin as completed his somersault into the middle of the room. Both Faris and Skara let out a startled gasp as they realized in unison this room was just as vacant as the last one had been.

She boldly strode into the middle of the room and stood beside Faris's balled up body as she spoke, "In the name of our Goddess what is going on?" Skara demanded as she spun around in place and took in the complete emptiness that surrounded her.

"I don't know!" Faris snapped. "We were both there when one of my men said Namir had been staying here."

Faris's look of surprise decided Skara's next plan of action better than anything she could have asked for. "Leave your last two soldiers here. You and I shall explore the rest of this pathetic little town and find out where he has taken refuge." Skara seethed as she paced out of the room.

"Tali will not be pleased," she thought to herself in fear. "First we fail to kill the girl, now this. What else can go wrong?" Skara wondered to herself as she overheard Faris pass her instructions on to the last of his little contingent. Her teeth gnashed together as she dove back into the shadows.

Hessa looked at Aves and the gypsy that accompanied her in confusion. She still could not wrap her mind around the fact they were both there and the gypsy had admitted to knowing her mother personally. "So how did you know my mother again?" Hessa did her best to hide her full curiosity from her tone.

A smile creased his overly attractive features as she asked. Somehow the combination of this grin and the twinkle in his eye reminded Hessa of a fox that managed to get caged with the chickens for the night.

"She was an old friend of my mother's," he said a little too quickly.

Hessa knew Aves studied the man's every move just like she was, but it did little to ease her fears about the man. All she could tell was he was guarded. She really hoped Aves could discern more.

"In fact, my mother was well acquainted with all of your parents," he added. All of them felt the tension increase a little as if his knowledge of their parents were some sort of taboo.

"How many parents does she have?" Aves asked mockingly. Hessa knew she was trying to pin down exactly what this gypsy knew.

"I meant my mother knew both Hessa's parents and your own." Onas clarified as he shot a knowing look at both ladies. "But how did this conversation become about me and what I know?" He asked somewhat jovially. "I thought you came all this way to retrieve your friend."

"I am," Aves admitted somewhat ashamed.

"Well then, I guess I am done here," Onas said over his shoulder as he turned to leave.

"Not quite," Hessa replied. She was pleased when he stopped in mid-step. "Please allow my sister and I resolve a few things before you go. She may need an escort."

"But I've come to bring you home," Aves interjected a little downtrodden.

Hessa felt her sister's hazel eyes bore little holes wherever she looked, so she returned the look. She realized it was the first time she really looked at Aves since she had stepped foot on her mother's property.

"What if I say no?" Hessa asked somewhat confused about the shift in Aves's demeanor. Aves blinked back a wave of tears and was obviously confused, so she added, "I have a lot to take care of here." With one sweeping gesture, she motioned to the house and the property. "I have also found things Natlia, my mother, needed me to finish for her." Her voice was laden with the same determination that filled it when she found her mother's journal and she knew it.

"So it's settled then? You have decided to leave us?" Aves asked. Everyone heard the heartbreak in her voice. Hessa hated how it made her feel, but she remained silent and let her sister speak. "So in the note you left, you meant everything in it then?" Aves's words sounded foreign. As if someone else spoke out of her mouth and it confused Hessa completely.

Hessa looked from Aves to Onas and back as she said, "I meant everything I said in my note, but I never said I would be gone forever. I certainly didn't say I was planning on leaving either you or our father. All it said was that I now owned a house and that I needed to go so I could find out what else I didn't know about my mother." Her explanation sounded harsher than she intended, but she felt overwhelmed and cornered.

Aves stared at Hessa in obvious disbelief. "You know Armani is your father?" Aves finally asked after she regained her composure. "How long have you known?"

"I just found out today," Hessa replied evenly. The confused look still dominated Aves's face, so she added, "I read about it in my Natlia's journal. When did you find out?"

"Father told me this morning. I didn't expect you to have found out." Aves pouted. It was very apparent to everyone that she wanted to surprise Hessa with this little bit of information.

"Now that we have settled that," Onas said smoothly. He timed is interruption well and took complete control over their conversation, "can we return to Ellsted. I have a few things I need to take care of and I'd rather do them soother as opposed to later."

"You mean our people," Hessa said with a knowing grin. She studied Onas's handsome features as she spoke and was amazed. Not only was he comely, his skin hid the telltale signs of aging extremely well. The little lines around his eyes and lips were all but invisible.

"Aye, I do," Onas replied merrily.

"You mean Natlia was a gypsy?" Aves asked incredulously.

"She was," Hessa agreed with a slight nod of her head, "as

is Armani." Hessa heard Aves's gasp and instantly realized her half-sister had no idea of their father's true heritage.

"Was," Onas interjected. "Armani was numbered amongst our familia, but he chose to shun us and embrace a different path. A mahrime path." Onas practically spat these last few words in contempt.

"What do you mean? IS my father a gypsy or not?" Aves asked completely perplexed by the conversation.

"Do you know why?" Hessa asked completely enthralled by Onas's knowledge.

"You mean what influenced him to leave?" Onas asked subtly as he gauged Hessa's reactions to his words. "No. I just know he broke our liri and was exiled."

"So my father isn't a gypsy?" Aves interrupted again as she tried to get a straight answer.

Both Onas and Hessa turned and looked at Aves in Unison. Hessa saw the fear that loomed behind Aves's eyes and felt her heartbreak. She glanced back to Onas for help as she started to help Aves understand, "Aye…"

Onas held his hand up and quickly silenced both girls. "No, he is not one of them and please refrain from naming any of our people with that slur. We are the Dekka or Dekkari. Our heritage is true and our lineage can be traced back to the first kings of Cennicus!" Onas's temper visibly flared and it was obvious that he did not care.

"We are sorry for any insults," Hessa said hurriedly. She hated being left in the dark, but she knew better than to insult those that have agreed to help her family. Even if she had no idea why Onas had agreed to help in the first place. She would do her best to make sure he would be willing to help in the future if they needed him to.

"Neither of us knew it was an insult," Aves cut in skillfully.

Hessa marveled at how well her sister tuned into her own thoughts and completed them.

"No offence taken," Onas conceded as he took a deep

breath to give his pride a chance to recover. "You both needed to understand that you are better than the geje. Your familia, brethren to me, as much as Armani was, if not more so."

Hessa felt her heart skip a little as she momentarily locked gazes with his soulful hazel eyes. If she had any doubts why Aves had chosen him, they were driven out. "I thought she was in love with Nurn," she caught herself thinking. Although his eyes swept from hers to Aves's and lingered there longer, Hessa knew this man could be more trouble than he was worth.

"Your father's sins are not yours and you're welcome to reclaim your heritage. That is if you wish to."

"I am not going to abandon my father," Aves said sternly.

Hessa knew that Aves was aware of Onas's intentions just as much as she knew that he was not a threat. At least not directly. She was just a little confused at the odd body language Aves assumed every time she addressed the man. While she became more formal and distant in her speech, she all but clung to the man physically.

"I do appreciate your offer, Onas. But, you see, my father is the only family I have. I cannot just abandon him, especially not now. Our lives are being ripped to shreds. He needs me." Tears welled in Aves's eyes as she turned from Onas and looked at Hessa. Her words came out haltingly as she said, "He needs both of us. It really hurt him when he heard me read your note. He cried and I have never seen him do that before."

Hessa's heart sank at Aves's words. It was almost too much for her. She knew her sister wanted her to reply, to say something, so she did.

Hessa's words quietly slipped from her lips and she felt her heart release a little bit of its pain as she said, "I never meant to hurt him. I hope you understand that. But I had to come here. I had to find out what my mother was like. Who she really was. All that I've ever known of her are the rare stories our father would offer." Her eyes met Aves's briefly. Her pain was apparent and Hessa could not take more than a couple seconds of it. Seeing it, even for that long, tore at her soul.

"Again, I didn't think my note was that bad."

"It was," Aves assured her half-sister. She carefully reached into her pouch and retrieved it as if she sought to justify her presence here.

Aves meticulously unfolded the pages. The crisp sound of the tight creases broke the silence that had built itself around them eerily. She paused once more to clear her throat before she read the note aloud,

> "I'm leaving. Don't try and find me or stop me. I've been kept as a slave for far too long.
>
> In my mind, I can forgive the fact that you've treated me this way, but my heart will ever remain jaded toward you for your actions. Neither of you once took the time to truly think about how I felt, unless it was to further your own position with someone in the community.
>
> Armani, I know you must've either cared for my mother greatly or despised her. That much is clear since you never once brought in another servant. Natlia was your cook, your maid, your seamstress, your errand girl, and your stable hand. While she was alive you made sure she was tasked more than humanly possible, yet, as I recall, she managed to abide by your every whim. I'm truly sorry I wasn't able to live up to your expectations as well as she had.
>
> Aves, dear cousin. Thank you for your hand-me-downs and little favors. If you hadn't insisted I go with you to Hornshir, I never would have known what it was like to live as you do. The idea that I can make changes happen in this world was beyond me until then. Sure I knew about how to take care of another, but not how to live for myself. This is the greatest, and most unexpected gift, you could possibly give to me and one I am sure you would take back if you could.
>
> I fear lesser people might look harshly back at the hard

work forced upon me by the two of you, but not me. I know that whether you meant for me to flourish as I have or not, the many years of training has only made me a better person.

So again, I thank you for the opportunity to see what freedom feels like and I wish nothing but the best for you two in your search for another woman to enslave. Hopefully, you will find one that doesn't mind the snide glances and subtle grabs as she cleans. Know that I will ever remain silent about how much Armani enjoys beating his help when no one is around. I know it makes him feel powerful, especially on those days the council sides against him.

I will always have a tender place in my heart for the two of you.

And it was signed Hessa." Aves's tone was flat as she read it. It was obvious she had read the letter's contents many times from the way the words flowed evenly through her taut lips.

"I didn't write that!" Hessa exclaimed vehemently. Tears welled up in the corner of her eyes as each word struck her face.

The note was succinct and cold, something she could never write. "The note I left was only one page," she begged. "In it, I said I was going for a day or two. I playfully asked you to stall your father so I could discover more about my mother. I also mentioned in it that she had left me her house and I needed to take some time to explore it."

Her words seemed to fall on deaf ears as she pleaded with her half-sister. "I would never lead a note like that. You know me better than that!"

"I thought I did," Aves admitted, "but that doesn't change what you put in your letter. I found it on your bed. No one, other than you, would go into your room. Besides, why would anyone replace your letter with a forgery?" Aves's questions cut Hessa to the bone and the girl winced as each word struck her.

"Because she is from a good family," Onas cut in to defend Hessa quickly. He smiled as Aves glared at him. "That is plenty reason, at least it seems that way in my experience."

"What does that mean?" Aves threw her question at Onas, much to Hessa's relief.

"How well do you really know your father?" Onas asked as he deftly dodged the issue.

"What does that matter?" Aves's temper was at the boiling point and everyone present knew it.

"It matters a great deal," Hessa cut in. "I'm sorry, but I don't think our father is as great a man as we believed." Hessa carefully took Aves hand and slowly guided her to a chair.

"What are you saying?" Aves demanded a little more timidly. "Why do you think our father is anything but the honorable leader he has proven himself to be?"

"That life is a lie," Onas sneered, "at least it is if you looked at the actions he took to get there." There was a malicious twinkle in the man's eyes that made Hessa feel a little uncomfortable.

"I don't want to hear about these lies." Aves cried. The large tears pulled at Hessa's soul as they tugged free from her sister's hazel eyes.

She felt caught between the two of them in. It was almost as if she was caught in a different world. The level of hatred that Onas exuded mirrored Aves's fear and horror perfectly. The fact that both of them pulled more strength from the same thing only made it more complicated.

"I am sorry, but I think it is about time you learned who Armani really is," Onas said somewhat sinisterly.

"You have no proof," Aves muttered helplessly. "It is all just words. Her knees buckled slightly as if she bore a weight a little too heavy for her, and she barely made it over to the chair before she collapsed."

"I'm afraid we do." Hessa cut in. Her words slipped out

before she really knew what she was saying. She knew her sister was desperately clinging to the image she had of their father. It was the only thing she really had left and she hated to take it from her. She just hated knowing that Aves clung to a lie.

"We have my mother's journals and," Hessa waived off Aves's objections before she could voice them, "we have a couple 'gifts' he gave my mother." She struggled to control her waring emotions so she looked down at her hands as she continued, "When you see them, you will see it proves his actions better than anything else can."

Aves's pleading look took a toll on Hessa. She watched as her longtime friend slowly descended into despair as each of Hessa's words hit her.

"I think we found him!" Faris called over to Skara.

The deep red rooftop glistened with dew. Each of them crouched so as not to draw unneeded attention to themselves, which was a difficult task during sunrise. Especially since the roof they were on directly overlooked Ellsted's central square.

"Where?" Skara asked as she crept deftly over to him.

"There," he replied as he pointed away from the Council Hall. "I see him in the smithy's courtyard." He said confidently. "At least I think it looks like him."

Skara squinted in the direction Faris's outstretched finger indicated.

The dazzling light as it played across the gems set in the ring on his finger caught her eye and momentarily distracted her from their task.

"I'll have to ask him where he got that ring," she thought to herself as forcefully refocused her attention back to their task.

"I don't see him," she growled.

"Over there, at the smithy," there was a superior tone to Faris's voice that rankled the fur on the back of Skara's neck as he spoke.

Her patience for this human wore thin as her eyes slowly adjusted to the brightness of the sunlight that met her gaze. It streamed over the horizon and exaggerated the obstacles that lay between her and the smithy with its stark light.

Her target's golden locks caught the gathering light just right to make him more visible, even at their distance. "You may be right," Skara smiled as she spoke.

She carefully watched him as he pulled a pail of water from the smithy's well. He moved with a certain grace she had not expected. The ease at which he managed to not only lift the bucket, but pour the contents into the two clay vases he had with him was unimaginable for a boy of his stature. Especially since the brownish red cloak he wore looked bulky.

"We may still have a chance to do our mistress's bidding," Skara purred. Her rough tongue flicked out and caressed her lips in anticipation of the hunt.

"It won't be easy to get at him there," Faris added as he surveyed the smithy cautiously.

"Why is that? From what I can see, aside from the wall, the place looks easy enough to get into." Skara snapped skeptically.

"Well for starters, the smith is a Calanari." His tone, though flat, was menacing as his words fell from his lips. "It also doesn't help that he fought in, and survived, the battle of Watchkeep," Faris recalled the last time he felt the wrath of a Watchkeep veteran and he did not want to relive the experience.

"The smith survived the Watchkeep massacre?" Skara said.

Her voice warbled nervously as her fingers played with one of the hilts protruding from her belt. Although she knew they were alone, she felt exposed by the openness of their position at the same time.

"He did," Faris replied. "From what I've been able to piece together, there are at least three of them in Ellsted."

"Three of the five? Here, in one place?" She fought against the rising tide of fear in her own mind valiantly, but she knew she was going to lose.

"Yes," Faris said calmly.

Skara could tell by the look on the man's haggard face that he had known this information for quite some time. Maybe ever since they first set foot in Ellsted.

Tension built between the two as a beleaguered silence built. There were too many secrets Faris had kept from her and she hated it. Likewise, she knew he felt the same way about her. Skara knew it was hard to trust someone with a secret agenda and both of them obviously had one.

"Why did you keep this to yourself?" Skara asked once she had managed to get a hold of her emotions.

"Because I had hoped that the only one we would have to deal with was Daffer, the inn keep. Now that's obviously not the case." The gravity in his voice was evident as he spoke. His words fell in hushed tones and lent to the feeling of exposure Skara had felt ever since she learned the truth about the smith. "This is why we need to have a plan in place before we go in to get the boy."

"Agreed," Skara nodded as she scrutinized what she could see of the building's layout from their vantage point. "What are your thoughts on infiltration?"

A skeptical and surprised look played across Faris's face as she spoke. She knew he would be taken off guard by her sudden interest in his ideas, especially since she had never really asked him for any advice before. But this time was different. If she hoped to kill their target and get out of the smithy alive, she needed to have him believe in their plan. Especially if she had to sacrifice him in the process.

"We need to ensure that Tipin is either away from the house or distracted before we make our way in." He looked over the courtyard again as he obviously thought about a plan of attack. "Any idea about where our target is sleeping in there?”

“None yet, but I plan on finding that out tonight after everyone has fallen asleep, Skara replied reassuringly. Her mind flew through several different scenarios on how she could infiltrate the smithy as they spoke about the final details.

“Good. Once we know that we can plan our path for extraction.”

Chapter Twenty-Three: Aurora

Namir set down the book he had been holding and rubbed his eyes. He gently pushed his chair away from the table and looked across the cluttered chaos of pages and books sprawled out in front of him.

Although it was morning, the room was only illuminated by the dim light thrown by the lantern on the wall. Miniscule shadows played across every surface that met his eye. Even these little subtle shifts of light and dark added to his frustration.

"So I guess the first thing we need to do is decide about which artifact we should go after," Haradine said as she took it all in as well.

"No," Namir refocused his attention away from her deep azure colored eyes to her soft lips as he continued his sentence carefully, "we need to figure out where all the artifacts so we can determine how best to retrieve them. I plan on collecting as many of them as I can. Only then can we be certain they don't fall into the wrong hands." His jaw was set as he finished his thoughts verbally.

"You want to collect *all* of the artifacts?" Haradine's jaw dropped as the meaning of Namir's words fully sank in.

Namir waited while she ran her slender fingers through her honeydew hair absently. He wanted to make sure she was ready before he explained anything else. Even in the feeble light, he could see the subtle lines of dread set in around the corners of her eyes and lips.

"If we can," Namir nodded. "Half of the problem will be finding them. I haven't come across a single location anywhere in your father's notes. There are only a few comments about regions and a couple place names scattered throughout. Occasionally he mentions a castle or a forest, but that's about all." He knew his exacerbation was evident and he did not care.

"Why do you need to get all of them again?" Haradine's eyes fixed on his as she asked.

He knew she struggled to understand him. She always did. For some reason, she found it very hard to decipher his intentions. Something which Namir found a modicum of pleasure in. He quickly decided to bury his growing amusement at her questions by thinking about the conflicting information in the journals.

After a long sigh, he finally answered, "Because I'm going to need all of them if I plan on claiming my throne," Namir said bluntly.

"Do you understand what these things are? These are items of power, not just some tools or weapons to be bandied about as you see fit. These artifacts contain the power of the Old Gods." Her tone was scathing and each word dripped with incredulity. "from the stories I've heard, you are lucky to have survived touching the one already in your possession."

"I know how powerful they are, which is why I need as many of them as I can get." Namir's determination was almost too intense for her to handle.

"But why?" Haradine exclaimed. The smooth line of her brow furrowed a bit in frustration. "Wouldn't one or two relics hold enough power to justify you as the rightful heir? Everyone seeing Zelios around your neck should know that you speak the truth. All of the legends, even among humans, tell of the power contained within that sapphire, ready for the heir to use in times of need. It just doesn't make any sense to think you would need more of them than that."

Her voice waivered with her pent-up emotions. Namir could tell the elf was almost at her breaking point and he needed to do something to break the cycle before it dragged her down farther.

"It isn't that simple. Even if it were, did the fact my mother had Zelios stop the last great war?" His voice was full of concern, but soothing at the same time. He desperately needed her to understand his reason, although he was still unsure why it mattered so much to him.

"That's different," she chimed in as if to defend her point.

Namir raised his hand to silence her and shook his head. "It's not. If people respected the rulers because of their power instead of plotting to get that power for themselves, there never would have been a war. To be honest, growing up there were few stories told about the relics your father devoted his life to protect. It was almost as if people weren't allowed to talk about them. So when they did, they spoke in hushed tones."

Namir took a deep breath as he allowed his gaze to fall from her face to her boots. Wearily he stepped over to the chair beside the desk and took a seat.

"Not every race has a memory as long as the elves. For us humans, a decade can change how things are viewed. Fears lessen over time, as does reverence. People need to be reminded of the need for their traditions constantly. Because if they are not, the lore of the past is quickly forgotten." He wanted to look at her. To see if she understood him, but Namir was afraid to let her see the fear he knew was etched into his features.

"But surely the power held in just three or four of the artifacts would be enough to rekindle that sense of need. You would be able to level any threat your enemies might throw your way." Haradine reasoned

Small droplets of tears fell as she spoke. He could hear them in her voice and see them as they soaked slowly into the soft leather of her boots. He knew she fought back the majority of them, but a few liquid emotions still made it past her control.

"Are you certain of that?" Namir's asked a little gruffer than he intended. His mind raced through their conversation as he formulated his response. He hated to bring any more misery to her, but he felt the urge to be heard. To be understood.

"Your father's notes link the origins of the last two great wars to the same forces that oppose my ascent to the throne. If he's right, if I am indeed up against the Darque Lords, I will need all the power from the Gods that I can get just to defend against them." He let his words sink in as his eyes scanned from her feet back up to her face and then across the walls of the room. "You, of all people, should understand what is at stake. If the keepers of darkness manage to win, we are all doomed."

"I know, and you are right. My mother and father both taught me about the Darque Lords. We would spend hours discussing how the Old Gods wrested control away from them originally to create the world as we know it." Her voice dropped to scarcely a whisper. It was as if she was afraid the shadows, kept at bay by their feeble light, would hear her.

"Why are you against my plan then?" Namir was certain Haradine could hear his pain, but a part of him wanted her to hear it. Then she might understand why this was all so important to him.

"Because it is flawed," her words slid slowly out of her mouth as if each word carried its own unimaginable weight. "You have no idea how dangerous the power you are trying to find is." Her eyes were raw and Namir found it impossible to look into them for very long. "If you are trying to gather these items just to prove that you are able to defeat the Darque Lords, you have already failed."

There was a subtle air of resignation in her voice that mingled with a sadness Namir could not fathom. He stared at the little telling lines around her eyes and the subtle downturn of her lips as she spoke for clues of her true intentions. None of which helped him understand the elf any better.

"Are you implying that I should just let them win?" Her idea was incredulous. How could she even think he could just not try to succeed? "They will kill thousands and enslave even more. All of that doesn't even begin to address how the will of the people will be destroyed."

"I know," she shook her head slowly as she spoke. This little gesture lent an odd air of gravity to her words. "Which is why you must succeed, but is this plan of yours the best way, sa'ouvant?"

"It's the only way." His words spilled out so softly it surprised even him. "If I hope to succeed, I will need the support of the masses. The people of every race must support my claim if I hope to keep the throne, once I am allowed to sit in it." His tone was harsher than he had intended, but the fire of passion burned at the edges of his vision and carried his emotions with them as he spoke.

"Careful," Zelios warned Namir mentally. "She knows the threat these artifacts pose well enough and she has witnessed their terrible power first hand."

"What do you mean?" Namir asked in his mind as the telling light blue glow of the amulet's power filtered through the fabric of his tunic softly.

"Her father devoted his life to preventing these powerful items from falling into the wrong hands. Before the wars began, many villages felt the power my brethren contain in terrible ways. Her village, like many others, was ravaged by people those that wielded the power of an artifact much like me. The Acwen leveled their temple and allowed the men using it to do to the elves of Erishai as they wished." Zelios's reply filled Namir's mind with its sound.

Before he could object, Zelios flooded his mind it with the

images of the atrocities. People writhing in pain as black flames danced along their skin. Priestesses raped in the streets as their oppressors, clad in dark robes, mocked their faith. Whole buildings crumbled into dust at just a slight wave of a hand.

"Is this real?" Namir mentally recoiled as the surreal horrors played behind his eyes. "Your brethren did this?" Namir thought in shock.

"We are tools and nothing more. Although we are imbued with the wisdom of our patrons, we must do as we are commanded to by our owners and our Gods," Zelios advised Namir silently.

"Are you okay sa'ouvant?" Haradine asked worriedly.

Namir knew she must have seen his reaction to what Zelios had shown him. He felt the muscles of his face slowly relaxed from the contortions of shock that had held them. Namir could only imagine what a sight he had been, which a look of fear on his face highlighted by the stark blue light of Zelios's power.

"I'm fine," Namir replied immediately as he thought his next question to Zelios. "So you have to do anything that I tell you to?"

"Not if it is against my instructions from my God or the purpose for which I was created. Otherwise, my will is tied to yours and yours to mine." Zelios's words faded from his mind as quickly as they appeared and left Namir a little confused.

"Explain that last part. Our wills are tied together?" Namir thought anxiously.

"The longer we are together, the more we are attuned to one another." Zelios explained briefly.

"Sa'ouvant, we need to understand each other if I am to be of any help." Haradine implored.

Namir heard the worry in her voice and he knew she needed him to respond. "This isn't over," he thought to Zelios as he forced the faraway look from his steel blue eyes. "I agree, which is why I included you in my plans." Although he tried to use a reassuring tone, he knew she still had too many reservations for it to be effective.

"I thought you originally wanted to gather a few of these artifacts," she started out hesitantly. Although each word started haltingly, they gained momentum as she spoke. "I was not prepared for you to say you wanted all of them. Please forgive my shock, but there is a reason for it."

"I know more about your reasons than you think," Namir said as he cut off her explanation succinctly. "Your entire village was destroyed. No, destroyed isn't the right word. It was obliterated in front of you. Your way of life decimated. All of this was at the hands of those wielding the Acwen." Namir took a moment to let his words sink in before he continued. "It's horrific, but it shaped you. This experience, though mortifying, turned you into who you are today. A dedicated warrior, skilled enough to conquer fear with the resolve to ensure that these things never happen to another person." Namir tried to soothe her with his tone, but he saw it had the opposite effect.

"Y-y-yes," Haradine responded haltingly, somewhat taken aback by his answer. He felt her eyes scrutinize his features as they spoke as she studied him. "Did my father write about it in his journals? Is that how you know?"

"No," Namir dismissed her question with a wave of his hand as he spoke. "It doesn't matter how I knew, the important thing is that know about it. I believe your concern is warranted." The look of relief that spread across Haradine's face was reassuring, so he kept the pause short as he continued. "But I still need to collect as many of these artifacts as I can. I just hope you can help me figure out how to manage all of them so no one gets killed unnecessarily."

"I would be honored, sa'ouvant." Her voice was reverent and matched her demeanor as she curtsied slightly.

With a slight hesitation, Haradine walked closer to the

table. Silently she scanned the upturned pages and opened journals her father had left behind as his legacy.

Namir knew this was the closest the elf had ever been to her father's life's work. The tension that manifested in the small gap between her and the slightly yellowed pages was palpable and unnerving.

He watched her timidly reach toward a page with a map scrawled across it. He was captivated by the obvious internal struggle she fought against. At the last minute, she resisted the temptation.

Her finger floated inches from the page as she turned and addressed him quietly, "My father once told me no one should have more than one of the relics. Not even if it meant stopping the Darque Lords from getting them." Namir felt her eyes dart up from his chest and lock with his steel blue ones. The deep azure blue shade of her eyes was mesmerizing as she continued, "I remember asking why, but he was hesitant to tell me. The only thing I could get him to say is that Gods are greedy and don't like to share the souls they have gathered."

Her response gushed out before she could hold it in check. There was no stumbling over words or tripping around the nuances she normally attempted to shy away from. It was raw and honest. Namir could tell Haradine was very pleased to be included in this decision, the subtle glow in her cheeks only confirmed it.

"Why did Aras feel that way?" Namir asked, more to himself than to either Haradine or Zelios.

"Because of the bond. Each of us forms a connection with whomever the Gods choose to possesses us," Zelios responded in Namir's head at the same time Haradine replied.

"He said each item united directly with the soul of those that wield them," Haradine's answer held a fearful hesitation in it. The soft warble in her voice was almost unnoticeable, but it was there nonetheless. "My father believed that a person can only, truly, devote themselves to one god or one mate. Those that possess relics of the gods can only be true to one at a time. I asked him why once and the only real answer he ever gave me was this. A soul can only handle so much. If it is divided, or pulled apart, it cannot sustain itself and will be destroyed."

"Interesting," Namir replied to both voices at once. "So, either I'm going to have to put this to the test or surround myself with an entourage of extremely loyal followers. Ones that will perform my every command." Namir mused. Sarcasm dripped from his words as he spoke them and he hated both choices sounded. "How many items are there?" He directed the question at Haradine and hoped, for the sake of his sanity, Zelios would stay silent.

"No, but Natlia noted the names of the items in a journal of hers before she died," Haradine answered obediently.

"Natlia? Hessa's mother?" Namir asked perplexed. "She was involved in this as well?"

"Yes. From what both of my parents have told me, and what I was allowed to see for myself, she was one of the six." She answered evenly. As she spoke she sat down at his feet and looked up at him.

Namir looked down at the half-elf in admiration. Not only was she beautiful, she was intelligent. But something was different. The more she spoke, the more submissive her tone became and he wasn't sure if he liked it. He was used to her being so much more aggressive. But, he had to admit, this docility held a certain charm as well.

Absently taking her hand in his, he said, "One of the six?"

"There were six people chosen to hide the relics. My parents were two of them. Natlia, the Shadow Walker, and the Divitian twins. They met periodically at the manor in Hornshir." Her words were spellbinding and Namir could not help but listen to the soft tones of her voice as she spoke.

"Well, it seems that we need to talk to Aves and Hessa then," Namir said as he started to clean up his papers.

He tried to hide the smile that pulled at his lips from deep within him when Haradine immediately picked up the pages that lay closest to her. Within a few moments, both of them were on their feet and placing the various books and papers into small piles that were easily hidden from view by other, less important things around them.

"Once we've eaten breakfast, we can walk over to the mayor's house. Hopefully, we can catch Aves and Hessa there. That way we will have enough time to review speech and make sure I'm ready for my council appearance." The words rolled off of his tongue before he even realized he said them. "That is, if you are still willing to help me with all of this." He hated making assumptions about anything, especially this.

If anyone had a reason not to help, Haradine did. It hurt knowing how much she lost. It was all the more uncomfortable knowing he was asking her to risk it all again.

The final board eased itself back into place as Namir stooped over the place he decided to use for the most important journals. Nurn had originally shown him it when they were younger and needed to stash the evidence of a prank he had pulled on Jaconis.

Thoughts of the oily rags and vials they concealed danced in his head as the ghostly aroma from almost a decade ago tickled his nose. Times were so much easier then. Less issues and more levity. Of all the things he missed about his two best friends, their ability to make him laugh stood out the most.

The subtle click as the tiny lock hidden under the adjacent planks pulled him back to the present. He easily shifted his weight so he could stand from the spot he had crouched for the last few moments.

He spared a quick glance at the half-elf and his breath caught as he did. The gathering light highlighted her honey-dew hair is just the right way that it created a heavenly glow about her head. His eyes traced along the highlights from her head along the soft curve of her neck down to the soft fabric of her chemise. Haradine was stunningly beautiful and he knew she knew it.

"I do," Haradine replied. A little smile tugged at the corners of her lips as she spoke and her azure eyes practically glowed as she spoke.

Namir was unsure if her response was to his thoughts or his statement. He really did not care which, he was just grateful she was there with him.

Without thinking, Namir swept his arm toward the door and nodded his head slightly. "Let's get something to eat," Namir said as he shot her a carefree smile.

"Of course," she replied on cue. Without a word, Haradine stepped lightly toward the door and descended the stairs to Tipin's kitchen.

As she did, Namir's eyes followed each and every step. He noticed her step seemed a little lighter and held a certain bounce he had not seen before. With each step, her hair shifted lightly in the breeze and her soft curves bobbed in the most tantalizing way.

Jaconis paced the floor of the devotional while he waited. His new robes rustled more than he was used to. He found himself stopping frequently just to make sure they were not dragging on the floor behind him.

The room was scarcely lit. No surprise there, the brethren preferred the comfort of the darkness over well-lit areas. With light comes scrutiny and, even when they were out in public, too much visibility always tends to cause problems. The darkness was something he was learning to embrace. There was something freeing about the nothingness that waits where others fear to go.

"Glad you were able to make it so soon," the deacon said as he entered. "As you know, the results of your tests have come back." The deacon's short dark hair was well oiled and matted to his scalp. He carefully adjusted his black robes instead of speaking any further.

Jaconis felt the deacon's dull brown eyes rest on his chest. The gaze only added to the awkwardness of the moment. The dramatic pause was on purpose and Jaconis understood why, for an added suspense. Alaster was well known for his ability to overdramatize everything.

"After twenty years of service to the faith, the main thing he could do was build anticipation and anxiousness around the smallest thing. Alaster has a penchant for making even the most normal thing seem miraculous. If a religion does not have these dramatic elements, it loses followers," Jaconis mused as he crossed the small chamber they were in.

He easily recalled a few of Alaster's lectures about the fallen churches. How each of them lost sight of those that helped it to thrive, their people. Religions, and by extent Gods, are nothing but the sum of their parts. If a community turns against the church, there is nothing that can be done to save it. These lectures were stunningly powerful, yet simple. Full of long pauses and riddled with a few great moments for introspection.

"Do you have any questions before we begin the review?" Alaster's gravelly tone was soft, yet commanding.

"What happens if I passed? Do I get fully inducted into the church, or are there more trials of faith needed before I can progress on my journey in Lotevilar's teachings?" Jaconis struggled with his own emotions as he asked. H knew that patience was one of the many teachings of the Goddess, but not knowing what to expect next was starting to take its toll on his psyche.

"Good questions youngling," the deacon nodded as he spoke.

Jaconis could tell Alaster really liked him by the small gestures he made every time they spoke. He noticed that the deacon rarely reacted toward the other acolytes in the same way.

"Your level of faith and devotion to the church's cause has been proven throughout these last few trials. If you have been deemed worthy, you would be allowed to accept your cassock tomorrow night at this time." The deacon paused for a moment before he continued,

Jaconis knew it was meant to add weight to this words, but he really was starting to get annoyed at his tendency to randomly pause when he spoke.

"We give all of our brethren a chance to decide if this is really what they want. You get one last day of life outside of the church to decide. If you chose to leave, then we would honor your choice, although we are saddened anytime a qualified candidate chooses to leave us." Another long, unnecessary, pause drew out the conversation long, "At the same time, if you choose to stay we would welcome you into our fold without any questions or reservations." He cleared his throat again and continued in his deep gravelly voice, "That is, if you have been accepted and passed all of your trials."

"I see," Jaconis replied pensively, "and did I pass?"

The deacon's smile broadened as he shrugged off Jaconis's impetuousness. "Let's find out," he said in a conspiratorial tone.

With the ease of a burglar, Alaster carefully removed an ornate wooden box from the shelf next to the cistern. The wood was polished and smooth, yet underneath the clear lacquered finish, Jaconis could see a deep, almost blood, red sheen to the wood. As the deacon placed it on the podium, he noticed the Goddess's sigil inlaid at the center of the lid in silver.

There were other markings on the lid as well, but Jaconis had a hard time making them out. They were darker than the wood. To his amazement, it looked almost as if someone had written through the smooth finish. He was unable to read most of the words, but one stood out. His name had been added just under Lotevilar's symbol.

The box had always been there. Ever since his first memory of this room, he had seen it on the shelf where the deacon had retrieved it from. The fact that his name was there, written under the lacquer as if it had always been there was disturbing.

"How did you know?" Jaconis stammered as he stared at

the box. "How did you know I would try to join your congregation?"

Alaster looked at Jaconis as the boy spoke. A look of sympathy and understanding crossed the older man's features as he said, "All things are foreseen by Lotevilar. Nothing is hidden and nothing can be done without Her knowledge."

"So you're telling me that box, it has always had my name on it?" Jaconis asked completely enthralled.

"Yes. These boxes were made a hundred years ago. Before the great wars engulfed Cennicus. Long before the Old Gods left. Lotevilar Herself shaped them from the trees in the heart of the Darque Woods." He paused as if to add more emphasis. "Before we accept someone into the trials, we first see if they have a box. If not, we turn them away."

"But if you know the names of those selected by the Goddess, why not just gather them when they are young? Raise them in the faith instead of letting them struggle and suffer without it. Wouldn't that make more sense?" Jaconis could not hide his bitterness as he spoke.

Alaster put his hand on Jaconis's shoulder gently. "It's not done that way because Lotevilar has ordained it otherwise. You see, She needs you to suffer before joining the fold. Your journey is unique and without the things you went through, you couldn't be who you are. She needs you, how you are when you approach your obligation. That is how She will use you best."

The words were hard for Jaconis to hear. Pictures of Lysanta's face contorted in pain from both labor and death filled his mind as he listened to Alaster's words. He closed his eyes in a desperate attempt to push the memories from his mind. Even now, after all these years, he felt ill-equipped to handle the pain of losing her.

"Death must be felt to be understood," the deacon said softly as if he had read Jaconis's mind. "Especially the death of those we hold the dearest. How could you hope to understand the levels of pain Lotevilar teaches if you have not experienced the worst one yourself? Lysanta, your mother, served her purpose. She gave birth to you. You were the sole reason for her existence. She lived long enough for you to be able to witness her final gift to you, the gift of pain. The pain her death brought has forged you into the young man you are today."

There was a tenderness in Alaster's voice, as he spoke, Jaconis had not thought possible. Although he was known for the drama he added to moments, he was not known for being soft. In fact, it was the opposite. Jaconis had heard all of the stories about how depraved and cruel Alaster was.

"Now, if you are ready, I can help you find an answer to your last question. We can both learn what path Lotevilar has set for you."

"How does he know so much about me?" Jaconis wondered as the man spoke. His head swam with images and words. Thoughts and dreams slipped away and swirled in the boy's mind as the barrage of information pummeled him in irresistible waves. By time Alaster finished speaking, the only thing Jaconis could do without losing control of himself was a simple nod of acceptance.

The deacon smiled comfortingly at the boy and lifted the lid ceremoniously. Jaconis's eyes probed the velvet lined interior and settled on an ivory scroll case. Its smooth off-white surface seemed to attract the light and magnify in just the right way to make it glow.

"Go ahead, pick it up and see what journey awaits you," Alaster said encouragingly.

The ghastly image from the other side of the glass turned in unison with Aves. No matter which way she turned, it matched flawlessly. Dead misted greenish blue eyes stared back as Aves stared in shock. She felt emotionally numb as she stared at her reflection in horror.

"Our father knowingly gave this to Natlia?" Even though it was the third time she asked, she hoped they would tell her it was all just a joke. A mean and cruel joke, but a joke nonetheless. If not a joke, maybe they would say something to prove it was not true.

"I have it on good authority he knew what it was," Hessa replied evenly. "I know it's hard to understand or to believe, but it is true. There is so much he has kept from us. So many secrets and, if you think about it, this all explains why. It makes sense," Hessa said pleadingly to her half-sister.

"Has Amani ever talked about the wars and his roles in them?" Onas asked as Hessa's questions tapered off. When both girls shook their head he added, "Ever wonder why not?"

"Why are you so certain he hasn't?" Aves snapped bitterly.

"Because of who he is and what he means to the Dekki," he said somewhat defensively. "We always hoped he would make amends for his transgressions and take his rightful place amongst our familia," Onas explained.

"I thought you said he was exiled," Hessa asked. Her disbelief was obvious by her tone.

"I did," Onas agreed. "That doesn't mean he couldn't make amends and be allowed back in."

"Why is it so important that he does?" Aves asked, still somewhat in shock by everything."

"Your father was supposed to lead us," he said nonchalantly. "He just decided that being the head of our familia was not enough for him. The thought of power corrupted his mind and he got greedy. After the war, he saw a way to get more power than he would with his own kind. So he chose to betray us and ran off with a geiji." The contempt in his voice was apparent.

"You are referring to my mother," Aves said in contempt, "and I would appreciate it if you did not refer to her that way."

She knew her tone was aggressive, but she could not make herself feel bad about it. Everything he said conflicted with everything she knew to be true. On top of it all, his contempt for her mother was too much for her to accept quietly.

"Although I would love to discuss our heritage, let's talk

about something a little more productive," Hessa said quickly. Her timely comment diffused the building tension in the room swiftly. "You came to take me back to Ellsted, right?"

"Aye," Aves nodded, still somewhat chaffed by Onas's comments.

"Ok then, I agree to go back to Ellsted with you two, but I have one condition. You both must help me find something." Hessa's tone was flat and it worried Aves with its emotionlessness.

"What are you looking for?" Onas asked. His arched eyebrow and the way his tone raised abruptly as he finished his sentence let Aves know how curious he was.

"Is it something here in your mother's house?" Aves asked immediately after Onas's question.

Hessa smiled at both of them with a somewhat triumphant look. "No, it is not here," her half-sister said conspiratorially, "but it's close by. My mother wrote about an artifact of historical value in her journal. From what I can decipher, it's in a cave not very far from here."

"Did she say what the artifact was?" Onas asked. His curiosity was obviously raised.

"Well, not exactly," Hessa said as she shot a sidelong glance away from Aves.

From the moment her posture shifted, Aves knew she was lying. What she couldn't figure out is why. Aves took a deep breath and watched her half-sister carefully. She noted everything from the way her hair moved in the almost nonexistent breeze to the subtle shifts in her weight as she leaned from one foot to the next. Something would give away why Hessa was lying.

Her mind drifted to the many classes the girls attended with Namir. Carness's were always the most fun, especially since she was able to watch Nurn exercise. She felt the blood start to rush into her cheeks and she chided herself for it.

"That isn't what I was trying to think about," Aves said

silently. "There was a class Allair taught. What was it?"

Hessa glanced again toward a small table against a wall. There was a small pile of papers and a pen, nothing else. It was really quite simple, but it was all Aves needed to spark the memory. "The arts of negotiation! She must be sending me a message she doesn't want Onas to know about." The revelation was a rewarding one.

"She wrote something about it needing to stay hidden. From not just the enemies of the crown, but also from those she loved the most," Hessa confessed cryptically.

"If it is so important that it remain hidden, why do you want to go get it?" Aves asked skeptically. She struggled to keep it out of her voice, but she saw the hurt look on Hessa's face and she knew she failed.

Aves just couldn't help herself. Everything seemed so different now. Her father wasn't the man she had thought he was. Namir was destined to rule Cennicus, Halin was lost and everyone in town carried on as if they hadn't noticed. Even Jaconis being gone was unusually disturbing. On top of it all, Hessa really was her half-sister. The girls had toyed with the idea when they were younger, but now it's true.

"I know what you're thinking, sister," Hessa said carefully. Aves knew her simple statement had visibly shaken her because she could see it in Hessa reactions. "And you're right. I think it is odd both Namir and I have found something about our heritages no one ever expected. And, like Namir's amulet, my mother wrote about this artifact as if she was somehow personally tied to it. So yes, I am curious to see what it is. Even if by so doing means I need to go against her wishes. Somethings were not meant to stay hidden forever, and I think this is one of them."

The way Hessa's chin jutted out as she spoke let Aves know she was trying to sound inspiring. In fact, the more she spoke, the better her posture became. Overall the effect worked. Aves felt a small desire to help her half-sister find this thing.

"So when do we start?" Onas asked excitedly.

Aves could not help but get swept up in their excitement. "After we find this artifact, we are going back to Ellsted. Right?"

"Straight away, I promise," Hessa agreed. "Thank you for understanding." Aves was surprised as Hessa wrapped her arms around her and gave her a big hug, but she also found it comforting.

Chapter Twenty-Four: Reunions

Landolin carefully watched the shadow as it moved through the darkness below him. He strained his elven eyes as he struggled to discern anything unusual about the thing.

"This must be how humans feel in the dark," he thought to himself helplessly.

He held his breath so as not to draw attention to the sheltered corner of the ceiling he tentatively clung to. A soft snuffling sound helped him determine where the thing in the shadows was. Landolin's eyes narrowed into slits reflexively as he probed the dark recesses of the tunnel where it explored the shadows in its search for them.

"It's some sort of nassarid," Landolin thought to himself frantically. Beads of sweat formed across his forehead as he clung directly above it. "Gienna mentioned the church of Lotevilar was evil, but she never mentioned they could be associated with the masters of the nassarid hordes." He thought furtively. I just hope it is not a lupine mix."

The little vials of perfume tied into the little pockets of his cloak tugged at the edges of his mind. He knew there had to be some way he could use them, he just had no idea how. Distracting it was the obvious choice. The issue was a distraction only helps when there is a reason. Something to distract a target from, not toward. Distraction in and of itself was useless.

Landolin took a moment to steal a glance at where Gienna stood, waiting as bait. Stoic. Perfectly still and ready, just like they planned. The only problem was the nassarid seemed more intent on lurking in the darkness instead of easy prey waiting for it.

That's when inspiration hit. Silently Landolin reached into his cloak and untied a vial. One of the smaller vials slid from its secure pocket and rolled down to the tips of his fingers. Timing would be everything, so he waited.

He knew it would not take too long and felt a small twinge of relief as he saw his opening. The creature's head swiveled away from Gienna again. With a quick snap of his wrist, he easily lobbed the vial toward his sister and silently hoped she would not catch it. His muscles eased a little as the sound of shattering glass echoed off of the walls around him.

The shadowy figure instantly froze and waited. Several long tense moments passed as it stayed completely motionless. Then Landolin saw it catch the scent of the perfume he had thrown. It took a long deep breath and then swiveled directly toward Gienna.

Landolin pulled his cloak close to him as he felt the thing's eyes slip over his location for a final time before it practically flew at his sister.

"Here it comes," Landolin cast his thought into his sister's mind as a warning. He knew the warning was unneeded, but it comforted him to send it.

"Thank you," Gienna thought back as she effortlessly pitched herself out of the creature's reach.

Darkness smothered him on all sides as Halin groped his way through the tight passage. He had stumbled upon some new caverns and he felt the need to explore them. What he hadn't planned on was getting lost. Well more lost than he had already been.

He chided himself under his breath for losing his way. “I know it’s easy to get turned around in these tunnels,” he muttered, “I just should have been more careful. I bet Namir wouldn’t be as lost as I am.” He said dejectedly.

Thoughts about the last time he had tried to explore the caves flooded into his mind. All of the abrupt turns that had clawed at the remnants of his clothes was almost more than he could bear. Then the sudden drop he had barely managed to avoid. “If I wouldn’t have stumbled, I’d be a gonner.”

As if to remind him, Halin felt the floor shift subtly under his boots. Like an electric shock, panic coursed through his muscles and he turned. The next thing he felt was the coarseness of the floor as it came up to meet him. The worst part is it moved faster than he had expected it to. The solid thump as he impacted it echoed briefly down the tunnel. Not only was he winded, again, but his ears rang from the noise.

Without effort, Halin deftly replayed his most recent stumble back through his mind. His foot had caught on something, a rock or an odd bit of stone. Nothing that should have made him fall like that. At least not that fast.

“It’s not like I was running,” Halin thought darkly to himself.

He struggled to keep his frustration in check. His lack of sleep did little to help him keep it all straight. Neither did his hunger. The growling pit in his stomach gurgled as if to remind him that it had already been far too long since he last ate.

“This cold will be the death of me!” He muttered to himself under his breath as he rolled onto his back to catch his breath.

“No, it won’t,” the darkness uttered.

“Who’s there?” He called out nervously.

He forced himself to be still as he tried to focus on the sound. Long seconds turned into minutes as the moments splintered into a timelessness of nothing but silence and darkness.

"Tayant, I promise to do your bidding for the rest of my life if you get me out of here and back to those I love." Halin prayed as he slowly stood up. Although his voice carried a little bit of sarcasm, his soul ached for his goddess to answer his prayer.

As if in response, he felt an overwhelming need to sit. The world spun, slowly at first, as his own weariness threatened to overcome him and his knees buckled.

In his mind, he could faintly hear his brother's voice, although Halin couldn't quite make out what Nurn was trying to tell him.

"How can you be so sure?" Halin asked. He turned slightly to try and find where his brother was. Although there was a part of him that knew Nurn couldn't possibly be there, Halin ignored it and waited for his brother to respond.

Nurn's smiling face faded into Halin's weary mind. The hulking body loomed above him and offered him a hand. Somewhere, in the back of his mind, he heard his brother's deep laughter. As if this whole thing had been a joke at Halin's expense.

That was all he needed. He felt a new wave of strength flood into his body as he heard Nurn's laughter inside his head.

He slowly sat up and ignored the pain in his stomach and face. Somewhere, deep inside, he realized how comical this all must look. A bumbling boy lost in the dark. Having conversations with people that weren't there.

He struggled against his own imagination as he grappled with the reality of the situation. Halin couldn't help it. He laughed. He laughed in spite of himself and he laughed at the pain he felt in his heart. Just the thought of Nurn being around was bittersweet.

The rough wall felt damp and clammy as he steadied himself against it carefully. Within moments, the floor shifted and he reached out wildly for the other wall. He knew it had to be close and cursed under his breath as his raw knuckles found it closer than he expected. The wall vibrated and moved ominously as he struggled to stay upright.

"What was that?" He whispered to himself as the shaking slowly subsided. Only the soft sounds of pebbles as they fell from far above him and the ever-present darkness replied.

Without any thought, Halin deftly unsheathed his dagger and slowly extended in one fluid motion. He cautiously moved it from side to side in an attempt to find the other wall. With his free hand, he kept track of the wall he was already pressed against.

The jagged edge on the wall scraped his hand unexpectedly. After a few breathes sucked through his teeth, Halin managed to regain a little bit of his composure. He cursed his foolishness under his breath as he reached out again, this time with a little more care.

He quickly discovered that the wall was a little easier to find, now that he had met it in a more intimate manner. The scrapping sounds of his dagger helped him keep track of the wall on the other side of the narrow tunnel. Halin had to laugh inwardly as he realized the other wall seemed smoother than the one he had run his hand along.

It seemed like forever, but he finally managed to find it again. With a little more finesse, Halin brought the tip of his dagger to rest against the wall a span away from his extended hand.

The memory of how he discovered that scraping the tip of his dagger against the rough surface of the cavern walls created enough sparks to see, however briefly, flooded his mind unbidden. An odd pang of remorse was disrupted by the shrill sound metal on stone. The resonating sound peeled through every aspect of his reality and forced him back to the present.

He held his breath as he squinted. He had found the combination a valuable one before. When he squinted just right he found ways to see some of the details in the walls. At least it did before, but not this time.

Somehow, as the feeble sparks flew into the shadowy darkness around him, they faded before he was able to see anything. Even the momentary glow emitted by the leaping sparks failed to dispel any the gathering gloom.

A pit formed in his stomach. With each passing moment, the feeling his only idea was a failure, became an ever-increasing reality. He had hoped for just a bit more light. Or closer walls. Something, anything, to help the glow actually reveal something about his surroundings.

He chided himself darkly. What little hope he felt of figuring out which way to go was extinguished as fast as the pathetic sparks were engulfed by the darkness. Halin tried several more times, with the same results or worse.

"The passage must get larger," Halin muttered as he slowly resheathed his dagger.

A whispered string of self-abusive profanities escaped his lips. They were followed by an ensemble of horrible thoughts and poorly decided upon plans. After a few moments of this, Halin lowered his head and slowly regained a modicum of control of himself.

"Blasted caverns!" Halin let his frustration echo off of the cavern walls around him in a cathartic explosion. "If only I could have curbed my curiosity," he cursed under his breath.

His mind focused on the thing that lured him into these new tunnels. It was a familiar strain of music. Halin had no idea where he had heard it before. A dream, or maybe it was something his mother had sung to him.

He tried to replay the strain of music over again in his mind, but all he could manage was a few wispy and fleeting notes. What he could recall definitely seemed familiar. The more he thought about it, the more he was certain it was a song from his childhood. His mind slowly filled in parts of the tune and then it hit him. Allair sang to him when he was younger and about to go to bed. The song of the Keepers of the Watch.

The dark lyrics of the defense of the realm snaked through his mind and he felt helpless. Although they were the defenders of the light, the song was a melancholy one. He shrugged it out of his head as quickly as he could, but not before the end of the chorus played its final phrase.

"Bright sword shining devouring the light. Fierce edge gleaming killing the night." He couldn't help but let his voice sing it in hushed tones. In his mind, his mother sang it with a deeper alto tone that he managed to harmonize with perfectly.

A part of him hated how easily he had fallen for the music's insipid pull. There was something about it that made him throw all of his fears aside and follow it deep into the darkness, farther than he would normally go willingly. It seemed the closer he managed to get to its source, the farther he was from anything he had come to know.

"Only one choice," he muttered again. Even his voice was devoured by the darkness. No echo and no response other than the muted nothingness.

He cautiously placed a trembling foot forward. His hand gripped the edge of the wall. Halin hoped there would be a floor to touch and his foot hovered above where he thought it should be. To his relief, the floor was waiting for his foot right where it should have been.

Frustration ate at his nerves as he blindly groped at the air beside him. He hoped to find some clue to the size of room he had entered. His sore hand still clung to the wall at the edge of the tunnel he just left. He desperately wanted to find another wall, but he was afraid to venture too far into the cavern in case he got turned around.

"If this is a big cavern, why isn't there an echo?" Halin said loudly.

He waited for a response eagerly. But there was none. Nothing. Not even the sounds of shifting rocks. No response from the deafening silence that surrounded him.

Tentatively, he let go of the wall and stepped further into the cavern. His hands sought for another wall. With every step he grew more confident that it was a very large room. After several more steps, the tips of his fingers brushed something smooth and hard.

He quickly reached forward and pushed his palm against the cold stone. Without a second thought, Halin placed his injured palm against it as well. He let out a sigh as the coldness seeped into the burning wound. The soothing effect was immediate and very welcomed.

He groped up as high as he could reach but still failed to reach the top of the stone. Its surface was remarkably smooth and curved. He ran his hands down it, to see how far it extended. To his amazement, although it went all the way to the floor, it tapered to a point. At its base, there was a pool of water.

"Cave water is some of the freshest you can find," he recalled Namir telling him on one of their excursion from Ellsted.

Namir, Nurn and himself were all exploring one of the caves carved into the bank by the river. Namir had explained this to his brother and him when they were trying to figure out if the water in the cave was safe to drink.

"How do you know?" Halin recalled asking Namir.

"Saril taught me," Namir had replied aloofly.

Namir always had a way of making Halin feel inadequate or stupid. Something that he really didn't care for, but had no way to stop. Even now, in his own mind, Namir's knowledge was helping him.

Halin lowered himself down and sat next to the small puddle. He stuck his finger into and slowly moved it toward him to find its edge. Then he lowered his parched lips to its surface and sucked a little in. Just enough to quench his thirst, but not enough to drain it completely.

"I may need to take some of this with me," Halin muttered to himself. "There is no telling when I might find more."

Without a second thought, he ripped a piece of his shirt off and dropped it into the puddle. "That should work," he thought to himself as he pulled the dripping fabric out of the water. With his good hand, he placed the wet cloth into one of his empty leather pouches. With his other hand, he steadied himself and slowly stood up.

Inwardly Halin marveled at the size and girth of the stalactite. Not only was it enormous, but it was perfectly smooth. He was careful to only move a few paces around the monolithic stone. He didn't want to get turned around.

Then he slowly stepped in the direction he thought he had originally headed. Deep down Halin knew that without light he had no way of knowing exactly which direction he was heading, but he was pretty sure he was right.

After another few steps, his fingers brushed another smooth surface. Cautiously he explored this one and decided that it was a stalagmite. Like the stalactite, it was huge. The taper as he reached up along its surface is what gave its nature away.

"How large is this cave?" He wondered as he maneuvered past it and continued along his path.

After another few steps, he came upon another one. It wasn't as large, but it was big enough to make him negotiate a path around it. The farther he went, the more of them he found. They practically littered the floor.

A few times they were large enough that Halin thought he had finally found the opposite wall. Each time he was crestfallen when he realized he was wrong. The minutes stretched on forever as Halin explored the inky blackness. He fought against an all-encompassing feeling he would never find his way out of this cavern.

The feeling started to become more of a certainty when he finally came across it. A wall. An actual wall and Halin almost walked away from it before he realized what it was. The absolute smoothness of the stone seemed exactly like the stalagmites. If his finger had not happened to brush a minute seam joining two of the stones together, he never would have known.

Halin slowly traced the wall down to the floor. The transition was nothing less than miraculous. The wall seemed to meld perfectly with the floor, almost as if the tunnel was carved in one piece from the stone by a master craftsman. Instead of the roughhewn stones he had become accustomed to in the rest of the caverns and tunnels, this one was perfectly smooth.

Halin was amazed at the level of craftsmanship. He found it almost impossible to detect where one stone ended and another began. The seams were almost impossible to find, but he finally found one.

He took his time to stand as he slowly traced the block in front of him. The one block was almost as tall as he was and it was square, perfectly square. The immense level of craftsmanship obviously needed to create it and then join it together in this fashion was not lost on Halin.

He drew his dagger tentatively from its sheath. He felt a pang of guilt as he placed its tip against the smooth surface of the wall. He knew he needed some light, but he hated to mar such a perfect stone.

"Tumere forgive me for what I must do," Halin whispered his prayer as he defaced the glasslike surface with a quick flick of his wrist.

Nothing. Not even a sound. He was both amazed and frightened by this prospect. Halin had a feeling that the sparks he hoped for would fail to appear, but this was worse.

"Where am I?" Halin wondered out loud completely bewildered.

"You are near," the voice resonated through the stone around him.

Halin froze. It felt as if the voice surrounded him. Time ground to a halt and barely inched ahead in spurts as he tried to turn his head. Halin fearfully waited for whoever was with him in the cavern to speak again.

With each agonizing second that passed, Halin realized how unlikely it was that he was going to get a response. When he finally found his voice, he thought he would try another tactic.

"Where, exactly, is that?" He croaked painfully.

His muscles tensed on their own in anticipation of the near deafening reply, but there was nothing. No sounds.

Disappointment replaced his tension and he forced himself to relax. To his surprise, everything seemed to shift back to the way it was before. He even found it easier to move. Halin had secretly hoped to find the source of the voice when it answered his question, even if the prospect frightened him.

"Hello?" He ventured again in another attempt. Knowing full well that his only answer would be the deafening silence.

She threw herself at the door and madly clawed at its clasp in mock fear. As she did, she felt her attacker recover and lunge at her once more. Deftly leaning to left, she managed to dodge its attack. She quickly followed up the lean by bending over backward and then swiftly pivoting into a crouch before she leapt to where she had stashed her weapons.

It was going to recover quickly, so she had to use her time well. She only had a few moments to get clear of the first layer of the trap. She needed to signal her brother now.

"Now!" She screamed as loud as she could.

Her fingers barely closed through the loop of the rope she had tied around her belongings. Skittering stones rolled against the smooth flagstones under her feet. The threatened to throw her off balance. Na matter what happened, or how she moved, Gienna knew she had to get past the first thin line etched into the floor. It's where the first passage of the deadly blade hidden in the ceiling would fall.

The beast's high pitch scream quickly followed hers and she wondered if it had figured out her their plan. The distinctive leathery sound of its wings as they unfolded only punctuated her predicament.

As she darted across the open surface, she glanced over her shoulder. "I hope I have enough time," she thought to herself.

The wicked gleam from its red eyes penetrated the darkness

as the creature clawed at the stones around it. It seemed unfazed about its failed lunge at her. Deep grooves were left behind as its claws used every surface to redirect its momentum.

At first, the soft red glow from its eyes leant a sense of warmth. That passed quickly as the thing tore through the air and vaulted toward her. With one flap of its large wing, the beast almost covered the entire distance she gained.

Pebbles and debris clawed at her as they flew along the gust of wind her attacker's wings dislodged from the cavern around them. The beast's eyes bore through her skin and exposed primordial fears she believed she had grown out of. Fear about the darkness and the things in it.

Gienna quickly turned her focus away from the creature and back to her footing. She had to get past the barely visible line in the floor before the wall-like blade fell. There was nothing for it. If she failed, she would be dead. There would be no second chance.

"Just a few more steps," Gienna thought to her brother.

Hurriedly she shielded her eyes from the dust kicked up by the nassarid behind her. The small thread of panic threatened to overtake her, so she tamped it down expertly.

"You won't make it!" The thing screamed its high pitched wail as it flew at Gienna's back. Its claw-tipped fingers reached greedily toward her long brained scarlet hair. "No one trespasses here and lives!"

Gienna tucked and roll as she felt the bite of its claws pierce her leather jerkin. Her shins and knees scraped the hard ground as she stopped her momentum and abruptly darted sideways. The creature's talons scrape against the stone she had been in front of a few moments prior.

Blood oozed from her many scrapes and cuts as she kicked off a wall and flipped over the thing. It screamed in surprise and she took some solace in its anger. With another high pitched scream, it lunged at her just as she recovered her footing.

Gienna could not help but marvel at how the thing managed to recover from its failed lunges so fast. "It's bad enough that it is faster than I am.," she thought to herself as she shimmied against a wall, "but how it seems to know where I am in the utter darkness is unnerving."

"Focus," Landolin's thoughts formed in her mind unwanted.

She really hated when he did that to her. Although, she supposed, he probably found it as annoying when she did it to him. Another failed lunge from the beast snapped her back into the moment.

Without thought, she sprang into the air and curled up into a ball. When she felt the tug of gravity slow her down, she instinctively kicked off the wall beside her and flew over the beast.

This time she was close enough she could have touched it. The rank scent of seat and feces infiltrated her nose and almost gagged her.

Gienna studied the creature's body in the split second she passed over it. Her eyes were drawn to its wings. They sounded draconic, yet they looked batlike.

Although they spread out well past the span of its arms, they were attached from its back to the creature's elongated fingers. The large flaps of skin stretched between the fingers to create large webbed pockets that it must use for lift. To her surprise, none of its fingers had anything sharp about them.

The talon's that clawed at her must have to have been on its feet, because there was nowhere else they could have been. Other than its dripping fangs, which were sharp enough to cut her, she could not see anything else the beast could have used.

She had barely landed when she saw it pivot in mid-lunge at an impossible angle. Before she could take another breath, the beast had altered its course. The sound of its clawed feet as the creature launched off the wall behind her forced Gienna to drop quickly in order to avoid its claws again.

"It is too fast," she thought as what little air she had in her lungs was knocked from her by the floor as she impacted it harder than she planned.

The nassarid wasted no time. She was still sucking in breath frantically when the beast dropped on top of her. Its razor-sharp talons pinned her wrists to the floor. Horrified, she watched as it spread its wings above her. It reminded her of how hawks shielded their prey from other predators.

Its rancid breath washed over Gienna's face and she struggled to keep her stomach in check. She wanted to retch, but managed to choke back the urge to empty her stomach. Her arms were pinned as the beast stood on her biceps. All she could do was stare helplessly into the beast's glowing red eyes.

Another wave of nausea threatened to overwhelm her as a single strand of saliva dripped from its maw toward her cheek. Her silent screams echoed in her head as it lowered itself closer. The rancid scent of its breath mingled with the beast's overwhelming musky sweat as it hovered mere inches above her.

Gienna struggled to maintain some semblance of sanity. Her mind reached out desperate to grab a hold of anything she could tether herself to. Anything that could anchor her outside of the looming nightmare about to devour her.

The soft owl-like whoosh of the fletching as the arrows whizzed passed the beast. The rhythmic strum of her brother's bowstring accompanied the arrow's passage. Although she struggled, the beast took little notice of her brother's attempts to help her. That is until one of his arrows managed to hit its mark.

The razor-like edge of the arrow's steel tip ripped its way through the leathery membrane of the thing's wing. Pain contorted the beast's face and Gienna found it oddly comforting. Its horrific scream, although high pitched, mingled with the rhythm of Landolin's assault to form a macabre composition of sorts.

Two more arrows flew through the beast's wings as its cries of agony all but deafened her. Writhing, the creature turned to face the direction where her brother's arrows assaulted it. Defiance marked its features as it screamed at the oncoming arrows.

Even more arrows skittered against its metal-clad chest. She studied the thing's armor as best she could. Thankfully the little sparks from the arrows as they deflected off of its armor provided her a little more light. Although battle scared, the armor looked familiar. Gienna just wished she had a better look at it.

To her relief, the creature's grip slipped a little as it staggered backward in pain. Gienna took the newfound opening. She arched her back and twisted against it. With a whip-like buck, she managed to jerk just enough to topple the nassarid off. A wet thump accentuated the beast's fall.

She struggled against the numbing pain and deadened nerves to get to her feet. Almost all of the feeling had fled her arms and her legs felt rubbery and non-responsive. Then she fought against a wave of nausea as she stood up shakily.

"Hurry," Landolin's voice slipped into her mind.

There was a sense of urgency in it she could not place. Her senses were assaulted by everything all at once and there was too much to focus on for her to appreciate his concern.

"I am!" She snapped back silently.

"I'm not sure how much longer I can delay the trap." His words were oddly strained, as if he struggled with something. Then it sunk in and Gienna finally recognized what he had been trying to convey.

Her eyes riveted on the thing as it writhed in pain only a few feet from her. The dust the beast threw up as it avoided arrows stung her eyes and burned her lungs. Her breathing was still a little labored from her recent exertions and she did her best to push it out of her mind.

Meticulously Gienna followed the thin rope she had tied to

her possessions. She only paused long enough to slide her hand into her pack and find the hilt of her dagger. Without any delay, she unsheathed it and spun toward the creature.

"This will only take a moment," Gienna thought back. She did her best to hide her fear. Landolin had enough to think about without adding worry to his list.

Silently she padded up to the creature. She knew it was in misery. It was no longer standing. Instead, it was hunched against a wall. Its only real movement was caused by its labored breathing. Although she moved silently, she knew it heard her approach. As if response it howled at her in pain as she approached.

Brackish blood oozed from its many wounds and added a bitter iron scent to the vile potpourri that surrounded it. From where she stood, she could see the many rips in its wings. The leathery membrane was cleft in a variety of places. Even the hideous creature's oversized ears were cleft by Landolin's arrows. Pieces of broken shafts protruded from the creature's hide and their other halves littered the ground around it.

The number of arrows Landolin had fired was staggering. Somehow Gienna thought he managed to fire off no more than six arrows, four at best. But, judging from the broken and shattered shafts on the ground as well as those protruding from its chest, she could tell he had loosed almost his entire quiver of arrows at the beast.

"I have come to put you out of pain," she said as she stepped up to its side slowly.

The creature let out a deep and gurgling laugh as she spoke to it. She could tell it hated her. The burning embers it had for eyes did little to hide how it felt. For some reason, this bothered her.

"You are not safe," it spat in a raspy voice as it eyed Gienna warily. "Your pathetic attempts to kill me only prolong the inevitable." Flecks of blood mingled with spittle as it sprayed its words at her.

"It is already evil enough," she thought as she mentally

withdrew from the nassarid. “Why must it entice my hand so?” She noticed how the eerie smile that creased the beast’s lips gave it an even more sinister appearance.

“That’s what everyone tells me,” Gienna said as she lowered her blade to the upper edge of the delicate choker it wore around its throat. Before it could reply she quickly pulled its keen edge along the edge of the choker and used it as a guide. “So far I have outlived all of them. This time shall be no different.”

The bright moonstone in the center lost its luster as the nassarid’s blood cascaded down from the wound. She allowed her eyes to watch the effect to give the creature the final privacy as it passed. She waited a few more moments after the gem took on a reddish hew before she peered into its eyes. The red glow had faded from them and left the milky tracks as a witness to the creature’s fleeing consciousness.

Something inside of her stirred as she turned, so she hesitated. The choker gleaming temptingly in the darkness and Gienna had to fight hard to resist the fleeting desire to claim it as her own.

“Let it take its treasure with it into the afterlife,” she thought to herself bitterly as she turned to leave.

“Are you about done?” Landolin scolded Gienna in her mind.

She could hear how much he was exerting himself to hold off the final part of the trap. Little fingers of guilt reached up and closed around her heart. She knew she should not have taken so much time to ensure their attacker was dead, she had to be certain it couldn’t come and get them. Something about this nassarid was different than any of the others she had ever encountered. Whatever it was, she knew she did not like it one bit.

“Maybe it was the certainty in its voice,” she rationalized as she hurried toward her brother’s location.

She moved as quickly as she dared to, but it still was not fast enough for her liking. Whatever Landolin had managed to do was the only thing that kept the walls at bay.

It was either long blades from the ceiling or moving walls. She was not completely sure how all of the trap worked. All she knew is her brother had managed to stop it from cutting off her way out.

"Just a few more platforms and I should be able to make it to him," she thought to herself wearily.

Instinctively as she was about to climb onto another ledge, she stole a furtive glance back to reassure herself the thing was not behind her and her heart froze.

Its body was missing. Her mind raced back through the details and she almost stumbled. The urge to go back and search for it was overwhelming.

"Maybe I turned a corner," she thought frantically.

"You should be on a straight path," Landolin replied to her thoughts. His message was so clear. Too clear. She knew right away he was confused by the frantic nature of her own thoughts. "Calm down and compose yourself," he instructed helpfully. "You are sending your thoughts wildly. Everyone within range of us will hear you. That is, if they are trained to hear them," he sent a soothing feeling into her mind along with his last few words.

"Thank you, dear brother," she thought in response.

Her stride naturally lengthened the more she thought about how much he was straining himself. She knew the trap needed to be sprung so they had a chance to get away.

A smile sprung to Gienna's lips involuntarily as she saw her brother clinging upside down to a stalactite by his legs. Seeing him this way reassured her somehow.

She could plainly see the steel capped end of his collapsible staff was wedge firmly into the trap's gears. What she could not see immediately was how he had wedged the other end against his shoulders. The tension of keeping the staff in place, holding himself upside down while firing arrows at the beast firmly set into Landolin's features. Every muscle of his lean frame was taught as he fought against the strength of the gears. His quick thinking had bought her more time than either of them intended and for that she was grateful.

Relief seeped into her weary muscles the closer she moved to her brother. The small waves quickly turned into a flood. The rhythm of her feet increased their staccato tempo as she sprinted toward him.

When he shifted slightly and dropped from the ceiling, she was a full run. Not even seeing his staff dislodge itself from the gears before she was close enough to clear the final wall did much to lower her spirits. At least not until it all could sink in.

She pressed herself harder. Gienna knew she needed to move faster than she was if she hoped to make it passed the final blade wall. Her legs pumped faster and her breath, already short, came in labored puffs. Her eyes widened as Landolin nocked and sighted another arrow, this time right at her head.

"What is wrong with you?" She shrieked as she threw herself into a sideways roll.

As soon as she felt the wall against the bottom of her foot, she kicked. This helped increase her speed and added just enough erraticness to make it harder for him to hit her. Before he could recover, she angled directly at him.

The edge of the blade wall shimmered in the darkness above her. From the corners of her eyes, she saw it start to lower slowly from the ceiling. She had to move faster.

"Leap left," Landolin's voice sounded oddly alien to her.

Without pause, he leveled the arrow at her again. His cool demeanor and emotionless face only added to her fear. This time the arrow was aimed at her chest.

She darted to her right and then zagged back on course after his arrow skittered off the stone wall to her left. He missed, but barely.

Gienna spared a brief glance toward the ceiling. She

looked just long enough to see the blade was still descending. It was odd that it had not fallen farther. Then she saw it.

There was a second blade. Unlike the one from the ceiling, the second one rose from the fine line etched in the floor. She easily calculated where the two blades would meet based on their speed.

Without hesitation, the elf adjusted her trajectory. She had to clear the spot before the blades could block her path. She knew it was going to be close, but she had no choice.

"If I can just move a little faster," she thought to herself as a wave of adrenaline washed over her.

"I said left!" He chided as another arrow skittered off to her side.

"And let you kill me?" She glared at her brother.

The distance was closing, but not fast enough. Tears stung her eyes as she suppressed her emotions. Everything felt unreal.

"I am not trying to kill you!" He screamed in her mind.

She could hear his pain. It seethed behind each word and tore at her psyche. No matter what it seemed like, she could hear the truth of his intentions. He believed what he said, no matter how far opposed his actions seemed to be.

"Tuck and roll! Now!" His instructions were excessively clear and forceful.

"For someone that isn't trying, you are doing a good job at it!" Gienna shot her words back at him like a bullet. Each marked for his heart and she felt their individual impact as they struck him.

No matter how much she wanted to rebel, she knew better than to disobey him this time. Her dive toward the ground helped her build the momentum she needed. Fluidly she collapsed into a ball as the floor impacted with her arms.

Well placed kicks at odd angles allowed her to gain more speed before she untucked and bolted toward Landolin. The extra momentum carried her back into a standing position seamlessly.

The closer she made it to her brother's location, the less stable her footing became. Tiny pebbles greeted each step and forced her to slow down or fall. Small stumbles threatened to become so much more. Each step only added to the risk.

As soon as she regained her footing after each stride, she gauged the distance to the closing opening again. Each time she realized she needed to move faster not slower.

"I'm not going to make it," the thought rang through her mind unbidden.

Her crimson hair matted with each ragged breath she pulled in between her teeth. Every bead of sweat forced her to move faster. Her muscles ached as her legs pumped methodologically beneath her.

Another shift of stones. New pains erupted from her ankles and shins. Her struggle to make up some of the lost distance her maneuver had cost her only accented Gienna's growing anger at her brother.

The darkness next to her shattered as another of her brother's arrows sped past her head. This time she saw the glint of the bronzed head as it missed her eye by mere inches. The sting of the fletching as it clipped the soft skin of her temples did little to ease her mood.

Reflexively Gienna turned her head to see where the arrow hit. Only darkness and dust met her prying eyes. An unexpected gust of wind from behind her only added to her confusion. Although she managed to keep her momentum, she felt her foot slide as it hit a patch of gravel.

Her whole body shifted, so she crouched and locked her knees. Within seconds she was in a controlled slide. Still on target, but not moving nearly fast enough. Her mind whirred as she tried to figure out how to break the slide and gain some speed by running.

The leathery sound of something moving where her head would have been, if she hadn't stumbled took her by surprise.

Something was still behind her. Hunting her.

Gienna glanced around in shock. "It can't still be alive," she thought in disbelief. Her thoughts filled with the feeling of its hot sticky blood as it coursed over her hands. Memories of how the overly hardened skin separated neatly under the edge of her knife filled her mind. "It can't be."

She glanced over her shoulder as panic filled her limbs. With a tight chest, she saw it. The blood-red glow as the beast bobbed in pursuit. Erratic was the only way to describe its flight. But somehow, it had overtaken her. This revelation reenergized her.

A sudden surge of adrenaline launched her forward. Only a few more steps and she would be safe. The gap between the razor-sharp blades was almost closed and she was still about a body length away from it.

"Jump!" Landolin screamed.

His voice was almost deafening as it shattered the impossible silence of her plight. He leaned far enough through what little space remained that his torso was fully visible. His hands stretched toward her. Fingers outstretched. Close enough to touch. A wave of relief as cascaded through her veins as she felt his strong hands close around hers.

Landolin heaved as she tightened her grip on his wrists. She could tell he pulled as hard as he could. Her clothes caught on the edge of the blades as she twisted and forced her way through to safety.

Then, impossibly, she was through. Both of them impacted the wall behind Landolin hard enough to knock the wind out them. The only thing either of them could think of was the fact neither of them had been caught in the scissor-like blades of the trap.

Gienna forced herself to turn. Bits of cloth and leather met her eyes. She knew both of them were tattered without looking. There was far too much fabric and armor scrap for them not to be. Even though her eyes struggled against the darkness and her own fatigue, she fought to see the beast.

A loud thump shook the ground under their feet and quickly pulled Gienna's attention away from the spot of ground her eyes were fixed at and back to the wall she had just squeezed through.

The sight that met her eyes was gruesome. The nassarid's face glared at them locked in an expression caught between hatred and horror. She watched somewhat detached from herself as it struggled against the blade walls in alternating attempts to squeeze farther through and pulling its head back out. The sheer animalistic fervor that possessed it was heart-wrenching.

The red glare from its stare locked onto Gienna's garnet eyes. The eerie glow slowly faded and was replaced by a look of despair and utter desperation. She could not take it.

The whisper of her sword as it freed itself from her scabbard added a haunting tone to the scene. Absently she brushing her brother's concerned attempts at restraining her aside and made her way to the pathetic creature.

The blades slowly carved their way through the thick skin covering its shoulders. Jarring lurches drove the blades deeper. The only thing that hampered their closure was the beast's bones. Somehow the nassarid managed to push its way farther in than she thought it would.

"I will not let you die this way." Her voice was filled with remorse. "It is undignified for a warrior such as you."

Gienna's blade flashed quickly before its eyes and its horrific features twisted into a maniacal smile. Somehow she imagined it laughing as her sword found its mark. A dull melon-like sound as the severed head hit the floor was the only appreciation she received or needed.

"It's done," Landolin said as he walked over to his sister and placed a reassuring arm on her shoulder.

"How do you do it?" Gienna looked up at her brother completely lost in her emotions.

Tears streamed down her face as she cleaned the blade of her sword off with a piece of cloth she kept specifically for this task. Little tremors ran along her arms and hands as she did so.

"These were once innocent animals before they were forced into their new lives. Weren't they?" Her emotions fogged her thoughts. "Beasts are above this sort of enslavement.

"I take souvenirs." Landolin's voice seemed more distant and cold than Gienna thought it would be.

She felt his fingers close around her shoulders. He was strong, stronger than she was. She let him turn her toward him and was thankful when she felt his arms pull her into an embrace.

"It never gets easier, but at least I have a way to remember those that have been afflicted involuntarily." His voice was oddly reassuring. "The souvenirs also give me a gentle reminder of what steps will be needed to exact revenge for these souls as well." He pulled away and glanced down at Gienna's hand as he continued. "The choker is a good choice, as long as you don't decide to sell it." His tone held a very matter of fact quality to it.

"What choker?" Her voice caught as Gienna followed his gaze to her hand and saw the choker dangling from it. She looked at it for several long moments confused. "But I didn't take it," she said somewhat defensively. "Although I would never sell it, it is far too beautiful for that," she added somewhat playfully. Somehow the thing managed to get into her hand. She was not sure how it happened, but she was glad it did.

Sorting and reattaching everything while she was spent from the recent run for her life proved time-consuming at best. She knew her brother was giving her space and time to get collected. Just like she knew they could not really afford to spare her the luxury, but she appreciated it.

"I'm almost ready," he soft voice was scarcely a whisper, yet it sounded painfully loud to her elven ears.

Her fingers fumbled against the multitude of ties and

hooks. She took her time to reattach her weapons properly in their original locations on her assorted belts and harnesses.

"You might think of carrying less blades," Landolin offered impishly. "After all, two should be sufficient for any situation that might arise. That is, if you're skilled enough."

Loose strands of her hair caught in the slight breeze, so she absently tucked them behind her ear. She smoothed the wrinkles from the surface of what remained of her clothes as she replied, "Unless the target is a bit far. That's when the quantity proves itself useful."

She knew her brother was trying to ease the tension that had built between them, but she was not quite ready to let that happen. At least not yet.

"Are you ever going to tell me why you had to try and kill me?" She blunted the edges of her words as best as she could.

"I had to. The thing kept dodging the arrows when I shot wide." His joviality was still strained and Gienna knew she had carried it on long enough.

"Next time, warn me."

"You didn't feel it bearing down on you?" He asked astonished.

"No, I thought I had already killed it. Everything was so silent. I could barely hear your arrows as they missed their mark." Her hand fluttered to the scratch along her cheek as she spoke.

"I am sorry for that," Landolin offered quietly. His hand, like his words, softly overtook hers and brushed lovingly against the wound.

"It's alright," she lied, "I just need to remember how bad of a shot you are."

"Right," his smile fought hard to break past his entrenched scowl. "I will remember that next time we have a nassarid hunting you."

"You do that. Besides, I think this turned out fine. The beast is dead. We are alive. I have a great souvenir to remember the moment by and you finally made something bleed with an arrow." She knew better than to look, so instead, she smiled at the imagined wound her brother mimed as she spoke.

Slowly Gienna raised the choker in front of her. She carefully inspected the leather that composed most of its bulk and then studied the surface of the moonstone cabochon. It was beautiful. Even in the almost pitch blackness of the tunnels, a sliver of pale light reflected within its opalescent layers.

"It will look just fine with your outfit," Landolin teased as she played with the choker. "I know that is what you were wondering," his voice dripped with sarcasm and she could not care less.

"I wasn't trying to decide if it would," she rebuffed. "I never put anything on that I haven't thoroughly inspected. You never know if there is an enchantment on it or if it has been laced with poison." Although her words seemed logical, she knew he would see the playful twinkle in her eye.

"Here let me help with that," Landolin said with a knowing grin as he snatched the choker from her hands. "Turn," he made a quick twirling motion with his hand and she giggled.

"It has been quite some time since anyone helped me put on a necklace," she smiled as she swept her crimson hair away from her neck.

"Or anything else for that matter," her brother chided as he slipped the choker around her lithe neck and fastened it securely. "That is odd," the amazement in his voice was a little unnerving. Especially after his previous comment.

"What is?" Gienna asked perplexed. Her finger slipped across the stone's smooth surface as her words fell from her lips. Something tickled the back of her head as she let her hair go and she dismissed it immediately.

"It fits so snugly. Your neck size and the nassarid's must be the same," Landolin said somewhat snarkliy. "I always said you were a brute, I just never imagined I would see the day that I was proven right."

"You are terrible," she replied playfully, her hand still on the stone. It was cool to her touch and she could not help but trace its smooth contours. "But we do need to be going."

"Very well," Landolin agreed as he collapsed his staff and slid it into the case fastened to his hip. "I am glad your mood has changed. Now let's see if we can find the others and our way out."

"Do you think either of them are still alive?" Gienna leveled a stark stare at her brother as she spoke. "After all we did find the beast in the middle of a blood filled room eating something."

"I know," his voice held more tension than he usually allowed, "but we have to be sure."

His tone was strict and Gienna knew better than to press the subject. Besides she had a new choker, what did she care if her brother wanted to search for his comrades?

She shrugged her shoulders as she motioned for Landolin to lead the way. Another tickle in the back of her head tugged for her attention as Landolin passed in front of her. She fought the urge to think about it until she was sure he was well ahead of her. Once she was certain he could not see her, she reached up and touched the moonstone again.

"Yes?" she directed her thoughts at the center of the stone. She felt silly, but she knew she had to try. There was something odd about the stone. She refocused her thoughts and tried to contact the stone again. This time she tried to talk to it like she did when she shared thoughts with her brother.

"Thank you for freeing me," the otherworldly voice erupted in the back of her head. It was distorted and quiet, but it was there.

"You're welcome, I think," Gienna replied.

She was amazed at how natural it seemed to communicate with the stone. She felt another odd sensation in the back of her head. It was not pain, but it was like nothing she had ever experienced before.

"Do you have a name?" She asked a little worried about the new tingle that shot through her entire skull.

"I do. I am the Maugutie. I am yours now. Do not worry, I will protect you forever." There was something different about the voice in her head this time. It sounded feminine, yet somewhat bestial at the same time.

Gienna felt a thread of fear wind through her soul as she delicately traced her finger backward from the moonstone across the leather of the choker. A deep feeling of dread settled into her mind as she searched for the clasp to the choker. It was not there.

"What are you?" She thought frantically.

"I am the Maugutie of Eternal Life." The voice had a jovial, yet sinister tone to it. "I am a gift from the gods. Do not fear, we are now bound together forever. You are lucky for you will never truly die." Its response did little to ease Gienna's fears.

"I am an elf and am already untouched by death," she thought haughtily at the amulet.

"Not like this," the thought resonated through her skull, "even elves face the ravages of time and, although some concessions have been made, the realm of the living is cut off from all elves after a time. For you, this will not happen." Part of her soul yearned to hear these words and it worried her.

"But the beast that wore you last died." Her thoughts were now laced with despair as she realized her new fate.

"No, death did not claim him. Do not fear, I am not here to force you to do anything other than what you are fated to do." The voice filled Gienna's head and forced her thoughts to go silent.

She was happy that Landolin did not seem to notice her internal struggle. She hoped he could not see the blood-like tear make its way gently down her cheek. Somehow she knew it was blood, although not hers. Just like she knew the creature's soul was trapped under the surface of the stone cradled in her bosom.

Gienna walked in silent turmoil as she felt the artifact merge with her mind. Odd burning sensations darted along the underside of her scalp as new and unbreakable paths were forged to bind her even more with the Maugutie.

Deep down, Gienna longed to touch her brother's mind. To let him know what was happening. But she knew better. Somehow she sensed that if they did connect, the Maugutie might lay claim to him through their shared a psychic bond.

Epilogue

Skara sniffed at the wind softly. She enjoyed every moment of the tingling sensation that accompanied the aroma of her prey. Each note blended together to create a tantalizing blend that set her senses on fire. Skara knew that her target was just below her and she could hardly wait for her vengeance. She pushed the thoughts of impropriety from her head as she traced Allair's movements through the dwindling number of people that lined the streets.

"Humans are strange," she thought to herself. "They have the ability to adapt to almost any climate, but they purposefully lock themselves indoors instead of enjoying the crispness that comes with the cold."

"She isn't on our list," Faris reiterated for the third time. Although he whispered, Skara jumped as if he had yelled. "Do you really think it is prudent to do this?"

"She stopped us from finishing our target in the square. She is alone and an unprepared. This is the perfect time to set the record straight." Skara snarled at Faris as if she could intimidate him into silence. "Besides, she is one of the two that is usually around our second target."

"My orders said to only kill those that we have to and to leave the rest alone." Faris's hesitation to go against their orders was apparent on both his face and his tone.

"Fine, go back to the smithy and keep an eye out for either of our primary targets. If you see either of them, and you have a clean shot, take it and get away. Make sure that you only use the arrows and bolts that our lady has given us." Her instructions, like her intentions, were perfectly clear.

Faris nodded his understanding and said over his shoulder as he left, "At least wait until I am well away before you attack. I don't want any part of your revenge."

Skara nodded her agreement and waited impatiently for him to go. "At least I won't have to smell his stench for a little while," this thought raced through her head and brought a smile to her lips as she patiently watched Allair move from one shop to the next. She saw her prey look down the road and then move toward yet another business, but not enter. Skara watched intently as Allair loitered out front of the shop for a few minutes, glance down the road, and then casually walk in the direction she kept looking toward.

"Who is she tailing," Skara hated only one thing more than someone stopping her from her task, not knowing. She tried to tamp down her curiosity, but failed. "I need to make sure it isn't a trap," she justified to herself as she stalked her prey.

ACKNOWLEDGEMENTS

Well, it's that time again. Time for me, as the author (more of a director really), to let the world understand how much support it really takes from others to make this book a reality.

For starters, I need to thank Derek Savage and his whole family: Tabitha, Kai, Keeley, and the rest of the Savage Clan. Although I will thank him again as we get into the Beta Readers section, and his pool table was still very instrumental, his ability to keep me just sane and grounded enough, in reality, to focus on the writing was amazing.

While it is true the bulk of this fine work was written before my slight dip into the dark recesses of depression that comes along with major life changes, the revamp, tear down and recreation of it didn't. Savages, thank you for the long nights and longer allowances for me to visit. Your support is instrumental. Especially the sanctuary your house represents for me.

The next person that needs to be thanked is my, now ex-wife, Tami Harrison. She put up with so many hardships while I struggled through the writing process. I'm sorry things couldn't have turned out better between us. Thank you for looking out for our boys and know that I will always struggle and strive to make sure that our children are always taken care of.

John Williams, your work is still visible on the maps and I doubt that will ever change. Look me up. I'd love to work on special projects relating to this series and others. I know that without your blood sweat and tears, I would have had to use the map I created as a kid. It wouldn't have been anywhere as nice as yours nor would it have been as cool looking.

Ofelia Garcia, I need to thank you for your input on the cover design. Your keen eye really helped me create an amazing image that I feel fully represents this chapter of the story perfectly. I also need to thank you for all of the sanity creating distractions that you provided. Your interventions made it much easier to craft the final product.

There are two people I need to also mention. Without these two, *Shadow Play* would still be part of *Shadow Flight*. The book was getting way too large and their timely advice and discourse allowed me to see the logic, and the relief, that came with splitting the book into two pieces. Liana Serrano, thank you for the initial push to split it. Without this voice of logic, I never would have ever thought about it. Arley Smith thank you for being the sounding board and motivational vessel during the editing process.

The next group of people that I need to mention is my beta readers. Sorida Gallegos, Marc Tucker, Derek Savage (see I told you I'd mention him again), and David Camden-Britton. All of you helped in your own special ways to flesh out the story.

Sorida, I hope you love Sori. I promise there will be more of her in the upcoming books. Your support throughout my odd creative process has been much appreciated.

Marc, thank you again. For all of the years that I've known you, you have always been an inspiration and a creative sync that I have relied upon to get things done.

Derek… what can I say that hasn't already been said? I'm glad that my writings have inspired you and Tabitha to create stories of your own. I hope I can be as much of a help to you as you have been for me. I know that I can never replace all of the many hours I used of your time to discuss nuances of what I'm trying to accomplish. Your wisdom and ability to map my arcs are still amazing to me. While we did still spend many hours in your bonus room shooting pool and discussing the book, I think your smoker has helped the creative juices as well.

David, or should I say Groovy, your need to have the grammar be as pristine as possible was a godsend to me and I am forever indebted to you for it. I also feel the need to focus on the fact that even when you were going through some really hard times of your own, you were available to me for what I needed. I am amazed at your giving nature.

The final group that I want to thank is a rather large one. This group encompasses everyone that has helped me explore some of the finer things that my local area has to offer. From the extremely helpful waitress at Applebee's in Modesto to the amazing staff at Kimoto Sake & Sushi. Without your expertise, I doubt that I could have stayed as focused on the final edits of this project.

Thank you all.

About The Author

A Reiki Master and accomplished author, John Harrison lives in central California and enjoys spending time with his family when he is not trying his hand at literary endeavors.

His current projects include: *Shadow Guard* (the fourth novel in the Shadow Saga) and *Bella Rouge* (a standalone novel based on "Unholy Trinity"—a short story published in Michael Moorcock's New Worlds Magazine).

John has been writing since he was in elementary school. His family and friends all love his imagination and his ability to weave a good story in a very short time. His professional writing has ranged from business processes to short stories and now novels.

For more information about John, or to find other works released by him, check him out on the web:

www.amazon.com/author/johnaharrison

http://jalbertharrison.wix.com/author-page

www.ingramcontent.com/pod-product-compliance
Lightning Source LLC
Chambersburg PA
CBHW051008180726
48291CB00006B/2027